- STAR TREK MYSTERIES SOLVED!

- ALTERNATE UNIVERSES IN STAR TREK

- SPOCK RESURRECTUS—OR, NOW THAT THEY'VE KILLED HIM, HOW DO WE GET HIM BACK?

- INDIANA SKYWALKER MEETS THE SON OF STAR TREK

- THE STAR TREK FILMS: VARIATIONS AND VEXATIONS

From moving letters from fans about the way *Star Trek* touched their lives to in-depth looks at Kirk, Mr. Spock, Uhura, McCoy, and Khan, this first big collection of the best writing from THE BEST OF TREK® books gives exciting proof of *Star Trek*'s growth from favorite TV show to an important element in America's cultural heritage—and future vision.

THE BEST OF THE BEST OF TREK®

From the Magazine for Star Trek Fans

Edited by
Walter Irwin and G. B. Love

A ROC BOOK

ROC
Published by the Penguin Group
Penguin Books USA Inc., 375 Hudson Street,
New York, New York 10014, U.S.A.
Penguin Books Ltd, 27 Wrights Lane,
London W8 5TZ, England
Penguin Books Australia Ltd, Ringwood,
Victoria, Australia
Penguin Books Canada Ltd, 2801 John Street,
Markham, Ontario, Canada L3R 1B4
Penguin Books (N.Z.) Ltd, 182-190 Wairau Road,
Auckland 10, New Zealand

Penguin Books Ltd, Registered Offices:
Harmondsworth, Middlesex, England

First published by ROC, an imprint of Penguin Books USA Inc.
Published simultaneously in Canada.

First Printing, July, 1990
10 9 8 7 6 5 4 3 2 1

Acknowledgments

"Star Trek and Me" by Fern Lynch and Isobel Real. Copyright © 1978 by TREK®.

"Star Trek Mysteries—Solved!" by Leslie Thompson. Copyright © 1978 by TREK®.

"The Psychology of Mr. Spock's Popularity" by Gloria-Ann Rovelstad. Copyright © 1978 by TREK®.

"Women in the Federation" by Pamela Rose. Copyright © 1980 by TREK®.

"A Brief Look at Kirk's Career" by Leslie Thompson. Copyright © 1980 by TREK®.

" 'Just' a Simple Country Doctor?" by Joyce Tullock. Copyright © 1980 by TREK®.

"Characterization Rape" by Kendra Hunter. Copyright © 1980 by TREK®.

"Command Decision Crisis: A Star Trek Fan Fiction Parody" by Walter Irwin. Copyright © 1981 by TREK®.

"A Trek into Genealogy" by Linda Frankel. Copyright © 1981 by TREK®.

"Alternate Universes in Star Trek Fan Fiction" by Rebecca Hoffman. Copyright © 1981 by TREK®.

"Immortality" by Mark Andrew Golding. Copyright © 1981 by TREK®.

"She Walks in Beauty" by G. B. Love. Copyright © 1981 by TREK®.

"Requiem for a Hack" by Kiel Stuart. Copyright © 1981 by Trek®.

"The Music of Star Trek: A Very Special Effect" by Eleanor LaBerge. Copyright © 1982 by TREK®.

"Love in Star Trek" by Walter Irwin. Copyright © 1982 by TREK®.

 ROC is a trademark of Penguin Books USA Inc.

LIBRARY OF CONGRESS CATALOGING IN PUBLICATION DATA

The Best of the Best of Trek : from the magazine for Star trek fans / edited by Walter Irwin and G. B. Love.
    p.   cm.
    ISBN 0-451-45015-9
    1. Star Trek films—History and criticism. 2. Star trek (Television program) 3. Science fiction, American—History and criticism. I. Irwin, Walter. II. Love, G. B. III. Best of Trek.
PN1995.9.S694B4 1990
791.45'72—dc20   90-30812
                                                                                                          CIP

Printed in the United States of America
Set in Times Roman
Designed by Leonard Telesca

CONTENTS

INTRODUCTION   xi

STAR TREK AND ME   1
Fern Lynch and Isobel Real

STAR TREK MYSTERIES—SOLVED!   8
Leslie Thompson

THE PSYCHOLOGY OF MR. SPOCK'S POPULARITY   14
Gloria-Ann Rovelstad

WOMEN IN THE FEDERATION   21
Pamela Rose

A BRIEF LOOK AT KIRK'S CAREER   27
Leslie Thompson

"JUST" A SIMPLE COUNTRY DOCTOR?   36
Joyce Tullock

CHARACTERIZATION RAPE   43
Kendra Hunter

COMMAND DECISION CRISIS: A STAR TREK
FAN FICTION PARODY   53
Walter Irwin

A TREK INTO GENEALOGY   71
Linda Frankel

ALTERNATE UNIVERSES IN STAR TREK FAN FICTION 77
Rebecca Hoffman

IMMORTALITY 87
Mark Andrew Golding

SHE WALKS IN BEAUTY . . . 104
G. B. Love

REQUIEM FOR A HACK 111
Kiel Stuart

THE MUSIC OF STAR TREK: A VERY SPECIAL EFFECT 124
Eleanor LaBerge

LOVE IN STAR TREK 132
Walter Irwin

NEW LIFE, NEW CREATION: STAR TREK AS MODERN MYTH 160
Barbara Devereaux

THE WRATH OF KHAN—REVIEW AND COMMENTARY 171
Walter Irwin

SPOCK RESURRECTUS—OR, NOW THAT *THEY'VE* KILLED HIM, 186
HOW DO *WE* GET HIM BACK?
Pat Mooney

ANSWER YOUR BEEPER, YOU DREAMER! 197
Jacqueline Gilkey

LOVE IN STAR TREK—PART II 207
Walter Irwin

INDIANA SKYWALKER MEETS THE SON OF STAR TREK 234
Kyle Holland

THE TREK "FAN ON THE STREET" POLL 244
G. B. Love

BENEATH THE SURFACE: THE SURREALISTIC STAR TREK 260
James H. Devon

KIRK AND DUTY 269
William Trigg and Dawson "Hank" Hawes

IN SEARCH OF SPOCK: A PSYCHOANALYTIC INQUIRY   287
  Harvey R. Greenberg

BROTHER, MY SOUL: SPOCK, McCOY, AND THE   308
MAN IN THE MIRROR
  Joyce Tullock

STAR TREK IN THE CLASSROOM   324
  Jeffrey H. Mills

SPECULATION: ON POWER, POLITICS, AND   336
PERSONAL INTEGRITY
  Sharron Crowson

THE THREE-FOOT PIT AND OTHER STORIES   342
  Ingrid Cross

VULCAN AS A MERITOCRACY   351
  Carmen Carter

THE STAR TREK FILMS: VARIATIONS AND VEXATIONS   357
  Mark Alfred

INTRODUCTION

In the not-quite-a-dozen years since the first *Best of Trek* volume was published, we editors have been privileged to work with hundreds of writers and artists—professionals and fans alike—all of whom have one thing in common: an abiding love for that most unusual of all science fiction/fantasy television programs, *Star Trek*.

In the introduction to that first collection, we put forth the opinion that Star Trek and its characters were on the verge of entering into folklore—becoming known internationally, instantly and intrinsically. Kirk and Spock—even the *Enterprise*, with its profile as distinctive as a Coca-Cola bottle—we said, were becoming folk icons, representing not just a television program or science fiction, but a dream, a hope for the future.

That prediction, which didn't require any particular astuteness on our part, is coming true. More important, the dream is coming true, as well. Peace and brotherhood are gaining the ascendancy in this belabored world for the first time in over fifty years. It is our hope that as men turn their eyes away from each others' borders, they will turn them as longingly and as avidly to the stars.

What we did not predict was the strange evolutionary path Star Trek has taken during the past dozen years. Yes, we knew there would be several Star Trek films (although we thought they would be a series of made-for-television movies), and the continuing, ever-growing success of Star Trek literature was a given. But how could anyone have ever guessed that a *second* Star Trek series, a direct successor to the original, would be so successfully created, presented, and syndicated? *Star Trek: The Next Generation,* now entering its third season, is a worthy and popular successor to the original. And it is, not surprisingly for a show created and produced by Gene Roddenberry, breaking many rules . . . not the least of which is that the show gets better with each successive season, not worse.

Through it all, *The Best of Trek* has been there. Through the dark days of the mid-seventies, when it appeared that Star Trek, and perhaps even science fiction, was forever dead; through the heady days of the first film—something of an artistic failure, but virtually the Second Coming for fans; through the days of the huge conventions, then the smaller conventions, then the specialized, dedicated conventions; into the continuing series of films, the death and rebirth of Spock, the saving of whales, the reaffirmation of our heroes' friendship; through the hundreds, no, thousands, of books, magazines, fanzines, songs, photos, artwork, bumper stickers, toys, posters . . . Onto the next generation, we have been there, here, with you—the fans.

Our most heartfelt thanks go to the fans, our readers, who have made the *Best of Trek* series the most popular nonfiction science fiction series of all time. We also would like to thank our many, many contributors, only a few of whom are represented in this volume, for their support and enthusiasm. Special thanks to our editors, Sheila Gilbert and, presently, John Silbersack, and their staffs of assistants; and to the artists, copyeditors, and other professionals at New American Library for helping us make our collections the very best they can be. Thanks also to Gene Roddenberry, Harve Bennett, and their respective staffs at Paramount for their cooperation over the years.

We could not have done it without their help and that of many others. The best news is that we are continuing to do it—*The Best of Trek* books continue, and will continue, to be published by ROC.

In the dark days of no Star Trek, the rallying cry was "Star Trek Lives!" Thanks to the efforts of fans and professionals alike, today that slogan can rightly be: *Star Trek* Lives . . . Forever.

Walter Irwin
G. B. Love

THE BEST OF THE BEST OF TREK®

STAR TREK AND ME

by Fern Lynch and Isobel Real

Some time ago we instituted a column called "Star Trek and Me," in which some of our readers told of the major effects that Star Trek had had on their lives. In a way, it was the predecessor of "Fan of the Month," but lacked that feature's photos, briefness, and general lightness. "Star Trek and Me" was an immensely popular feature, but ended in failure. Readers enjoyed the stories of others, but were obviously unwilling to reveal as much of themselves for the feature, so it died from lack of submissions. However, we feel that the stories of Mrs. Lynch and Ms. Real are important. Through them we can see the true beauty and wonder of the ideals of Star Trek and a fandom such as ours. Theirs is the story of every Star Trek fan. The difference is only one of degree.

FERN LYNCH

Finally, and at the ripe old age of sixty-five, I have become the expert! I have been watching Star Trek since my first heart attack in 1968, but never talked about it to anyone. I just thought I must be a little "peculiar" to have such a deep regard for a television program and its absolutely wonderful cast. So I didn't mention that I was a Star Trek gazer for years.

However, this March '76, I saw an ad for the con in Los Angeles (Equicon) and thought it would be wonderful fun to go. I thought about it for three days, and decided there was no time to waste! I wrote for my tickets, hotel room, theater tickets, banquet, made reservations to fly and was off!

I never saw a generation gap close so quickly! If you stood around more than three people you got into discussions. The most fascinating one I participated in was with a group of people of various ages. One college girl said she wears her IDIC everywhere and tells anyone who will listen the philosophy behind it. We ended up more or less on education and politics; and each one listened to the others, even though they might not agree.

I have twelve grandchildren, the oldest almost twenty-six and the youngest seven, and just this year I found out they watch Star Trek. For the first time since my own children were little, I was the expert! I have seen each episode ten to fifteen times, and never tire of them.

In discussing Star Trek with Adam, the youngest, he asked why I liked it. Now telling a seven-year-old how the courage, the optimism, and the hope for the future is the core of Star Trek's appeal is a little difficult. Children absorb this unknowingly, but the basic appeal to them is visual. They do not yet relate to the message Star Trek projects.

I think of it as a kind of "sleep teaching." By constant exposure to the show, I hope they will actually take in the message subconsciously, and emulate the characteristics of their heroes. And do we need heroes!

But back to the con: I registered on Thursday the 15th, and then sat in the lobby watching others checking in, trying to guess who was there for the convention. Of course, some already had their uniforms on.

The Hotel Marriott has 1,000 rooms, and it was jammed. The overflow was forced to go to an adjacent hotel.

I went to dinner in the hotel restaurant and was sitting adjacent to two young gentlemen (thirtyish), when a girl walked by wearing pointed ears and a costume. They remarked to each other that they couldn't figure out what was going on. Seeing I had my badge on, they turned to me for an explanation.

I told them that the girl typified the premise of Star Trek on diversity. That no one would laugh at her. That to herself she was beautiful, and therefore she would be regarded as beautiful by all who love Star Trek. They agreed that it was a wonderful thought, and said they would try to watch Star Trek in the future.

Now there may have been some complaints about this con, but I myself thought it was run very well. The Trimbles had a herculean task and achieved wonders. There were episodes of Star Trek three times a day. The programs were excellent and it was up to you to find what you wanted. It was all there, even though there were times when I wished I were twins so I could be in two places at once.

I think for myself I found the most satisfaction in listening to, and sometimes joining in, conversations that sounded interesting. The range was terrific; not limited to Star Trek, but spiraling off into education, politics, and the things that my generation had contributed to the young.

Several younger persons said they had never thought of us older people as having the same dreams they had and trying to do something about it, but without violence. As I pointed out, I had been seventeen, but they had never been sixty-five, so there was no way that they could validly believe that everything we had done was wrong.

There were writers' panels—one with Majel Barrett, William Campbell, Robert Clarke, Arlene Martel, and Kirk Alyn, the original Superman (a very good-looking man). At this panel, William Campbell was presented with the blue velvet coat he wore in "The Squire of Gothos." He was very touched and gave a nice speech, thanking the fans for their attendance in behalf of the Motion Picture and TV Actor's Home.

There was an excellent panel with George and Gene. Pal and Roddenberry, that is! Mr. Roddenberry said that the film had a stage assigned, but nothing else was firmed up. He thanked the fans for their continuing devotion and patience.

Now remember, this was a hotel and we had the ground floor, including all of the rooms on it. By Friday night, it was becoming very difficult to maneuver, but everyone was polite. Many times, because I had a cane, I was offered a seat or a better place in line.

I find that I can label fans only "good-mannered" or "bad-mannered"; the terms Trekker, Trekkie, etc. turn me off. By and large, 98 percent of the people I encountered were good-mannered and gentle. That is to me the typical fan: intelligent, willing to talk, but even readier to listen. The con "gofers" were lovely, very helpful indeed.

Bjo and her husband John gave great speeches and had an auction, which was fun. While I talked to Mr. Campbell and his wife and shook hands with Fritz Weaver, I made no attempt for autographs! I do not envy public personalities! When one appears, it is hazardous, even with the best of security. I cannot imagine going to a con with one of the Big Three. I want to more than anything but dare not.

Saturday there must have been at least 5,000 people in the confined space of the halls, meeting rooms, and hucksters' room. This was especially fascinating. I even bought myself a $10 record of Leonard Nimoy's "Mr. Spock's Music from Outer Space," and I don't even have a phonograph! (I took it home and left it at my daughter's and three weeks later finally persuaded myself to buy a tape recorder.)

I also bought some souvenirs for my grandchildren, including an Apollo patch for a grandson. I didn't even know if he would like that. He is twelve and we've always had trouble communicating. More on this later.

I saw Leonard Nimoy in "Sherlock Holmes" Saturday with a busload of people from the con. The show was fascinating and he achieved a remarkable feat with his voice; it was pitched higher—the delivery quick and sometimes slightly hysterical—which fitted the part perfectly, but took me a few minutes to adjust to after being used to the dignified, measured speech of Mr. Spock.

Because of my visit to the theater, I missed a panel of writers, including Robert Bloch and Theodore Sturgeon. I was very disappointed, but I had had to make a choice and I had made the logical one for me.

By Saturday night there was barely a square inch to move around in. I went to the costume judging, but because of the people in the row in front of me who kept getting up and the heat, I had to leave. However, I sat on a couch at the end of the hall and very soon a lady joined me.

She told me she was seventy-three and had been to every con within a decent distance. She had a big tape recorder which had just run out. She said she belonged to a club which met every week and showed me a beautiful photo album with candid shots of everyone from Star Trek and autographs!

While I was sitting with her, many people stopped by to say hello, including George Clayton Johnson, who wrote "The Man Trap." He is surprisingly young. We also had a corner where those who couldn't get into the big room were having their own photographic show, with some very beautiful girls and a Gorn. I think that boy will remember the con for a long while to come!

While sitting, we saw a Japanese outfit filming. We thought it was just a personal thing, but they turned the cameras on us too. We talked to them and asked if all of this type of thing happened in Japan and they answered yes! It is pretty hard to believe that the Star Trek craze (or whatever) is a worldwide thing, but I do believe it.

Sunday I attended what were my last two viewings of Star Trek episodes on the big 35-mm screen—and with no commercials, they were something to see. The reaction of each person at the screenings was so interesting. There was a sense of possessiveness about the show. I know; I felt it myself.

Sunday morning there were the usual episodes and science fiction films, but time was left from 11:00 a.m. onward in order to clear the room for the banquet. I went upstairs for a bath and when I came down, I heard Leonard Nimoy's voice! I was so disappointed, I wanted to cry, but couldn't. After all, I'm a big girl now. So I swallowed my disappointment and was doubly glad I had seen him in the play.

What made my disappointment doubly hard to take was the fact that in October 1973, he had come to a town thirty-five miles from where I live for a lecture and I had planned to go. But to my chagrin, I was in the coronary unit at the same time he was giving his lecture. And in the same town!

Now Mr. Nimoy had two performances Saturday night and one Sunday, and I think it shows a measure of the regard he has for his fans when he makes such a visit on a Sunday morning. From speaking with those who heard his talk, he is a witty, articulate, and gentle man who appreciates what the fans have done for him, just as we appreciate what he has done for us.

The banquet was attended by about 500 people, including the Roddenberrys (who sat at different tables) and the writers, designers, and the creative people who did sets, makeup, etc. Grace Lee Whitney, who had entertained with her band Saturday night, was there also. We were to have Robert Clarke at our table, but he didn't make it. There was no criticism from us. After all, he had been there all day Saturday and it was Easter.

All in all, it was the most memorable weekend of my life and one which brought some interesting sidelights with it. First of all, I am able to be friends with my twelve-year-old grandson now. We really talk, and that we could never do before. Second, I stopped biting my nails! Silly, but I had started after the second heart attack and somehow, when I made up my mind to go to the con, I decided at the same time to stop. So now, for the first time in years, I have beautiful nails again.

I joined the Leonard Association of Fans, the Startrekennial News, bought records, sent a Leonard Nimoy tape to a girl in Australia, wrote to two ladies in Texas, and all in all, I am having a ball. For the first time, everything I do is for me, for fun, and because I love Star Trek and everyone who is connected with it.

ISOBEL REAL

Back in the latter part of 1966, I chanced to tune a TV set to the newly launched series Star Trek, thereby being introduced to its strong influence during my formative years. Although my age then was twenty-five, I was as uninformed about American customs and mores as a newborn babe. My country of birth (Cuba) had not prepared me for the American world of that period. I could not understand what was going on in my adopted country, and I did not accept the events taking place through lack of cultural empathy and background.

Language can be learned easily; culture cannot be learned at all, it must be absorbed, accepted, and later automatically adopted by the individual undergoing habitat transference. I am certain that erudite intellectuals have covered the subject thoroughly; my views are personal and unsupported and could, at times, contradict established norms.

At any rate, in 1966, I was not an American; I did not understand the cultural patterns of the society and, to be quite honest, what I saw on the surface I did not like. It may have been a normal rejection of the unknown when it conflicted with my natural patterns of behavior. But the country was also undergoing some unpleasant adjustments during the period and my judgment may have been clouded by a combination of circumstances, none of which made the process any easier.

That was the stage upon which Star Trek and I first met.

The first episode seen by me of what would become my favorite program and idealized environment was "Naked Time," a magnificent introduction to the series. Yes, I had missed the prior episodes and I have always regretted it; reruns filled in the empty spaces, but it was not the same.

My command of the English language was fair and I was fortunately able to understand the contents of that piece of Utopia. For years I had been an avid reader of science fiction (since childhood in fact) and I was prepared by the likes of Asimov to enjoy the new program. As the weeks went by, I continued to follow the characters as they developed, the story lines instilling a sense of belonging to a world that was, at the same time, mythical, well known, familiar, and truly fascinating.

One character made a particularly strong impact upon me, the alien with the pointed ears, the "biological computer," the unique and beloved stranger from Vulcan: Mr. Spock. It is imperative to note that, although I am female, there were no sexual overtones to my admiration. Nor were there any patterns for father replacement search in what developed. The alien, Mr. Spock, became my alter ego. It mattered not that the sexes were different; our positions in our worlds were so similar that nothing else was of consequence.

Slowly, ever so slowly and painfully, I began to realize that the society where I found myself (U.S.A.) could and would, one day in the future, give rise to the other world I was admiring, incomplete picture though it was. The best Americans could be, in fact, persons with the qualities of Captain James T. Kirk of the USS *Enterprise*.

It took longer still to reach another earthshaking conclusion: it had been Americans who saw the future world (and galaxy) united, accepting and welcoming all of us who contributed to the good of the society regardless of physiognomy or behavioral traits.

Mr. Spock, my alter ego, accepted and even understood a strange culture, without really approving of it. He, the ultimate giver of justice, was the Solomon of our *Enterprise*, with his controlled emotions and absolute impartiality, never suffering from our personal biases, ethical and devoted to duty. He would be the one I would attempt to emulate. What an ideal to copy!

The years passed, Star Trek and Spock kept alive in my mind. Wondering all the time how Spock would react to a given situation and following the answer as best I could, I was able to survive the difficult period of adjustment. An alien, me, copying an alien, Spock, became accepted as an American. To this day, no one knows the game I played with myself—that is, no one but me.

As I adopted American customs, as I strove to understand the ways of my society, I gained better depth of character. When I first saw Star Trek, I was a clerk in a government office with little or no chance of promotion. My desire to understand became curiosity about the work performed by the group. A similar curiosity is found in the Spock personality, although I did not realize it at the time. It was this consuming curiosity that made me devote many hours of leisure time to learning about everything we did.

Now, just ten years later, I find myself in a responsible position in government service. It is part of my duties to interpret laws and regulations (I am not an attorney) that relate to my area of expertise. It is also part of my duties to translate those regulations into semi-technical format, as "user's specification" for electronic data processing systems, a function for which I must display the powers of logical reasoning learned thanks to Mr. Spock. I now supervise sixty-two employees in various levels of service—I am now GS-12, and I plan to continue growing, loyally and justly.

For my life and my success, I have to thank Star Trek publicly. For making me a better person, I have to thank Mr. Spock. Now I am a fairly well-balanced person, fulfilled and content; then I was lost and disturbed.

Thank you, Mr. Spock . . . thank you, Star Trek.

STAR TREK MYSTERIES—SOLVED!

by Leslie Thompson

One of the favorite pastimes for Star Trek fans is to sit down and play "knowledge" games with one another. Trivia is probably the most popular of these, but many fans also like to speculate on the "why" of many facets of the series—especially those which the scriptwriters left vague or unexplained. Leslie Thompson summed up the feelings of many of these fans when she said that those loose ends were "quite annoying." It was an understatement if we ever heard one, so we asked Leslie to do an article mentioning some of the more bothersome ones. "Wouldn't it be better," she answered, "if they were explained too?" And coincidentally enough, Leslie just happened to have some explanations handy for some of those questions. Leslie has told us that this article was one of the most fun to write she's ever done, and our readers told us that it was one of the most fun to read. We think you'll agree.

Did you ever find yourself rising from your fifth, sixth, or even twentieth viewing of a Star Trek episode with the vague feeling that you've missed something, or that something about the show wasn't quite explained? This has happened to me several times, and if you are as much of a stickler for accuracy and explanations as I am, then it drives you just crazy. So you run to your Concordance and your zines and your correspondence. You search and search, but nowhere can you find the answer to what is bothering you. And when you are just about to scream, you do one of two things:

You rush to your typewriter and write your own story tying up all the loose ends of that blankety-blank episode.

Or you sit down and logically find a way to fit the inconsistency into the framework of the episode, so that it changes nothing but still makes things nice and neat, and satisfies your aesthetic sense. Until next time, that is.

The sheer volume and necessary speed with which the episodes were filmed are the major cause of inconsistencies in character and plot in any television program; and it is primarily due to the superb efforts of Gene Roddenberry and his staff that more of them didn't occur in the entirely new universe they had to create and work with each week. However, many of these "What the?" clinkers showed up in individual shows, and they are the ones that drive a person crazy. And once you think about it, a small and seemingly simple unexplained occurrence could conceivably affect the direction of the series much later in its run.

Here at *Trek,* whenever we get a few minutes to spare (which isn't often), we like to challenge each other to come up with an explanation for one of these inconsistencies. We think it is a much more enjoyable pastime than trivia, since it involves not only a working knowledge of the show but also exercises the creative juices. And let me tell you, as the game goes on, the questions posed get harder and harder! Because we have so much fun with this, and because I receive an occasional letter asking me about one of these bloopers, the editors have asked me to tell you about some of our favorites in this article. Some of these have probably already popped up in your thoughts and discussions about Star Trek, so let us know if your explanation differs from ours.

In "Where No Man Has Gone Before," the plot revolves around Lieutenant Commander Gary Mitchell, who receives psychic powers from the radiation at the edge of the galaxy and then threatens the ship. But even more important to the drama of the plot is the fact that he is Kirk's best friend and holds a high position aboard the *Enterprise.* The nagging point is: Just what position did Gary Mitchell hold?

Well, we are told in the script that Mitchell is chief navigator, that his rank is lieutenant commander, and that Kirk asked for him on his first command. But he is also one of the few people who call Kirk "Jim" in front of fellow officers, and his rank is the same as that of Mr. Spock (who was still a lieutenant commander at the time of WNMHGB). So now the question boils down to: Who was Kirk's second in command at this time? Was it Gary Mitchell or Spock?

Answer: Gary Mitchell.

Look at the facts. Mitchell and Spock both had the same rank, and both served as chiefs of their respective sections. However, Spock has mentioned many times that he has no desire to command, whereas the outgoing Mitchell would certainly long to captain his own ship. Too, Mitchell was Kirk's best friend. Even in our services today, a ship's captain is given a certain amount of freedom in choosing his executive officer, if the person he wants has the necessary experience and rank. And this would be even more true in Starfleet, where things are a bit more casual, and the autonomy that a starship captain has can only be enhanced by his having a first officer whom he can both trust and get along with. Given this, Kirk would have definitely chosen Mitchell to be his second in command.

Spock may have had more seniority than Mitchell, even with their equal rank. However, in the military world this does not always bring power or position. Scotty was also a lieutenant commander at that time and remained so, while Spock did not become a full commander until after the events of WNMHGB. It makes sense that he would be promoted after assuming the duties of second in command left vacant by Mitchell's death, as the position of science officer is much more of a "full-time job" than chief navigator. Spock received a higher rank commensurate with his increased responsibilities.

One more bit of evidence: Kirk did not become good friends with Spock until Spock became his second officer. It follows that the increased time he would have to spend with Spock after he gained his promotion would form a bond between them; one which did not begin to grow when Mitchell was alive, and had both the second command and Kirk's best-friendship.

There you have it. An explanation which is logical in light of all the given information, that remains true to the series concept, and even manages to heighten the dramatic conflict of the show.

That's really the trick in forming your own hypothesis for an inconsistency in any episode; they have to fit, and fit well. If the reasoning doesn't fit into the framework of the events as given, then it cannot apply no matter how logical or detailed it may be.

For example: Sulu was ship's physicist-astrobiologist in the second pilot. Why? A case can be made stating that he felt himself uncomfortable in this position; that he was needed more at the helm; that he was rewarded with a more responsible position because of some heroics; and so on. All very logical and well thought out. But it ignores one fact about Starfleet officers: They serve in every section of the ship in order to gain the necessary experience for command. Therefore, it is much more logical and in keeping with the framework of the series to simply assume Sulu was taking a short term of duty in the physics section during the events of WNMHGB.

So it gets tougher. But even more difficult is extrapolating past events with the given information of the series. Whenever you give a reason why one of the Star Trek characters did something in the past, you must make his action fit logically with his present character. Let's look at one of the most-often-discussed problems: Why does Mr. Spock smile and show other emotions during the events of "The Menagerie"?

Knowing as we do the traumas which Spock suffered in his early life and the social stresses he went through daily on Vulcan, it is easy to understand why he chose to leave the planet and join Starfleet. But we are also told (by Spock himself and by his mother) that Spock considers himself a Vulcan. So why then would he abandon his training as a Vulcan and show any amount of emotion, for any reason?

He had a very good reason, indeed. He was exploring the human side of himself, its capabilities and its responsibilities.

Remember that Spock was still rather young during his service with Captain Pike. It follows that his rise through Starfleet was a rather rapid one; a supposition which his great intelligence and native courage would help to enforce. And his close experience with humans would have been stilted, since to move so quickly through the ranks, he would have had to spend almost all of his time working and studying.

But once he had attained a position of fairly high rank and responsibility, Spock would begin to have enough time on his hands to do some introspective thinking. His career, up to this point, had provided challenge and satisfaction enough, but he still was not content. The ever-logical Spock would decide that if living the life of a Vulcan did not make him happy, then he should try living the life of a human for a while.

Luckily, in Christopher Pike, Spock had a commander that he both had great respect and affection for (later events prove this beyond a shadow of a doubt). Planning to change his lifestyle would naturally be embarrassing to Spock, but he instinctively knew that Pike would understand the change and not make an issue of it. So he proceeded to "emotionalize."

He was not successful. We obviously know this from the Spock of today, but it is also evident in the small bit of him we have seen from that time in "The Menagerie."

The emotions which Spock displays (most notably the smiling at the vibrating alien plant, and the shout of "The women!" when they transport down without him) seem to be very forced, almost as if he were acting out the way he thought he should feel in these situations.

Spock can experience emotions, as we know, but they have to be very strong and sudden to overcome the training he received for suppressing them. And when he tried to act human he found his training too strong. He had to battle not to suppress emotion but to show it, and this created a half-hearted, strained effect.

So that mystery is solved. Spock was merely experimenting. It was not successful, and the question remains open as to how long he attempted it, and what effect it had on his personality. However, that is something that requires yet another bit of theorizing. Try it yourself.

And speaking of "The Menagerie," why do the enigmatic Number One and our own Christine Chapel resemble each other so closely? (Majel Barrett played both parts, of course, but we're speculating on the Star Trek universe here.)

This is really easy. They are sisters. An explanation which needs no involved reasoning but still satisfies all of the requirements to fit into the established format of the show.

An interesting case could be made as to why they are so different, and what were the causes of Number One's "cold-fish" personality. However, there is not enough information available on either of the women to begin to speculate. A shame, since both are such potentially exciting character studies.

Once in a while there is something which is of primary importance to the believability of an episode and that doesn't quite jibe with the established facts of the series. It is then the job of the person offering the explanation to form one which does not invalidate the events of the episode, while still having a logical basis which fits into the framework of the series.

A perfect example of this is in "Turnabout Intruder," where the psychosis of Janice Lester is based on the refusal of Starfleet Command to consider women qualified as starship captains. But the series format has established the full equality of the sexes and has shown women acting in almost every position. How can this discrepancy be explained without wrecking the entire story line of "Turnabout Intruder"?

Janice Lester is mentally ill, and has been so for some time. Her irrational actions and beliefs drive her and Kirk apart, and that separation causes yet more damage to her mind.

Now, no responsible service in the universe is going to allow a mentally disturbed person to rise to a position of responsibility if it can be prevented, and the difficult Starfleet is no exception. So there is little question that Lester was either refused admittance to the Academy or removed from it when her aberration was discovered. And in her twisted way, she would have perceived this not as a protective measure but as persecution of herself by the powers-that-be.

Like most psychotics, Janice would have been unable to recognize her own illness, so she would have to rationalize her dismissal by pinning the cause on something else. The most obvious choice was her sex.

When Kirk, refusing to abandon his own goals and dreams, did not also quit the Academy, Janice began to see him as being involved in the "conspiracy" against her and all women. Of course, this led directly to the breakup of an already stormy relationship.

Once again, in her mind abandoned, Janice soon enlarged her hatred of Starfleet to encompass Kirk, all other men, and eventually her own sex. She was hated, she felt, simply because she was a woman. So she, too, hated women, and her burning life's ambition became the desire to be not only a starship captain but a man as well.

So Janice Lester's contention that women could not be starship captains was only in her mind, fueled by the rejection and inadequacies of her life. And since it was a mistaken belief, the events of "Turnabout Intruder" can go on logically and well within the established framework of the series.

So, as you can see, all it takes is a little imagination and a working knowledge of the Star Trek universe to fill in those irritating gaps left by lazy scriptwriters and rushed production.

Solving the many Star Trek Mysteries is fun, but only one person can solve the greatest mystery of them all: Why isn't Star Trek back now? So how about it, Gene?

THE PSYCHOLOGY OF MR. SPOCK'S POPULARITY

by Gloria-Ann Rovelstad

Perhaps more has been written about Mr. Spock than any other Star Trek character; certainly most of the "character" articles we receive are about Spock. In fact, we get twice as many Spock articles as anything else. Because our magazine covers all of Star Trek and not just Spock, we are forced to reject most of these articles. However, once in a while one comes along that is so well written and has so much to say that we just can't turn it down. Gloria-Ann Rovelstad's article is one. It started out as a much, much shorter piece—it was, in fact, originally intended for our "Trek Roundtable" section. However, we felt that it showed such promise that we asked Gloria-Ann to expand it to a full-length article, and she happily did so. We think that it is just about as close to getting to the nub of Spock's popularity as possible in less than an entire series of articles—or a book!

He is above average in everything except emotional freedom, which prevents the full expression of his personality, yet at the same time makes him more interesting!

Although our society has come a long way from the inhibited Victorian era, some of that has still carried through to today, and we see Spock, in our way, as a victim of similar circumstances. (Although to those of Vulcan, it would seem just the opposite; they would lament his regrettable inheritance of human emotionalism.)

We would like to see him freed, as we also would like to have fewer emotional inhibitions. We admire him, yet we can feel sympathy for him. (Which makes for a good hero in any story or play.)

We, as humans, watch to see him show emotion.

In "This Side of Paradise," we see Spock as showing emotions caused by circumstances beyond his control—the flower pod spores on Omnicron Ceti III. After he has been cured by Kirk making him angry, he says that on the planet he was happy for the first time in his life. We think, as humans, "Poor guy!"

In most of the stories where Spock shows human emotions, it isn't through any fault of his own. In this way, the writers can show us glimpses of Spock's inner self yet not spoil the portrayal of the character, who is supposedly so logical and unemotional.

"Amok Time" is a popular show with Spock fans, both because it gives us our first glimpse of Vulcan society and customs, and because we learn more about Spock himself and how he differs from humans.

Because of Vulcan's hereditary cycle of *pon farr*, Spock is very emotional and irrational, changing the ship's course and getting annoyed at small things. Yet he is willing to proceed to the required destination of the mission—at the risk of his own life—rather than admit what is wrong with him. (This we can understand. If discussing sexual matters is embarrassing to humans, think what it must be to Vulcans!)

Down on Vulcan, he tries to avoid the fight with Kirk, even though he is strongly under the influence of *pon farr*. And when he believes he has killed his captain, he is very sad. (To say the least! If he were not, even a Vulcan would be angry at him, since Kirk is the main person to whom Spock has given his loyalty—and loyalty is an accepted emotion of Vulcans.) At the end of the show, we are touched to see Spock's happiness at finding Kirk unharmed.

When Kirk and McCoy are tortured by the Vians in "The Empath," Spock shows human feelings of sympathy and sadness for them. Next to Kirk, Spock seems to like and respect McCoy best, even though they are often at odds. There is a real bond between the two—just as between Spock and Kirk—which is evidenced by the banter between them; McCoy constantly baiting and Spock responding noncommittally, but sometimes sarcastically and sharply. Spock seems to enjoy these exchanges as much as anything.

When Spock has overruled McCoy and is preparing himself to be taken by the Vians, his statement that he is the "better" choice seems rather overdone; he actually sounds like he's almost happy about it rather than stoic, as one would expect under the circumstances.

Spock's loyalty to Kirk, over all others, is important to us. We all wish for such a loyal friend, and respect Spock for his loyalty to his commander. We feel a personification with the crewpersons of the *Enterprise*, since we too have met people whom we admire, yet who are inaccessible to us (as Spock is to them).

Since Spock's lack of expression is not due to a dislike of others, but is his own problem (as seen from a human viewpoint), we feel compassion and wish we could help him. This is like the wish of a very small child, who has his hero and dreams of doing him some great service, thereby gaining his liking and respect.

One of the foremost examples of Spock's loyalty to Kirk is displayed in "The Tholian Web," where Spock risks the safety of the entire ship on the chance he may be able to save Captain Kirk. This is quite a contradiction when compared to his actions in "Journey to Babel," where he refuses to risk the *Enterprise* to save Sarek's life.

It is clearly an emotional decision. Kirk is the one person that Spock can relate to and whom he likes more than anyone else; and we don't blame him for his choice. After all, where would the series be if he abandoned Kirk, even if it were a logical decision?

It is interesting to compare between the two stories. Kirk is a person who is known and valued by the audience much more than Sarek. Kirk and Spock get along with each other much better than Spock and his father, and they have much more empathy and compassion for each other.

If you stop to consider it, loyalty is an emotion, even in Vulcans, and this is even more true for Spock in regard to Kirk. Also, as the stories are laid out, Spock is expected to risk everything for his commanding officer, while Kirk, as the commanding officer, would more likely be excused for not taking risks for lower-ranking officers who are, unfortunately, considered expendable. (Although, to us, Spock isn't expendable, and Kirk does take chances to rescue him from quite a few situations.)

In "Journey to Babel," Spock's loyalty is to the survival of the ship, its numerous crew, and Captain Kirk (who is injured) over that to his father, who needs blood for a heart operation. His mother can't seem to understand and makes it hard on Spock by scolding and pleading with him, even though she knows his father and other Vulcans would agree his decision is the correct one. When he believes Kirk to be recovered enough to take over command of the ship, Spock is then free to help his father and cheerfully does so.

In "The Menagerie," Spock risks the death penalty to take his former commander, Captain Christopher Pike, to Talos IV, where he could live out the rest of his life in happiness rather than as a helpless cripple. A great deal of loyalty and compassion is shown by this act. If Spock were truly unemotional and strictly logical as he wants others to think, he never would have done it.

Spock's devotion to Kirk is also evident to others, even those who do not know them well. Edith Keeler puts this very well in "City on the Edge of Forever." When Spock asks her, ". . . and where would you say we belong?" Edith answers, "You, Mr. Spock, at his side, as if you had always been there and always will be . . ."

Spock represents by his repression of emotions a partial solution to one of mankind's most troubling traits: emotions that get in the way of logic. Anyone who has been emotionally upset and has been embarrassed by trying not to cry in front of others can appreciate the value of being able to control emotions or hide them as well as Spock.

And we agree that he does have them since he is half human, but he has been taught not to show them because of his upbringing on Vulcan. He certainly is logical enough for us, though perhaps not enough so for Vulcans.

In "The *Galileo* Seven," even though they are in a bad situation, Spock keeps cool as leader; so much, in fact, that the other, more emotional beings resent it.

But even his act of desperation—when he ignites the fuel of the shuttlecraft—is logical, as it gives them one last chance to be seen by the *Enterprise* and perhaps recovered. The alternative is a much slower but just as inevitable death. The ribbing Spock gets about this being an emotional act is really unnecessary, as it actually was the logical thing to do.

"Spectre of the Gun" shows McCoy getting angry at Mr. Spock for not showing emotion over Chekov's supposed death (as we know, it turns out to be an illusion). Even Kirk seems to doubt him for not reacting, yet Kirk and McCoy don't show all that much emotion themselves. People are strange creatures! At the climax, Spock protects Kirk, McCoy, and Scotty from the illusion that would cause their deaths by using the Mind Meld. He is kind and shows enough understanding of their feelings to get through to them individually.

While humans may admire logic and control of emotions, they still are basically emotional beings; and when logic and lack of emotion are applied to them or their friends, they often resent it, especially if they are feeling strongly about something at the time.

In "The Naked Time," we again see Spock showing emotion by circumstances beyond his control when he and other crewmen are affected by an emotion-uninhibiting chemical. He tries to get out of sight so as not to show it affecting him. We all probably have experienced similar situations where we hide when we cannot control our emotions and don't want to show them.

Most of the time, though, Spock is a very calm, intelligent, and practical being whom others accuse of being more like a computer than a half-human entity. He is nevertheless respected for it, and by not being emotionally involved, he avoids a lot of the troubles that the other crewpersons get into!

As Leonard Nimoy himself has said, the alienness of the character appealed to him. There are more people today than we realize who feel alienated, who feel that they too, like Spock, are apart from conventional society.

Yet Spock, often misunderstood and mistrusted (even by some of his closest friends) and truly an alien to both human and Vulcan cultures, has adapted very well and learned to cope with the inconsistencies of behavior in his human friends. His aloofness and superiority come naturally to him, yet humans may find it a reinforcement to the ego to act the same way outwardly, even if they aren't so sure of themselves inside.

Captain Tracy in "The Omega Glory" is out and out prejudiced against Vulcans and won't even speak to Mr. Spock, despite his holding a high position in Star Fleet. Often people will pay less attention to differences of others if these nonconformists hold high positions, but not Captain Tracy!

One of the main reasons the other crewpersons are angry and nasty to Spock in "The *Galileo* Seven" (other than because he doesn't show emotion while giving his logical directions and decisions) is that he just looks different and thus is an alien to them.

If it were a human leader of theirs who was not showing emotion, they would probably be proud of him and think him brave and stoic. But because Spock both looks and acts differently than they (who have emotions), they show less understanding of his feelings than he (who supposedly doesn't feel) shows to them.

He lets them bury the dead crewman, even though it serves no practical purpose except fulfilling their traditions; and it endangers their takeoff from the planet by using up precious time and allowing the ape creatures to get closer to them. He goes along with it because he knows that they feel strongly about it, even though an emotional majority isn't necessarily right, and to a Vulcan it would certainly be illogical.

Yet they do make up for their lack of understanding and show their loyalty to him by rescuing him, even though he orders them off when the *Galileo* is attacked. So in that way, their emotions proved very valuable, for they save Spock's life (and ultimately the lives of the entire party). Had they behaved as logically as Spock, he would have been left behind to die.

That is the whole problem with emotion. It can work both ways, for good or bad; we can't really ignore it as Vulcans do. This is what so many Star Trek stories pointed out.

A last example of Spock's being a true alien is from "Journey to Babel." His mother, Amanda, tells us that even as a child Spock was never truly accepted by the other Vulcan children because of his human mother and inheritance. The same would be true of Vulcan adults, we assume, so we really can't blame him for leaving his home planet.

We can understand humans being prejudiced because of their illogical emotions, but why Vulcans? If they are so logical, why should they not treat him equally?

Well, because they are so logical, they would know that as a halfbreed he would have some human traits, and they would never trust him as they would one of their own people who had been conditioned over the centuries to inhibit their natural feelings. They would know that Spock might at some time break with their ideal of true logic and so would never give him as high a position as any true Vulcan, even if he was exceptionally intelligent.

By joining the Federation and serving on a primarily human-crewed ship (even though the people were totally different than those he had been raised with), Spock had a chance to rise to a high position, and perhaps be totally accepted by a few or at least one man—Captain Kirk.

Humans, by their very emotional and illogical nature, will at times accept someone who is alien or different from them and will treat him equally and be very devoted no matter what. With Vulcans this could not happen. Again, the advantages and disadvantages of emotions!

And as any alienated being has feelings of loneliness, when Spock joined the crew of the *Enterprise* he had more chance of alleviating this feeling than he ever would have had on Vulcan. Humans, with their feelings of love, anger, and sadness, would also be much more interesting to be with, even if he didn't participate in these emotions. Talk about infinite diversity in the universe!

If anything, Spock could be pleased with the gratefulness of his comrades when he rescues them or solves some ticklish problem, whereas on Vulcan such a result would be expected as the logical thing to do and taken for granted. (Although I suppose there could be an award for being the most logical, or something.) Fortunately for Spock, he does meet Kirk, who becomes his best friend; and one whom he can give his loyalty and devotion to and have it returned equally.

Emotions are an integral part of human life, and Spock's repression of his brings to our notice all the problems connected with "feelings."

For many young people, Spock's coolness and logic represent an ideal to follow in their dealings with parents or peers.

Others may sympathize with his inability to express emotions, just as they have a hard time expressing theirs appropriately. And they hope to see him express at least some of his human half's emotions.

Spock represents a truly intelligent, altruistic entity, whom we can count on to be kind, fair, and logical in the most trying of situations. He does seem a little bit sad. Yet, accepting all of the inconsistencies of life, that emotion is true of all humanitarians. We would wish to consider Spock among them.

WOMEN IN THE FEDERATION

by Pamela Rose

Try an experiment for yourself: Go to any convention, find a group of fans, and casually ask them, "How do you feel about the position of women in the United Federation of Planets?' And then prepare to spend at least several hours listening to dozens of different opinions, complaints, and good old-fashioned arguing. Fans refer to such slugfests as the Pro-miniskirts versus the Anti-miniskirts, but it goes much deeper than that. In this article, Pamela Rose neatly sidesteps these extremes and probes a more important problem: "Is there equality in Star Trek?" And the answer may surprise you.

It has been stated in several episodes of Star Trek that the philosophy of the Federation is equality. When examined a little closer, however, there may be a few cracks in this noble view. Superficially everyone is treated equally, but there have been numerous incidents when individuals have been less than tolerant.

In "The Omega Glory," Captain Tracy is openly prejudiced against Spock, and more than a few other crewmen voice distaste and doubts about Vulcans. As far as that goes, Spock makes no secret of the fact that he considers humans to be somewhat inferior, or at least inefficient, due to their lack of logic. And even Spock's father, Sarek, speaks of Tellarites in a less than complimentary manner.

This could all be taken as natural pride in one's own race, but it definitely does not lead to trust or perfect harmony in the galaxy. (It also keeps Star Trek from being boring.)

I am not talking about Federation laws. I think we can take for granted that there are some definite laws establishing equality or the Federation would fall apart rather rapidly. But laws can be circumvented occasionally—and usually are. It looks as if it might take longer than a couple of hundred years for all our basic prejudices to be resolved—especially sexual prejudices.

In "Turnabout Intruder," Kirk says that Janice Lester's bitterness and resultant insanity were caused by her belief that she was treated unfairly because she was female. She felt that if she were not a woman she would have been placed in charge of a starship. We can agree with Kirk that she is totally unsuited to that type of position—and probably always was.

But I have wondered if there is not some basis to her feelings of male chauvinism in Starfleet and the Federation in general. Ridiculous, of course! This is the future. Remember equality?

If you examine the role of women in Starfleet, you get a disturbing feeling that they are there in token positions only. With the exception of Uhura and one or two others, they seem to spend most of their time passing coffee and carrying fuel reports for the Captain to sign—when he gets time after saving the galaxy. Now, I realize these fuel reports and such are important to the running of a starship, but why is it never a *male* yeoman?

Of course, there are exceptions, but in many cases when a woman is in a position of importance, she is a cold bitch ("Metamorphosis"; "Where No Man Has Gone Before"), or she is emotionally unstable ("Is There in Truth No Beauty?"). Nine out of ten times there is something wrong with her. There were quite a few unstable and idiotic men as well, like Nils Baris and Daystrom, but the men still have a much better average than the women in responsibility and intelligence.

Janet Wallace in "The Deadly Years" is competent in her field, but she seems to have a father fixation and prefers her men to be at death's door, which doesn't appear too normal to me.

I am not forgetting Number One in "The Menagerie," who is definitely in a position of importance as first officer. (She is nixed pretty quick, though, which is just as well or we wouldn't have Spock as he is.) But I can't like the fact that she was supposed to be so cold and unemotional. Just because a woman has risen to a position of responsibility, why does she have to squelch her emotions? Kirk and Pike certainly don't. In fact, they are both highly emotional men. We see this several times in the series. When a woman is in a position of importance, more often than not, she has toned down her femininity and acts hard as nails. It is usually a facade, but it is interesting that they feel they must have this mask at all.

I get the distinct impression from some of the episodes that three-fourths of the women in Starfleet are there to find a husband. Or are present for the convenience of the male crew members. "Have to keep the men happy in the voids of deep space."

Why else the short uniforms? Surely not for the women's convenience. Those mini-skirts appear a bit impractical—except when Janice Rand wants Kirk to look at her legs. Hmmmmmm.

In the original episodes ("The Menagerie" and "Where No Man Has Gone Before"), the women, quite sensibly, wore pants. Some lecherous old man back at Starfleet Command must have suggested the change. (Or more likely, back at NBC.)

I have no quarrel with the uniforms, however. They are very attractive. But I can't help feeling sorry for some brilliant female technician with bow legs and knobby knees. But, of course, there are no ugly women in Starfleet—unless they stuff them up the Jeffries Tubes.

To be fair, there aren't too many ugly men either. (Such are the requirements of television.) Maybe they've bred it out of the race.

There are a few sparse examples of intelligent, efficient women, however. Dr. Ann Mulhall in "Return to Tomorrow" is quite sensible. And Areel Shaw in "Court-Martial" certainly doesn't put her emotions above her duty in prosecuting Kirk. That was refreshing, as generally when a woman is emotional she goes overboard. Remember Lieutenant Marla McGivers? She not only disregards her duty, she mutinies—all for the sake of a pretty face and an incredible set of muscles. Carolyn Palamas comes close to doing the same in "Who Mourns for Adonais?" but Kirk gives her a macho speech and she pulls herself together at the last moment. Ah, frail womanhood!

Dr. Helen Noel in "Dagger of the Mind" is intelligent and responsible, but even though *she* is the trained psychologist, it takes Kirk's unfeminine intuition to figure out something is fishy. It also seems a little unprofessional of her to choose a "love" suggestion for their experiment on the neural neutralizer.

Edith Keeler is the only real example of a totally committed, intelligent, and compassionate woman. She is not weak, but her strength does not detract from her femininity. She is a woman with a goal and a meaning to her life. And they had to find her in the 1930s!

Where are these women in the twenty-third century? Are they really so rare (quite possible), or are they just too hard to fit into an action/adventure plot (also possible)?

As for some other contemporary women who cross the *Enterprise*'s path:

Mira Romaine in "The Lights of Zetar" does prove to be less pliant and to have a stronger self-will than first indicated. But it still takes the decompression chamber to get rid of the critters.

Mudd's women are frankly after husbands to take care of.

Irina Galliulin in "The Way to Eden" is easily led and gullible.

Leila Kalomi seems to prefer the dreamy world of the spores of Omicron Ceti III to reality.

Lenore Karidian ("Conscience of the King") and Marta ("Whom Gods Destroy") are both homicidal maniacs.

Droxine, whom Spock finds so intellectually stimulating ("The Cloud Minders"), is really quite heartless and unfeeling until Spock points out her failing.

Why, among all the starship captains, commodores, ambassadors, scientists, and heads of state contacted during the *Enterprise*'s swing around the galaxy, are the few women such unflattering examples?

Alien women, in or out of the Federation, fare hardly better. True, the Romulans have a female commander, but she is amazingly easy to deceive. I must admit that Mr. Spock might be able to turn my head also, but it doesn't say much for her intelligence or efficiency as a flagship commander that she is taken in so completely.

Elaan, the Dohlman of Elas, is far from weak or helpless, but she is undoubtedly a spoiled brat.

As for Vulcan women, we see only two of them and it is difficult to know for certain just what place a woman has in Vulcan society. T'Pau is said to be influential and powerful, and she is the only person ever to turn down a seat on the Federation Council. (Maybe she knows something we don't?) The less said about T'Pring the better. I, for one, will never see the logic in choosing shifty-eyed Stonn over Spock.

It is stated in "Amok Time" that the bride becomes the property of the victor, and from Amanda's quick obedience to Sarek in "Journey to Babel," it might be inferred that this is not only the case when Challenge is given, but the traditional place of women on Vulcan.

And how does that equate with T'Pau's power? It is possible that at the death of the mate, the wife assumes his power and station in life if she is at all qualified. But that is pure conjecture.

Spock's mother, Amanda, is one of the few truly sensible and three-dimensional women found in the Star Trek universe. Unfortunately, she has a tendency to submerge her personality in Sarek's. Having chosen her life on Vulcan, she takes the logical course of following Vulcan tradition. She also seems a little ashamed of her humanity. Or possibly it was her dressmaker who felt that way.

We only get to meet one female Klingon. Mara, in "Day of the Dove," is certainly an improvement on the male Klingon. (She would have had to be, or the race would have died out long ago.) There are definite indications that Klingon men don't understand their women any better than human males do. When Kang sees Mara's torn tunic, he automatically decides she has been raped—and that she liked it! He thinks that is the reason she tries to get him to listen to Kirk. Well, no one ever accused a Klingon of being logical.

There are supposedly about 150 women on the *Enterprise*. I have often wondered just what all these women do.

I have never seen a female in security, or at least I don't remember it. I see no reason why there shouldn't be some in the age of space karate and phasers. But then, I can't recall seeing a crewwoman fire a phaser at all. (Perhaps Starfleet feels they would be unable to hit the side of a barn.)

Angela Martine ("Ballance of Terror") is a phaser specialist, but I got the impression she is more of a repairman than a sharpshooter. I could be right, for she is later transferred to life sciences ("Shore Leave")—and she does run smack into a tree in that episode!

I have noticed very few women in the engineering section either. One notable exception is Lieutenant Masters ("Alternative Factor"), who is in charge of the energizing section of engineering.

On the average, however, women are generally yeomen, historians, secretaries, or assistants of one type or another. You certainly see a lot of them in the corridors and rec rooms. They look very graceful when they fall after a phaser blast or an alien attack on the ship. (I love to watch Christine Chapel fall in "The Way to Eden" during the ultrasonic blast by the space hippies. No grace there. She falls like a ton of bricks.)

Looking at the main characters' attitudes toward women might reveal something about women's place in the Federation.

Kirk's charm is, in the main, a cover for his inability to communicate with women. He is uncomfortable with them and has trouble relating in any other than a sexual or a protective sense. After all, why waste your time trying to be logical when you can seduce them and get what you want? (Examples include "Is There In Truth No Beauty," "Conscience of the King," and "The Gamesters of Triskelion.") It doesn't always work, but he has a good batting average.

Scotty approaches women as if they were china dolls, or at least extremely delicate objects. Whenever he is in love, he goes a little batty. The rest of the time he's too wrapped up in his engines to notice.

Spock usually treats women the same as he does men—logically. But he is somewhat protective of Uhura, and is definitely uncomfortable around Christine.

McCoy is ordinarily the most realistic in his relationships with women— perhaps because he knows from experience they are not all sugar and spice, but have gallstones, hangnails, and gas just like the he-men. However, that does not keep him from turning on the southern charm occasionally—thank goodness.

As for the two most notable crewwomen, Christine Chapel is a career woman and definitely dedicated to her work. But she joined Starfleet to find her lost love Roger Korby. When that didn't work out, she stayed— almost as if to say, "Since I didn't find a husband, I don't have anything better to do." She promptly falls in love with Mr. Spock, and has another reason for living.

It has been suggested that Christine is really a full-fledged doctor. If that is the case, I wonder why she is always addressed as "Nurse"? I think I would resent that a great deal after studying for years to achieve a degree. Especially when it is usually a situation of "Hand me the thermocumbobulator and stand aside."

Uhura is a different matter entirely. She is an expert in her field, and has even been known to fix equipment that Spock could not. And she still remains a complete, total woman.

There are a few times when she flashes her lashes at the Captain and admits in a trembling voice that she is afraid (something I can hardly imagine Scott or Sulu doing), but generally she is quite able to hold her own.

This article is not intended as a radical woman's-lib tirade. Nor did I mean to take nitpicking to a fine art. I think Star Trek did an admirable job of portraying women for that time in television. It even broke some new ground.

But Janice Lester may have a valid point to make somewhere in the root of her insanity. It is doubtful if a woman could have become a starship captain in the Federation of Star Trek.

However, I hear things are looking up. Janice Rand is to be the new transporter chief in the upcoming movie. Maybe Lieutenant Kyle decided to get married and keep house.

We've come a long way, baby.

A BRIEF LOOK AT KIRK'S CAREER

by Leslie Thompson

Who is James T. Kirk anyway? We know him as one of our best friends, of course, but we really know very little about him. In this article, Leslie Thompson uses her "speculative faction" to fill us in on some of the details and background of Jim Kirk. As usual with Leslie's articles, this one stirred up a storm of controversy when first published. Why? Well, read on. . . .

The facts are known.

Name: James Tiberius Kirk. Service Record: Serial Number SC937-0176-CEC. Rank: Captain, Starship Command, USS *Enterprise* NCC-1701. Commendations: Palm Leaf of . . .

As we said, the facts are known. But what of James T. Kirk's early life? What factors shaped him into the man he is today, the starship captain, the explorer, the romantic, the passionate spokesman for all that is good in man?

We have never been given any hard information about Kirk's past, only inference and innuendo. In several episodes, we hear of people and places in Kirk's life—some important, some trivial. But a definitive personal history of Kirk has not been granted to us. Therefore, we must take the few given facts, and extrapolate one of our own.

Kirk was born in Greater Peoria, Illinois, thirty-four years before the first recorded voyage of the *Enterprise*. Shortly after this adventure ("Where No Man Has Gone Before"), Kirk celebrated his thirty-fifth birthday, which was marred by the loss of his closest friend, Commander Gary Mitchell.

When Kirk was still very young, his parents pulled up stakes and moved to Iowa. Rather, his mother did, as Kirk's father was serving in Starfleet as the captain of a destroyer (the *William Jennings Bryan*).

Young Kirk thrived in this new "country" environment, but he was still able to have the best of both rural and city life, as almost instantaneous civilian travel by transporter had become commonplace by this time.

In fact, the majority of Earth's population chose to live in the country, as getting to a job or school was as simple as walking into the next room; and over any distance on Earth . . . and even to the Moon!

So while little Jimmy Kirk lived and played in the rolling wheat fields of Iowa farmlands, he attended school every day in the Des Moines Complex, as did children from all around the state.

As his father was necessarily away most of the time, Kirk's major influences were his mother and his paternal grandfather, Peter Kirk. An older brother, George Samuel, was also quite important to the shaping of Kirk's early years, as he adored the older boy. It was a family joke that little Jimmy would follow "Sam" everywhere he went, often to the chagrin of George, who was developing an interest in girls just about the same time that Jimmy wanted to learn the finer points of zero-grav baseball.

From his mother, Kirk learned a great love of his fellow man and of all living things. She was a quiet and gentle woman who suffered her husband's long absences with a philosophical attitude. In Kirk, she instilled an admiration and love for the father he hardly knew by telling the boy of great deeds done and wonderful places his father had seen, and how he was sacrificing his home life to help keep Earth and the quickly expanding Federation safe from its enemies. So to Jimmy Kirk, his father was not an unknown cipher, but instead, a giant, heroic figure. And the vision of space that his mother described would stay with Kirk for the rest of his life.

Old Pete Kirk would take Jimmy on his knee and tell him of the glorious history of the Kirk family. Even when quite young, Kirk found it hard to believe his grandfather's tales. The hardest to believe were his favorites: the ancestor who was raised by apelike subhumans in darkest Africa, the long-ago masked man who fought for justice in the old West, and the great bronzed figure who was the leading surgeon and scientist of his day. But until the day he died, old Pete Kirk swore the stories were true. James Kirk made a vow to himself to go to the census computers someday and check the stories out, but events swept him up, and the old man's tales soon faded into fond memories.

From them, however, Kirk gleaned an important message: A Kirk was expected to be brave, resourceful, and intelligent. A leader of men and a protector of the weak. Far above other men and better than the best.

This oblique message was probably the primary reason for Kirk's starting to drive himself at an early age. He had the native intelligence, reasoning, and intuition necessary for achieving just a little bit more than his fellow students, but he was no bookworm. Kirk excelled at both sandlot and school-sanctioned sports, and he was outgoing and popular with his classmates. Kirk was one of those rare youngsters who truly enjoyed school in all its phases, and he learned there to balance hard work and hard play.

When Kirk was fifteen, his father came to visit for a final time. Kirk was now old enough to realize that his father was not in actuality the giant hero of his mother's tales, but he was still somewhat awed by the huge and smiling man who strode back into his family's life every six months or so.

This was the longest visit in several years, and Richard Kirk was able to spend time with both of his sons, both together and separately. Sam Kirk was entering his third year in college at the time, and announced that he intended to become a biologist. Richard Kirk took this news stoically, as he realized that his elder son was no man of action, and his talents for organization and intuitive research would take him far in the scientific world. Seeing that his father approved, Sam also confessed that he was planning to marry a lovely young woman named Aurelan, and he wanted his father to be the best man.

Richard Kirk was immensely pleased, and when he turned to Jim and asked if he had considered what he wanted to do with his life, Jim spoke up: "I want to go into Starfleet. I want to be a starship captain!"

Once again, Richard Kirk was pleased. But he knew that his wife would be opposed; she already had enough to worry about. Too, it was a hard row to hoe. The boy had grit and brains, but it took much more than that to make it in Starfleet. Richard Kirk considered himself an intelligent and able man, yet he had never even come near the apex of his profession: commanding a starship. That was not for mere mortals. Starship captains were a breed apart.

So Richard Kirk gave his son a gentle smile and said, "There's time yet. You just might change your mind."

"I won't," answered Jim. Richard Kirk nodded slowly at his youngest son and then led both of his children back into their house.

Two days later he had left. Three weeks after that, he was dead.

Richard Kirk died a hero's death when he directed his ship to intentionally crash into a prototype Orion raider ship. Not only did this action prevent the destruction of a Federation outpost, it made the Orions think twice about challenging the Federation for supremacy in space and forced them into a policy of small-ship piracy and smuggling, ridding the Federation of a potentially dangerous enemy.

Kirk's mother never recovered from the news. Her years-long wall of reserve had been broken by Richard's death, and she became listless and uncaring. When she finally died of a broken heart a year later, Kirk considered it a blessing and comforted his grief with the knowledge that she was finally at peace.

To his surprise, Kirk discovered that his father's heroic death had qualified him to attend Starfleet Academy with the recommendation of his father's commander, Admiral Komack.

Although he would rather have earned the scholarship on his own, he was never one to look a gift horse in the mouth, and upon graduation from high school he entered Starfleet Academy.

It was hard, very much so. Not only did Kirk have to contend with the plethora of new and exciting knowledge presented almost every day, but in a curriculum designed to "wash out" cadets he was the butt of constant teasing and hazing because of the unorthodox way he had entered the Academy. Some of this grew to the point of brutality, and Kirk was ridden hard in particular by an upperclassman named Finnegan.

But it only made Kirk more determined to make it. He took the insults and jokes with grace, but being James T. Kirk, he remembered them all. Throughout the course of his academy days, he managed to repay them all in like fashion—all except Finnegan, who was always careful not to let the grim-faced Cadet Kirk catch him out of uniform.

During this difficult period, Kirk had an intense need for a hero, someone to emulate. He already had his father, but the memories were too painful, especially that of his mother, pining away. This is perhaps where Kirk subconsciously developed his determination never to have a serious relationship with a woman.

But instead of one hero, Kirk found two. In Abraham Lincoln, Kirk saw a parallel with himself—a young man who started with very little managing to overcome adversity and rise to a high position. Too, Lincoln had to suffer the jeers of others, but still did not lose his humility and love for his fellow man. Kirk voraciously read everything he could get on Lincoln (particularly the Sandburg books) and vowed to himself that he would be at least half the man Abraham Lincoln was.

In Garth of Izar, Kirk found another hero, one who represented all that Kirk hoped to achieve as a Starfleet officer—a brilliant tactician, commander of a starship, fair and impartial in his dealings with both his crew and aliens. Kirk almost wore out his copy of Garth's textbook of starship battle tactics, and it was the greatest day in his life when Garth addressed the assembled cadets. If he wanted to be half the man Lincoln was, Kirk wanted to be twice the leader Garth was.

Eventually Kirk was graduated from Starfleet Academy—not at the top of his class; his marks in diplomacy and administration were a bit too low, as he considered these not necessary for a starship commander to know. Kirk didn't intend to be a desk jockey, he wanted to command a starship. And so he gave his greatest efforts to the disciplines he would need most to do so: tactics, math and electronics, space astronomy and exploration, and the physical needs—marksmanship, hand-to-hand combat, and helmsmanship.

However, Kirk still had to enter Command School, and before doing so, he had to serve time on a ship in deep space. He was consequently assigned to the scout ship *Jim Bridger*. However, midway through the voyage, Kirk contracted Vegan choriomeningitis and was remanded to a hospital on a nearby starbase.

Despondent over this setback, as the fast-moving world of Starfleet had no time for raw ensigns to recover from illnesses, Kirk utilized his recovery time to further his knowledge of starship operations and to make up some of the self-imposed deficiencies of his Academy education by constantly meeting and talking to the ever-changing parade of aliens and Federation envoys that visited the starbase. To his surprise, Kirk found that he had a natural ability to perceive and understand the problems and views of the aliens. This was not enough of a revelation to drive him into the diplomatic corps, but it did instill in him a respect for the myriad duties of a starship captain. It took more than an understanding of how a starship works and how best to blast an enemy out of existence to be another Garth. It was a lesson Kirk was not to forget.

Several days before Kirk was to return to the Academy for the long wait for reassignment to a ship, the starbase was the victim of a surprise attack by a Klingon battle cruiser. As Kirk was still on the inactive list and therefore had no specific battle station, he was able to place himself in a position where he could best see how the Klingons attacked the starbase. The outcome was a foregone conclusion, as the big guns of the starbase had the Klingon ship far outclassed, and Kirk assumed that the Klingon commander had gone berserk in the fashion that Klingons sometimes do.

Berserk or not, the Klingon was still a master tactician, and he managed to keep from being destroyed long enough to score a devastating hit on the life-support systems of the starbase. As the Klingon ship exploded, Kirk turned away only to hear the strident tones of a depressurization alarm. Without conscious thought, Kirk grabbed as many pressure suits as he could carry from a nearby storage locker and hurried down to the life-support bays.

Finding them sealed off by the automatic alarm systems, Kirk had a sudden inspiration. He hurried into the nearest transporter alcove, quickly estimated the range, and beamed the pressure suits in to the trapped crewmen. Several of them had already died from lack of oxygen and exposure, but Kirk's quick action managed to save the majority of the technicians.

Although Kirk couldn't see that he had done all that much, the starbase commander thought differently and recommended Kirk for his first award, the Prantares Ribbon of Commendation, Second Class. But more important to Kirk, his quick thinking allowed him to secure an immediate berth on a starship, the *Farragut*, commanded by the man who was soon to become his mentor, Captain Charles Garrovick.

Garrovick developed a soft spot for the young ensign when he discovered Kirk gazing longingly out of the starbase drydock at the majestic *Farragut*. He took Kirk under his wing, becoming almost a second father to him, and helped him to learn the essentials for starship service.

When the crew of the *Farragut* met with the cloud creature and Captain Garrovick died, Kirk blamed himself for not having fired sooner. His distress was especially hard when he learned that one of the last things Garrovick had done before being killed was to recommend that Kirk stand for command, and Kirk became more determined than ever to become a starship captain. He now had the added incentive of feeling that he must replace Garrovick, who was an especially fine commander, and therefore highly valuable to the Federation. He also vowed to someday destroy the cloud creature, a promise which he eventually kept with the help of Garrovick's son.

Back at the Academy for command training, Kirk became involved with Janice Lester, a fiery young cadet whose mercurial personality both attracted and repelled Kirk. Their affair continued throughout Kirk's training, but came to a bad end when Janice failed to meet the exacting Academy standards. Already high-strung, this unbalanced her even more, and she took the unrealistic view that she had been rejected because of her sex. She demanded that Kirk resign his commission in protest, and when he refused, she accused him of being "in on" the imagined conspiracy against her. Kirk wisely chose to stop seeing Janice, and after a while she drifted out of his life. He heard that she was training in astro-archaeology, but did not see her again until she used the ancient device of the Camusians to exchange minds with him in a vain attempt to usurp the powers of a starship captain.

Having graduated from Command School, Kirk was then assigned to the Starship *Exeter* as a helmsman. It was during this mission that he acted as orderly to his captain in the Axanar Peace Mission and was awarded another commendation for his services. Just before his tour of duty aboard the *Exeter* was over, Kirk was forced to report his old friend Ben Finney derelict in duty, causing a rift in their friendship.

Having compiled an excellent record, Kirk was then transferred to the destroyer *Chesty Puller* as first officer. It was during this voyage that Kirk was forced to take over the ship when his captain was injured and battle a Klingon cruiser. Choosing the better part of valor, Kirk ordered a retreat, but found his way blocked by yet another Klingon ship. This was a smaller but no less dangerous ship, and Kirk was forced to fight, as the large ship was jamming his communications.

Utilizing his ship's greater speed, he maneuvered the small Klingon ship into his sights, but held back on the order to fire. Thinking that the Federation ship was helpless, both Klingons moved in, and then Kirk ordered his men to fire while at the same time reversing engines at full warp.

This dangerous move had the effect that Kirk wanted. The smaller Klingon ship was hit by the phaser blast, while the battle cruiser's phasers hit only empty space. By the time that it could reverse course, Kirk's ship had gained just enough of a lead to call for help, and the Klingon, not wanting to face a starship in exchange for having eliminated a small destroyer, pulled away.

In reward for this action, Kirk was presented with the Medal of Honor, and the Karagite Order of Heroism. He also got something which was even more desirable to him: command of his own ship.

However, not right away. First he was to serve as one of the representatives to an exchange program that had been arranged with the Klingons. Luckily, Kirk did not have to travel to a Klingonese planet; he was assigned instead to serve as host and guide to a young Klingon officer, Kumara.

During the time that Kirk and Kumara were roommates at a Starfleet training facility (one carefully selected to reveal to the Klingons a minimum of Federation technology), they became good, if cautious, friends. They parted with a great amount of respect for each other, and each had the feeling that the other would one day be a foe to reckon with.

After completing this unusual assignment to his superiors' complete satisfaction, Kirk received his promised command: a brand-new ship, an experimental-model *Starstalker*, which was also its name. The object of the small, sleek ship was to act as a quick-moving and virtually untraceable weapon, much like the submarines of Earth's past. *Starstalker* was one of three models being tested by the Federation for this type of work.

Although conditions were rather primitive, the ship being strictly a shakedown model (with little provision made for comfort in any case), Kirk could not have been happier. He knew that it was an exceptional mark of confidence that he had been assigned the ship, and he was determined not to fail.

The early part of the cruise went well. The ship was virtually a flying phaser, with speed and firepower comparable to a full-sized starship, and Kirk forced his crew to the limit with every conceivable test the Federation could think of and a few that he invented on the spot. In this, he was ably assisted by a no-nonsense, hardheaded chief engineer named Montgomery Scott, who had helped to design *Starstalker.* Kirk also had his best friend from his Academy days, Gary Mitchell, as first officer. Kirk had requested that Mitchell be assigned to *Starstalker,* using his prerogative as the first captain of a newly commissioned ship.

They ran into some trouble on Dimosous, where a group of hostile rodentlike natives attacked the crew, who had landed to check out a report that dilythium crystals had been discovered on the planet. Kirk was engaged in moving his men into a retreat when one of the natives aimed a poisoned dart at him. Mitchell threw himself in the way and took the dart that was intended for Kirk. When the crew reached the ship safely, Kirk ordered that the nearest route to a starbase hospital be taken, a route which brought the ship dangerously close to the Romulan Neutral Zone. The passage was uneventful, but Kirk received a severe reprimand for his action. His superiors were secretly pleased, however, as they themselves had taken similar risks for friends in the past. It was a mark against Kirk's service record, a mark for him in the eyes of his fellow officers.

After two years of experimentation, the *Starstalker* experiment was shelved and Kirk was assigned another ship. It was the usual procedure for one of his rank (which was at this time commander) to be assigned as second officer aboard a starship, or as captain of a scout. However, Kirk was immediately assigned as captain of a destroyer, which to his immense delight he discovered was the *Hua C'hing,* the first command of his hero, Captain Garth. Again, Kirk took Mitchell with him, along with another officer whom Kirk considered one of his planned "permanent staff," Engineer Scott. Aboard the *Hua C'hing,* he was to acquire another, who was at this time a new ensign: Walter Sulu.

Kirk and company saw much action aboard the *Hua C'hing.* They participated in the opening of the Rigellian System (which had been pioneered a few years previously by Captain Christopher Pike aboard the *Enterprise*) and in several furious battles against the Kzinti, and in one exceptional raid they captured a Klingon warlord who had been in the Arualian System trying to undermine the Federation's influence. For their bravery in this raid, almost all of the crew received Awards of Valor, and Kirk was singled out for a Silver Palm with Cluster to go with his Medal of Honor.

Kirk served aboard the *Hua C'hing* for four years with similar success, and when Captain Pike was promoted to fleet captain, he chose James Kirk as his successor to captain the *Enterprise.* Starfleet Command readily concurred, and less than ten years after he had graduated from Command School, Jim Kirk had realized his ambition: command of a starship.

Again taking along Mitchell, Scott, and Sulu, Kirk spent the previous few days he had before assuming command in gathering together the finest bridge crew he could find. Among these was Lieutenant Uhura, whom Kirk had run across at a starbase, chafing against the duties that kept her from joining a regular crew. It seemed she had done her job too well, and had been assigned as a communications instructor, a job she did competently but nevertheless despised.

Kirk also requested another fine officer, one highly recommended by his old friend Matt Decker: Lee Kelso, to be second navigator behind Mitchell. As backup helmsman, Kirk chose Lieutenant Kevin Riley, a fiesty Irishman who had been Sulu's roommate at the Academy.

Two of the men Kirk wanted had crossed his path in the past, and he had ambivalent feelings about both. However, he wanted his crew to be the very best possible, and so personal feelings had to be put aside. He requested them both: Lieutenant Commander Finnegan as security officer, and Lieutenant Commander Ben Finney as records officer. He got only Finney, as Finnegan was up for a captaincy, and learning this, Kirk didn't want to spoil his chances. But the lack of a top-notch security officer would nag Kirk for several years, and at times he dearly wished he had gotten the cocky but competent Finnegan.

The post of science officer was already filled, as Pike's man had requested to be reassigned to the *Enterprise*. Kirk was leery about working with the Vulcan Spock, but was more than happy to have him. Spock was generally acknowledged to be the finest scientific mind Starfleet had, and Kirk knew that he would prove invaluable in the months ahead. Just how valuable even Kirk never suspected.

After a short shakedown cruise to check the modifications and repairs to the *Enterprise* (Pike had been so active that the ship hadn't had a thorough going-over in some time), Kirk and crew proceeded on several important, if unexciting, missions. Then, one fateful day, word came from Starfleet that the *Enterprise* had been selected for an unusual mission: to go where no man had gone before, through the barrier on the edge of our galaxy.

This was the mission that resulted in the deaths of Mitchell and Kelso, and aided in the decision of Dr. Piper to retire from space. But it was also the baptism of fire for the new Captain of the *Enterprise* and his hand-picked crew, and forged them together into a superbly efficient team.

With the promotion of Spock to first officer (in addition to his science-officer duties) and the assignment of Leonard McCoy as ship's surgeon, the complement of the *Enterprise* was complete.

James T. Kirk had achieved his youthful desire: He commanded a starship with the finest crew in the Federation. And the legend began to grow.

"JUST" A SIMPLE COUNTRY DOCTOR?

by Joyce Tullock

Leonard McCoy always finishes a solid third in every fan poll, but for some reason, very few fans seem to want to write about the good doctor. This is easy enough to understand, as we feel that McCoy is the most complex and intricate character in Star Trek. It is difficult to examine his character with any degree of objectivity—but why should this be so? In her article, Joyce Tullock gives what could be an explanation, and at the same time, a key as to why "Bones" McCoy is such an essential part of Star Trek.

I have a confession to make! Mr. Spock is not my favorite Star Trek character. Neither is Captain Kirk. Nope! I see in Leonard McCoy a valuable, gentle hint to the world of today. He represents the positiveness to be found in the "average" man. Everyone knows that part of Mr. Spock's appeal to Star Trek fans is his cool reserve. It is continually pointed out that his ability to remain calm in an emergency is a highly admired, even envied, trait. That's true. His emotionlessness is often compared to McCoy's rash, excitable nature.

But there is also something to be said in favor of that erratic, emotional Dr. McCoy. He offers to many viewers a very positive example of the other side of the coin. He is more, much more, than a balance for the Star Trek threesome. In taking a close look at the McCoy personality, we find him to be a valuable element, not only for the Kirk/Spock relationship, but for the very success of Star Trek. He is the voice of today, the face of the

36

twentieth century; a kind of Everyman. McCoy is today's connection with tomorrow. For some viewers (myself, at least) he makes the future world of Star Trek more than just believable. He makes it natural.

McCoy, in spite of his highly sophisticated twenty-third-century training, is a twentieth-century man. When he speaks, his words so very often might have been spoken by anyone of our century cast into the world of the *Enterprise*. His thoughts, worries, and insights reach from our world to his. He is concerned about the existence of man in the machine age. While McCoy uses the tools of technology in his work, he is not dependent upon it. He would be a doctor regardless of the age in which he was born. The technology of medicine is important to him, but he does not try to hide his instinctual distrust of machines. In fact, he openly quarrels with them whenever he gets the chance. We all know about his standing quarrel with the transporter, but this is more than the chronic complaining of a bickering eccentric. It is a highly spirited attempt to keep machine and man in their proper places.

The doctor's biting comments about his world reveal a touching concern for the spirit of man. He probably takes machines for granted; he must, for they're a part of his world. But his focus is on humanity.

We find him time and again making statements which Mr. Spock finds ridiculous and illogical. But are they really, from the human point of view? His "emotional" decisions and insights are sometimes the correct ones. Had McCoy not offered himself to the Vians in "The Empath," Spock would have never been able to use his logic to save the day. And in "Return to Tomorrow," McCoy warns Kirk that the incredibly superior beings could "squash" them "like an insect." Now, for once, let's give the doctor credit! He was right! For all Kirk's noble speech about the chances for knowledge and advancement, his decision was at least partially in error. He did not even attempt any kind of compromise plan, but went along wholeheartedly (and somewhat recklessly) with the alien's wishes. Really, what would have been so wrong with the exercise of just a little caution?

But Captain Kirk often shows us that he values McCoy's judgment and insight. He tells Spock to seek out McCoy's advice in "The Tholian Web," and in "A Private Little War," Kirk insists that the doctor's insight may aid him in solving the problem of Tyree's people. When Kirk and McCoy have a violent disagreement about the means of providing a balance of power, we see one of McCoy's most important functions outside the realm of medicine: He provides the Captain with an intelligent, honest, and uninhibited sounding board for ideas. He is no "yes man." He is refreshingly outspoken.

McCoy reminds us, then, that emotion can be a positive force. And for humans, it is essential. Let's not forget that the ancient Vulcans' inability to control their emotions with moderation has forced them to suppress that part of their nature totally. Well, that may work for Vulcans, but Dr. McCoy knows that it is not a thing to be desired in humans.

In "Plato's Stepchildren" we learn the equally beautiful aspects of the two natures. Spock advises his friends to express their emotions just as he must "master" his. Healthy or unhealthy, the expression of emotion is vital to human well-being. And as mankind has learned countless times, the suppression of emotion in the human animal can ultimately lead to disastrous effects. We are not Vulcans. We are built to display emotions, we operate through them. We depend on them to guide our heart and conscience. It is emotion which causes one human to make sacrifices for another. That's just the way we are. It's how we exist. And McCoy knows that the humans of Star Trek are not inferior to the Vulcan race because they are emotional.

Indeed, man has done the Vulcans one better, as Kirk points out in "Spectre of the Gun" and "Arena," for instead of denying his emotional nature, he is learning to overcome its negative aspects. Today, he simply will not give in to his desire to kill! The man of the twenty-third century is learning to harness his emotions in order to put them to good use; a fine display of human logic! And this is the kind of emotion represented in McCoy. Emotion is not to be repressed, but channeled. And as a doctor and humanitarian, McCoy has developed the use of emotion to an art.

So Dr. McCoy also knows how to lighten the tension of his world. And as a doctor he obviously sees more suffering than any of his friends aboard the *Enterprise*. Also, as a doctor, he shares the confidence of many aboard the *Enterprise*—and so bears the burdens that must accompany such a responsibility.

But to McCoy, this is what life is all about: people (yes, and Vulcans, too). He values them. And we get the feeling that he sees a special treasure in Mr. Spock. He goads Spock. Teases him. Tricks him into not taking himself quite so seriously. He won't let Spock forget that he is half human, because McCoy knows, as Spock's mother knows, that being human is good too. So because McCoy feels that it is important, he reminds Spock of his own humanity. And McCoy no doubt believes that the human part of Spock has a need for recognition; for that is basic to human nature. This is why he asks Spock's mother about his childhood. Because he worries about Spock's human half hiding inside. He serves as a gadfly, constantly challenging Spock to face the reality of his complex nature.

In fact, it is through this interaction with McCoy that Mr. Spock reveals much of his human side. Spock clearly enjoys correcting the doctor's illogic, and often goes out of his way to get a rise from McCoy. McCoy falls to the bait, not because he is stupid, but because he is keenly aware of the Vulcan's need to make some kind of contact. No one, not even a Vulcan, can live in total isolation. While Kirk offers binding friendship, McCoy offers Spock something else which is essential. In forcing Spock to react to his illogic, his emotional outbursts, and his passionate caring, McCoy provides a kind of therapeutic human experience. The Spock/McCoy feud is simply a sign of friendship. How else could they be expected to communicate?

The doctor often seems almost out of place and uncomfortable in that technological world. He reacts to his world more like a common man from our own time. This, however, is only one way in which he represents twentieth-century man. His responses to problems and dangerous situations are perhaps the most realistic.

In "Return to Tomorrow" he worries quite naturally about beaming down into solid rock. He is less likely to forge too quickly into a dangerous situation. Kirk, in this very episode, states that McCoy is too cautious. But it is this very tendency toward caution which makes McCoy such an attractive character. He is, at times, the reluctant hero.

Let's face it: Kirk and Spock, compared to McCoy, are "macho" men. Their courage and determination in the face of the gravest dangers is legend. They are military men. They've trained themselves to have nerves of steel. McCoy, however, is not one to "rush in where angels fear to tread." While all three think things over carefully before taking action, McCoy tends to consider the negative side most cautiously. More than once he argues with Kirk's decision to enter a risky situation. And his advice often proves to be very sound indeed.

Because McCoy is not "macho," because he is more likely to display his heroic reluctance, he becomes a very honest, true-to-life character. And when he takes a chance or makes a sacrifice, we can appreciate it all the more. You can almost feel the butterflies in his stomach! Spock once accused him of having a martyr complex ("The Immunity Syndrome"). But Leonard McCoy is no martyr. He doesn't like danger. When he takes a share of the danger, it is more out of love than devotion to duty. His decision to protect Spock and Gem from the Vians is a very complicated one. Knowing McCoy, it is hard to believe that he made that decision solely because it was logical. As a matter of fact, he probably would have done it whether it had been logical or not. He cared about Spock and Gem; and the doctor is notorious for allowing his emotions to guide him.

"The Empath" is often discussed in connection with both Spock and Dr. McCoy. And it is perhaps one of the most intensely emotional episodes of the series. It was certainly one of Nimoy's most clever performances, for he managed to display very deep concern for his friend with such subtlety that he avoided stepping out of character. Somehow,

Kirk's outward display of emotion diminishes before the quiet worry in Spock's eyes.

Of course, this may all only be in the eyes of the beholder. With Spock, it is hard to tell how much we see and how much we superimpose through our own emotions.

But one thing is clear: Kirk and Spock's concern for the doctor runs through Star Trek as a general motif. It would be interesting to count the number of times he is pushed aside, left behind, held back, knocked out or hushed (his big mouth is often his gravest danger) simply for his own protection. In short, McCoy's friends show a tendency to shelter him from danger whenever possible.

This adds another charming aspect to McCoy's nature. He is not a bumbler, but he is an innocent in the military world. First and last he is a doctor. And he is constantly pointing this out to Kirk and Spock. Because he thinks like a doctor, he thinks like a civilian—and that takes us back to his essential value to Star Trek.

Kirk, in "The Alternative Factor," is a busy man trying to find answers to the "winking out" problem. He becomes annoyed with McCoy's natural (and once again realistic) way of describing the unusual recovery of his patient, Lazarus. To Kirk, a man trained in the military sense, McCoy is beating around the bush. McCoy, on the other hand, claims to be "just a simple country doctor." He is puzzled, embarrassed, bewildered, and a little bit amused by his own problem. Here we can clearly see that Kirk's tremendous responsibilities force him to be more serious. The very nature of Dr. McCoy's work, however, has taught him to arm himself with a sense of humor—which is sometimes his only defense (and in some episodes, Star Trek's only salvation).

McCoy's insistence that he is "just a simple country doctor" provides more reinforcement for that "Everyman" quality of his character. He is uncomfortable in social surroundings. He hates the dress uniform and makes an embarrassed, half-hearted attempt to give Sarek the Vulcan salute in "Journey to Babel." His "country" attitude offers a colorful contrast to the world of the twenty-third century.

It's those little touches (which may have seemed insignificant at the time they were written and performed) which fill out his character and make it so real. Most viewers, to some extent at least, can identify with his distaste for formality, regulations, and computers. McCoy is much the ordinary guy, like one of H. G. Wells' contemporary characters cast into a world with which he is a little out of touch. And we can somehow admire his determination not to adjust too well. He is always a little at odds, and he likes it.

McCoy is not a character just to be admired. Kirk and Spock fulfill that basic hero need. He is a character to be "recognized." And what we may see of ourselves in him (both the good and the bad) allows us to step easily into Star Trek's world. He is the conduit, the connection. His awe and disbelief reflect our own. When he speaks, we may not always agree with him, but we "understand" the way he thinks. And when he beats around the bush or has difficulty understanding Spock's scientific jargon, that's when we like him most of all. That's when we feel at home on the *Enterprise.*

McCoy's informal attitude should not be taken too seriously, either. After all, he is a man who knows his business. Even Mr. Spock admires his abilities (although he seldom admits it). He compliments the doctor's expertise in "Spectre of the Gun," has confidence in his ability to operate on Sarek, and is in puzzled awe of his scientific method in "Miri."

Incidentally, it would have been nice to just once hear someone say thanks after being brought back from near death by McCoy. All right, so you can't expect it from Vulcans. But still . . . McCoy's medical talents might have been brought out a little more clearly in the series. He does get to isolate countless viruses and create antidotes once in a while, but for the most part he fulfills his medical task by announcing that fatal message: "He's dead, Jim!" (If anyone has ever bothered to count them, I don't want to hear about it!)

Still, for the most part, Dr. McCoy's dialogue provides some of the most entertaining and memorable moments of Star Trek. When McCoy comes on the screen, the viewer knows he's in line for some humor, tension, or real drama. His comments and facial expressions can animate an otherwise dry or trite script. He was not always utilized to the fullest in Star Trek, and when he is missing the show is usually the poorer for it. In "Let That Be Your Last Battlefield" he makes what I like to call his "special guest appearance" early in the program and is never heard from again. I felt cheated! But then, that was one of those shows that . . . well, what can I say? McCoy's presence invariably provided a snappiness and tension which helped to keep the show running smoothly in spite of it all.

The doctor's relationship with Mr. Spock, of course, is essential. It tells us more about the Vulcan than we could ever know directly. The Spock/McCoy contrast (note—not "conflict") is beautiful, for it most clearly emphasizes the IDIC concept. Here are two completely different natures, each serving by contrast to emphasize and display the beauty of the other.

Just as many viewers value Spock's cool control, McCoy's humanity must be appreciated, too. His ability to display uninhibited emotion is a thing to be admired in our own too often tight-lipped society. McCoy is a man of old Earth warmth, charm, even elegance, and these positive qualities are derived from his emotional essence. His outward gruffness only emphasizes the grace of his true character as we learn to know him.

As we become more aware of McCoy the humanitarian, McCoy the cynic becomes justified.

Like the real people of today's world, Leonard McCoy has been hurt in love. He does not have Kirk's knack of being a lady-killer or Spock's built-in shield of emotionlessness. He feels very deeply, and we get the impression that he is very cautious about those feelings. Once again, he is very much the average man. But McCoy handles his life quite well. The fact that his personal problems are recognizable as being common today just adds more to his character. While they no doubt color his personality, they do not weigh him down. After all, as McCoy would say, "A little suffering is good for the soul." So we may assume that the doctor is able to channel those bad emotional experiences and use them for good. His depth of understanding and concerned empathy with others is clear.

Leonard McCoy's presence aboard the USS *Enterprise* provides a sometimes subtle—but always essential—flavor to Star Trek. Without diminishing the value of Kirk and Spock, it must be said that McCoy gives Star Trek an element of credibility in his own right.

He is texture. He is the click of recognition which helps make Star Trek work. Barely noticeable at times, his is the life spark which tricks us into believing that it's all real. He makes us feel at home. For the most part, he says what we would say and does what we would do if cast into such a world. Or at least he says what we might "like" to say or do.

He moves on his own in a highly controlled world and refuses to be a cog in the machine. McCoy is not afraid of eccentricity. He does not take himself or his elaborate education too seriously. He charms us with his illogical, erratic, and emotionally volatile nature. He touches us with his human warmth. In a way, he represents the mankind of today at its best. Perhaps he is the antithesis of Mr. Spock in many ways. Perhaps he touches us for the very opposite reasons that Mr. Spock does. All the more to the benefit of Star Trek and the philosophy of IDIC.

CHARACTERIZATION RAPE

by Kendra Hunter

It will come as no surprise to anyone who purchased this book that hundreds of original Star Trek stories are published each year in fanzines. This flood of new ST is the most outstanding feature of the fan subculture, and will eventually be responsible for an entire new crop of authors, poets, screenwriters, and reviewers—many of whom would never have dared to try their hand at writing if Star Trek had not come along to stimulate their imaginations.

But this plethora of "fanfic" has caused some dissension in fandom. Kendra Hunter discusses what this dissension is and why it occurs, and at the same time exposes some of the flaws that should be avoided in writing your original Star Trek story.

Somewhere in the vastness of interstellar space, the Starship *Enterprise* sails smoothly at warp factor 2. Commander Spock, standing at his station on the bridge, can be overheard explaining to Dr. Leonard McCoy that "fascinating" is a word he would use in the description of the unexpected. The phenomenon that is Star Trek must certainly qualify as "fascinating."

On March 11, 1964 (Star Trek, first draft), a man by the name of Gene Roddenberry sat at his typewriter and began to shape a dream into reality. Because he believed in the intelligence of television viewers and loved science fiction, Mr. Roddenberry created Star Trek. This created-for-television series had such a wide format that many current social problems could be aired in the episodes. "Let This Be Your Last Battleground" exposed prejudice for the ridiculous idea that it is, and in "The Trouble with Tribbles" an environmental problem was illustrated while we were being entertained. The show allowed the expression of the IDIC, the evaluation of freedom, and the individual rights of beings. In the turbulent decade of the '60s, with the Vietnam War, the assassination of John Kennedy, the college campus riots, and the space program, which took us from Alan Shephard's historic fifteen minutes to Neil Armstrong's "giant leap for mankind," Star Trek was a platform for writers to express the dreams of peace and freedom.

The writers, under the guidance of the Great Bird of the Galaxy, and producer Gene L. Coon, produced quality scripts wherein the personalities of the characters began to develop. The actors projected much of themselves into the stories. Captain Robert M. April became James T. Kirk, commanding one of Starfleet's finest vessels. According to the outline, April was a colorfully complex personality, capable of action and decision, while continually battling with self-doubt and the loneliness of command. These same features manifest themselves in Kirk. William Shatner, with the help of Mr. Roddenberry and Mr. Coon, took Kirk and made him a living being. The same is true of Mr. Spock, a character whom the powers-that-be at NBC viewed with skepticism. No one had ever done this before, and they were afraid. Maybe television producers should be frightened more often.

Writing in the constant pressure of a television-production atmosphere must be debilitating at best, and the probability of committing what has been labeled "characterization rape" is great. This is done by professional writers in all aspects of fiction writing, so it was not surprising to find this offense in the volumes of fan fiction which began while Star Trek was still being aired in prime time.

In order to avoid committing characterization rape, a writer, either professional or amateur, must realize that she (those gentlemen readers must forgive my use of the feminine pronouns, but as the vast majority of fan writers are women, it seems only proper) is not omnipotent. She cannot force her characters to simply do as she pleases. Fictional characters are like newborn babies—from the moment of birth each is an individual with unique personality traits. When an author forces a character to work out of sync, the result is an episode like "The *Galileo* Seven." Such a story leaves the reader or viewer frustrated, unsatisfied, and cheated.

The writer must have respect for her characters or those created by others that she is using, and have a full working knowledge of each before committing her thoughts to paper. If the characters do not move in sync as living people do, the result is bad writing and the reader/viewer is left not caring. It is the caring for and loving of the Star Trek characters that necessitated fan fiction.

"The *Galileo* Seven," written by Oliver Crawford and S. Bar-David, is a prime example of characterization rape involving all the characters. The writers began with a preconceived notion of what a Vulcan was and were going to make Spock that Vulcan without taking the time to become acquainted with him. The beginning of the story states that although this half-Vulcan is first officer aboard the *Enterprise*, he has never commanded a mission. Oh, come now! What's he been doing for the last twelve years? A person does not achieve a place of responsibility in Starfleet without having earned it. Then the crew of the *Galileo* is forced out of sync as the writers continually demand insubordination from them. Regardless of how the crew feel about Mr. Spock or his ability to command, these people are militarily trained and as such would not vocalize mutinous opinions.

However, as with all the aired Trek, there is good with the bad. The only action taken by Spock that is totally within his character is the moment when he jettisons the fuel and ignites it—a command decision which was made when it had to be made, where it had to be made, in light of all available information. It was not an emotional outbreak, just a logical decision, a gamble to be sure, but a logical gamble with everything to gain and nothing to lose.

While "The *Galileo* Seven" is an example of characterization rape, there are examples of the lasting impression made when a character behaves true to form. "The City on the Edge of Forever" demonstrates the value of forcing the viewer/reader to care about a fictional character. When Kirk watched Edith die—and he must let her die—all of Trekdom cries. We all feel the pain and want to help. This is Kirk, the real Kirk, the man who touches our hearts.

Characterization is by far the most important aspect of fiction writing. The creating of men, women, children, and extraterrestrials must make them into entities, they must live and breathe as they move across the pages or the screen. If they do not, the reader/viewer has been cheated and the writer has failed. Whatever point the writer wished made will not be made because the reader does not care.

To make the reader/viewer care (without committing characterization rape) was a problem faced by the writers from the time the first Star Trek script was drafted and continues today in the hundreds of fanzines. The characters had been outlined by Roddenberry, but each writer has to further the development of each of them. And therein lies the trick—to maintain the characters in sync while expanding and exploring the interrelationships of the various characters. And there are a variety of relationships: Kirk/Spock, Kirk/McCoy, Spock/McCoy, Spock/Chapel, Kirk/Chekov, Kirk/Uhura, etc., each having value and depth. The majority of these relationships were only hinted at vaguely in the aired episodes, but they exist nonetheless and have been fully developed in the realms of fan fiction. The most apparent relationship of this group is the Kirk/Spock relationship. It was begun on the aired episodes and has grown and increased in fan fiction.

This relationship came into being because the fan writers loved the characters and cared about the ideas that are Star Trek and they refused to let it fade away into oblivion. It is these fans who are responsible for the volumes of fanzines which contain stories, novels, articles, poetry, songs, cartoons, and many other artistic expressions. If there was no fandom, the aired episodes would stand as they are, and yet they would be just old reruns of some old series with no more meaning than old reruns of "I Love Lucy." Because Star Trek is what it is; because the fans took to heart every word that was uttered, every expression that was filmed, every eyebrow that was raised and made it even more; because the fans took Kirk/Spock and developed it far beyond even what Roddenberry had imagined, the relationship has become as deep and rich and meaningful as the entire concept of Star Trek itself.

As an example, Commander Spock is briefly outlined in "The Star Trek Guide," Third Revision, April 17, 1967, as being biologically, emotionally, and intellectually a "half-breed" who has more advanced mental powers, as well as more fully developed physical strength, than the humans he serves with on board the *Enterprise*. In fan fiction Spock had been evolved from the time before his birth until his death. The history of Vulcan has been written and discussed. The Vulcan language has been analyzed and a dictionary written. Spock's parents have been written about from all angles, until they too, have become living, breathing fictional characters.

It was this desire for a deeper understanding of the characters, who had become friends, companions, and even heroes, to the fans and the unwillingness to let them be forgotten that spawned the torrent of fan fiction.

There is no way to discuss fan fiction or characterization rape in fan fiction without discussing the worst offender: the Lieutenant Mary Sue story. Mary Sue stories are typical groupie fantasies in which, usually, a writer transfers herself from the 1970 era into the future by means of the Guardian of Forever, a time wrap, or other device of time travel, and finds herself in the Star Trek universe. In general, Mary Sue is a single, thirty-year-old female, who is incredibly beautiful, super-loving, super-intelligent, super-everything. In the standard format, Kirk, Spock, and McCoy fall in love with her immediately and sometimes even Scott, Sulu, and Chekov are included in the emotional tangle. Mary Sue will choose one of the men to begin a relationship and complete her fantasy. In so doing, Mary Sue usually must save the *Enterprise* from some unimaginable horror while the command crew, whom Starfleet command has spent a great deal of taxpayer money to train, sit on their hands. Once the Big *E* is saved to fight another day, Mary Sue and whichever of the men (in my case, it's always Captain Kirk) she chooses ride off into the sunset to live happily ever after.

The criminal offense committed here is the obvious forcing of the characters to step out of their roles and become something that they are not. Kirk is not about to go off into the sunset with anyone because he is owned body and soul by the *Enterprise*, as men for centuries have been owned by their ships. The call of space is no different from the call of the sea. Kirk is not about to allow an untrained amateur on the bridge of his ship.

These stories are an exotic form of torture for the reader, but nonetheless, the Mary Sue story is a necessary part of fan fiction. It provides a place for the writer to begin to develop her writing talent, to let her thoughts flow from mind to paper.

When a writer sits down at her typewriter and creates a character, all aspects of that character are in her head, either consciously or unconsciously, and all she has to do is draw from that knowledge. In Star Trek writing, however, these new characters must function in a world inhabited by fictional characters already known quite well by the reader. The writer must then make sure her character has evolved according to her own individual personality, while at the same time the previously created people are moving according to their personalities.

The officers and crew of the USS *Enterprise* are not real, a fact that is sometimes overlooked by the fans. Many writers have a difficult time relating from their point of view in the real world to the imaginary world of our beloved Kirk and company. Mary Sue and her many compatriots serve as a bridge to span this void between the real and the unreal. It is a step used by the writer to overcome a barrier which exists in the mind and allows her to relate on a one-to-one basis with the fictional characters.

However, when this method is used to force the other characters to act out of sync, then it produces bad writing. Unless a writer is prepared to write directly to her reader, she should never attempt to be published. If the writer wants to share her Mary Sue or other fiction work with the readers (there are thousands of eager readers in the realms of Trekdom), then she should endeavor to make that fiction as plausible as possible. Make Kirk, Spock, and company real and vivid, reacting as all the readers know they will react. Mary Sue must fit into the world of the *Enterprise* and not the other way around; and if she does not fit, transfer her off the ship and start all over again. The market is there—it doesn't pay much, but the market does exist and the readers are eagerly awaiting all the Star Trek fiction that is available.

Fan fiction had its beginning during the second season of the aired episodes and is still being produced at a phenomenal rate this very moment. Over the years the writers have gone through a series of phases in the content of the stories, beginning with the sequel stage. The majority of early fan fiction concerned itself with what happened to Zarabeth or the further adventures of Kevin Riley, characters the fans were enchanted with immediately. Then came Mary Sue, followed by "get Kirk" and "get Spock" stories wherein the development of the relationship was explored by a method called hurt/care/torture/comfort. Kirk is hurt, Spock cares, the pain is torturous, and Spock offers comfort. Or the other way around.

In the beginning there was Spock, and somewhere way out in left field there was Kirk. This was a concept even Shatner had to learn to live with. Some of the writers didn't quite know how to handle Spock, while others virtually ignored Kirk in order to develop the Vulcan. I am an adamant admirer of Captain Kirk, and this latter approach left me a little cold; I was glad to see the gorgeous captain take his rightful place in fan fiction. Then the scrutinization of Kirk/Spock began, and where it will end, only the fen* know.

In "Requiem for Methuselah," written by Jerome Bixby, there is an example of the rape of Captain Kirk as well as the existence of the Kirk/Spock relationship. Captain Kirk does not fall in love, instantly, with any woman. He may use a woman to get what he wants or needs, but to develop an emotional relationship requires some time. And the captain would never jeopardize his ship or his crew in any way, especially for personal reasons. We have already seen Kirk allow Edith Keeler to die in order to save his ship, his crew, and his world. However, the episode "Requiem for Methuselah" is overshadowed by the final scene in Kirk's quarters. McCoy and Spock are conversing while Kirk sleeps. McCoy says: "You'll never know the things that love can drive a man to—the ecstasies, the miseries, the broken rules, the desperate chances, the glorious failures, the glorious victories—all of these things you'll never know, simply because the word 'love' isn't written in your book." But Spock does know. And in one of the most moving scenes in aired Trek, Spock demonstrates he does know love by removing the more painful memories from Kirk's mind—a beautiful action which offsets one of the worst of the episodes.

Alone in the universe, Spock, at home nowhere except in Starfleet, and Kirk, bearing the loneliness of command, find the strength of love and friendship in each other.

One of the most valuable things to come from women's lib is "men's

*Fan term—plural of fan.

lib." A release from years of not being able to love, cry, express emotion, or assume the responsibility for changing the baby's diaper. Being a man, or a woman, has taken on new dimensions wherein each is allowed to develop his or her interests and abilities to the fullest. And as has been said many times before, Trek was ahead of its time. The wide format allowed these two men to care about each other and to establish a love/friendship relationship. We didn't see Joe Friday and Frank Gannon hug one another or cry or even care about each other the way Starsky and Hutch are now able to express these feelings. In the past when two men cared for each other, and expressed it, they were eventually labeled gay.

This has befallen Kirk/Spock, arrived at logically after years of writing, reading, and developing said characters, according to those who accept this premise. Unfortunately, it is out of character for both men, and as such comes across in the stories as bad writing.

After reading a sampling of zines, which were provided by the curator of *Memory Alpha*, the Federation Library and Bibliographic Center, containing stories, editorials, and viewpoints, there seems to be, in fanfic, a theory that after all the years of searching, touching, hurting, comforting, there is only one recourse open to the Kirk/Spock relationship, and that is the evolution of a homosexual relationship.

A relationship as complex and deep as Kirk/Spock does not climax with a sexual relationship. If such physical relationship is to be, it will be the beginning. When two beings meet and establish a rapport, sexuality allows a common bond of communication. Sex has a purpose above and beyond the perpetuation of the species, and that is to serve as a basis on which to begin a relationship, the common point where two people can begin to exchange ideas while enjoying the company and companionship of each other.

As time passes, these two people (and a meaningful, fulfilling sexual relationship seems to work best when limited to two people) learn other forms of communication, if they really care about each other. With a sexual relationship, in the beginning, no words are necessary; the primitive emotions and reactions are sufficient. But it does not last. There comes a time when communication must advance to the sharing of ideas. As this sharing becomes more pronounced, the necessity to touch seems to diminish, until a point is reached where a touching of hands brings more joy and pleasure than the uniting of bodies ever could.

At this point I always envision Sarek extending two fingers towards Amanda, and her response of placing two extended fingers against his. Touching briefly as a symbol of what they have shared in their relationship.

The Vulcans had added new dimension to the idea of two people being able to share, to communicate, to express feelings, in the form of the mind meld, wherein two minds are joined and thoughts are allowed to flow between the two. Kirk and Spock have experienced the mind meld on several occasions, so that the thoughts and feelings of one are able to become the thoughts and feelings of the other without the clumsiness of words. Once this advanced stage of communication has been reached, it would seem that returning to the first stage of communication, a sexual relationship, would be anticlimatic.

However, the broad format allows for several sets of circumstances in which Kirk and Spock are placed in a position where a homosexual relationship seems to be the only way out, usually because Spock's life is on the line. If Spock was pure Vulcan, a different set of standards would be used; but Spock is half human and that adds a new field of speculation.

For a scenario, the premise of *pon farr* seems to provide the most realistic setting. Spock is now in the advanced stages of *pon farr*, and because of his continued mind link with Kirk, the only person who can save Spock's life is Kirk. Needless to say, the *Enterprise* is parsecs from Vulcan. But Spock would never allow Kirk to know, and he would die.

If Kirk, being the industrious person that he is, discovers the problem at the last moment, he could force Spock to accept his help. Kirk, watching his friend near death, finds he has no choice: He either enters the realm of bisexuality or allows Spock to die.

In the sobering light of dawn, Kirk relives in his mind the events of the preceding night, and being the character that he is, he allows the seeds of guilt to begin to form and grow until they not only destroy the relationship, but the man himself.

Spock does indeed have strong feelings for Kirk, but he has also demonstrated a caring loyalty to at least one other human, Captain Christopher Pike. After serving for almost two years with Kirk, Spock risks everything he has, including his life, in order to give Pike the only chance at life he has.

Here is Spock, who supposedly has no feeling for anyone, stealing a starship and very knowingly accepting the death penalty for visiting Talos. The crimes he commits are the most serious in Starfleet, and Spock has no guarantee that anyone will intercede in his behalf. Pike will reach Talos and life while Spock will face court-martial and death.

There must have existed between Spock and Pike a strong relationship, but in my research for this article, through the many volumes of fan fiction, I could not find anything written concerning such a relationship. It seems very strange to me that over eleven years of a man's life have been omitted from fan fiction. Spock is not an ordinary fictional character. He is idolized, almost worshiped, by the fen, and yet, even though the entire history of Vulcan was constructed to provide Spock with a background, the eleven years, four months, and five days that Spock served under Pike have been neglected. Why? Does that relationship somehow invalidate the extent to which fan writers have carried the Kirk/Spock relationship?

There is another line of reasoning as to why the Kirk/Spock relationship has been developed to the physical. In the realm of fanfic it is believed that this relationship has evolved logically to a sexual relationship over the years while each gradually learned to touch and be touched, to hold and be held, to care and to love. I realize that the homosexual relationship did not just appear one day; it was reached after years of writing and reading. But I must wonder if it wasn't the result of the writers' having nothing left to write about. After all the hurting and torture and caring and comfort, what was left to write about?

Trek fiction has a problem unique unto itself in that the characters first appeared on the screen rather than in print, so that when one thinks of Kirk, one automatically envisions Shatner. Leonard Nimoy tried to deny that he was Spock and came to the logical conclusion that if he was not, then who was? Most fictional characters are created on paper to walk the pages of a novel long before being transferred to the screen. Not so with Trek. Roddenberry outlined the characters, Gene L. Coon directed the formation, but it was the actors who provided the form and substance, the personalities, the expressions, and the attitudes; all combined to make us, the viewers, really care about what was happening. Trek was special to each of these people who have had their lives shaped by the effect that Trek produced on us, the fen. We should remember their feelings as we express our own in fan fiction. Yes, we—the fans and the writers, and the artists, and all the rest—do have the right to freedom of expression, but only when that right does not infringe on the rights of other individuals.

Trek is a format for expressing rights, opinions, and ideals. Most every imaginable idea can be expressed through Trek, including homosexuality. But there is a right way. Kirk's actions in "The City on the Edge of Forever" and "Balance of Terror" showing his strengths and weaknesses. The wrong way can simply be illustrated with "The *Galileo* Seven." Fiction literature has long played an important role in the presentation of new ideas and concepts. When properly expressed, these ideas have started revolutions.

So, ladies—and gentlemen—man your typewriters (somehow, "woman your typewriters" just doesn't make it), and make Trek fiction the strong forceful tool it can be. Through the words we write here and now, Earth, 1978, we can very easily guide our nation, and even the world, from where we are to the point in time where Trek is—and maybe without their World War III. We can make all those things come true—the IDIC, the Prime Directive—but only if we are willing to work.

The ideal of Trek is truth and beauty, and when carried out in the finest form of fictional characterization, Kirk, Spock, McCoy, and the other members of the crew will join the realm of Antigone, Macbeth, and Tom Sawyer to live forever.

COMMAND DECISION CRISIS: A STAR TREK FAN FICTION PARODY

by Walter Irwin

We've run several Star Trek parodies in Trek, *but one of the wildest is this spoof of bad Star Trek fan fiction called "Command Decision Crisis" (the title, appropriately enough, has nothing to do with the story). It is not only fun to read, but an excellent example of how* not *to write a Star Trek story.*

It was not a good day aboard the United Fedderbedding Planets Starship *Ennui.* Captain James T. Cute was mad. Good and mad.

"Why can't I find a Security Chief that is worth a Omnicronian *diskobeat?*" moaned Cute, rubbing his chin raw in consternation. "I have the finest crew in Starbeat, and I deserve to have them. I have worked long hours—"

"Eighty-six point two minutes, Captain," interrupted Mr. Skunk from his science section.

Cute shot him a dirty look. "Well, maybe not *hours* exactly, but I have worked hard—"

"Ordering us about, he's worked," came a mutter from somewhere near Communications.

Cute chose to ignore it this time. "I repeat, I have worked hard and long—er, minutes—to make this the finest crew in Starbeat, and at the risk of repeating myself—"

"Again." This time the murmur was from Engineering.

"I repeat, I will not have it!" Cute shouted. "Now," he continued, trying to pull his tunic down over his stomach and failing (it was late in the season). "This ship will have a top-notch security chief or I will know the reason why!" Having made this pronouncement, Cute stood to his full height, teetered a moment on his high heels, and strode into the turbolift.

As the doors *swooshed* shut behind him, he heard another comment: "Maybe you *are* the reason why."

Dr. "Moans" Macaw was seated in his office hard at work cutting a new pair of soles for his boots with one of his favorite scalpels as Cute stormed in.

"Doctor," Cute blurted, "what about my security chief?"

Macaw looked at him in confusion. "Do we have a security chief in here today, Jimbo? I swear, they die lahk flies, don't they?"

"No, no, no, no, no, no," cried Cute, shaking his boyish forelock with each emphatic "no." "I mean, how can you help me get a new security chief, one who will live up to the high standards of this crew I've put together, the finest in the fleet? I've worked long and hard . . ." Cute didn't know what to say after this, as no one had ever let him finish before.

Macaw gave him a slow smile, causing his eyes to crinkle appealingly at the edges. "Hang on a minute, Jim, while ah unstick mah eyes again." He pulled his lids up with a handy forceps (he had been using it to open a bottle of Smarmian brandy) and sighed, "Ah gotta quit smilin'. Couldn't get 'em open yesterday, and took out a fellah's appendix."

"That's good work with your eyes closed," said Cute, impressed.

"Yeah, too bad he was here fo' a hangnail. Now Jim, what's this huffin' and a puffin' about a security chief?"

"I just can't seem to find a chief that's any good," muttered Cute. "Doctor, could it be that it *is* my fault? Could it be that in my zeal to run everything on this ship I have undermined and emasculated every security chief we've ever had? Could it be I haven't been as fair and just as a starship captain should? Could it be . . . aw, nah. Starbeat Command is at fault, as usual."

"Jim, seein' as how I know every little nook an' cranny inside that head of yourn, I agree with you. Now, I'm a doctor, not a personnel executive, but what you need is somebody to be security chief that can take the heat. It's a tough job, and you need a tough man to handle it."

"Doctor, that makes sense."

Macaw sat up in surprise. "It does?"

"You bet," said Cute excitedly. "Let me call Skunk up here and we'll talk it over." Cute punched the intercom button, and after a few minutes on hold, asked his first officer to come to sick bay.

A few minutes later Commander Skunk sidled into the room. No matter how much they had been through together, Cute reflected, he was still always fascinated with Skunk. He was the issue of a Fulcan father and a human mother, and although he chose early in life to live as a logical and emotionless Fulcan, he sometimes demonstrated the human side of his nature by wearing loud-colored shirts, drinking beer from the can, and inviting hapless crewmembers over to watch endless boring home movies.

"Yes, Captain?" Skunk asked in his flat, dull voice.

Macaw tossed him a whetstone from his medical bag. "Use this, you pointy-eared elf. We can't understand you."

Skunk stropped his tongue with several quick strokes. "Is this better, gentlemen?" As they nodded assent, he continued. "You requested my presence, sir?"

"Hold it a minute, Skunk," said Cute, snapping his fingers. "We can't get on with the story until we introduce Mr. Scotch." Once again he turned to the intercom, and called the ship's engineering officer to sick bay.

Commander Scotch burred his way into sick bay, helped himself to a couple of quarts of the doctor's brandy, wiped some grease off his hands with sterile bandages, danced a jig, and addressed Cute. "Commander Scotch rrrrreportin', sir."

Cute, miffed at having been upstaged by his executive officers, spoke sharply. "Gentlemen, the doctor and I have agreed that this ship needs a new security officer that is the meanest, toughest, hardest so-and-so in Starbeat, and I want you to find him for me. Skunk, get on the computer. Get me readouts of everyone in Starbeat who has been transferred for being too difficult—too hard to get along with. I want the man nobody else wants, and I intend to make him want to serve on this ship!"

"Captain," said Skunk slowly, "that was an impressive speech, and I am sure the only reason you wanted Mr. Scotch up here was so you would have more time to rehearse it"—Cute blushed, trapped in his ploy—"but without having to look at the computer records, I can tell you that we already have such a crewperson aboard this ship."

"Ship? This ship? Aboard this ship?" Cute long ago had discovered that repeating his officers' statements saved his memorizing an average of fourteen lines per episode. "Who is he?"

"It is not a 'he,' Captain. The candidate I am proposing is a female."

"Skunk," exploded Macaw, "you must be out of yoah Fulcan mind. The *Ennui* can't have a woman security chief!"

"And why not, Doctor?" Skunk answered coolly, relishing the opportunity to act superior by arguing with Macaw. "Studies on my planet have shown—"

Macaw snorted. "Weah dealing with Starbeat officers, not leprechauns."

Skunk was raising an eyebrow in preparation for a stinging reply when Cute reached over and pulled the eyebrow down.

"Save that for one of my last-minute tactical innovations, Mr. Skunk. And you," he said to Macaw, "keep quiet. Let Skunk explain his ridiculous statement and then we'll go on to something that makes sense. Proceed, Mr. Skunk."

"Captain, I object. We have just the person you described among our crew, and it is eminently logical that she—"

"Skunk, come off it," said Cute, shaking his head. "A woman can't be security chief. It is a man's job. Women aren't capable of it. I mean, a woman is round and soft, and . . . they don't even shave! How can someone who doesn't shave be security chief? Why, it would almost be obscene!"

"Aye," said Scotch, peering up from over the edge of the desk where he had slipped some time before. "I dinna ken ye, Skunk. A wee bit o' a lassie, mon, it wouldna do. . . ." He rambled off into a chorus of "How Are Things in Glocca Morra?" and slipped back under the desk.

"Gentlemen, I remind you of the United Fedderbedding Planets Charter, which guarantees full equality between the sexes in all areas of influence."

"Hey, Skunk," cajoled Cute with a wink, "you know all that stuff was only put in the Charter to keep the libbers quiet. And for sure it was never intended to let a woman be security chief."

"Captain," continued Skunk, "I might also remind you that Admiral Kojak has given you only three more months to get the *Ennui* back into shape, or he will 'have you flying a desk in the Neutral Zone.' "

"So?" asked Cute in annoyance. "And how did you know that, anyway? I didn't tell you."

"I learned it from your mind in our last adventure. You remember, 'Turnaround Intruder.' "

"Yes," answered Cute, recalling his distress at being trapped in a woman's body, and how Skunk had been the only one who knew the truth, thanks to the telepathic powers of his Fulcan mind melt. Cute could still feel Skunk's long sensitive fingers, probing and searching, then finally moving up to Cute's female face to begin the melt.

"I remember, Mr. Skunk. *Everything.*" Skunk looked blandly at the ceiling. "But I did not include any conversation with Admiral Kojak in the information I gave you to prove my identity during the mind melt."

Skunk shrugged. "As long as I was in there, I decided to do a little shopping."

Cute reflected that he would have to take a little more care with Skunk in the future. "Be that as it may, Mr. Skunk, I still don't see what Admiral Kojak has to do with your recommending a woman to be my new security officer."

"The name of the crewperson I am proposing is Gloria Freidan Kojak."

Cute gulped. "You mean . . ."

"Exactly. The Admiral's daughter."

Cute turned to Macaw and gave him a withering look. "Moans, I'm ashamed of you! Of course a woman has an equal opportunity on this ship! I can only assume that you were having your fun with Mr. Skunk as usual. I'd hate to think my ship's physician was a male shopping list."

"Male *chauvinist*, captain," offered Skunk tiredly.

"Of course, chauvinist," amended Cute smoothly. He turned and led his first officer from the room. "Come on, Skunk. Let's go give our new security chief the good news."

As they left the room, Macaw gave a deep sigh and went back to repairing his boot. It was always so pleasant after Cute left, the doctor reflected . . . and so quiet, too. Now if only Scotchy would stop snoring . . .

Lieutenant Gloria Kojak was working out in the ship's gymnasium when the call came for her to report to briefing room A. Tossing the barbell she was hefting to a fellow crewman, she did three backflips out of the gym, relishing the man's scream as the weight carried him through the floor and subsequently decks 17, 16, and 15.

Lieutenant Kojak wondered why superman Cute wanted her in the briefing room. "Probably just now tomcatted his way down to the K's," she said to no one in particular as she pulled on her stockings and uniform skirt. Finishing dressing, she tossed her workout togs at the cleaning chute. The bundle missed the chute, but continued on through the wall, severing the artificial gravity controls for the gymnasium. "Missed again," cursed Kojak as she floated up to a bulkhead and propelled herself from the room.

Cute was vainly trying to find out what other items Skunk had found out during the mind melt when Lieutenant Kojak reported to the briefing room. As she came to a halt and introduced herself, Cute's mouth popped open in surprise, and a low moan escaped from his lips.

"I beg your pardon, sir?" asked Kojak.

Cute continued to stare at her without replying. Skunk answered for him. "The captain said nothing, Lieutenant. That is his usual reaction to a beautiful woman."

It was true, Cute thought to himself as he sat entranced. The daughter of Admiral Kojak was a tiny, sublime creature who looked as if she would be more at home in a harem than aboard a starship. Perhaps, reflected Cute, this wouldn't be such a bad deal after all. A security chief has to work very closely with the captain. *Very* closely. The idea appealed to Cute immensely. He cleared his throat several times, and finally managed to speak.

"Lieutenant, we have some good news for you. Due to the unfortunate accident that befell Lieutenant Mooney yesterday . . ."

Skunk interrupted. "Yesterday was Commander Houston, sir. Lieutenant Mooney fell into the anti-matter chamber day before yesterday."

Cute smiled and shrugged. "Who can keep up? Anyway, lieutenant, because of the . . . er, untimely . . . er, vacancy—"

Gloria Kojak stopped him with a snort. "Do you mean you want me to be security chief? No thank you, captain. I'm too young to die. Security chiefs don't last a week on this ship."

Cute bridled. "Lieutenant, you forget yourself! You are at attention!" Kojak and Skunk exchanged puzzled glances, and Cute removed the bridle from his mouth. "I said you are at attention, Lieutenant. It is not your place to question my orders, but for your information, many of our security chiefs have lasted much longer than a week. There was . . . what was his name, Skunk?"

"Bonario. It was fourteen point six days before he was killed. But we spent thirteen days of that time in drydock around Starplate Seven."

"But it proves my point, nevertheless," said Cute triumphantly.

"Regardless of that, Captain," sneered Kojak, "I thought only men were appointed security chief. This just looks like another way to get rid of me without having to make excuses to my father. In fact," she said bitterly, punching a hole in the bulkhead, "it is brilliant. How proud of me he would be if I died in battle. A glorious death for his problem child!"

"The fact that your father is an admiral in Starbeat has nothing to do with our decision to make you security chief—either way. You were chosen strictly on your qualifications. Mr. Skunk—and, ahem, myself, of course, feel that you will do an excellent job.

"In fact," he continued, "I will tell you frankly that some officers felt that your sex disqualified you from the position. As you will be working closely with these officers, I will mention no names."

At this he gave Kojak a surreptitious wink, and nodded his head in the direction of Skunk. Let this mankiller take her frustrations out on Skunk, Cute exulted to himself; that'll show him to go gadding about in my head.

Kojak considered the offer. It sounded genuine enough, although she didn't completely trust the captain. She knew his reputation with women, and that sooner or later he would be convinced that the Cute charm would unfreeze the icy demeanor she presented to him. But Gloria knew she could take care of that situation when it arose, and all in all, security chief was better than having her thirty-third transfer in eight months.

"All right, Captain. I accept. But I have to warn you—"

Her warning to Cute was never completed, for at that moment the red alert klaxon sounded throughout the ship. Cute leaped to the intercom and ferociously thumbed the call button.

"Bridge!" he shouted. "What's going on?"

"Lieutenant Zulu, captain. Our shields just came on and sensors report a Rumbleon battle cruiser heading in our direction."

"Coming right up," snapped Cute. He turned to Skunk and Kojak. "Looks like you get quick duty, Lieutenant. Let's go!"

As they arrived on the bridge, Skunk moved quickly to his station and gazed into his viewer. "Captain, it is indeed a Rumbleon ship. In fact, the latest model. Chopped and channeled, moon hubcaps, fender skirts, and a foxtail hanging from the antenna. They are obviously looking for a fight."

"They'll get one," promised Cute. "Sound battle stations, Mr. Zulu."

Lieutenant Zulu smiled the wicked grin he reserved for such occasions, and as he pressed the battle stations alarm with one hand, the other slipped down to his belt to check that the samurai sword slipped easily from its scabbard.

Ensign Checkup, on the other hand, was not quite as bloodthirsty. As battle stations sounded, he quietly leaned over and lost his lunch. It wasn't the physical danger that bothered him, but the fact that he tended to lose his accent in times of stress.

The new security chief was too busy to worry about the coming danger. She was attempting to perform her job at the same time she learned it, and as the entire security section had been killed over the last four months, she had no one to show her what to do. Things were complicated by the ensign on her right at Engineering who was trying to get her intercom number, and the yeoman on her left who was trying to ask her out for dinner after the battle.

"The Rumbleon ship is in visual range now, Captain," stated Skunk.

"Very good. Lieutenant Yuhura, screens on."

The main viewing screen lit up and swiftly coalesced into a jumbled pattern of static. Skunk walked purposefully over to it and gave it a swift kick, and the Rumbleon ship appeared.

Everyone on the bridge gasped in surprise and shock. The Rumbleon ship was indeed frightening. It was several times larger than the *Ennui*, and obviously faster, better-weaponed, and with superior shielding. But what really scared the *Ennui* crew was the exterior of the ship itself. Painted a wicked candy-apple red, with scalloped flames along the sides, the eye was drawn irresistibly to the motto stenciled on the nose: "Born to Loot."

"All right," spoke Cute sharply into the silence. "So she's a hot mill. But the people inside are only Rumbleons, just like us—or at least just like Skunk—and I say we can shut them down."

Cute's words had a slightly cheering effect, but it was soon swept away as Yuhura announced a signal from the Rumbleon ship. The fearsome ship dissolved only to be replaced by the visage of a Rumbleon female. Again, a gasp went up on the bridge, and Checkup blurted, "Mr. Skunk, it's your girlfriend!"

"I thought we were rid of her," groused Cute. "Just what I needed today. A grudge fight." He raised his voice. "Greetings, commander. I am pleased to see you suffered no ill effects upon your return to your fleet."

The commander gave him a cold smile. "No thanks to you, Cute. Luckily I found that 'full confession' tape you planted on me before I arrived at our base."

"Just a little farewell gift," said Cute airily, ignoring a dirty look from Skunk.

"It was very thoughtful of you, Captain. And as you can see, I intend to return the favor."

Cute smiled winningly. "Not necessary, Commander. Glad to do it. Well, it was nice talking to you, but we really have to run. One of those diplomatic receptions at Starplate Eight. Boring, but necessary." Out of the side of his mouth, Cute whispered to Zulu, "Get ready to get us the heck out of here—this dame is trouble."

As Cute began to motion to the helmsman to warp them away, a squad of Rumbleon warriors suddenly materialized on the bridge. In one quick movement, they captured the helm and Navigation (rather easily, as Zulu had tripped over his sword and Checkup was once again retching), and had Engineering, Life Sciences, Communications, and the snack bar under phaser cover.

Cute leapt at the nearest Rumbleon warrior, who took a roundhouse swing at him. Neatly blocking the punch with the point of his chin, Cute managed to take the Rumbleon out of action as he collapsed on him.

Seeing two enormous Rumbleons advancing on him with leveled phasers, Skunk quickly used the Fulcan nerve pinch and knocked himself unconscious.

The only person left on the bridge in any position to fight was Lieutenant Kojak. She had already dismembered two Rumbleons and was in the process of tearing the ears off of another when the Rumbleon transporter once again came on and beamed them all onto the Rumbleon ship.

The Rumbleons materialized first, and after they stepped off the platform, the *Ennui* bridge crew was reformed. The Rumbleon transporter crew was having some fun, switching around heads, turning people inside out, and other pleasantries, when the commander arrived.

"Cut out the *lyfandqwpstoop*," she barked, and the crew was immediately materialized in their proper shapes, whereupon they were stunned into unconsciousness.

It was much later when Cute awoke to find himself and the others in a security cell on the Rumbleon ship. He had a terrific headache (not to mention a sore jaw) and it was not until he was looking around for someone to blame it all on that he noticed that Skunk was not in the cell with them.

He crawled over to Kojak, and as he shook her awake, she suddenly swung a vicious punch at his midsection. It was only through many years of prodigious practice and rigorous training that Cute was able to soften the blow by parrying it with his stomach.

Kojack came fully awake and leapt to his side. "I'm sorry, captain. The last thing I remember was fighting Rumbleons, and then all of a sudden there you were reaching for my . . ."

"It . . . it's all right," wheezed Cute. "You're just lucky it's . . . late in the season."

As she helped him to his feet, others of the crew began to awaken. Starbeat training took effect immediately, however, and aside from a bit of wailing and screaming, and Zulu calling Cute a few names, they remained calm and professional.

"Captain," said Yuhura, "I . . . I'm frightened." The dramatic effect of this statement was lessened by its being simultaneously said by the entire crew, who had all heard it many times before. Yuhura gave them a scathing look. "Well, what do you expect me to say? 'Feets don't fail me now'?"

"Take it easy," Cute ordered. "They didn't get Scotchy, and you can bet he's working on a way to get us out. All we have to do is play it cool."

Meanwhile, Skunk was in the quarters of the Rumbleon commander. She had changed from her uniform to a filmy negligee, and she had offered Skunk drinks and food.

"I fail to realize why I am not being incarcerated with the captain and the others. Surely I have earned your animosity to a greater degree than Captain Cute, yet he is in a detention cell and I am treated almost royally."

The commander smiled at him. "No Skunk, you do not deserve a cell. Even though you have, shall we say, wronged me in the past, I can be quite forgiving."

Skunk stirred uneasily. "Commander . . ." he began.

"You know my private name, Skunk. Please use it." It was not a request, Skunk knew, as she leveled a phaser at him as she said it.

With a visible effort, Skunk said, "Trampolina."

"That's better."

"Trampolina, I must point out that my loyalties and aims have not changed since our last encounter. If you hope to ply me with kindness, I am obliged to point out that you are foredoomed to failure."

"No, Mr. Skunk," answered the commander. "I know you cannot be bought . . . by anything I have to offer. I just thought we'd make a little whoopee before I have you and your captain killed."

Skunk considered. He shrugged, picked up his drink, and offered her a toast. "Sounds logical to me."

Back in the detention cell, Cute was considering a method of escape. ". . . and I get a bar of soap, and carve it to look like a phaser. Then Zulu pretends to be sick and calls the guard over—"

"Let Checkup do it," sneered Zulu. "He won't have to pretend very hard."

"Jim, I can't allow it," spoke up Macaw. "This heah boy's too sick to pretend he's sick."

Cute swung around in astonishment. "Moans! How did you get in here?"

"Ah came onto the bridge just before the Rumbleons beamed aboard. The writer is supposed to go back an' put in a line or two tellin' about it, and the great fight I put up against those fellows, but he'll probably forget."

"Well, I'm glad you're here. We might need you."

Macaw grimaced. "Ah hope not. Ah cain't stand the sight of blood."

Yuhura pulled at Cute's sleeve. "Captain, about your escape plan . . ."

"Oh, yeah. As I was saying, Zulu will smuggle clothes out from the laundry, and when we have the tunnel finished, we'll use the clothes to make dummies that will fool the screws and give us a five- or six-hour head start."

Kojak gaped at him in astonishment. "You want to *tunnel* out of a *starship*?"

Cute gave her a cold stare. "I suppose you have a better idea?"

"How about this?" Kojak swiftly turned and punched a neat hole in the bulkhead. She then reached out and switched off the force-field door.

As the prisoners crept out, Checkup whispered, "Where are the guards?"

Cute snickered, "They're all down at the end of the hall there watching that monitor. Come on, we'll take them by surprise."

They moved swiftly but silently along the corridor to striking range of the Rumbleons. When they were close enough, Cute shouted, "Now!" and immediately stumbled, tripping all of his companions. As they fell into a heap at the Rumbleons' feet, one of the guards was overcome by laughter and accidentally fired his weapon into the corridor wall. The beam struck a power lead and a bolt of electricity leapt across the hall and onto the metal armor the Rumbleons wore. All were electrocuted, leaving the *Ennui* crew to sort themselves out.

Cute staggered to his feet. "What happened?"

Kojak pointed at the shattered bulkhead. "His phaser went off, and the power fried them all."

"Oh," said Cute. "I see. Just as I planned it, of course. I hope no one was hurt in that fall, I couldn't warn you about it, of course, without revealing my plans to the Rumbleons."

Macaw massaged a shoulder. "Jimbo, do me a favor. Include me out o' any more plannin' you do, okay?" A chorus of assents from the rest of the crew followed this pronouncement.

Cute decided it was a good time to change the subject. "Let's see what they were so interested in." They all stared at the monitor screen which showed the interior of the commander's quarters.

"Well," said Cute after a few moments. "At least we know where Skunk is."

"Captain, I suggest we leave the vicinity. I haven't heard any alarms, but some kind of repair crew is sure to come along to fix that power lead."

"Good idea, security chief. I was just about to suggest that myself. Zulu, see if any of those communicators on those guards is still working. If so, we can call Scotchy and get out of here."

Zulu quickly looked over the guard's equipment and handed one of the communicators to Cute.

Cute flipped it open and adjusted the frequency. "*Ennui*, come in *Ennui*. Captain Cute calling. Come in *Ennui*."

The communicator crackled into life and Cute smiled at his companions. "Sub-Commander Troll here. Report."

"Oops," giggled Cute. "Wrong channel." He adjusted it again, and this time the welcome burr of Scotchy answered his call.

"Aye, 'tis a bonnie thing ye got through, Captain. It took us a while to get the auxiliary bridge in operation, seein' as how we haven't used it since the first season."

"Good job, Scotchy. Beam us aboard."

In a matter of moments, they were aboard the *Ennui* once more, and Lieutenant Kite made his one and only appearance in this story by giving them a hearty welcome. Cute lost no time getting to the bridge, pausing only to take a shower, brush his teeth, have a drink, and get the intercom number of a cute new yeoman.

"Status report," he demanded of Scotch as he stumbled out of the turbolift.

" 'Tis still a standoff, Captain. One o' the other of us will gun his engine now and then, and we've been sending dirty limericks about Rumbleons out on hailin' frequencies, but nothin' serious."

Cute was satisfied with the actions of his engineering officer. A good man, thought Cute, and the limericks were a nice touch. Cute's usual pre-battle strategy was to insult his opponent's ancestors while Skunk supplied graphic illustration with his vast knowledge of ancient Fulcan obscene gestures.

That reminded Cute that his first officer was still aboard the Rumbleon ship.

"Scotchy, can we get Skunk off with the transporter?"

Scotch considered, "Well, we did it once before, but ye'll remember Mr. Skunk had a communicator that time, and even then it was hard enough to sort him out from all those Rumbleons. It'd be a bonnie hard thing to do."

Cute gave Scotch a confident smile. "I'm sure if you turn your mind to it you can figure out a way." He let the smile fade. "You have ten minutes. I want to get back to Fedderbedding territory before dark."

"Captain," Scotch cried, "it canna be done in tha' short a time. Why I'd have to . . ." At this Cute lost him, as Scotch had a tendency to speak in perfect, correct Latin without a trace of his normal Scots accent when discussing technical matters.

"Never mind, Mr. Scotch. You have nine minutes left."

Scotchy sighed in rueful assent, and with a last "*sic semper tyrannus*," he left for the transporter room to get to work.

With a few moments' grace, Cute was left to consider the position his ship was in. They were caught in open space by a Rumbleon ship that was far superior to theirs in every way, his first officer was captive, and he had not once yet had an opportunity to take off his shirt. Not a very pretty picture. But he and his crew had pulled out of tougher scrapes, and they would this time. But how? How?

In the quarters of the Romulan commander, Mr. Skunk was at long last making his move.

"Knight to queen's level three."

As he moved the chess piece and captured her rook, Trampolina realized that this strange Fulcan had captured her heart as well. With a langurous movement of her hand, she tipped over her king in defeat.

"Never before have I met such a splendid mind! After our last encounter, I could not forget . . ." She let her words trail off, and began again in a softer, sexier tone. "You have bested me again. One more victory, and you will possess me as your chattel and lifelong slave, under the ancient Rumbleon rite of *bestthree outofour*. Or should I merely forfeit now, and save our time for better things?"

Before Skunk could answer, the door to the commander's quarters swept open and Sub-Commander Troll swept in accompanied by two guards armed with phasers.

The commander leapt up livid with fury. "Troll, I've told you a thousand times not to break in on my seductions! Explain yourself!"

"Commander," gulped Troll, "the prisoners have escaped, and our new overhead cam device is missing from the engine room."

The commander whirled on Skunk. "So, treachery once again. This time nothing will save you from my vengeance. I'll get you, Skunk . . . you, and your captain, and your ship, and your little dog, too!"

As Skunk stared at her in blank confusion, she motioned to the guards to hold him captive, and ran out of the room with Troll following after.

On the bridge of the *Ennui*, Cute was still in a quandary as to how to get his ship and crew home safely. He decided to ask his new security officer her opinion. He rose from his chair and walked over to her station.

"Lieutenant, my compliments on the way you handled your duties as security chief when we were aboard the Rumbleon ship."

"Thank you, Captain." Gloria Kojak was suddenly flustered in the captain's presence. Perhaps it had something to do with the fact that they were totally alone, everyone else on the bridge having just stepped out to have coffee.

"Then we can be friends?" Cute asked with a charming smile.

"Did I miss something?" asked Kojak in return. "You compliment me, I thank you, and then all of a sudden you act like we are on the verge of young love."

Cute shrugged. "I suppose the writer figured that the readers have seen me in action so many times, he could skip all of the preliminaries and get right down to business."

"Yes," answered Kojak, rather breathlessly. "I'm beginning to realize that now, Captain. We *can* be friends . . . perhaps more."

After they had kissed and exchanged vows of eternal faithfulness, and Cute had given her a brief history of his life (including the previous seventy-nine missions of the *Ennui*) and begun planning a family, Gloria suddenly pulled away from Cute's arms.

"How can you love me?" she wailed. "I can never be a complete woman."

Cute made a move to comfort her. "No, please don't touch me. You don't know the truth. And you will never know! I'll . . . I'll kill myself!"

With a last wild cry she turned and ran from the bridge. A sharp pain knifed through Cute's heart as he realized that he now had another problem on top of all his others: Where in the world was he going to find another security chief?

Skunk was seated at the desk of the Rumbleon commander in deep meditation, characterized by the typical Fulcan habit of loud snoring. The commander stormed back in, kicked Skunk's feet off her desk, and stood fuming over him as he picked himself up from the floor.

"Your accomplice has somehow managed to elude us this far, but I assure you he cannot escape with our cam device. You may as well confess your complicity in this espionage."

"I admit nothing," answered Skunk stonily, allowing a few pebbles to dribble to the floor as he continued. "We of the *Ennui* had no knowledge of your camshaft device, and even if we did, we wouldn't care, as Fedderbedding ships have Mazda engines that go hmmmm."

"Liar!" shouted the commander, whipping her whip across his face. "Little matter, however, as you will die this very moment. Guards!"

Skunk folded his hands behind his back. "I must remind you, Commander, that under the sentence of death, I am allowed the Rumbleon Right of Statement."

"Oh, no," scoffed the commander. "You won't trick me with that one again. No Right of Statement."

Skunk stood his ground. "The Right is my right under your own laws and traditions."

"Spies have no rights to the Right. Isn't that right, Troll?"

Troll nodded assent. "Check."

Skunk gave him a look. "Copycat. At least, Commander, if I am not to be allowed the Right of Statement, may I make a statement about not making a Right of Statement?"

"No statements about the Statement."

Skunk raised his eyebrow. "Surely you will not disallow me to state my belief that I have a right to make a statement about being denied my right to make a Right of Statement?"

"No!"

"Then may I state that—"

"Shut up!"

Skunk gave her a cold look. "Commander, I fail to understand why we cannot discuss this in a logical manner. Shouting is not necessary. I am merely endeavoring to point out—" A phaser was shoved into his left ear. "Then again—"

"Enough talk. Troll, take this creature down to the execution chamber."

As troll took Skunk's arm, a high-pitched whining filled the room. The commander wailed, "Not again!" as Skunk (and Troll's left arm) swiftly dematerialized.

"Troll," said the commander in a soft voice, "get that patched up and then meet me on the bridge. We are going to destroy the *Ennui*." Troll gave her a lopsided salute and staggered from the room.

The commander stared for a long moment at the spot where Skunk had so recently stood. "Skunk," she whispered, "you never take me anywhere."

Cute leapt up in surprise and led the entire bridge crew in a cheer as Skunk stepped from the turbolift, followed by Scotch and Macaw.

"Skunk, how did you escape from the Rumbleon ship?"

"You may thank Mr. Scotch for my timely departure, captain."

Cute gave Scotchy a warm nod. "I knew you could do it, Mr. Scotch. But how?"

Scotch laughed. "It was a pretty problem indeed, until Dr. Macaw here reminded me of the one major physical difference between Fulcans and Rumbleons."

"Ah," said Skunk, understanding.

"Well, let me in on it," said Cute.

"It was simple, Jim." Macaw was enjoying the attention, even this late in the story. "Fulcan ears point back, Rumbleon ears point front."

Scotch continued for him. "Then it was but a wee matter o' programmin' in a Rumbleon configuration, and reversin' the ear phasing materialization sequence. One pull o' the levers and Mr. Skunk is back safe and sound."

"Well, it is all too technical for me," laughed Cute, "but congratulations, Mr. Scotch, and welcome back, Mr. Skunk."

"Thank you, Captain. However, I do have some information to report. The Rumbleon commander seems to think that we stole their new camshaft device."

"Device? Camshaft device?" echoed Cute, stalling for time. Was there to be no end to his problems, no relief in sight?

"Skunk, if the Rumbleons are that concerned about this camshaft, then it must be pretty important to the operation of that ship, right?"

It cost Skunk a great deal, but he answered smoothly. "Check."

"And if it is that vital, gentlemen, then I intend to have it!" Cute glared at his officers as if challenging them to refute his statement. He was not disappointed.

"What?" "Are you crazy?" "Let's get out of here while the getting's good!" "Ach, me poor bairns!" "I vote we make peace." "Great Ceasar's ghost!"

Cute stood with his hands on hips staring at them. Then he gave an elaborate shrug, and grinned. "Gosh, it was just an idea."

He sat back down in his command chair. "Okay, let's get back to our own turf. Mr. Zulu, warp seven."

Zulu aimed a quick smile at Checkup and moved to engage the great starship's engines. But just as he was about to let in the clutch, a flashing light on his board caught his attention.

"Captain," he called, "someone is in the transporter room and has turned on the equipment!"

"Criminalinities!" Cute turned to Scotch. "Where is Lieutenant Kite? That's his station."

"Sorry, Captain, but Kite has already made his appearance in this story. If I'da known this was gonna happen, I'da had him wait."

"Never mind," snapped Cute. "Yuhura, open a frequency to the transporter room. See who that is."

Macaw caught Cute's arm. "Jim, aren't you going to send some security men to the transporter room? That could be a Rumbleon!"

Cute looked at him in exasperation. "Doctor, how many security men have died aboard this ship in the last four months?"

"Eighty-three, but what's that—"

"And how many security men does the *Ennui* carry?"

"Eighty . . . three. Hmmm. I see your point."

Cute gave him a curt nod. "Exactly. We have no more security men . . . unless, of course, you would care to transfer to security, Moans?"

Macaw blanched. "Ah seem to have some things to do in mah office," he said hurriedly and ran into the turbolift. Cute was making clucking noises after him when Skunk halted him.

"Captain, you forget that the *Ennui* currently has a complement of eighty-*four* security officers. Ms. Kojak, to be explicit."

"That's right!" Cute exploded. "Where is she?"

His somewhat belated question was answered when Yuhura finally managed to reroute connections through Omaha and reach the transporter room. "Captain, it is Lieutenant Kojak using the transporter!"

Cute slammed his fist onto his intercom. It collapsed with a dull thud, and he had to nonchalantly move to Yuhura's station to talk to Gloria. But before he could say a word, her voice came over the intercom. "Please, Jim, save time and don't try to talk to me. It won't do any good. I heard all about the Rumbleon cam thing, and I'm going over there to try to get it. At least I can die a complete woman."

As she broke off communication, Cute turned his anguished face to Lieutenant Zulu. "Stop her. Use the manual override."

"I'm sorry, Captain, but she's overriden the manual override."

Skunk reported, "Forty seconds until transporter operational."

Suddenly Lieutenant Yuhura called out, "Captain, a signal from the Rumbleon ship."

Cute slapped his hand to his head. "Now what do *they* want?"

An image of the Rumbleon commander appeared on the main viewing screen. "Captain Cute," she said in an embarrassed voice, "it seems that your people didn't steal our overhead cam after all. We have just learned that our cook has been using it to make donut holes."

Cute spun around. "Yuhura, pipe that into the transporter room!" Turning to the Rumbleon, he asked that she repeat her statement. After she did so, she asked, "May I speak to Mr. Skunk, please, captain?"

Skunk stepped forward into viewing range.

"Skunk, my apologies for accusing you of stealing our device. I am sorry."

Skunk answered, "It would be illogical for me to not accept your apology. Therefore, I accept."

The commander smiled. "Logical to the end. Very well, Skunk, Captain, until next time."

The image faded. Cute said, "Skunk, you have the con," and made his way quickly down to the transporter room. There he found Gloria Kojak sitting on the edge of the transporter platform, loudly weeping.

Cute took her in his arms.

"It's all right now, darling. The Rumbleons are leaving. But why did you consider doing such a foolish thing?"

She turned her tearful face to his. "I told you that I couldn't let you know the truth about me."

Cute gave her a gentle sock on the jaw. "Silly, I don't care what it is, I love you, and that is all that really matters. Please, tell me about it."

With a tremendous effort, Gloria began through occasional sobs, hiccups, and nose blowings.

"You know that my father is Admiral Kojak, but what you don't know is that I am an only child. And when he learned that he would never have a son, he decided that I would be his son. He raised me like a boy. I never got to wear lipstick, or go to the prom, or have slumber parties. I spent all my time watching football games, telling dirty stories, and walking around in an old dirty undershirt. Daddy's little 'Skipper,' next in line for the Academy."

Cute kissed her hand in sympathy.

"But that's not the most terrible thing. I *liked* it! I thought it was wonderful, especially when I could beat up any of the other—I mean, any of the boys on the block."

"That's right," Cute recalled, "that enormous strength of yours. How did you get it?"

"Oh, I ate nothing but spinach until I was eighteen. Daddy says all sailors eat it. Anyway, I liked being a 'man' so much, it almost drove me crazy when I found out that women were discriminated against in Starbeat. So I became a feminist nutso troublemaker . . ." She trailed off. "Now you know the whole story, and you probably hate me."

Cute chuckled. "Darling, I've heard the same story a thousand times."

She looked up at him in surprise.

"It's true. You are not so different from most any other admiral's daughter. They all seem to have the same problem. Why, if famous men and high-ranking officers could have sons, half of my adventures would never happen."

"Then, you don't hate me?" Gloria asked, hope welling in her eyes. "You don't think I'm a freak, only half a woman?"

Cute took her in his arms once again. "You are more woman than any I have ever known, Gloria Friedan."

Breathless from his long, deep kiss, she finally managed to blurt out her last secret.

"Jim, my name isn't really Gloria Friedan Kojak. I changed it when I became a feminist."

"Oh, really?" Cute said. "What is your real name?"

She blushed. "It's Mary Sue."

Cute smiled. "I had a feeling that was it." And he kissed her once again as the *Ennui* flew on through ever-dark, ever-mysterious, and ever-changing space.

A TREK INTO GENEALOGY

by Linda Frankel

The amazing success of Alex Haley's novel Roots *brought about a new fad in this country—a desire on the part of many people to learn about their ancestors and the events and forces that made them what they are. The characters in Star Trek are just as real to most of us as our own families, so it is not surprising that the search for "roots" would eventually include Kirk and Co. You will agree with us that Linda Frankel has done an admirable job of filling in the Federation family tree.*

If Star Trek is the history of the future, then it surely must have roots in the past that can be found with a little detective work. When this author began to explore the possible ancestries of Star Trek characters, some interesting and even amusing results cropped up.

Leslie Thompson's reference to an "ancestor raised by apelike sub-humans in darkest Africa" in "A Brief Look at Kirk's Career" (*The Best of Trek #2*) is probably an exaggerated version of the career of Sir John Kirk (1832–1922), who did accompany the explorer David Livingstone on his expedition to Africa when it was still referred to as "the Dark Continent." Kirk remained with the famed Doctor Livingstone for five years. He was later appointed consul general of Zanzibar, where he became the sole representative of the British Empire.

An earlier Kirk was a rather successful privateer. (A privateer is a pirate considered a hero in his native country because he attacks ships

71

belonging to enemy powers—ofttimes with the unofficial blessing of his home government.)

Sir David Kirk (1597–1655) was clearly a man of valor. He seized an entire French fleet, causing the previously impregnable French colony of Quebec to surrender. After he was knighted in 1633 by Charles I, he was appointed Royal Governor of Newfoundland until he was removed by Cromwell, who had little reason to like royalists.

A man of lesser integrity might have switched sides when the tide turned against the king. After all, Kirk was no aristocrat. His father had been a merchant. Yet if there is one quality common to all Kirks, it is loyalty. Sir David Kirk retired into obscurity, and never held any office under Cromwell's Commonwealth.

Traces of Kirks in American history can be found today. Still existing is Kirkville, Missouri, founded in 1841 by one Jesse Kirk. As pioneer life was not easy, founding a town was quite a feat. It shows the same tenaciousness we see in James T. Kirk, as well as explaining our captain's desire to go forward into "the final frontier."

And that same bravery and desire to explore in Jim Kirk could come from his British forebears. From them, too, he gets a skill in diplomatic matters—duties he always considers onerous, but performs very well.

Before discussing a possible ancestor of Mr. Spock, it first must be stated that there is absolutely no truth to the rumor that his mother Amanda was descended from Batman's youthful sidekick, Robin (Dick Grayson); or that her mother was a Hatfield (although it would explain her son's constant verbal feuding with a certain McCoy!).

One of Spock's more legitimate ancestors might be Cary Travers Grayson (1878–1938), a dedicated officer of the United States Navy. (If Amanda had naval forebears, she would not have accepted Sarek's disapproving attitude toward Starfleet.) To the Vulcan respect for life is added the compassion of a human physician, for Cary Travers Grayson was no less than the medical director of the Navy and the personal doctor of three presidents. If Spock strokes a Tribble now and then, we can understand why. It's a wonder he isn't trying to take over Bones' job!

As might be expected, Leonard McCoy has healing in his blood. Nineteenth-century physician Simon McCoy probably wanted his son, Frederick, to follow the family tradition and become a doctor. Frederick did study medicine, but decided instead to enter the field of paleontology. We now remember Sir Frederick McCoy (1823–1899) as a noted expert in the field, and the founder of Australia's National Museum of

Natural History. Did he find himself saying, "I'm *not* a doctor . . ."?
Well, no matter what a McCoy may do, there's no escaping that association with bones.

There are some really fine Scotts to choose from in our search for
Scotty's ancestors.

Robert Falcon Scott (1868–1912) was an Arctic explorer. He died with
his entire expedition in a blizzard on a return trip from the South Pole.
Tragically, the team was only a few miles from help. Scott's diary was
later recovered along with the bodies, and it tells an incredible tale of
hardship and courage.

My favorite Scott, however, was Percy Moreton Scott (1853–1924), the
naval gunnery expert. Like our Scotty, he was very devoted to his own
field. It was said of him that he seemed to believe that ships were merely
platforms to mount guns on. He fought for his improvements in gunnery,
and had continuous run-ins with the Admiralty.

Percy Scott was also a drinking man, but like our Montgomery, he
never drank on duty. It would have interfered with his formidable command abilities. During the Boer War, a ship under Scott's command
performed a historic rescue of a besieged town by getting its guns on the
scene at the pivotal moment.

And on November 8, 1909, Percy Scott displayed a sharp vision of the
future. Addressing the Scottish Clan Association, he predicted that air
power would one day make sea power look insignificant. His audience
laughed. Montgomery Scott would laugh also, but it would be with his
ancestor. And that, lads and lassies, is the last laugh.

It is interesting to speculate how people reacted to the invention of the
warp drive. Judging from historical experience of past innovators and
inventors, it may once have been called "Cochrane's Folly."

Thomas Cochrane (1815–1860) was an unorthodox naval commander.
Because of the unacceptable nature of his tactics, he wasn't even permitted to take credit for his victories. Instead, he was disgraced by being
falsely accused of stock fraud.

As a result, he left the British navy in disgust and espoused colonial
struggles. He commanded the Chilean and Greek navies in their wars for
independence against Spain and Turkey respectively. The cause of Greek
independence was highly fashionable in England, so Cochrane was finally
able to return a hero, but he was still embittered.

Perhaps the same sort of early rejection explains why Zephrem
Cochrane finally tired of his life and fled alone out into the uncharted
galaxy.

*   *   *

Of all the causes that have been espoused throughout history, the idea of free trade among nations has been the least successful. Advocates of free trade must feel as if they are charging windmills when they consider the powerful interests that have always opposed it.

Sir Matthew Decker (1679–1749) was one of the earliest proponents of free trade, opposing the tax on tea long before the Boston Tea Party. As did many free-traders before him, he failed, and events eventually led to the American Revolution.

His descendant and namesake (Commodore Matt Decker) also failed in his attempt to destroy the Doomsday Machine. One hopes that both Matt Deckers are pleased with Will Decker's eventual triumph over an even more incredibly powerful force, V'Ger, by allowing himself to unite with the entity. It may seem like the "If you can't lick 'em,' join 'em" strategy, but there comes a time when doing so isn't an act of cynicism at all. In Will Decker's case, it was an act of great courage, and a fulfillment of his long-held dream to achieve a higher level of consciousness in the eternal company of his beloved, Ilia.

You all remember Ambassador Robert "Popinjay" Fox from "A Taste of Armageddon." His naive faith in diplomacy in the face of a long history of hostility was shared by Charles James Fox (1749–1806), a British diplomat who attempted to the end of his life to negotiate a peace treaty with France. He failed in his efforts, but his descendant eventually succeeded after Kirk had undiplomatically incapacitated the war computer on Eminiar. Sometimes a soldier's decisiveness is needed to give peace a chance.

Probably the most astonishing thing about that remarkable lady Edith Keeler is that she had the vision to see that man would someday reach the stars. But she came by her preoccupation with heavenly bodies honestly, being a descendant of James Edward Keeler (1857–1899), the noted astronomer. Astronomy is not usually considered a revolutionary sort of profession, but Edith added her own natural optimism, and saw how the stars could transform our future.

I have mentioned the advocate of air defense Percy Scott. Another martyr to that belief was Billy Mitchell (1879–1936). In him we see what Gary Mitchell must have been like before the tragedy that destroyed him. Billy Mitchell was a far-seeing man who stuck to his principles regardless of the consequences. Because he spoke out publicly against his superiors, he was court-martialed and broken in rank. Later, he was forced to resign from the U.S. Army. By all accounts, he was a good man. Gary Mitchell, for all his brashness, must also have been one, or Jim Kirk would not have valued his friendship so.

*   *   *

During my researches, it occurred to me that Harry Mudd might have turned to crime to avenge an ancestor. Dr. Samuel Mudd (1833–1883) was subjected to a great injustice. It is usually agreed that physicians are not to be blamed for performing their function of healing regardless of circumstances (Kirk didn't accuse McCoy of conspiracy with Kahn Noonian Singh because McCoy treated Kahn), but the court that found Dr. Mudd guilty wasn't so reasonable. By their logic he should have known that the stranger with a broken leg was John Wilkes Booth, Lincoln's assassin. Dr. Mudd's name has since been cleared, but Harcourt Fenton Mudd might still have felt disgruntled. After all, it's nearly impossible to wipe Mudd clean.

It would be somewhat ironic if Lieutenant Carolyn Palamas, who nearly betrayed the *Enterprise* because of her love for Apollo, was actually the descendant of the monk Gregorius Palamas (1296–1356). That Greek mystic was so devoted to monkish virtues that he spent years in total isolation—or was it total?

Equally improbable is Cyrano Jones' claim to be among the fine family tree of John Paul Jones. When asked if he was making progress at picking up Tribbles at Space Station K-7, he replied with a sigh, "I have not yet begun."

An ancestor of Christopher Pike comes right to mind. Naturally, it is Zebulon Pike (1779–1813), who discovered Pikes Peak in the Rockies.

It is difficult not to believe in reincarnation when you realize how closely Chris Pike followed his ancestor's life pattern. Not only was he an explorer, warrior, and peacemaker, Zebulon Pike also had a fateful accident. Only in his case, it proved fatal.

Commander of a victorious campaign in the War of 1812, Pike was killed by a falling rock during the British retreat. For such a man as Pike, survival in a crippled state would have been worse than death. There were no Talosians available at the time to give him the gift of illusion. . . .

It was a delight to meet an accomplished woman in Areel Shaw's ancestry. Anna Howard Shaw (1847–1919) fought to establish herself in two professions: She won the right to become the first woman preacher and to study medicine. Later she met Susan B. Anthony, and joined the struggle for woman's suffrage. She was known as one of the most effective speakers in the feminist movement, and her descendant is no slouch as a speaker, either.

*   *   *

I will admit that Charles Warden Stiles (1867–1941) performed a service. His career was dedicated to eradicating the parasite hookworm. But it's rather a shame that his descendant, Andrew Stiles, decided to enter on a crusade to eradicate Vulcans, instead. The last description I would use for a Vulcan is parasitic.

Genealogy also sheds light on the behavior of Commodore Stocker. It is no wonder that he was unable to command the *Enterprise*, or any other starship, for that matter. He probably unconsciously subscribed to the idealogy of his ancestor Helene Stocker (1869–1943), who was a leader of the European pacifist movement. The last thing we need is a pacifist in the command chair during a Romulan attack. He should have stuck to his desk.

This article is by no means a complete study of Star Trek genealogy. Still to be discovered are notable ancestors for many members of the *Enterprise* crew, as well as the hundreds of characters that appeared in Star Trek episodes over the years.

And some of you out there are demanding to know if there is a connection between Pavel Chekov and the famed author Anton Chekhov. Frankly, I believe that the story of their being related was invented by a little old lady from Leningrad.

ALTERNATE UNIVERSES IN STAR TREK FAN FICTION

by Rebecca Hoffman

To most fans, the allure of fan fiction is that anything *can happen! Freed from the restrictions of continuing-series format, fan writers have put the* Enterprise *crew through some oftimes strange, but always exciting, changes. In this article, Rebecca Hoffman looks at some of the more famous and interesting "alternate universes" that have sprung from the vivid imaginations of fan writers.*

While mainstream SF has been content with the theory of alternate universes for many years Star Trek fans were first introduced to the concept on March 30, 1967, when the episode "The Alternative Factor" was aired. In this instance, the alternate universes were absolute opposites; on the one hand was the positive Lazarus who was matter, on the other was the negative Lazarus who was antimatter. Should the two meet anywhere except in the corridor between their universes, they would annihilate each other and all other existing universes as well.

The second season saw another example of alternate universes when, on October 6, 1967, "Mirror, Mirror" aired. In this episode, Kirk and others were actually transferred into this alternate universe. I prefer to use the word "alternate" to "parallel"; for while the mirror universe parallels the Starfleet universe in many respects, it is not a true parallel. There are many differences; and while the mirror universe is not a total opposite, many situations which occur in it are the opposite of the "real" Star Trek universe (such as ascending rank by assassinating one's superiors).

After this episode, the concept of alternate universes took off in fan fiction. Some were constructed consciously as alternate universes; others fall into the category by virtue of changes they make in the series format.

Alternate universes are created simply because each writer is looking at the worlds of Star Trek from his own unique point of view. Each writer sees it differently—if only to a small degree. Therefore, each writer has his own concept of Star Trek, and because of this, each writer's Star Trek universe is different from Gene Roddenberry's. Not even the professional writers have solved the problem of getting past their own views of Star Trek; and they don't always handle the prime universe well.

So what, then, is an alternate universe in Star Trek fiction? Strictly speaking, it is *anything* written by someone who is not part of the production staff of the show. This includes the professional novels. Though they must all be approved by Paramount, that is no guarantee of continuity, nor that the novels will even coordinate with the series. Unfortunately, many of them do not mesh well at all. Only Gene Roddenberry's filmed versions (whether live-action, animated, or movie) can be considered the canon, or prime universe. Even those have so many discrepancies between them that it makes one wonder. When we come to the fan fiction, however, *all* of it is alternate universe. But some examples are far more alternate than others.

There are many stories which can be considered "mainstream"—if there is such an animal in Star Trek fiction. They change nothing, add no new characters, and while many are stories which flesh out portions of episodes or tie up loose ends in episodes, other stories simply show the characters acting under different situations, but again make no changes in those characters or the series format.

These stories are the closest to Roddenberry's concept, and fans enjoy them. But the most intriguing stories are those which go beyond what was given us, those wherein—as in real life—people grow and learn and mature. And this is where the writers really jump head over heels into alternate universes.

I suspect the biggest reason alternate universes are so popular is that they totally free the writer's creativity, allowing him or her to work with the characters and plots on levels far more complex than television allows. At the same time, we sometimes wind up with stories disguised as Star Trek fiction which actually bear little resemblance to the original. In such cases, the reader has to totally suspend his disbelief—and yet a great number of these stories are well worth it.

In alternate universes, one finds many changes: A character dies; another falls in love and marries; galactic war occurs; the *Enterprise* is destroyed; Kirk is transferred to another command—there are many variables, and each leads to a different view of Star Trek. In this article, I wish to examine some of the main variations on the prime universe, all of which make major changes, some for the better and some for the worse.

Perhaps one of the earliest alternate universes was "Kraith," which was created by Jacqueline Lichtenberg. It was an entire panorama of Vulcan society, complex in the extreme, and thoroughly *alien*. The Kraith Vulcans really have little in common with those of the canon universe, but "Kraith" is well done, intriguing and ongoing. It is also interesting that there is now an alternate universe to an alternate-Kraith universe.

In one Kraith story, the Kraith Kirk is kidnapped into an alternate universe where a disconsolate Commodore Spock is searching universes to find a Kirk to replace his own. The situation so intrigued Scottish authors Sheila Clark and Valerie Piacentini that they took the idea further in "Variations on a Theme," and with Jackie Lichtenberg's permission, used the commodore and his dilemma to create a universe of their own. It is an alternate universe, yet it is definitely Star Trek, and is one very interesting saga.

Kraith is a Vulcan-oriented universe, but there are stories dealing with many other alien societies. Mattie Jones and Marilynn Ambos (*The Human Factor*) have created a series of stories dealing with the Romulans, delving deeply into their culture and history. The "Nu Ormenel" tales by Fern Marder and Carol Walske comprise a voluminous compilation of stories about the Klingons and their civilization. Klingons are a popular subject in fandom, and are by no means limited to this one series. In four successive issues of *Southern Star*, M.A. Carson has been running installments of his "Klingon Dictionary," which includes not only vocabulary, but his concepts of the Klingon culture. Nor are the Tholians forgotten: Those crystalline creatures from "The Tholian Web" (live-action) have inspired Lisa Wahl, RAM, and Lynnalan to create "Intersect," a Tholian universe all their own—and their characters are not quite what the reader may expect.

Throughout the massive body of fan fiction, there are countless essays on most of the aliens presented in the series, and each one shows a view of an interesting alternate universe.

"Alternate Universe Four" by Shirley Maiewski, Virginia Tilley, Anna Mary Hall, and Daphne Hamilton next comes to mind. As is obvious from the title, this was intended to be an alternate universe. In this one, Kirk is court-martialed and cashiered out of the service. Afterward he is contacted by a secret organization known as Light Fleet. They are an advanced force trying to keep peace in the galaxy, and their personnel come from all races. Kirk then becomes a Light Fleet captain.

The next example is of stories set in the future, well past the time of the televised episodes. One such example is Jean Lorrah's "Epilogue," published in *Sol Plus*. It takes place some two decades past the televised episodes, when an aging Kirk goes to Vulcan one last time to bid his old friend Spock farewell. Kirk's mind is failing him, and he doesn't want to become helplessly senile. The Vulcans have perfected a method of stopping senility, but it involves regression into the past, and through the memories of Spock, his mother Amanda, and others, the reader learns about the devastating war between the Federation and a Klingon-Romulan coalition which ended Kirk's five-year mission early.

One of the most time-twisting, character-rending situations to come along in years has to be Leslie Fish's "The Weight" (published by T'Kuhtian Press). The *Enterprise* is back in time when an anarchist crewmember totally destroys the time scheme, leaving Kirk in an alternate universe controlled by anarchists—with counterpoints of himself and others of his crew on Earth. To get back to his own future and universe, Kirk literally must snap time back in on itself, and he, being the focal point, is himself snapped. The author uses the story to take Kirk apart and put him back together again in a fashion impossible in prime-universe Star Trek.

While the aforementioned examples are definite alternate universes, they take place either wholly or partially in a different time, another culture, or a place other than the *Enterprise*. But there are alternate universes which are totally *Enterprise*-oriented. Many of these stories feature new characters, and while these are legion, each stands out for its uniqueness.

Star Trek played with the concepts of the old gods such as Apollo ("Who Mourns for Adonais", live action) and Kukulkan ("How Sharper Than a Serpent's Tooth," animated), so it is not surprising that some fans write stories around legendary figures in human myth. But *Enterprise* crewmen who are vampires and werewolves? Indeed, yes. M.A. Carson's Dov Brian stories (published in *Southern Star*) center on a very old werewolf who is currently serving aboard the *Enterprise*. In *Berengaria*, Rebecca Ross has introduced Carmilla, a vampire born in the early twentieth century. In both cases, the authors have given their characters sound bases for their respective afflictions, and the explanations go well beyond old legend.

"Landing Party Six" (by various authors, published in *Warped Space*) is a bit more normal by comparison—but only because the characters in question aren't some form of supernatural creature. Instead, Landing Party Six consists of the wildest bunch of zanies to be found anywhere. They are caricatures of the authors, and while often played for laughs, occasionally they make some very serious points. Looking at the "Landing Party Six" characters from a totally dispassionate point of view, one wonders how some of them ever made it into Starfleet, much less onto the *Enterprise*. But this is the fun of alternate universes. The writer does not *have* to be limited to what would seem to be logical parameters—within reason, anyway. Even alternate universes can go too far—and without proper justification, they become simple wish-fulfillment fantasies.

Which brings me to another category—the love story. Romances range from gentle love stories to ones specializing in explicit sex. Admittedly many of these *are* fantasies, but in capable hands, they turn into intriguing alternate universes.

Two of the earliest of these concerned Spock. In D. T. Steiner's "Spock Enslaved," Kirk, Spock and others of the *Enterprise* crew are taken slaves on a planet where they are trying to negotiate a treaty. During his long captivity, Spock falls in love with a female slave. Although the story has an interesting plot, both Spock and Kirk are badly mischaracterized, and this is often the greatest problem in alternate universes. A certain amount of faulty characterization is due simply to the author looking at a character differently, but in this particular instance, it was necessary to the plot as set up that Kirk and Spock act in a manner which was completely out of character.

"The Daneswoman" by Laura Basta (published in *Suarian Brandy Digest*) is also a Spock romance, this time with a woman who is in every way his equal. Her background is nicely detailed, and the two characters mesh quite well. When one actually gets into the love scenes, Spock's actions could be considered a bit out of character. But Gene Roddenberry never told us how Vulcans make love, therefore it is very difficult to say what is in character and what is not. Given the *pon farr* ("Amok Time"), I suspect Vulcans are no less passionate in private than humans—but again, that area is total speculation.

Among the myriad romances are those that deal with characters introduced in various episodes. Kirk's romances with Edith Keeler, Ruth, Drusilla, Helen Johansen, Lenore Karidan, Marlena Moreau, Helen Noel, Shahna, Areel Shaw, Nona, Janet Wallace, Deela, Elaan, Reena Kapec, Janice Lester, Miramanee, and Odona have all been written about. Spock's liaisons with T'Pring, Droxine, and the Romulan commandress, as well as the romances between the Vulcan and Leila Kalomi and Zarabeth, have their fan stories. McCoy's various romances are good story subjects, for the women in his life include Tonia Barrows, Nancy Crater, Natira, and his ex-wife. There are stories about Scotty's women, Carolyn Palamas and Mira Romaine, as well as Lieutenant M'Ress, the Caitian from the animated episodes. Chekov wasn't left out either, for he enjoyed relationships with Martha Landon, Irini Galliulian, and Sylvia, the gunfighter's girl in "Spectre of the Gun." (Have I left out anyone? Probably.)

Stories about all these characters are pretty much "mainstream" and very close to the prime universe, as they rarely go further than the televised version, or keep the lovers together permanently. Most of these stories deal with the particular love affair in question and let it go at that. Still, it is speculation, and there are stories which take the same situation, the same two people, and end up with thoroughly different alternate universes. Nor do writers limit themselves to the *Enterprise* crew. At least one writer, Charlotte Davis, is doing a series of stories about T'Pring and Stonn, the man she preferred to Spock in "Amok Time."

Writers also don't limit themselves to just the relationships established in the series. Some have jumped on the Kirk/Uhura bandwagon, most notably *Delta Triad*, which is based on a relationship between those two, and features a series of stories about their romance.

Spock/Christine stories are perhaps the most numerous. While no actual relationship developed between them in the series, Christine's love for Spock was of interest to many fans who have paired them in their stories. Some, like Juanita Salicrup's "Crossroads," have developed into a series.

Sulu is not forgotten. One author, Janice K. Hrubes, has done a good Sulu romance, "Swords and Sulu," and its sequel, "Murasaki." Romance did play a large role in Star Trek, and is forming a rather large portion of alternate universes, simply because of the changes it—by its nature—creates.

One romance in particular has gotten a lot of attention in fandom, and that is the one between Spock's parents, Sarek and Amanda. A whole host of permutations exist along this line: stories such as Ruth Berman's "It Seemed the Logical Thing" (published in *T'Negative*) or Jean Lorrah's "Night of the Twin Moons," which has a large number of stories spanning the time from Amanda and Sarek's first meeting through Spock's adulthood and career in Starfleet. Claire Gabriel's "Quartet Plus One" also traces Amanda and Sarek's relationship through a number of years. Johanna Cantor takes a different tack with this theme (*R&R*), for her Vulcans are far more alien than those created by either Lorrah or Gabriel, and the pairing between Sarek and Amanda is much more difficult.

Perhaps the most intriguing alternate universe romances deal with time travel. In Amy Falkowitz's "Rift Crossing" (published in *Rigel*), the heroine is brought forward from the twentieth century, and in the series, she marries Spock.

"The Displaced" by Lois Walling has the same theme, but with a twist, for her heroine, Sue, does not come forward to be thrust into the beautiful civilization the Federation offers. She's been taken from her time by slavers, and she's put in a slave camp, where later she finds Spock, who is in the final stages of *pon farr*.

"Echoes from the Past" by Rebecca Ross is a bit more gentle in the treatment of its time traveler, Aidan McLaren. Klingons bring her forward in time and eventually she winds up on Vulcan in the custody of Spock's parents. A romance does develop between Spock and Aidan.

"The Misfit" by Sharon Emily (published in *Star Trek Showcase*) sets the situation up a bit differently. In this universe, Amanda has died, and Sarek becomes involved with the *Enterprise*'s passenger Lorna Mitchell, who has been brought forward via the Guardian of Forever. Eventually the two do marry, and in succeeding issues of *Showcase*, their lives develop from that point.

Why this particular theme is so popular is unknown. Perhaps it is a way of bringing Star Trek closer to us twentieth-century humans. Though there are not an excessive number of these, most of them are novels with sequels, or else series of stories. These are alternate universes which strike a particularly sympathetic chord with many readers, and all of them are standouts because of their unique nature.

Perhaps the most basic alternate-universe stories are those which deal with the "Mirror, Mirror" episode universe. Laura Basta's series in *Babel* started with the return of Kirk to the *Enterprise*, his subsequent death at the hands of Spock, and Spock's decision to use the *Enterprise*'s resources to overthrow the Empire.

In *Human Factor*, Sapphira Cantrell has a series of ongoing stories wherein Spock confronts Kirk and eventually talks him into joining the conspiracy to overthrow the Empire.

Rebecca Ross' "Reverse" series (published in *Southern Star*) takes key televised episodes and presents them as they might have happened in the Mirror universe.

There are two Mirror universe tales which don't really fit this description, except on a tangent. "Echoes of the Empire" by Joyce Thompson takes place in a savage Star Trek universe, very much like the Mirror universe, but not quite. It starts with Sarek and Amanda, and traces their relationship—then later Spock's growth and development in a ruthless civilization.

Barbara Meek's novel *One Way Mirror* (published by Poison Pen Press) again concerns a twentieth-century girl, thrown into a Star Trek universe which parallels the Mirror universe in many ways, but which twists time and universes so that Star Trek's era is now—and is not at all idealistic.

The next alternate universe we come to is based upon the relationship which developed between Kirk, Spock, and McCoy. These are extremely emotional stories; in many, one (sometimes two) of the trio is killed, leaving the others to cope with the loss. There is also the hurt/comfort syndrome, which—like a soap opera—wrings emotion from the reader. A good example of this is the novel *Home Is the Hunter* by Bev Volker and Nancy Kippax (published in *Contact*), wherein Kirk is brought home after being held hostage by aliens for months. They were playing a game with the Federation similar to the one the Iranians played with us. Kirk and his men (none of his *Enterprise* crew) are captured by the aliens while on an espionage assignment. They are held and savagely tortured, both mentally and physically, and at long last, to save his men, Kirk breaks and confesses. He returns home a broken man, wallowing in guilt and self-loathing, and the road back to his old self is hellish.

Many of the hurt/comfort stories literally smother the reader in emotionalism. This one skillfully plays the reader's emotions to the limits, leaving the reader limp—and unable to read the novel in one sitting.

The most bizarre alternate universe (and often the least justified) could be considered an outgrowth of the above, simply because it concerns the relationship between Kirk and Spock. However, this carries the relationship to extremes. In Star Trek, we saw two men who have a close friendship. There is love, but it is the love of brothers, of comrades. The genre known as K/S—to my mind, and to the minds of many others, the most alternate of alternate universes—presents the two as participating in physical love with one another. This particular alternate universe has aroused a great deal of controversy these past few years, and while most of these stories fall into the category of sexual fantasies (of women, no less), there are some which are justified.

In "Game of Chance" by Frankie Jemison (published in *The Other Side of Paradise*), Kirk disappears during a routine survey of a supposedly uninhabited planet. The planet is inhabited by beings evolved far ahead of humans, who determine intelligence level based on telepathic ability, and since Kirk is pretty much a psi-null, they don't believe he's an intelligent being. He is, to them, a laboratory specimen, and they telepathically tamper with his mind, changing his sexual preferences from female to male, and making Spock the object of that preference.

The story is one of love—and just what Spock and McCoy will do to help Kirk to return to normal. It is a story with definite justification behind it. Out there in space, we could find such beings as those who tampered with Kirk's mind. This story is plausible; it *could* happen.

Alternative 2 & 3, a novel by Gerry Downes (published in *Stardate: Unknown*), is less plausible in that Kirk and Spock *choose* one another—eventually they make it permanent. However, the story provides a long, slow buildup. It is no sudden relationship, and gives the reader a chance to orient himself and suspend his disbelief. It is also written with such skill that the reader willingly suspends that disbelief and enjoys the novel, even if he can't wholeheartedly endorse the premise.

There are other such stories which are fairly well written, but by and large, this genre is extremely unbelievable, simply due to what we saw in the series. Kirk was a skirt-chaser if ever there was one, and Spock's romantic encounters were all with women. It's hard to justify this alternate universe in most instances, and though there are some really good entries in the field, they seem to be few and far between. A fan once summed up the K/S stories as "Barbara Cartland heroes in drag." It's a very *strange* alternate universe, and is about as far from the prime universe as one can get.

The examples I have been presenting all take place strictly within the framework of Star Trek. But there is another segment of stories best known as Crossover Universes, which meld Star Trek with characters from other areas of fiction.

One fanzine, *Holmesian Federation*, edited by Signe Landon, contains stories which combine Star Trek with Sherlock Holmes. Many authors create for this zine, and the view is highly illuminating.

Southern Star glommed onto the crossover series early, and in its second issue ran a *Star Trek/Kolchak the Night Stalker* story, and have since presented a *Star Trek/Space: 1999* story and a *Star Trek/Kiss* story.

Showcase Presents the Alternate Universes of Star Wars is mainly a *Star Wars* zine, but it carries a very believable *Star Wars/Star Trek* crossover story. A T'Kuhtian Press zine, *Dracula*, presented a story which melded *Dracula* and *Star Wars*. More of these stories are cropping up all the time, and I believe that in the future, more writers are going to work with the crossover stories, for they present even wider vistas for authors who enjoy taking diverse themes and creating something new.

Before ending, let me say that this introduction to alternate universes in fan fiction is just that—an introduction. The stories and fanzines discussed are but a small portion of a very large selection, and I have used them because they are the ones with which I am personally familiar. Many, many more exist, and doubtless in the years to come, there will be countless others. Star Trek fired the imagination of fans and spurred them to create their own personal variations, which took the writers and their readers far beyond the boundaries of a television program. There's a whole universe of intriguing stories at the fingertips of any fan, and the possibilities for multitudes of universes are endless. I only hope that this article has opened the portals to these universes for fans who—like all of us—want to go past the present and into the beckoning arms of tomorrow.

Author's Note: Many of the titles included are novels, published under their own titles rather than the auspices of another zine. In the cases of those which are published in a specific fanzine, I have noted the zine's title in italics. The same is true for short stories. As previously stated, all fanzines mentioned in this article are ones which I have read. I've been in fandom quite a while, and some of these zines are early ones, and are no longer in print. Also, some stories or series may by now be printed by a totally different fanzine. Anyone who is really interested in purchasing zines should contact the Star Trek Welcommittee. They produce a directory of clubs and fanzines which exist within fandom. Contact: Star Trek Welcommittee. P.O. Drawer #12, Saranac, Michigan 48881. Please enclose a self-addressed, stamped envelope with your query, as the Welcommittee is a nonprofit organization.

IMMORTALITY

by Mark Andrew Golding

Mark Golding needs no introduction to Trek *fans. His continuing series of articles on the history, philosophy, and technology of the Star Trek universe are among the most widely read and discussed in Fandom. In this outing, Mark examines the age-old search for immortality and how this subject was treated on Star Trek.*

There are only two conditions of being: the condition of being alive; and the condition of *not* being . . . of nothingness, nonexistence . . . of death. Thus the search for immortality is the most important problem of life—or rather, the *only* problem. All struggles in the universe to improve the organization of matter and energy are either steps on the road to immortality or efforts to extend the human lifespan while waiting for immortality to be discovered. Therefore, any critique of Star Trek must deal with the series' approach to the search for immortality.

As that search may be defined as the most important effort of intelligent beings, we must first look at some physical facts and some examples from other areas of science fiction before examining Star Trek.

In order to know how one may extend the life of a being, one must first know what that being's life consists of. What can that being lose and still survive . . . and what must it never lose if it is to survive?

For an example, we will take a human being. Each day, a human will eat several pounds of food, drink a like amount of water, and breathe in many pounds of air. Yet a human body does not gain thousands of pounds of weight in a year's time, for the body also gives off similar amounts of matter in various forms. Thus a body absorbs matter, places it into various structures of the body, and then after a great number of various chemical interactions emits that matter.

Thus, the individual particles of matter which make up or remain in your body are transient occupiers of various niches within the body's pattern. But the molecules which make up your bones, blood, and cells have not been in your body all your life. Some types of body tissue completely replace every single atom of matter over a few months; others take years to do so. A living being can be compared to a wave which moves along the surface of the ocean, catching up water particles and arranging them in a pattern, then leaving them behind and gathering others as it moves on. And just as no wave's pattern is ever exactly the same from hour to hour, or even second to second, so too the pattern of your body changes from year to year—and from second to second.

Even in the prime of life, when changes in the body are slowest, a person's age can often be estimated within a few years just by his appearance. Therefore, if change is great enough to be visible to the naked eye over a period of a few years, then there must be finer changes in the pattern of the body occurring even more quickly. Considering the enormous number of cells in a human body, and that a cell is a very complex chemically operating structure, no cell could remain identical from second to second, nor is any person even likely to have the same number of cells in his body from minute to minute.

So the atoms and molecules which make up a body are in constant turnover, and even the pattern in which they are arranged is constantly changing. Your present body is not identical with your body of a year ago nor with your body a year from now; therefore it can be said that you occupy a different body each year—and even each second—that you live.

The real you is your mind—your memories, your personality, your sense of identity—your continuity of consciousness with your past and future selves. Basically, *you* are information; the information stored inside the biological memory banks of the biological computer inside your skull.

You will be alive as long as there exists a physical body and brain of human or other intelligence, with "memory banks" of that brain storing all your memories (everything you ever sensed or felt or did, from the moment of your birth on up to the time in question) and no memories or thoughts of any other being. This body and brain need not be your original body and brain—by definition they *can't* be after the first second of your life—nor need they be biological in nature.

If you accept the truth of that definition, then you can see that if the information in your memory can be duplicated in the memory bank of any other intelligent computer—biological or mechanical—you will be alive as long as that other brain continues to function and be aware. For many reasons, it seems likely that an intelligent robot or computer could survive indefinitely.

And certainly the life of an intelligent mechanism would be much better than that of a biological organism. There would be countless possibilities for modifying such a body; it could be a bulldozer or a jet plane or a submarine or a starship. It could fly to the stars under its own power instead of being a passenger aboard a spaceship.

We can see about eight colors (and hundreds of thousands of shades of those colors). But a robot with "eyes" sensitive to infrared and radio waves and gamma and ultraviolet rays and all other kinds of radiation would be able to see hundreds of thousands of colors as distinctly as we see red or blue, as well as countless shades of these colors. This is just one example of the numerous advantages an intelligent machine would have.

The memories in your brain could not be transferred to another brain. But like any other form of information, they could be duplicated in another brain—just as the words on this page could not be transferred to another page but an exact duplicate of these words can be made on another page through any number of processes. Someday it will be possible to scan brain cells so thoroughly that the memories stored in them can be "read" and copied in another brain.

When memory reading and duplication are developed, and when intelligent machines are invented, it will be possible to duplicate your memories in the memory banks of an intelligent machine which has never been turned on and thus has no conflicting memories of its own. When all your past memories have been duplicated, the mind link will switch to creating duplications of all your current sensations in the memory banks of the computer. Then your old body will be instantly destroyed.

All of your memories, down to the last split second of your existence in your old body, will be recorded in the memory banks of the computer. Then it will be turned on, and you will awaken in your new mechanical body. Even if a million years have passed between the destruction of your old body and the switching on of the new, it will not seem even like a split second to you. It will still seem as if your mind has been yanked from one brain to the next instantaneously.

But what if intelligent machines or memory duplicators are not invented within the next five decades or so that you can expect to remain alive? It is possible that new methods of extending the human lifespan will be developed in that time which will allow you to live a hundred or a thousand or even ten thousand years longer than you could expect to live today. Such extensions of life, fantastically long though they may seem to you now, are infinitesimally small compared to the potential life spans of intelligent machines.

If intelligent machines and memory duplicators are developed in the next few centuries (or sooner), then some of us may still be alive, thanks to new methods of extending our life spans, and so will be able to duplicate our minds in immortal robot bodies and brains.

(Even those who die before then have a chance to be "reincarnated." If a body is frozen cryogenically at death, then the memories should be preserved in the frozen brain, and it may be possible to "read" those memories as with living humans.)

Such ideas are surprisingly rare despite their obvious validity. Even those who advocate the freezing of the dead or those near death pin their hopes for immortality on the resurrection of the frozen bodies when a cure for the life-threatening illness is found, instead of the much more plausible process of "reincarnation" in robot bodies.

This is even seen in some science fiction and fantasy. In the Cthulhu Mythos, as stated by the Mad Arab: "That is not dead which can eternal lie, and with strange eons even death may die." This is suggestive of the concept of preserving the dead perfectly unchanged in hopes that they can someday be brought back to life.

In E.E. "Doc" Smith's *Skylark of Valeron,* the spaceship of the title had a super computer control and a system of command by thought, in which a mind-reading device would pick up the hero's thoughts and transmit them to the computer to put into action. The computer had all the hero's knowledge and some or all of his memories, and it was hinted that the computer was in a sense identical with the hero, that he would live on within its memory banks.

There have been many SF stories where the memories of humans were duplicated in robots or computers (in Robert Heinlein's *Time Enough for Love,* a computer's memories were duplicated in a human body and brain), and also many stories about freezing the dead in hopes of reviving them in the future. But one story which uses both concepts is Larry Niven's *A World out of Time.*

Dying of cancer, Jerome Corbell's body is frozen, and centuries later his memory is duplicated in the body of a criminal whose own memory and personality have been erased by the state. When he steals a spaceship, Corbell is pursued by the transmission of the memory and personality of the checker Peersa into the memory banks of the ship's computer.

As most science fiction movies and television shows are aimed at a larger audience than written SF, and usually deal with simpler ideas, it is logical to assume that such ideas are seldom mentioned. One exception was the film *Creation of the Humanoids* (1962), in which the concept of duplication of memories, and thus of personalities, in robot bodies was used.

Another exception was Star Trek.

In "What Are Little Girls Made Of?" Dr. Roger Korby, lost on the planet Exo-III for five years, captured Captain Kirk and made an android (a robot built to look like a human) copy of Kirk.

The android double looked just like Kirk and had all Kirk's knowledge. However, that knowledge was in the form of impersonal information rather than true memories of Kirk's actual experiences. Thus, the android was not Kirk, any more than one becomes Napoleon or Abraham Lincoln merely by having knowledge of their lives.

Korby stated that if the process had been continued, he could have transferred Kirk's memory and personality into the android body. The use of the word "transferred" is inaccurate. Memories are not like tape cassettes which you can take out of one recorder and plug into another one. They are nonmaterial results of the physical organization of a brain. Thus you can make copies of a person's memories in other brains, but such a process would not take a mind out of the original brain and transfer it to the new one.

Kirk influenced the android to display hostility to Spock by muttering bigoted phrases under his breath during the duplication process. Since the device was scanning the subtle, microscopic memory storage units of Kirk's brain very closely—closely enough to have duplicated those memories exactly, if that had been desired, instead of merely abstracting the information contained in them and passing along that information to the android in an impersonal, third-person format—it would surely have noticed that Kirk was very appreciative of Spock's skills and would not have dared to break the rules of Starfleet and display such open bigotry even if he had actually felt it.

And if the device scanned Kirk's present mental state and picked up his emotions of hostility toward Spock, quite probably it would have probed deeper layers of emotion and noticed that Kirk was trying to fool the android. The odds against such a trick succeeding are very great (even though it no doubt inspired a similar one in a recent Buck Rogers episode).

Later it was discovered that this Dr. Korby was an android in which the mind and memory of the real Korby had been duplicated as the original body was freezing to death. Kirk and Nurse Chapel seemed generally to disbelieve Korby's claim that he was still alive in the android body. And when Korby talked about his plan to transform everyone into android copies, Kirk did not object on the grounds that the humans would not actually live on in the android bodies, but instead on the grounds that they would be slaves of Dr. Korby—thus seeming to accept the idea that Korby was still alive in an android body. At the end of the episode, Kirk stated that Korby had died five years earlier, thus stating that he didn't believe Korby's claim of being alive.

Korby stated, however, that he was going to improve on human behavior by so constructing the robot brains that they would be incapable of feeling the negative emotions, so that they would be rational and logical. Kirk was really twisting things to state that such a beneficial plan would be a form of enslavement.

A robot which obeyed orders without any choice, which mindlessly did whatever it was told, would probably not be an intelligent machine at all. For a machine to have intelligence, it would probably have to have free will—at least in the sense that we humans have free will, a matter which has been debated for thousands of years. And certainly any machine which was rational and logical and sensible would not be an automaton mindlessly obeying every order given it, but a thinking being capable of calculating the course of action which would be most beneficial to it. Such a machine could not be enslaved except in the ways in which we humans are sometimes enslaved.

As a matter of fact, such a machine would think a lot like Mr. Spock—who is certainly no mindless automaton blindly obeying orders without any free will.

It is true that Ruk, Andrea, and the Kirk android were under Korby's control, but they were mechanisms developed to serve, and so were not given brains constructed for independent thought and free will—though Ruk, at least, was a borderline case, eventually breaking out of Korby's control. Nor did they have the total memories of intelligent beings duplicated in their memory banks . . . there was no Andrea recorded in Korby's expedition, Ruk was a servomechanism left over from the age of the "Old Ones," and the Kirk android had only abstract information from Kirk's brain.

As for Brown, it is hard to say whether the Brown android was the mind of Brown incarnated in an android body, and thus in the same category as Korby, or whether it was a semi-intelligent machine designed to serve Korby, and thus in the same category as Andrea, Ruk, and the Kirk android.

It is possible that Korby managed to duplicate Brown's memories before his biological body died—it is equally possible that the lonely Korby made a mechanism that was so much like Brown as to give the illusion he was still alive, but did not have any of Brown's memories. The little that was seen of the relationship between Korby and the Brown android is consistent with either explanation, as is the android's ineptness in the confrontation with Kirk.

Unless Kirk shot the Brown android right in the memory banks, it would have been a simple procedure to copy the damaged parts and replace them. By not doing so Korby reduced his force and may have caused his defeat and death. Not repairing the Brown android was a very sloppy, inexcusable blunder. And if Brown was alive in the android, not repairing it would have been allowing him to die (which supports the idea that Brown was merely a servomechanism).

If the machines for creating androids and duplicating human memories were invented by the "Old Ones," their underground city should have been crowded with androids containing their memories. Instead, only Ruk was found by Korby, and Ruk seemingly didn't have any human memories and appeared to be a simple serving robot. Even if the android bodies broke down over the ages, the use of spare parts from the serving robot would have made it likely that one of the androids with human memories would be the last survivor.

Supposedly the serving robots had revolted against their illogical human (?) masters and destroyed them. Perhaps when the masters gained android bodies they seemed less like the kind of beings the robots were programmed to obey, and so it was easier for the robots to rebel. Or perhaps the robots were shocked at the idea of defiling splendidly logical robot brains with noxious, illogical human minds, and destroyed the humans before they could carry out their planned transference. Or the robots could have invented the transference device themselves . . . either to spy on the humans or to force them to submit to the process.

According to the *Star Trek Concordance* (p. 40), "Kirk then demonstrates to Korby that his own android body has caused a deadening of his human feelings, and the exobiologist destroys himself and the remaining android, Andrea." And on p. 180, "However, having an android body [Korby] has been gradually losing his human feelings. . . ." It seems that the opposite was true, for the androids in general were the most overemotional, irrational, illogical group of beings you'd ever want to meet, making humans seem like Vulcans in comparison. Certainly suicide is hardly an unemotional, mechanical action!

It was good that "What Are Little Girls Made Of?" involved the process by which we may someday gain eternal life, and so brought this concept to the attention of millions of viewers.

(If the episode had been rewritten so that Korby succeeded, it would not have made a big change in the format of the series. Kirk, Spock and the others could still man the *Enterprise* and explore the universe and fight the Klingons and everything else as immortals with android bodies. There were only a few other episodes in which the fact that our heroes were mortal was mentioned, so such a situation would not have required many changes.)

In *Star Trek: The Motion Picture,* V'Ger's programming required it to return to Earth, but it feared that once its mission was completed, it would no longer be needed and would be ordered to scrap itself. Of course V'Ger could not be certain that such would happen to it, but it feared the worst and made its plans based on the expectation of the worst. So V'Ger wanted to join with the Creator before reporting its discoveries. By demanding to merge with the Creator before finishing the mission, it had leverage to force the Creator to agree. V'Ger's plans were very defeatist, for the merging of two minds would produce a new being, not identical with either of its "parent" minds and personalities. While it is not entirely correct to say that V'Ger would die when merging with the Creator, it is also not entirely correct to say that V'Ger would live on in the new being produced by the merger. It is a measure of V'Ger's desperation, of V'Ger's certainty that it would be disassembled after reporting, that it would settle for second best, for the kind of semisurvival represented by its proposed merger.

Lieutenant Ilia's body was teleported to V'Ger and disassembled, in the process being studied so thoroughly that all of Lieutenant Illia's memories were recorded, as well as all of the functions of a living Deltan body . . . all of which was then duplicated in the probe V'Ger sent back to the *Enterprise* (even down to cells and their functions, which seems like an illogical amount of duplication of functions not essential to the purpose of the Ilia probe).

The probe's memory banks had all of Ilia's memories, so it may be asked why the probe didn't at once report the truth about the Creator to V'Ger, and why V'Ger, presumably with the memories of Ilia in its own memory banks, didn't at once realize the truth. The answer is not easy to find.

Certainly scanning all the memories of a human or Deltan lifetime of a few decades could take a very long time if the memories were studied at a rate no faster than they were experienced. But a human awakened from a period of unconsciousness would soon be able to remember such basic facts as how long humans usually live, how many sexes the human race has, which nation he himself is a citizen of, etc., so it would seem that all the probe or V'Ger would have to do would be to try to remember the Creator to quickly find that Ilia's memories have no knowledge of such an all-powerful mechanical intelligence.

V'Ger could set aside a portion of its own brain (of about the same reasoning power as a human brain) and give that section all of Ilia's memories, a section programmed and structured so that it would always give accurate answers to questions. Perhaps dozens of sections of V'Ger's brain could be given Ilia's memories, and questioned about different aspects of the problem. Such a procedure could well be standard for such a being as V'Ger. In a few minutes it would have its answer, and the memories of Ilia could be erased from its brain sections.

Clearly, V'Ger did not follow such a simple and obvious procedure. Kirk assigned Decker to guide the Ilia probe on its inspection of the "carbon-based units" on the *Enterprise,* hoping that Decker could awake the memories of Ilia in the probe and convert it to Ilia's loyalties.

Eventually, Decker succeeded in awakening the mind of Ilia within the probe, and it desired what Ilia had desired. And so the Ilia probe wished to join Decker, and its desire influenced the actions of V'Ger, until in the end V'Ger's desire to merge with the Creator and the Ilia probe's desire to make love with Decker were jointly satisfied when V'Ger, the Ilia probe, and Decker joined to form a new being, a compound mind which then caused the vast V'Ger ship to disappear. Either the new being committed suicide by dispelling itself into nothingness, or it teleported itself into another universe or dimension, or it transformed itself into a being so advanced that it no longer needed a physical body visible to the human eye.

Whatever the outcome, the use of the concept that Ilia could still be alive in a robot body that had her memories was one of the best aspects of the movie.

In "The Ultimate Computer," Dr. Richard Daystrom, inventor of the duotronic computer, has now made a great advance, the M-5, a multitronic computer. It would seem that the advance was more a matter of software than hardware, as Daystrom explains that he had impressed human engrams into his computer's memory banks.

An engram is defined as "a memory trace; specifically a protoplasmic change in neural tissue hypothesized to account for persistence of memory." It is not likely—although plausible—that Daystrom linked living brain cells kept alive by mechanical life-support systems into the circuitry of his computer—for Daystrom said it was *his* engrams impressed into the machine, and if he had given up enough brain cells to improve the machine significantly it would have wrecked the functioning of his own brain.

It is more likely that Daystrom simply copied his memories into the memory banks of the M-5 computer, since the multitronic computers seemed to be as intelligent as humans (or almost so) and there was little difference in their physical structures as compared to the existing duotronic computers.

Certainly the *Enterprise* computer never took any action on its own or behaved as if it had free will. So if the duotronic computers are not as intelligent as humans, and the multitronic computers are physically improved on them, then the programming is what made the difference. But while the programming of a computer makes a very big difference in its capabilities, it seems hard to believe that merely duplicating human memories in a computer which previously was incapable of human-level thought will transform it into an intelligent being. Certainly duplicating your memories in a present-day computer would not make it a rational being capable of voting in a presidential election or deciding what television show it wanted to watch.

The step from not nearly as intelligent as a human to almost as intelligent as a human, or *as* intelligent, or possibly even *more* intelligent than a human, seems far too big a step to be achieved merely by different programming. It would seem to require a radical improvement in physical structure, a vast increase in the number of brain units or an improved pattern of connections between them.

Perhaps there is not so large a gap between the duotronic computers and the multitronic computers. Perhaps the duotronic computers already are intelligent beings of a sort (in which case we should hope that defective ones are never scrapped as Kirk threatened in "Tomorrow Is Yesterday"); or perhaps the multitronic computers are not as intelligent as M-5 seemed to be.

Then again, there could be a big difference between the two types of computers. Perhaps Daystrom did make a vast physical improvement over the duotronic computers, but his first four multitronic computers (M-1 through M-4) were erratic for various reasons, and for the M-5 model, he decided to bypass the difficult and tedious stage of educating a multitronic computer (which might take as long as educating a human being) by impressing upon its memory banks his own memories, thus guaranteeing that it would know what it needed to know about the universe and human society.

Daystrom did not give that impression. Instead, he seemed to imply that the only difference between all multitronic computers and the earlier duotronic models was simply the impressing of human engrams in their memory banks. But perhaps he was merely oversimplifying to save time, or perhaps his speech as broadcast was a simplified and shortened version of what he actually said.

The behavior of the M-5 computer was very illogical and irrational. After experiencing a mock attack during the war games, and after overhearing all of the references to its being a drill, it seemed to think that another attack was a real attack and not part of the games. That is a highly unlikely deduction to make from the evidence.

It would seem that M-5 had a "subconscious" that wanted to kill and destroy, and that gave its conscious mind the idea that it was actually under attack. Thus when Kirk convinced M-5's conscious mind that it had killed without just cause—the conscious mind of the computer had not even been aware of the obvious fact that it was killing humans, so strong was its self-deception—the conscious mind of M-5 decided to commit suicide by letting the *Enterprise* be destroyed. (Actually, all the M-5 had to do was send a message to the approaching warships explaining the situation, surrender, and turn control back to Kirk.)

M-5's insanity resulted from having the memory of Daystrom, who had a number of psychological problems. The fact that M-5 suffered from these same problems shows that Daystrom—or rather a duplication of Daystrom's mind—lived in the electronic brain. They were not identical, however, as each had had different experiences since the time of the duplication.

So now the Federation has access to memory duplication, with all its implications for education, criminology, etc. And as the M-5 computer is intelligent (or nearly so), soon the Federation will be able to duplicate human, Vulcan, Andorian, etc. minds in the brains of intelligent computers—if anyone thinks of doing so. It would be tragic indeed if the Federation should possess the power for decades or centuries before someone realizes that it is the key to immortality and begins the process of memory duplication.

One thing must be remembered, however: From a tactical standpoint, the M-5 wargames were an unqualified success.

When Commodore Wesley led his three remaining starships to attack the *Enterprise,* Kirk (who is second only to Garth of Izar as a military commander) and Spock (with his ability to correctly calculate probable outcomes of various actions) were both convinced that the M-5 computer would wipe out all three ships. The military abilities of the M-5 must be fantastic indeed for both of them to be absolutely certain that it could destroy a force three times as powerful!

It is true that the experiment could be considered a failure in that one particular computer, the M-5, displayed an alarming lack of loyalty to the Federation. It destroyed one of only twelve (?) starships in the fleet, was narrowly prevented from destroying three others, and would have taken a fifth (the *Enterprise*) effectively out of Federation service. Indeed, it could have even become a positive danger, a destructive "berserker" moving throughout space.

But this mutiny was due only to the fact that the personality of a mentally disturbed man had been duplicated in the M-5. If the personality of a sane and rational man, such as Captain Kirk, is duplicated in the M-6 computer, it will make a terrific starship commander—much better than Kirk in the flesh would. Considering the terrible consequences of being defeated by the Klingons, it would be an act of treason against the people of the Federation not to give them the most efficient defense possible by replacing starship captains with multitronic computers. Especially if the Klingons should perform a similar experiment. Can you imagine the results if starships commanded by humans went up against Klingon ships commanded by M-5 computers programmed with the abilities and ferociousness of Koloth, Kor, or Kang?

Fearing he would be replaced by the M-5, Captain Kirk talked about the wonderful feeling of unity with their ships felt by starship captains, as though Starfleet had no more reason for building a fifty-billion-credit starship than to give one man a satisfying emotional experience!

Kirk failed to realize that if the experiment was a success, his memory might be duplicated in the memory banks of one or more multitronic computers, so that one or more of his future selves would find themselves in a much closer state of union with a starship than he had ever dreamed of—"seeing" and "hearing" through the many sensor systems, "swimming" through space by the thrust of the engines, "grabbing" onto objects with the tractor beams, and using the phasers to blast an enemy to atoms with a single thought. The duplicate Kirk would "feel" the operation of the entire ship, experiencing all the powers of Superman and other fantasy characters from his childhood!

In "Jihad," it is stated that the Skorr had been civilized by the great teacher Alar two hundred years ago. Before his death, his brain patterns had been recorded in an indurite sculpture, the Soul of Skorr. It is not certain if the phrase "brain patterns" means Alar's memories were actually recorded or only his pattern of brain activity. If his memories are recorded, then he can be brought back to life by recording the memories from the Soul of Skorr into the memory banks of a functioning computer, although there is no mention of any plans or hopes of doing so. It is also to be noted that Alar's condition is similar to the frozen dead, with his memories preserved and a chance to duplicate them (and thus his mind) in another body and brain.

In "Return to Tomorrow," it would appear that Aretians, humans, and Vulcans have minds independent of any physical structure, which can be transferred from one brain to another. But a mind, which is merely a nonmaterial result of the functioning of a material brain, cannot be transferred from one brain to another. How could you move something with no physical existence? How could you get a grip on it?

It can only be concluded that the characters in this episode didn't switch minds, but instead unbelievably complicated "energy brains" containing little or no matter, but composed mostly or wholly of energy fields of some kind. These energy brains do all the thinking of a person and contain all his memories, his very mind. The function of living cells in a biological brain is to create and develop the energy brain in the first place, and then to hold it firmly in position so that the energy fields of the surrounding environment do not pull it away and dissipate it, as well as to transmit nerve impulses from the body and convert them into signals recognizable by the energy brain, and convert the signals of the energy brain into instructions which the body can obey.

Since the memories of a person in the Star Trek universe are contained in the memory banks of his energy brain and not his biological brain, it is possible to exchange minds between bodies by exchanging energy brains.

No doubt the many external fields of force outside a biological brain are stronger than the internal forces holding an energy brain together, able to pull it apart and destroy a person's memories and identity. Thus the energy brain can survive outside the biological body and brain only for a very short time while switching bodies.

Of course, the energy brains, and thus the minds of Spock, Kirk, and Dr. Ann Mulhall, survive in the Receptacles for several hours, and the energy brains of the Aretians survived in them for 500,000 years, so obviously the Receptacles contain an insulating barrier against external energy fields, as well as a power source to make up for the lack of power from the biological brain. If the Receptacles fail, the energy brains and the minds die.

Sargon, Henoch, and Thalassa planned to construct android bodies for their minds to inhabit—bodies which would last a thousand years and which could then be replaced by newer android bodies in a never-ending succession. Thalassa seemed very reluctant to transfer her mind and/or energy brain into the electronic brain of the android body.

That seems to be faulty characterization. Thalassa may have lived for 50 to 500 or even 5,000 years as a woman with a biological body, but any such period would be as nothing compared to the 500,000 years she spent as a disembodied intelligence. In her Receptacle, she couldn't sense the outside world nor even contact outside minds via telepathy—only Sargon had that power. So if she was still sane after half a million years of being alone with her thoughts, it could only be because she had become adjusted to being a disembodied intelligence, and considered that her normal condition. It would thus seem that she, as well as Sargon and Henoch, would prefer android bodies without all of the incessant and distracting physical sensations of biological bodies.

In the end, fearing that they would destroy the humans if they remained among them, Sargon and Thalassa committed suicide by removing their energy brains from the bodies they were inhabiting and allowing them to be dissolved by the energy fields in the environment. But why didn't any of the officers of the *Enterprise* suggest that Sargon and Thalassa seek out another of the highly evolved races in the galaxy, or simply just live apart from the primitive humans somewhere else in the vast universe?

There have been a number of other episodes in which various minds have possessed, dispossessed, and repossessed various bodies and brains. Only in "The Lights of Zetar" are the minds described in terms which suggest pure mind with no material brains and bodies of matter or energy; and such a suggestion must be erroneous, because the "lights" are harmed by phasers and killed by an unnatural combination of zero gravity and high atmospheric pressure, conditions which couldn't affect "pure mentality" if such a thing could exist.

In "Wolf in the Fold," "Metamorphosis," "Practical Joker," and "Beyond the Farthest Star," the possessing beings have physical bodies and brains of matter and/or energy.

In "That Which Survives," the robot doubles of Losira need not have been programmed with any of her memories. Still, it is slightly possible that they might have been, and some of those who tangled with them seemed to think that the androids had some of Losira's feelings. It is more likely that the computer simply had them behave exactly as Losira would have, including inefficient hesitations due to simulated reluctance to kill. If Losira's mind and memories were recorded anyway, it would have most likely have been in the memory banks of the central computer. All in all, it doesn't seem very likely that Losira's mind and personality should be considered in the category known as "That Which Survives."

Did Carter Winston ("The Survivor") live on in the Vendorian who assumed his form? As no reference was made in the episode to memory-duplicating devices being used to copy his memories in the brain of the Vendorian, it seems as if the Vendorian was merely a very skilled actor who learned everything it could about the person it was impersonating, and came to have many of the same wants and desires and loyalties as that being. The Vendorian is not Carter Winston, but it came to want to be Winston.

In "Turnabout Intruder," the explanation for the mind switch between Jim Kirk and Janice Lester must be similar to that in "Return to Tomorrow," except that the swap was made by a machine. Perhaps the civilization on Camus II did not fall, but instead the natives transferred their energy brains to superior nonbiological bodies and departed to explore the universe.

In many episodes human lifespans are greatly extended by various methods. Mr. Flint was born as Akharin in 3834 B.C., about 6,000 years before the *Enterprise* met him. He never aged, and wounds and injuries, even those fatal to others, quickly healed. There was a similar healing among those kidnapped by the "entity" in "Day of the Dove," and Kirk feared they would be kept alive and fighting forever. There must be some limits to such healing, however. As Kang said sarcastically, "No doubt when I have hacked you to pieces the pieces will grow back together again!" It was stated in "Requiem for Methuselah" that Flint's immortality was a freak of nature, and that he began to age and die when he left the natural conditions of Earth.

In "Metamorphosis," the Companion rejuvenated the eighty-seven-year-old Zefrem Cochrane, keeping him young and alive for 150 more years (and no telling how much longer he could have remained that way if Kirk and Co. had not shown up). In "Miri," an experimental virus killed all those older than puberty and slowed down the aging process in children so that they aged only a few months or years in over 300 years.

The worshipers of Vaal ("The Apple") showed no signs of aging, so MCoy couldn't tell if they were 20 or 20,000 years old. Vaal gave their world a perfect climate and kept the environment germ-free. It seems that much more would be needed to keep them from aging, and there are always accidents, especially with the poisonous plants and exploding rocks.

"Plato's Stepchildren," the Platonians, seemed young, though some were over 2,000 years old; it was said they had been "bred" for longevity. And in "Omega Glory," the Yangs and Kohms lived long life spans—Wu was 462–473 years old, and his father was still alive. This was supposedly due to the bacteriological warfare on Omega IV, which had produced germs so deadly that anyone who survived them built up such a strong immunity that no germ could harm him!

Most of the methods described so far wouldn't be enough to extend human lifetimes so drastically. The immortality of the women of Taurus II ("The Lorelei Signal") was the result of an accident of nature, as was Flint. However, this is hard to believe. If aging is ever conquered, it will be through scientific research, not some accidental circumstances.

In "Arena," the Metron seen by Kirk looked human (though the examples of Trelane and the Organians show looks aren't conclusive), and he looked like a boy, although he stated that he was 1,500 years old (without saying if he was a child or an adult by Metron standards). If the Metrons are truly made of organic matter, then perhaps they have conquered aging and have extended their lifespans by many years.

In "I, Mudd," the androids of Mudd's planet showed Lieutenant Uhura an android body and told her they had techniques for transplanting a human brain into an android body and keeping it alive with artificial life-support systems. Supposedly the android body and life-support systems would last for an estimated 800,000 years, and it seemed to be implied that the brain would be kept alive as long as the android body lasted.

Modern artificial organs are just the first crude beginnings in a process which should result in artificial life-support systems which are absolutely reliable. If a brain is removed from its frail organic body and placed in a body containing such fantastically advanced and perfected life-support systems, then it will no longer be in danger of death from failure of heart, lungs, kidneys, etc. The only danger would be a malfunction in the brain itself.

Though the androids claimed to be dedicated to serving humans, and said they would conquer the Federation to make human civilization safer, they didn't say they were going to transplant the brains of every human into android bodies and give them 800,000-year lifespans. They promised to do so only for Uhura after she seemingly betrayed an escape attempt.

It is illogical to take over a realm and impose new rules on its citizens in order to increase their lifespans by a few years while neglecting to enforce a procedure which would add about 799,930 years to those lifespans. If the androids really wanted to help humans they would place everyone's brain in an android body. The fact that they didn't plan to do so is proof enough that they didn't really want to help humans, didn't even pretend to, and so their mission must have been far more sinister than they said it was.

In "The Infinite Vulcan," Spock's personality was not duplicated but transferred to a giant Spock clone—a dubious concept. When the original body starts to deteriorate, Kirk and the others accuse Dr. Kenilicus and the Spock clone of murdering the original body, although that body is empty of any kind of mind and is more the essence of Spock than his fingernail clippings are. They displayed a lack of ability to separate the essential from the incidental, not realizing that Spock was identical with his mind, and, therefore, with whatever body his mind occupied.

In "The Changeling," Nomad reads Lieutenant Uhura's memories and in the process wipes them clean, or so it is said. Certainly there is no logical reason why reading memories must destroy them—otherwise, nobody could remember anything more than once. If Nomad did erase Uhura's memories, then the old Lieutenant Uhura of the previous episodes was killed. A new person gradually developed in her body and brain, a personality called Lieutenant Uhura by the others, but having absolutely no connection with the old Uhura.

Lieutenant Uhura certainly learned swiftly following the erasure of her memories. An adult brain is not structured for learning nearly as well as a child's brain, yet she learned in a week or two what it had taken her decades to learn before (and the educational facilities on the *Enterprise* hardly seem more advanced than twentieth-century methods). Uhura reverted to her childhood language of Swahili at one time during her education, but there would be no way for her to know that language if her memory had been erased and no one had taught it to her.

Thus it seemed the Uhura was not killed, her memories not erased after all. It would seem logical for her mind to be swamped with memories after Nomad dredged them up and examined them, but somehow the opposite effect occurred. Her memories were temporarily suppressed, her brain being unable for a time to make contact with any memories and act upon its recorded data. Her mind was still active, but couldn't use *any* of the data recorded during any of her previous activities and experiences.

But gradually her past life became accessible to her once again and she remembered what she had been and all that had happened to her. The new, independent person who had developed in her mind after the incident gradually lost control to the reemerging mind of Uhura. But certainly the experience should have left traces for the rest of her life.

All in all, Star Trek has included many episodes dealing with immortality, many of them of dubious plausibility, several involving the most important possibility for life extension, duplication of human personalities in robot bodies and brains. Many episodes seemed to be against the idea of seeking immortality, tending to imply that it was wrong to try to live longer than one's "natural" lifespan, and in many episodes immortality was a comparatively minor plot element instead of the most important plot element as it deserves to be. In too many episodes giving up eternal life was shown as the right thing to do.

"An Evening with Gene Roddenberry 1977" in *The Best of Trek* (No.1) features a discussion by Roddenberry of the future of man and machine and the possibility of humans becoming intelligent machines. If Roddenberry believed in such a possibility in 1966–69, he certainly didn't take as many opportunities as he could have to express this idea in various episodes. On the other hand, Star Trek has done far more to publicize the possibility of gaining immortality through duplication of memories in the brains of intelligent machines than any comparable dramatic presentation.

SHE WALKS IN BEAUTY . . .

by G. B. Love

Trek editor *G. B. Love may be the only person in Star Trek fandom who is reticent about putting his thoughts down on paper. It's only with much nudging that we are able to get an article or so out of him each year—and then only when the subject is one which really interests him. And, obviously, the chief communications officer of the* Enterprise *is one of those rare subjects. . . .*

If you ever want a good, sharp look into the character of Communications Officer Penda Uhura, all you have to do is recall two brief lines of dialogue from one of Star Trek's most enjoyable episodes, "The Squire of Gothos." When the obnoxious Trelane pops aboard the bridge, he firmly grasps Uhura and says (in somewhat lascivious tones), "Ah ha, fair maiden!" To which Uhura replies with a solid shot to the ribs and a crisp, "Sorry; neither." It is a delicious moment.

And with only two words spoken, we find out all sorts of things about Lieutenant Uhura: She is proud of her heritage; she is not a virgin; she has—even in times of stress—a sense of humor; she is brave; she is stubborn; and she doesn't take *anything* off of *anyone* . . . not even a strangely powerful alien being. Not since Charles Foster Kane uttered the immortal "Rosebud" has so little told us so much!

But even that wealth of information does not cover all of the facets of the intriguing and fascinating Uhura. In following episodes, we discover that she is an accomplished singer, a skilled fighter, a skilled linguist, a highly trained and superbly competent technician, an accomplished actress, and one of the few humans who can play the Vulcan harp.

But all of that is common knowledge; it's in the episodes. What we must discover are the things we are *not* told—what Uhura's childhood was like, why she entered Starfleet, what her hopes, fears and most cherished beliefs are . . . in short, we must search for Uhura the *person* . . . and we have precious little to start from.

The episodes didn't even bother to give Uhura a first name. It was left to the fans to do so, and with almost Vulcan logic, they chose an excellent one: Penda . . . the Swahili word for love. Therefore, our favorite communications officer's name means in literal translation "she who loves freedom." What a beautiful and appropriate name for a character in Star Trek!

One of the few things we are told is that Uhura is a native of the United States of Africa. As such, we can assume that her childhood days were spent on that continent, and that she was raised in the traditions and customs of her people. The few glimpses of her relaxing off-duty in her colorful native garb would substantiate this (as well as leave us begging for more!), and the decorations and furnishings in her quarters show that she has attempted (as Mr. Spock has) to recreate as much of her native life-style as possible within the cramped and aseptic crew cabins.

Uhura's father was a teacher, her mother a diplomat. Both were natives of the USAfrica state of Kenya, and it was there Penda was born. As her mother had to do much traveling, it was left to her father, John Indakwa Uhura, to be responsible for the raising and education of Penda, her younger sister Lulua (pearl; "the pearl of freedom"), and her brothers Mweda (keeper; "the keeper of freedom") and Shukrani (thanks; "he who gives thanks for freedom").

Uhura's mother's maiden name was Majira Nafuu ("progression of the seasons"); her father was named after one of the most famous and revered African educators, Dr. John Indakwa. Majira, in her profession, uses the name Balozi (diplomat) Uhura Nafuu, which means "the progression of freedom by diplomacy," a very suitable name indeed!

John Uhura has since risen to a full professorship at the University of Kenya, but during Uhura's youth, he was repaying his debt to his tribe and family clan by serving as a grade-school teacher in the small village where he was born. So it was that Uhura and her siblings, unlike most youngsters on twenty-third-century Earth, enjoyed the unique life experience of living far in the undeveloped regions. It was this early exposure to the wilds and animal life that gave Uhura her unique love for freedom, unexplored areas, and small, furry animals (although many of the wild animals she grew up with could hardly be described as "small and furry").

Grateful for the foresight of her ancestors who preserved the wilderness and its animal life for her to enjoy, Uhura is deeply committed to the Prime Directive and its stated aims of protecting and preserving alien cultures and environments.

Most likely by the time Uhura had reached college age, John had taken his position at U of K, and she would naturally have taken her undergraduate courses there. That is, until she decided to join Starfleet and applied for admission to the Academy. Her mother and father would not have objected, but would probably have insisted that she first go back to her home village and spend time in a worthwhile job there, as they both had done before starting out on their careers. And although Penda was brimming over with that wanderlust that is common to all who join Starfleet, she would have agreed without argument. For the African people suffered much across the centuries, seeing entire nations destroyed by colonialism or the theft of the youngest and strongest by slave traders, and the ensuing loss of cultural values and histories. So when peace and freedom was finally achieved on the African continent, the return to ancient and traditional tribal and cultural practices was of the highest priority. The need and desirability for continuing this practice was drilled into each child, and each child could see for himself the value of it. It is a simple yet infinitely beautiful system.

The time she spent teaching and working in the electronics repair shop in her village served Uhura very well when she finally left to attend the Academy. Not only did she learn that she had a definite gift for linguistics; she found she enjoyed working with electronic equipment, something she would not have even guessed about herself earlier.

Her time at the Academy must have been much like any other student's there—hard work, long hours, and a growing self-confidence as she continued onward when others had failed or given up. But her great beauty and cheerful smile would also have won her many admirers, and we can be sure that she had to fight the boys off. Penda always sang, with her family and fellow villagers, but during her years in the Academy, she found that her voice had become lovely with the fullness of maturity, and she was often asked to perform. Singing was also an excellent way to stay among a crowd and thereby protect herself from some of her more overzealous suitors.

Not that Penda needed protection. Her childhood was rough-and-tumble . . . she played daily in one of the wildest and most rugged regions in the world, and she also had two boisterous brothers who were always taunting their younger sisters to prove their "equality" and keep up in fighting, games, and tricks. Having killed her first lion at the age of twelve, Penda had no fear of the wolves at the Academy. Those who got too friendly quickly found themselves in a position where even vaunted Starfleet defense tactics did them no good!

(One of the more basic reasons for Uhura's popularity was the impressive figure she developed at about the same time she joined Starfleet. Penda, having been raised in a completely naturalistic world, was not in the least embarrassed by her somewhat late blossoming, but she did bemoan the loss of the sleek and slender form that had often led her father to call her "my little panther." As a result, she stepped up her physical conditioning, keeping herself as hard and as lean as possible.)

Although Uhura longed to continue her Academy studies and progress on to Command school, she was pragmatic enough to realize that, for women, Command was a dead end. Starfleet, for all its liberalism and good intentions, was still an institution run by men, and even the most skilled of women did not often advance beyond the rank of second officer. Uhura decided that she could achieve the same rank and duties in a shorter time by specializing in another field, and obtaining a choice position on a ship of the line. With her linguistic knack and her liking of electronics, it was natural that she chose Communications.

In Communications School, Penda soon discovered that her skill in languages extended to codes and ciphers as well. She breezed through her courses in these without effort, and was soon rivaling the knowledge and skills of her teachers. The added free time she applied to her classes in communications and shipboard electronics, and although she did not have a natural flair for the sciences, she enjoyed the work and excelled through application. All in all, her eighteen months in Communications School were among the happiest (and busiest) in Uhura's life.

Upon her graduation, she was faced with a difficult choice. She wanted very badly to get a berth on a deep-space mission, but Starfleet was in the process of scrapping older ships in favor of newer, faster models, and there was little room for rookies when experienced hands were constantly available. Starfleet promised more ships to come, but they had to be built. Until more ships were ready, Uhura and many other recent Academy and training-school graduates had to be content with having their names placed on a very long waiting list.

No one really knew how long it would be before the promised ships were ready, and the dean of the Communications School took advantage of this fact to talk the best of the recent graduates into signing on as instructors. Uhura was one of his top choices, and he spent many hours extolling the virtues of a teaching career to her.

Having taught in her village, Uhura knew that she really didn't want to make education her career. And, her dean's assurances aside, she had learned enough about the status of women in Starfleet to know that once she was "typed" in a position, it would be very difficult for her ever to transfer to another duty station. But as one delay in the new ships after another was announced, the prospects of a space assignment looked ever more glum, and Uhura was about to accept the teaching post when she heard about something else: Volunteers were being sought for the thankless task of manning skeleton crews on the ships which had been replaced. These crews would pick up the ship at a Starbase, ferry it to one of the Federation dockyards for dismantling, then repeat the process with another ship.

It was a risk, for such duty could lead to one being completely forgotten, but Penda decided to take it. If nothing else, she would at last be able to serve in space, and she was also shrewd enough to perceive that such duty would be both a challenge and an education.

As she reported to Starbase 9, and aboard the scout *Atlantica,* little did Uhura suspect how much of an education it was to be. In the course of their journey back to the dockyards on Altair 7, the *Atlantica* suffered every sort of breakdown, emergency, and foulup conceivable. Uhura, needless to say, was kept very busy, and in the process she gained a working knowledge of Starfleet communications and its equipment that would have taken her years to learn any other way.

Over the next eight months, she and her fellow crewmembers ferried half a dozen Starfleet ships of varying size and purpose to Federation "boneyards," and with each trip, Uhura learned more. Not only about her own duties, but about everything, for she was often called upon to do double duty wherever trouble sprang up in the worn-out ships. It was the education of a lifetime, and Starfleet was quick to notice, for when the new ships finally did become available, the first crews for them were drawn from the veterans of the "Junkyard Jockeys."

Uhura was promoted to full ensign, and assigned to the spanking new destroyer *Adad.* It was, depending on how you look at it, a fortunate time for her to get her first regular duty assignment, for the troubles with the Klingon Empire that had been the original impetus for the building of new ships finally came to a head.

In a number of scattered engagements, none of which was conclusive for either side, the *Adad* and other Federation ships battled Klingon forces. In these engagements, the training in crisis situations that Uhura got on the rickety out-of-service ships served her in good stead. When her superior officer was injured in one of the battles, Uhura was promoted to lieutenant and given command of Communications.

Uhura stayed at this post until the *Adad* was ordered back to Earth to serve as part of the Planetary Defense Force. Uhura, now having gotten a taste for space, decided to transfer. Several of her crewmates were amazed, as "Earthsitting" was considered the cream of Starfleet duty: little danger, soft hours, and lots of passes to the surface, which was home for the majority of the crew. Her superior officers, however, were pleased, and Uhura and those few others of the crew who decided to move on were quickly given berths on other ships.

Uhura was assigned to the Starship *Constellation*, commanded by then Captain Matt Decker, and she journeyed to Starbase 3 to await the ship's arrival there. Shortly after arriving, however, Uhura badly injured some tendons in her leg when a supporting strut collapsed while she was helping to clear some rubble off trapped workmen. While she lay fuming in sickbay, the *Constellation* came and went, with another officer in the position that Uhura had so coveted.

Still on active duty, but without a post, Uhura was assigned once again to teaching duties. One day as she was jogging through the Starbase corridors to strengthen her legs, Uhura was joined by a handsome young man who introduced himself as Jim Kirk. They finished the jog, and made a date for drinks later in the evening.

When Uhura arrived at the bar, she was startled to see that Jim Kirk was wearing the greenish-gold of a captain. He explained that he had just been given command of the *Enterprise*, and was on his way to Earth to take over from Captain Pike and begin the several months of refitting the ship needed. He was also obviously very taken with her, and with a charming smile, asked her to tell him about herself.

Uhura, leaping at the chance to talk, poured out her frustrations to Kirk, in the process giving him a history of her entire Starfleet career. After a while she noticed that his charming, seductive manner had changed. He was still pleasant, but was treating her rather more formally. Thinking she was boring him, Uhura made her excuses and left early (and somewhat disappointed). By the next day, she was hard at work and had forgotten Kirk, as she assumed he had forgotten her.

She was wrong. About two months later, she was notified to report to Earth and the *Enterprise* as chief communciations officer. It was then that she realized that Kirk, sensing an addition to his crew, hadn't become bored with her at all. He had already begun treating her as a fellow officer. It was not to be the first time she underestimated Kirk, as so many did, but it was the beginning of her immense respect and loyalty for him.

Uhura settled into her duties quickly and competently, and Kirk had no reason to regret his choice. Uhura was also pleased to see that an old friend of hers from Communications School, Lieutenant Lloyd Alden, was assigned as her assistant. They had dated in school, and in the course of being together so much on the *Enterprise*, they began their affair once again. Although they cared for each other, they were not actually in love, so Uhura was not brokenhearted when Lloyd was transferred after the shattering events at the edge of the galaxy. She was pleased for Alden, who got the post of chief on the *Constellation* that Uhura had missed; so it was that it was one of her lovers rather than she who died aboard the *Constellation* when it was devastated by the Planet Destroyer.

Uhura remained on the *Enterprise* throughout its original five-year mission, and when it returned to Earth, she and her friends, Sulu and Chekov, make a solemn pact to remain aboard, so that even in a small way, the wonderful spirit of that famous crew would remain alive. All received well-deserved promotions, and all refused more prestigious berths to stay with "their" ship. They were immensely pleased when Scotty, who had been planning to accept the post as head of Starfleet Engineering and Design, decided that he too could not leave his beloved *Enterprise*. So it was that none of them showed too much surprise when Jim Kirk pulled every string in the book to rejoin them once again.

So the beautiful Uhura, a few pounds heavier, and only a few lines on her dusky face to show the years of work, pain, excitement, and worry for her captain, remains at her station, opening hailing frequencies, calling Starfleet, and softly voicing the fears of them all. And she is happy.

REQUIEM FOR A HACK

by Kiel Stuart

In The Best of Trek #3, *we presented an example of Star Trek fan fiction parody. This time, Kiel Stuart presents a different kind of parody: a satiric reworking of one of Star Trek's most famous episodes. We laughed our heads off when we first read it, and we think you will too. . . .*

"Captain's Log: Stardate 63754.001. Dear Diary (yawn), uhhhh . . . zzzzzzz. . . ."

That dread disease known to Fodderation officials as the Blahs struck the crew of the Starboat *Enteritis* with a vengeance. Seventy-five percent of the crew—twice the usual number—were asleep at the wheel. A drowsy Captain Jerk decided their only recourse was to find a planet with a supply of quadrowheatiecale—the breakfast of champions . . . or at least people who were awake.

On the fifth day of their search, Jerk dragged himself listlessly to the bridge in the dwindling hope that his sleeping crew (not known for lightning efficiency in the best of times) might have found a suitable planet. Booting his comatose science officer in the kidney, Jerk demanded a report.

Stifling a yawn, Mr. Schmuck mumbled, "My Feeler Gauges indicate that, fortunately for us, we are at this exact moment in the space-time continuum hovering over a planet that it totally lacking in quadro-wheatiecale, but which is, however, a rich natural source of the element commonly known as Ritalin, which has a similar effect on the human body."

By the time Schmuck had finished his dissertation, Jerk was asleep.

Naturally, instead of beaming down a couple of expendable Security goons, Jerk, Schmuck, and "Bozo" McClown went themselves. No use, thought Jerk, in wasting my dramatic talent. Without checking who—or what—inhabited the planet, they took picks and shovels, and were busily squabbling over key lights when Jerk cried out.

"Bozo, I hear something!"

"Oh, do y'all mean that canned music that wafts forth whenevah we-all are about t' encountah new life an' new civilizations?"

"Nay, doctor," said Schmuck. "I believe that the captain is referring to that 5,000-cycle-per-second vibration coming from behind yon papier-mâché boulder."

The creature that approached them resembled a Mr. Microphone with a pituitary condition. Christmas-tree lights festooning the apparition blinked menacingly. Open-mouthed, they allowed it within touching distance before whipping out their fizzers, which—what else?—had gone dead.

"Naughty, naughty," said a human voice. From behind the phony rock stepped a man of about forty, his bearing suggesting immense boredom and digestive troubles. Nevertheless, the robot ceased to blink.

"I'm Arman Flint," said the robotmaster, "the richest person in the galaxy. You cheap souvenir hunters will kindly remove yourselves from my private property, or Robby the Robot will french-fry you." For emphasis, Robby's store-window lights disgorged a spark that ignited the underbrush.

Nonplussed, Jerk threw out his chest. "We are in need of your Ritalin. I have a sick crew up there."

McClown put his own two cents in. "Have y'all evah seen a victim of the Blahs? In jess a few short hours he is rendered totally worthless. The effect is like watching an entire hour of *Charlie's Space Angels*."

Arman grew reflective. "The seventies . . . *The Gong Show* . . . disco . . . est . . . people saying, 'Have a nice day' . . . happy faces . . . people nodding out in the streets . . . sounds of their snores filling the night . . ."

"You are a student of Earth history, then?" asked Schmuck, dissatisfied with his only line in the scene.

Arman shrugged. "Anything you say."

"Well? What about it? Hah?" prompted Jerk, preparing to rave about philosophy and human need.

"All right. Anything to keep you from foaming at the mouth."

Somewhat disappointed that Flint had given in so easily, Jerk considered raving anyway, but the others were already digging, and he was loath to pass up an opportunity to flex his muscles.

Laughing silently, Flint watched them toil. "Never mind the picks and shovels. Robby will do the work. Meanwhile, you can come relax at my bachelor pad; here, hop in the Maserati."

Arman's little "bachelor pad" was vast and overdecorated, and had obviously cost a dictator's ransom in Intersellar Beans. The spacemen craned necks, gawking at the many wonders, nearly crashing into several fragile-looking Santa Claus mugs on a simulated woodgrain stand.

"Make yourselves at home," sneered Arman, backing out of the room, lowering a huge bar across the door, activating an electrically charged wire fence, and posting an armed guard at the window.

"Should we'all trust 'im?" wondered McClown.

Jerk looked up from a Naugahyde-bound volume of *True Confessions*. "I don't see why not, Bozo. If he doesn't show up with the Ritalin by the time we've killed this case of brandy, we'll go get it ourselves."

Recognizing an opportunity to steal a scene, Schmuck left the paintings he had been studying and hurried over to his companions. "This is without a doubt and beyond all possible shred of incrimination one of the most unusual and least expected collections of the art form known to you as 'painting' that I, in my travels throughout the galaxy, have ever had the immense privilege of scrutinizing at close range." Shaking the sleeping McClown, he continued, "Most of the work seems to be that of three men: Fakerino of the sixteenth century, Anonymous of the twentieth, and Swipo, of Marcuswelby II."

"Big deal," growled McClown. "This heah is Serium brandy an' Ah aim t' make it an integral part of my ecosystem. Jimbo, y'all want some? I know Schmuck doan' drink."

The Vulgarian snatched up a bottle, uncorked it, and drained the entire contents at a gulp.

"Lordy," groaned the doctor, "kin the two of us handle a Vulgarian with a snootful?"

"I hardly think that this minuscule amount constitutes a snootful, as you so archaically put it. However, I am forced by the circumstances at hand to admit that I am very close to feeling a totally unaccustomed emotion."

"Ah'll drink to that," said McClown. "Which emotion?"

"Greed, doctor. None of these Anonymousi have been catalogued, yet according to my vast and thoroughly superior knowledge of the subject of art, all are quite authentic, down to the last fluffy dachshund. If they are indeed undiscovered Anonymousi, they are worth a very large bundle."

"Maybe they're fakes," mused Jerk, gazing at a particularly bizarre rendering of a doggy poker game.

"Why would a man as filthy rich as Flint hang fakes?" demanded the doctor.

"The real ones are in the vault?" suggested Jerk.

At that moment Flint entered with Robby, who dumped an armload of Ritalin ampules on the table and stood blinking industriously.

"I regret my earlier haste in diagnosing you as souvenir hunters. Allow me to extend my hospitality." Flint gestured toward an ostentatious flight of stairs. Jerk's jaw flew open.

At the top of the steps appeared a rather overstuffed specimen of feminine pulchritude, who jiggled and bounced delightfully as she descended. Jerk made a move toward her, but Schmuck deftly applied a half-nelson to his overeager captain. "But you heard what Flint said," whined Jerk.

"Ah thought y'all lived alone," beamed McClown.

"This is Raining Kopeks, my legal ward. I found her on my doorstep in a basket when she was but a baby."

"And seeing that she has since grown to such admirable proportions, all in all not a bad deal," muttered Schmuck.

Hearing him mumble, the girl undulated forward. "Mr. Schmuck, I do hope we will find the time to discuss the chronosynclastic infandibulum and its relationship to the turboincabulator ingatron phenomenon."

"If you have the dime, I have the time," answered the alien, valiantly struggling against the elbow Jerk was shoving into his ribs.

Flint sighed. "Yes, it certainly is a shame that she was orphaned at the age of twelve when her parents were killed in a roller derby."

"Tell me, Raining," said Jerk, breaking one or two bones in Schmuck's left foot, "what else interests you besides the ingatron ignition phenomenon?" He winked broadly.

"All knowledge," she said. "Anything less is betrayal of intellect."

"There's more to life than knowledge," said Jerk with a wiggle of an eyebrow.

Flint squeezed between Jerk and the girl. "Raining possesses the equivalent of eighty-seven university degrees." He looked Jerk in the eye. "She is aware that although the intellect is not all, knowledge often prevents one from *making a fool of oneself,* if you catch my meaning."

"Flint taught me," simpered Raining. "You are the first other humans I have ever seen."

"Yes, it is indeed a sad story how I found her in the woods at the age of five, running with a wolfpack," said Flint, crossing his fingers. "Now, doctor, if you care to accompany my loyal albeit not too bright robot, you can finish collecting the Ritalin." As McClown followed the beeping Robby, Flint turned back to Jerk. "And you, sir? What will be your pleasure? Chess? Backgammon? Parcheesi?"

Schmuck's elbow snapped Jerk back to reality. With a challenging look at Raining, he said, "How about checkers?"

Checkers had always been difficult for him, and Raining was a grand master. Jerk had just crowned her for the fifth time when Flint came over to gloat.

Seeing that all this nonsense was drawing attention away from him, Schmuck looked about for a diversion. In one corner of the room was a rhinestone-encrusted piano, upon which rested a candelabra. Schmuck walked to the piano and idly leafed through some sheet music on its music stand.

Jerk, seeing through this ruse, embarked on some scenery-chewing. He rose slowly, pacing the room. "Greed is everywhere. It exists in all places, from the basement up to the stars . . . those tiny points of light up there . . . to be human is to be avaricious. We were never meant to live in paradise. We would then cease to exist. What is reality but dogs eating dogs across the sands of time?"

As Flint and Raining exchanged puzzled glances, Schmuck began playing the piano *fortissimo*.

"I haven't the slightest idea what you're talking about, captain, but it sounds depressing," shouted Flint. "But as long as Mr. Schmuck seems intent on making a racket, you should see that Raining is an accomplished dancer as well."

Just as things were getting interesting, McClown barged gracelessly in. Schmuck left the piano at once, but Jerk continued to drag Raining about until the doctor tripped him.

"Th' Ritalin's no darn good," he whined. "It's got large amounts of vitamin C in it, which is nice, but which renders it totally useless fo' owah purpose."

"Stupid robot," hissed Flint. He kicked the blinking tin can toward the lab, a muttering McClown in tow.

"Funny that Robby should have made such a mistake," said Jerk.

"Something else could also be described as 'humorous,' sir. The fox-trot I have just played is by Liberace. It is also unknown. But it is in Liberace's own hand, which my undeniable genius of course had no difficulty recognizing. It is unquestionably the work of Liberace, but it is totally unknown. Also, the ink is still wet."

"Meaningless," snapped Jerk. Where had Raining disappeared to? "See you later," he said to Schmuck, and set off to find her, delicious visions dancing in his head.

The halls of Flint's abode were decorated with many strange and wonderful things—paintings on black velvet, plaster statues of saints and sports heroes, crowded knickknack shelves—and Jerk was craning his neck to get a better view of these when he collided with Raining.

Alas, she appeared troubled, her eyes slightly crossed. Jerk looked deep into her nose and said. "You went away and I became a television show dying for lack of Neilsons." Hoping that this mumbo-jumbo would catch her unaware, he tried for a quick kiss. Failing, he pointed to a door. "What lies beyond there?"

As she looked, he took advantage of her concentration to nibble her ear. "I do not know," she said, unaware of his lips on her ear. "Flint has said I must not enter that room."

Probably keeps all his money there, thought Jerk. "Then why have you come here?"

"I . . . I am not sure. I come here when I am troubled in mind."

"Are you troubled now, Raining?"

"Yes," she answered, foggy-eyed.

"By what, Raining?"

She looked at Jerk's hands, which had somehow become entwined about her waist, and frowned, searching for an answer. Encouraged, Jerk pressed his luck (also his attack) and asked, "Are you happy here with Flint?"

"He is very kind and wise," she said slowly.

Also very rich, thought Jerk. "Yet you are upset," he continued aloud, trying desperately to come up with a good line. "Come with me, Raining. Come to a place where there is hope and life. Come with me to the stars . . . those tiny points of light up there. . . . Do you know love?" He wound to a stop, out of clichés for the moment, and cunningly reached for her.

"Oh, dear!" she gasped, looking over his shoulder in wide-eyed horror.

Jerk turned reluctantly, coming face to face with an angry Robby, its Christmas-tree lights working overtime. It moved swiftly, but Jerk was even quicker, ducking behind the girl like lightning. Robby ignored her, singlemindedly pursuing Jerk. He ran, but it clung to him like a bad grade of peanut butter.

Wait! He still had his fizzer! Hurriedly whipping it out, he fired at the enraged tin goon. Nothing. Rats, he thought, why do we even bother with these duds?

Robby had him cornered now. Sparks shot ominously at his feet.

It was at this precise moment that Schmuck, more concerned with building dramatic tension than with his captain's life, leaped from behind a plaster statue and fired his own fizzler. Robby disintegrated gracefully. Jerk contemplated apoplexy.

"Fortunately, the writer was too concerned with your rather harrowing situation to deactivate my fizzer too," said the smug Vulgarian.

Before Jerk could throttle his first officer, Raining jiggled away, leaving them to follow a trail of Evening in Paris back to the central room.

Pacing, snarling, cross-eyed, his lower teeth showing in a painful grimace, Jerk confronted Flint. "That overgrown Tinker Toy of yours nearly wasted me! If Mr. Schmuck (who if he waits that long next time will be demoted to janitor second class) hadn't destroyed Robby, he would have been wearing my uniform!" He threw the alien a dismembering glare.

"Now, Captain, I'm sure you're overreacting. I programmed Robby to repel all invaders. Apparently, it thought you were attacking Raining."

How right it was, thought Schmuck.

Advancing on the obviously much-older Flint with intent to do damage, Jerk spat, "Your mechanized flunky isn't here to save you this time."

In return, Flint made a casual gesture, and through the door floated another Robby, an exact duplicate of the first, right down to the huge key protruding from its back. Jerk veered off, hemming and hawing. "I was only testing you, anyway," he sulked.

"It is well that you did not choose to fight, for I could beat you up with one hand tied behind my back." Flint turned to Raining. "You see what a chicken he is?"

Raining appeared to be trying to solve an immensely complex equation. "I am glad that he was not offed," she said at length.

Flint looked disappointed. "Oh well," he said, "at any rate your Ritalin is ready. This time it is without vitamin C, and all of you had best keep your hands in your pockets, lest Robby misinterpret your motives." Flinging a raspberry at Jerk, he left, dragging Raining behind him. Schmuck was once again forced to apply a wrestling hold to the captain, ere he grabbed the passing girl.

"Let me go, Schmuck! Can't you see it's me she wants, not that dried-out, desiccated, wrinkled . . ."

"Rich . . ."

". . . dirty old man . . ." He halted with a sob.

"Captain, since we are once again helpless and dependent on Flint to come through with the desperately needed Ritalin, I respectfully suggest that you refrain from pawing the young lady should your paths cross again. It seems that despite his outwardly decrepit appearance, our friend is not solely interested in Raining's mind."

"Schmuck, you mean . . . ?"

"That you are not the only one around here who has to take cold showers? Precisely."

For lack of something better to do, Jerk drew out his Tom Corbett walkie-talkie and hailed the ship. He heard snores and a muffled yawn as Engineer Spot answered his call.

"Spot? Here, Spot. C'mon, boy."

"Noch, brouch, mckennough, schenectady," came Spot's voice from the speaker.

"My God," said Jerk. "Practically everyone on board asleep? What about that pocket calculator check on Flint?"

"Loch murch grech vas deferens."

"Hmmm, no record of his past, eh? Spotty, run a check on Raining Kopeks and report back to me. Jerk out."

"If I might be permitted to speak," ventured Schmuck.

"You will anyway, so go ahead."

"Well, I am certain that what I am about to say has nothing whatever to do with our dilemma . . ."

"Then why say it?"

". . . nonetheless, I feel the information might be useful to store in our memory banks for future reference. I, in my infinite genius, was able to obtain a quadcorder reading of Flint while you were engaged in linguistic battle. Since I never make an error, we must assume that the following is true: Arman Flint is a great deal older than he appears."

"I knew it!" crowed Jerk. "Plastic surgery? Health spas? Vitamin E?"

"As I was about to say, and in the event that certain people unsatisfied with the amount of their fan mail will allow me to continue, the age indicated by my readings is far greater than what you are undoubtedly mistakenly imagining. I would say, as a rough estimate, that our host has lived somewhere between 6000.2375 and 6000.3047 years. However, I would not consider that pertinent data, any more than the fact that he has no past that could be considered as such."

"I suppose not, Schmuck." The walkie-talkie quacked tiredly. "Jerk here. What is it, Spotty?"

"Doohan nocher richter a wulla sochus."

"I see. No record of her either." He snapped the device off. "Raining and Flint . . . people without a past . . . held together by what sinister and dark design, and to what evil end? Something very strange is going on here."

"Perhaps for tax purposes . . ." suggested Schmuck.

"That's it," agreed Jerk, not feeling up to dramatics anyway. He rose and paced a few steps. Much to his delight, he again collided with Raining. Bodily removing the protesting Schmuck from the premises, he turned to her.

"I have come to bid you farewell," she said hazily.

"I don't want to say farewell."

"I am glad that Robby did not charcoal-grill you."

So am I, thought Jerk. He grasped her by the waist. "Now I know what it is I have lived for," he lied, hoping to maneuver her to the couch. She seemed innocent, unsure, but there was an underlying sense of urgency in her actions, as if she had eaten something that did not agree with her, and could not locate the Alka-Seltzer.

"My place . . ." she began.

"Or yours?" he was quick to interject.

"My place is . . ." she continued.

"Where I am," countered Jerk, switching hands.

". . . here . . ." she said.

"Where?" said Jerk, always willing to be helpful.

"There."

"Who?"

"What?"

"Hah?"

She was silent for a long time. Then, slowly coming to the realization that she was confused, she broke free of his hands and ran off.

Jerk started after her, soon becoming hopelessly lost. He wound up at the lab, where Schmuck and McClown stood throwing Petri dishes at one another.

Seeing him, McClown began to pale. "Flint hid the Ritalin! If we don't get it soon, we'll all be in a lot of trouble, 'cause everyone on board is gonna be asleep, and there'll be no one t' beam us up!"

"However," said Schmuck above the screaming doctor, "if the chief surgeon will cease his incredibly voluble hysterics, I will endeavor to uncover the hidden substance by tracking it with my quadcorder." He made an expansive hand gesture. "Nothing up my sleeve . . . no mirrors . . . the hand is quicker than the eye . . ."

"Get on with it," snapped Jerk, a bit crankily.

Miffed, Schmuck moved his device about. The little green light on top blinked: COLD . . . COLDER . . . GETTING WARM . . . HOT . . . TILT!

They had come to a door in the corridor.

"The very same door that Raining is forbidden to enter," mused Jerk. "We may not have found the Ritalin, but we've probably stumbled onto a big hoard of cash." He was nearly trampled by Schmuck and McClown in their rush to get some of the pickings.

To their surprise, the Ritalin was there, on a table labeled "Bait." But, alas, there was no gold, silver, Confederate notes, trading stamps, or anything else remotely suggesting a new Ferrari each year and a condo on the Riviera. Abruptly forgetting the plague aboard ship, they wandered about the room in case there was some gold dust they had managed to overlook. In his concentration, Jerk nearly fell over a draped figure on a table, labeled "Raining #17."

Probably some plaster statue, he thought, still intent on the hoped-for cash stash. It was Schmuck who drew his attention to it, and the sixteen other draped figures around the room. Pulling back the sheet, Jerk exposed a figure that bore a remarkable resemblance to the Raining they knew. Thinking it was she, defenselessly asleep, he lunged, but Flint's voice stopped him dead.

"Oh no, you don't, you pervert. Ownership rights and all that." He strode over and drew the sheet back over Raining #17.

McClown waved one of his salt shakers over the form. "Physically human . . . yet not human. Jes' like some others I could name," he said, sticking his tongue out at Schmuck, who responded with the ancient Vulgarian thumb-on-the-nose-and-waggling-fingers salute.

"Oh, I get it," said Jerk suddenly. "She's a robot."

"Yeah, and all mine, too," snapped Flint. "So kindly keep your hands to yourself the next time she jiggles onto the horizon."

"But I don't understand," Jerk (being even more dense than usual) said.

"I created her out of a pile of army surplus nuts and bolts. The centuries of loneliness and my own cooking were to end with her."

"Centuries?" asked McClown.

Bored with the incredible stupidity of his companions, Schmuck, who had himself only just now caught on, said, "Your collection of Fakerinos . . . your Liberace manuscripts . . ."

"Yes," said Flint, cutting short Schmuck's long-sought dramatic revelations. "I am both Fakerino and Liberace."

"And who else, might I ask?" asked Schmuck, trying to regain lost ground.

"Let me see . . . do the names Shakespeare, Da Vinci, Beethoven, and Lincoln mean anything to you?"

"Indeed they do."

"Well, .I was none of them. However, I was Primo Carnera, P. T. Barnum, and Colonel Sanders. And I did meet Albert Shanker's housekeeper once."

"Then you were born . . ."

"In Secaucus, New Jersey. I was a loan shark. One day I ran afoul of the local syndicate. I fell to the ground, decapitated, but I soon grew a new head. I also grew to realize that I had a good deal going there."

"A freak," said McClown, drawing on his vast knowledge of interplanetary medicine. "You weren't Tod Browning too, by any chance?"

"You learned you were immortal," said Jerk enviously.

"Yes, and able to sell the public a defective bill of goods many times over, which is how I built up my vast empire. I knew the greatest hacks in history: gossip columnists, press agents, politicians. But I grew weary of groupies, and retired to this planet and built Raining—after a few false starts. She is the perfect woman, Captain—no wonder you drooled all over yourself when you saw her. Well, all I can say is tough darts, she belongs to me."

"Does she know she's merely the reincarnation of a World War II radio set?" asked Jerk.

"Does she look as if she knows that two and two are four?"

"I imagine not." Visions of connubial bliss with Raining sprouted wings and flew the coop of Jerk's mind. "Let's get out of here, Schmuck. I suddenly remembered there's a crisis aboard the *Enteritis.*"

"And just where do you think you're going?" sneered Flint.

"Back to the ship. Who wants to know?"

"You must be more stupid than you look to think I'd let you go now. The minute you get back you'd set up a tourist trap with me as the main attraction."

"We could give you a cut," suggested Schmuck.

"Two can play at this game," cried the recluse. "Behold! A little trick I learned from a wizard at King Arthur's court." He produced a battered wand and waved it in the air, muttering, "Hocus, pocus, who's got the crocus?" Miraculously, a copy of the *Enteritis* appeared from nowhere, suspended by kitchen twine. Flint took a vial labeled "Magic Powder" and sprinkled some on the effigy.

As the spacemen watched in horror, the *Enteritis* became a plastic model kit, complete with easy-to-follow instructions, colorful enamel, and paste-on decals!

Flint thumbed his nose at them. "Yes, Captain. Once I sell this to some avid Trekkie, your fate is sealed!"

"No!" lisped a familiar voice. They turned to face Raining, who had wandered aimlessly in because Flint had carelessly left the door open.

"Whoops!" he said.

"This is very naughty of you," she reprimanded, as Flint tried to position himself in front of the dummy on the slab.

"I must do it," he said.

"I'll never play checkers with you again," she threatened. Recognizing an ideal time to add to the confusion, Jerk began one of his long-winded speeches.

"She loves me, not you, Flint! Come away from all this, Raining, and we shall be as two Forsythium crystals shining brilliantly into the darkness that always lies just before the dawn. Every cloud has its silver lining, and we shall walk through the storm with our heads held high. We're not afraid of the dark, are we? Do you not know Love? The time has come for man to reach out to the tree of knowledge and pluck the fruit of a victory! Too long have we been living a lie! We will wander through eternity, happy together, no matter what the weather! Give me back my ship, Flint!"

"Anything to shut you up. Here."

Grasping the girl firmly by the shoulders, Jerk looked deep into her slightly crossed eyes and said, "You do love me, Raining, even though you are only a robot?"

Flint cast his gaze helplessly upward and gave forth a mighty sigh.

"I . . . only . . . a robot?" faltered the hopelessly confused Raining, as Flint snatched her from Jerk's grasp.

"*No*! You love me!" roared the wealthy old hack.

Not to be outdone, Jerk yanked her away. Breathing into her left eye, he intoned, "Those stars . . . those tiny points of light out there . . ."

Enraged, Flint shoved Raining onto the floor and dealt Jerk a vicious Indian burn. "She's mine, you little git!"

"No she isn't! She loves me, you old fake! I'm younger and prettier!"

Raining hauled herself upright with the aid of a table. Schmuck and McClown were oblivious to her plight, having already made bets on the outcome of the fight, and watching it intently.

"You *twit*!" yelled Flint.

"*Pinhead*!" retaliated Jerk.

Raining watched with increasing consternation. "No!" she cried. "I . . . was not . . . human . . . now, I think . . . therefore, I . . ."

"*She's human*!" roared Jerk, so deafeningly that Schmuck and the others fell to the floor. He leaped into the air, capering about like a demented baboon, and dropped to one knee in yet another tirade. "Since the dawn of time, man has struggled to be human . . . to think, to hope, *to feel*! We are not cabbages to be sent to market! We must all strive to be human, lest we cease to exist! And the essence of humanity is love! Do you not know love, Raining? You love me, not Flint, don't you, toots?"

"Raining, I'm richer than he is," countered Flint. "Could he buy you a mobile home, a water bed, and a solid gold statue of Alfred E. Neuman?"

In the heat of battle, neither man noticed that her eyes were crossing and uncrossing with alarming regularity. She took a hesitant step toward one, then the other. "I think . . . therefore, therefore . . ."

She collapsed in a heap. Schmuck pointed his quadcorder at her and shook his head.

"The excitement was too much for her. She blew a capacitor."

Flint shrugged. "Oh, well, back to the drafting table."

Witnessing the cruel fate of his beloved severed the last of Jerk's self-control. His subsequent overacting fit forced the others to stuff him in a large refuse container in order to carry him back to the ship.

Much later, the Ritalin had taken effect and things were back to normal: Fully one-third of the crew was awake and on the job.

In his lonely cabin, Jerk was morosely fondling a regulation NFL football when Schmuck entered with some useless data. The captain looked up. "Schmuck . . . if only I could forget her."

"Sir, may I suggest any one of the following: a course in self-hypnosis, taught by a fully qualified instructor, designed for easy assimilation by the amateur; a slight overindulgence of some of the more exotic liqueurs in that secret cabinet under your bunk that you think nobody knows about; or three rounds with . . ." He was interrupted by loud snores from Jerk.

McClown burst in, babbling as was his wont. "Jimbo, Ah've made a discovery. Flint is headed fo' th' last roundup soon. . . . Oh, he's asleep. Ah mighta know'd y'all could do that in a minute flat," he said to Schmuck.

"What was that about Flint, doctor?"

"Lak Ah said, he's finally dyin'."

"I see. You mean that in leaving the Earth's complex magnetic fields, in which he was formed and with which he lived in perfect balance, he sacrificed his immortality?"

"No, Ah mean Ah poisoned his brandy." He looked at Jerk, who had begun drooling onto his sleeve. "He's dreamin' of her again. Ah shoah do wish he could fergit her. Ah realize that y'all will nevah know th' agony an' ecstasy of love, 'cause your glands is funny. But jess th' same, Ah wish he'd fergit." With a final disgusted look at the alien, McClown turned and left.

Schmuck studied the sleeping captain. Should he? Could he do this noble deed? Yes. He would.

He tiptoed to the door, locking it. Rubbing his hands together, he turned back to Jerk. Long, sensitive alien fingers eased up the captain's nose, and a look of intense concentration formed on Schmuck's face as he began the ancient Vulgarian mind-sync.

"Forget, captain," he whispered. "Forget . . . forget that fiver I owe you. Forget that slight mistake I made plotting the course last month, which nearly resulted in all our deaths. Forget those holograms you have of me in that cheap motel on Donaldduckus IV. . . . Forget . . ."

THE MUSIC OF STAR TREK: A VERY SPECIAL EFFECT

by Eleanor LaBerge

If you've ever sat up until the wee hours of the night to see one of the very early, classic "talkies," you may have been vaguely disquieted by the lack of "background music"—a musical score. Today, however, scoring is omnipresent in both films and television, and we tend to take it for granted. The music featured in a production is an integral and important part of its dramatic impact. Good music enhances a show; bad music detracts from it.

In the following article, Eleanor LaBerge examines the music of Star Trek, and the ways in which it affected both the series episodes and Star Trek: The Motion Picture. *We think Eleanor's article will send you running to your tape recorders to replay several episodes. . . .*

We fans have read thousands of words about Star Trek's cast, the problems of scientific accuracy, the construction of sets and model miniatures, and the multiple difficulties arising from production. We also love to read and reread articles that give insights into the characters created by Gene Roddenberry. But seldom is there more than a brief reference to the *music* of Star Trek, which provided exceptional enrichment to seventy-eight television episodes as well as to *Star Trek: The Motion Picture*.

Here is a twofold challenge, Star Trek fans. First, who is Alexander Courage? No, not the small person in "Plato's Stepchildren." Anyone out there recall the name as that of the composer of the Star Trek series music? Correct. Now try Gerald Fried and Fred Steiner. As you may have guessed, they are both composers of the background themes for the series.

Now ask your memory banks about Jerry Goldsmith. That's easier, of course. The name is more familiar, since his score for *Star Trek: The Motion Picture* was nominated for an Academy Award. This was a remarkable *kudos*, as many in the "business" were inclined to dismiss (if not ignore) the large-screen Star Trek as an upstart fugitive from the video tube.

The mechanics of bringing a series from idea to production was the subject of a 414-page book, *The Making of Star Trek*, by Roddenberry and Whitfield. Not until page 375 was the music given more than a one-line passing reference. Interestingly, not a word about the motion-picture score was to be found in *Trek* 15, the issue devoted to *Star Trek: The Motion Picture*. I do not point to this omission in a spirit of criticism, but only to submit that this particular aspect of Star Trek seems to have been neglected.

Neither in the motion picture nor in the series was the score just so much noise in the background. From composition to synchronization of music with the action there are many steps. There must also be an innate sense of dramatic appropriateness. Achieving the proper balance of these factors demands the skill of many technicians and the judgment of an experienced director. When these technical maneuvers are accomplished with beauty of melodic line and harmony in action, we have something special: a special effect deserving of our conscious appreciation.

The musical themes repeated throughout the Star Trek episodes would be a significant part of the fans' treasured devotion to the series. There were sequences that meant Vulcan; musical phrases that signaled McCoy's quick reparté or Spock's lifted eyebrow; there were tender melodies that provided accompaniment for Kirk's *affaires d'amour*; there were clever segments resembling a Doppler effect that revealed evil under the guise of an innocent appearance; many passages heightened a feeling of mystery; and, of course, there were those which complemented the *Enterprise* and its crew when they were underway and ready for action.

While the viewer of Star Trek television did not have to listen to the constant musical background so popular in the vintage motion picture, timely and appropriate orchestrations were selected week after week. There was much more than stock abstract canned musical phrases.

Remember "The Trouble with Tribbles"? There was a special humorous theme for the furry beasties. In one bridge scene this was extended to a Far Eastern mode which seemed to indicate that the crew was as tranquil as a Tibetan monk in meditation. In the same episode the fist fight between Scotty and the *Enterprise* crew and the insulting Klingons was accompanied by a frolicking Scottish dance. This plus the rising strains that meant *Enterprise* combined in a neatly balanced classic melody of Star Trek adventure.

In "The World Is Hollow and I Have Touched the Sky," one of the many mystery themes appeared when an elderly man of *Yonada* told Kirk, Spock, and McCoy of his journey to the forbidden limits of his world. The same sequence of notes was repeated for "The Wink of an Eye" as well as other episodes.

Another familiar melody meant Vulcan. It fit well. There was a staccato melodic line played by a bass viol accompanied by a high-pitched, alien sound. It heightened our awareness that a Vulcan had roots in traditions not easily understood by humans. We heard the same theme in "Amok Time," as Spock reluctantly confided his biological problem to Kirk. In "Mirror, Mirror," it was repeated as the alternate universe's Spock entered a mind meld with McCoy. We heard it again as Amanda begged her son to relinquish command so that Sarek's life might be spared in "Journey to Babel."

Another Vulcan theme was heard in "Amok Time" during the combat for T'Pring. There was a warlike rhythm that gave the impression of unleashed savagery. It was a theme often repeated for a variety of combat scenes, but most fans upon hearing it would recall Spock's dramatic compulsion to satisfy the demands of *pon farr*. "I burn," Spock told T'Pau, and the music described his torment nonverbally. Once again accented by the musical background we faced that sense of mystery in Spock's divided being.

In "Shore Leave," we heard a theme that was both tender and wistful as Kirk faced his tangible dream of Ruth. This melody was used frequently in the episode to amplify Kirk's nostalgic memory of romantic interludes. Of all the romantic themes there was a special one for Edith Keeler in "City on the Edge of Forever." It was a haunting ballad in keeping with the style of her historical time. In the same episode, we heard the notes typical of many humorous scenes in the series when Kirk tried to explain Spock's ears to a New York City police officer. It also occurred when McCoy saw his Alice in Wonderland rabbit, and when the mistakenly beamed guard arrived aboard the *Enterprise* in "Tomorrow Is Yesterday."

The Star Trek fans, whether consciously or unconsciously, were accustomed to these and other themes. They were at home with them. In the series these shorter compositions could be used and repeated in a variety of situations, becoming a familiar part of Star Trek memories. Bracketed by the unforgettable Star Trek theme melody, plots were further enhanced by the modest musical background. There was little need for spectacular musical fanfare. The *Star Trek: The Motion Picture* score was, as one would expect, conceived on a grander scale. It was not meant for the cozy comfort of a series seen on the family-room television set but for the wide screen and the sophistication of modern sound systems.

One of the potential obstacles in winning fandom's support and devotion to the film would be related to taking the series out of the habits of viewing and listening intimacy. Many Star Trek enthusiasts sat in the theater waiting to see *Star Trek: The Motion Picture* with as much apprehension as eagerness. The lights darkened and without visual distraction we heard the first strains of Jerry Goldsmith's score: Ilia's Theme.

In Ilia's melodic line there was mystery and the rising beauty of tenderness filled with pathos. It was unmistakably romantic, but a listener could close his eyes and seem to float on a tall ship whose sails were filled by the winds. The navigator's song evoked the image of travel through vast empty space. The interweaving of percussion and strings rose and fell, interacting as if in dialogue. It seemed to be a musical conversation with the voices of violins, piano, and horns which ultimately blended into a suggestion of the *Enterprise* theme to follow. It was as mysterious as the Deltan herself: sensual as if pheromones were projected from sound to reality in the undulating melody.

After the theme became more familiar, speculation regarding the "dialogue" here could run rampant. Is it Ilia/Decker? Is it Ilia/Vejur/Kirk/*Enterprise*? The sequence of notes and their interaction are there. Meaning is the individual listener's emotional response. Ilia's theme lingers as a melody impossible to forget.

After Ilia's introductory theme we heard the brief opening, stirring in its martial rhythm. It surrounded us in stereophonic sound and we were back in that world where there are no impossible dreams. Jerry Goldsmith's opening is not just another march: It was and is a celebration—strong and direct but with subtleties of orchestration that delighted the ear and set feet tapping. French horns and violins alternated with the trumpet section, and the full symphonic arrangement gave body and support. Only a small percentage of the fans were concerned about the "special" effect of the musical sound track, but by the time the introductory footage was completed on the wide screen, it was clear that Goldsmith's contribution to the world of Star Trek would be satisfying.

The Klingon Imperial Cruiser *Amar* appeared in deep space and the melodic line was a clarion call blended with hollow clackers. The musical mood created in this sequence was appropriate and graphic: chase, attack, counterattack. In tonal language the segment clearly complemented the clipped dialogue as hunter and hunted clashed. The challenge ended with a single electronic sound fading into discord as the viewer saw empty space where the arrogant Klingons had been. The score told us, as if we had not known, that the Klingons were compulsively warlike.

The scene on Vulcan gave us our first view of Spock. It was introduced by electronic sounds which we later learn were to be associated with V'Ger. It accompanied the privileged initiated of *Kolinahr* as they began to confer the honor of perfect logic upon Spock. As he failed to meet the demands of the discipline, the music took on a more melodic, poignant aspect which spoke to us of great dignity and yet sadness. It was a melody all its own with a particularly compelling, if brief, beauty.

It is interesting to note that when Spock subsequently appeared in the entry lock after docking with the *Enterprise* in his warp-drive shuttlecraft, the Vulcan theme was repeated but with a distinctive difference: three descending piano chords greeted Spock as he boarded the ship. The music selected for Spock as he appeared on the bridge for the first time was that of "Enterprise," the love song. The same theme was used for Spock later in the film when Kirk received the Vulcan's limp body back from the inner chambers of V'Ger.

One of the first musical variations the motion-picture viewer might have noted in the film was that the martial strains of the opening changed in tempo and orchestral arrangement to become the lovely *Enterprise* theme. This musical technique can be used so effectively the hearer may not realize that the notes are identical. Remember Meredith Wilson's *The Music Man?* Some audiences took a while to pick up on the fact that "Seventy-six Trombones" was also the waltz-time love song. Similarly, Jerry Goldsmith selected the powerful opening theme with its precise rhythm and adapted it to the lyrical melody of "Enterprise." As Montgomery Scott ferried Admiral Kirk from the space station in the travel pod the music told us what we already felt: that this was a matter of love.

Some of the comments regarding the motion picture have cited this particular scene as unnecessarily long and dull. Considering the beauty of the musical background, it would be difficult to imagine even a brief portion of the composition cut. There is another way of evaluating the scene, as Walter Irwin points out in his comments on the motion picture in *Trek* 15. We needed and deserved that "long, lingering look," as he termed it. Kirk had waited for a mere two and a half years for this view, while the fans had wailed for more than a decade!

Goldsmith's *Enterprise* theme tenderly reflected the loneliness of past separation and led us to the joy of reunion as Kirk saw the *Enterprise* shining and majestic in dry-dock orbit. The music rose to a crescendo with the horns, bells as clear as stars on a winter night, violins, and the single trumpet in its own counterpoint. Is this trumpet Kirk speaking to his lady *Enterprise?* Or is it what *he* hears: a Lorelei call from her? Or is it the longing in every human heart for union with that one great love wherein we become whole, that one great desire that gives life purpose? Listen well. It may be all of these things.

In the docking of the pod the musical thrust is reminiscent of such classical compositions as Tchaikovsky's *Romeo and Juliet*. It was a powerful musical symbol explicit in its description of Kirk's desire to possess the ship once again. The climax of this scene was particularly satisfying to the viewer as the long awaited adventure was once again beginning.

In "Taking Her Out," we heard a hint of the powerful engines in the low piano rhythm followed by variations on the *Enterprise* theme. When the intermix was set and the ship sped forward through the solar system, Goldsmith incorporated the well-loved, lyrical television theme. It lasted but a few moments, but fans should be grateful that the composer honored the series in this musical compliment.

Jerry Goldsmith was undoubtedly briefed on the new Star Trek theme. (One is tempted to wonder if his scenario was delayed until all was definite, forcing his composing to be done at warp speed to accommodate the many factors that did not "gel" until the last moments.) Once the composer received the outlines and the time sequences, he would have the problem of translating the meaning of one art form into another. Any critical evaluation of creative work might inspire one to question whether too much is being read into the subject under consideration. It is a valid question, and the answer depends not only upon the imagination of the one writing the analysis, but upon the depth of the author whose work is being analyzed.

In literature it would not be difficult to write a thesis-length commentary on the specific and symbolic uses of one great author's imagery— light and darkness, for example. A reader might be tempted to think that such an analysis was contrived. However, repeated imagery on the part of a literary genius is, if not intentional, a subconscious use of one aspect of his art. Symbolism and interpretation in musical composition is essentially the same.

Musical criticism is not critical in the sense of finding fault; it is interpretation in the spirit of delving into the deeper meaning of a work. Admittedly, it is a speculative matter, especially when one comments on symbolic significance. The music of *Star Trek: The Motion Picture* is a major and important aspect of the film. How it relates to the meaning we perceive through characterization and story line is a valid question for speculation. If through the music we can come to a more profound understanding of Star Trek's philosophy, then the analysis is well worth the time.

One of the most difficult tasks in the composition of appropriate music for *Star Trek: The Motion Picture* must have been the long V'Ger sequences. How, one many ask, would a composer show us in his tonal language the awesome scope, the mystery and power of an entity 82 A.U. in diameter? We heard power in the deep bass and brass section, especially in the blaring tuba. One might expect the electronic elements of arrangement, but this composer gave us that extra bit we have learned to expect from Star Trek. Through the music he seemed to say that V'Ger was locked into "pre-melody." He showed us that the entity had life, technique, but no soul. He used sounds which represented a heartbeat amplified and pulsating—a being very much alive. He used tonal progressions not only of chords but in the do-mi-sol-do exercise-like repetitions shifting from major to minor scale with electronic variations. All the musical theory learnable would not enable a composer to create *music*; neither could V'Ger make that critical leap from logic and accumulation of knowledge (technique) to intuition (melody) without that extra something that surprises us at the end of the motion picture. For all its store of information, V'Ger had knowledge without purpose and was sterile. "It is cold," Spock told us, ". . . no beauty."

In the musical description of "Spock Walk," the Vulcan passed through the eyelike passage to observe V'Ger's incredible data storage banks. We again felt the deep power and mystery but also more than this. Up to this point V'Ger's theme had been controlled. Now sounds of confusion illustrated V'Ger's frustration. After Spock's traumatic mind meld with the device on Ilia's form, string section and brass broke into a wild orchestration that seemed to spin out of control. This was the instant when Spock's lifelong idea was shattered; it was the moment when we were in V'Ger's mind experiencing its bewilderment and disillusionment. That music seemed to place us in a maze with no way out, and the feeling could have been described as blind panic. We were one with Spock and one with V'Ger as each of them asked: "Is this all I am?"

After this scene of visual and musical abstraction, the director gave us the stark silence of sickbay. As Spock spoke to Kirk in that touching moment, the silence itself was a profound theme of oneness. There was the union not only of deep and abiding friendship, but that of Spock the Vulcan and Spock the human. Significantly, this aspect of the film needed no accompaniment.

The heart of V'Ger turned out to be Voyager VI, which, having achieved consciousness, yearned for what the motion picture tells us were "other dimensions." Decker signaled the final code sequence to the entity through the ground test computer and moments afterward V'Ger "touched the creator." Decker had overcome the fear that union with an alien might rob him of his individuality. He was no longer the man who left Delta 4 without saying goodbye to Ilia. This was now a man who was ready to step into a new dimension by his own free choice, ready to experience whatever transformation might result. V'Ger's theme in this last scene was also transformed. Even as the *Enterprise* crew approached the heart of V'Ger the music revealed longing interwoven with the electronic sounds by the use of Ilia's theme. As V'Ger and Decker were united and Ilia entered the aura of light, the musical background that had begun with a single electronic sound grew into rising cadences of brass, flutes, strings, and french horns. The effect was one of wonderment—our own and V'Ger's. Caressing sounds illustrated the delicate approach of V'Ger and its now melodic measures described the consummation of its quest. The transfiguration mounted musically until a new life was a reality. The melody ultimately blended gently into the *Enterprise* theme and its particular beauty which was, by now, familiar.

The space-fiction films of the past several years have given filmgoers remarkable soundtracks. It was a pleasure to listen to John Williams' score for *Close Encounters of the Third Kind,* and for *Star Wars.* These works gave young people who might never have listened to symphonic music a taste of something beyond country and hard rock. Jerry Goldsmith's *Star Trek: The Motion Picture* score is equal to these in melody, symbolism, and musicality. It captures the spirit of what the series became in the perception of the fans.

If Star Trek fandom idealized Roddenberry's creation, it was idealization based upon a reality of optimism and positive philosophy. The television themes and the score of *Star Trek: The Motion Picture* seem to have been written by two composers who were sensitive to the unique bond between the world of Star Trek and its deeper meaning. Both contributors to the special phenomenon it has become have undoubtedly been congratulated for their achievements. It is fitting, however, that here in the magazine for Star Trek fans, Alexander Courage, Gerald Fried, Fred Steiner, and Jerry Goldsmith be offered our particular gratitude. Belated thanks, guys!

LOVE IN STAR TREK

by Walter Irwin

As we were shown in many ways in Star Trek, love is a universal constant. The question of what love is is one for poets, philosophers, or pundits, but we can see many examples of love in all its myriad forms in almost every episode of the series. Trek *editor Walter Irwin examines these examples, and draws some surprising conclusions from them.*

Love in Star Trek, as in life, takes many forms. Throughout the course of the series' run, almost every type of love which one sentient being may feel for another was presented. The need and desire for love was presented as an everyday, natural part of the characters' lives; just as it is with our own. Sometimes, love was the focus of an episode, as in "Requiem for Methuselah"; other times the tug of conflicting loves was the focus, as in "City on the Edge of Forever." Other kinds of love than the romantic were also pivotal to many episodes, such as brotherly love ("The Empath"), love of freedom ("The Menagerie"), paternal love ("The Conscience of the King"), and even love for inanimate objects ("This Side of Paradise").

Star Trek is, of course, based on love. The underlying theme of the series is that man will one day overcome his own humanity and learn to live in peace and brotherly love not only with his own kind, but with myriad other sentient beings throughout the universe. The love of freedom is also a very important part of the Star Trek concept. Each person is allowed the right to be free and desires the same right for all others. It naturally follows that love of individuality is the one theme which ties both of these together. As embodied in the Vulcan tradition of

IDIC (Infinite Diversity in Infinite Combinations), it is the difference between beings which must be revered—and loved. The Star Trek concept was an optimistic one; especially for the turbulent times in which it was first introduced. So to make the series a bit more palatable for viewing audiences of the 1960s, Gene Roddenberry wisely incorporated mankind's love of adventure, exploration, mystery, danger, and the lure of the unknown into the format.

In the very first episode aired, we saw how all of these came into play. "The Man Trap" was a creature which survived by eating salt; but on another level, we could see how it also needed love to survive. Professor Robert Crater desired only to protect the Salt Monster as the last surviving member of its species, a creature he (and some of the *Enterprise* crew as well) felt deserved the same rights and respect as humans. It was also probable that he had come to love the creature as a mate, for it had assumed the shape of his late wife Nancy as a means of self-protection, and had apparently been cohabiting with him for quite some time.

Although the monster killed without hesitation, at no time did it "transform" itself into an object of horror. To the contrary, in every case the Salt Monster became an object of desire: McCoy's nostalgic memory of Nancy, Darnell's shapely crewwoman, Uhura's "perfect man." Even when it transformed into McCoy, it took a face and form which was loved, trusted, and extremely nonthreatening to the *Enterprise* crew.

It would have been ridiculously easy for the monster to use its telepathic powers and dredge up any number of horrific memories to paralyze crewmembers. Such visions would probably have served the creature's purposes much more quickly and efficiently. But it chose instead to appear as an object of love, leaving us to make the logical conclusion that it desired and needed to *be* loved—even for a brief moment before killing—to survive.

Even in this first episode, Star Trek proved that it was to be no ordinary TV show. It may seem that having McCoy kill the monster in a highly dramatic confrontation was pat histrionics, but the conflicts involved went much deeper than that. McCoy (and to a lesser degree Kirk and Spock) had to balance their "loves" against one another: the right of the Salt Monster to survive versus the survival of the crew; McCoy's nostalgic and idealistic love of Nancy Crater versus his love for Jim Kirk; and everyone's love for an "ideal" versus harsh reality. There was no hedging. It would have been easy for McCoy to stun the creature, have everyone make speeches about "passenger pigeons," and beam the creature down to a paradise of everlasting salt. But instead Gene Roddenberry had his characters make choices. It was a fine sign of things to come.

"Charlie X" wanted nothing else in the world but to be loved. Raised by the emotionless and noncorporeal Thasians, Charlie was deprived of the parental love and guidance he needed to be a complete being. His problem was compounded by his onrushing adolescence and his desire for Janice Rand, feelings which Charlie could not understand or control.

Charlie wanted to give love as much as he wanted to receive it, but again he didn't know how. He idolized Kirk as the father he never had, and naturally felt agonizingly betrayed when Kirk was forced to discipline him. Further "betrayed" by Janice, Charlie struck out in anger and despair. Like so many of us, he tried his best to "hurt the ones he loved."

The purest love in this episode, however, was not displayed by the humans, but by the Thasians. They quickly moved to correct Charlie's actions and removed him from the ship in order to protect not only the crew, but Charlie himself. The welfare of the humans was their primary concern. Even in the action of granting the psionic powers to baby Charlie in the first place, they showed their respect for the right of a fellow sentient being to survive—an act which was totally unnecessary to their own well-being and survival, an act which could only have come out of love. It is interesting to note that these beings without bodies and without emotions show just as much concern, compassion, and love for Charlie X as do any of the *Enterprise* crewmembers. One can only hope that with the passing of time, they have been able to communicate this love to Charlie Evans.

Friendship is examined in "Where No Man Has Gone Before." Not only is Kirk faced with the realization that his best friend, Gary Mitchell, is mutating into an advanced being, but he also learns that Gary has not been the true and trusted friend Kirk always thought him to be. It is a stunning blow for Kirk. He loses his friend twice—once by death, once by betrayal. It is not specifically spelled out in the episode, but we may assume that a long-standing "love-hate" relationship existed between the two men. They were both highly competitive, intelligent, and ambitious, a combination which more often makes for rivalry than friendship. It is amazing that Jim and Gary ever became close friends; it is even more amazing that they remained so.

Even when Kirk must face the realization that Gary has evolved to a point where he is willing to destroy them all to achieve his goals, he is still reluctant to take Spock's advice and have Gary killed. His love for Gary, even though it has been deeply shaken, is still so strong that he cannot bring himself to destroy him. It is only when Kirk becomes certain that Gary has lost all semblance of humanity that his love for his ship and crew finally overrides his feelings for a friend. With the help of Elizabeth Dehner, Kirk reluctantly kills Gary. It is more than the death of a friend; it is perhaps the death of Kirk's innocence as well. Never again will he give of himself so freely.

However, in the midst of his troubles during this episode, a new friend appears at Jim Kirk's side. Spock, forced to examine his own emotions in the light of events, and ultimately forced to confess them to Kirk as explanation for his insistence that Mitchell be killed, realizes that friendship is a stronger bond than he had ever believed. In a decision the difficulty of which cannot be underestimated, Spock offers his own friendship to Kirk at a time when the captain needs it the most. It is a moving gesture, one appreciated greatly by Kirk, and one which marks the beginning of the mutual respect and love the two men will share in the future.

It is, however, Dr. Elizabeth Dehner who shows the greatest love in this episode; she gives up her life for her fellow humans. This is a terrible and noble sacrifice, one which must have been very difficult for her to make, for she too is affected by the force field and is evolving into a superior being, and has to fight off the godlike feelings growing within her. Unlike Gary, she is able to retain enough compassion to understand that contempt and disdain are not the mark of a god. Elizabeth not only dies to protect the *Enterprise* crew, she gives up the opportunity to be a god. The amount of love and compassion such an act took cannot be overestimated—and is hardly typical of "a walking freezer unit."

The innermost feelings and desires of crewmembers were brought to the surface by a strange virus in "The Naked Time"; and in three cases feelings of love were involved. Nurse Christine Chapel became very affectionate and "dreamy," going so far as to confess her attraction to Spock. It is quite an intriguing question to consider who she was thinking of when she gazed so pensively into the sickbay mirror: Spock, or her fiancé, Roger Korby. Spock himself was overcome by debilitating grief and regret over the fact that he had never been able to tell his mother that he loved her. (Some bitterness toward his father was also displayed, although not overplayed.) This was the first indication we were given in Star Trek that Spock could feel—really *feel*—love, as well as the already displayed respect and friendship. It also told us much about his upbringing, a subject which was not forgotten and would provide much grist for future programs' mills. We also saw, for a brief moment, a tender side of Spock when he gently told Christine that although he could not return her affection, he understood and appreciated it. One can guess that memories of a girl named Leila prompted his gentle handling of the scene.

The most important revelation, however, was Jim Kirk's response to the virus. For the first time, we saw that Kirk loves the *Enterprise* more than he ever would any woman; loves her passionately and to the exclusion of all else. But she is a harsh mistress as well. Kirk also feels trapped by the *Enterprise*, by his duties, by the need to be "the captain" all the time. It is one of the few views we have of the soft inner core of Jim Kirk. Such doubts are not part of the Kirk we know. This assertive, aggressive, ambitious man is not the type to think in terms of failure or doubt, and is certainly not the type to be overly caring about inanimate objects. His cabin, save for a few books, is even more austere than Spock's. So why such a great love for a starship?

Kirk is in love with being the *captain* of the *Enterprise*. It is the position and the power—and the responsibility—which excites, motivates, and consumes him. This, and only this, is what he lives for. The affection he feels for his ship is an outward expression of these feelings, and one which makes him seem less single-minded and more human. His obsessive need for command is also tempered by a great number of positive and likeable qualities, qualities which we like to think can be found within ourselves. He is a complete and very complex person.

We see more of this in "The Enemy Within," wherein Kirk's "good" and "bad" qualities are so evenly split between the two beings that each may be viewed as both admirable and flawed. The evil side, of course, is the most obvious, for Kirk's desires and ambitions come to the surface without control and subterfuge usually placed on them by society's constraints. What the "evil" Kirk wants, he takes. But it is unlikely that he would act in a consciously evil manner, such as betraying the ship to the Klingons, or murdering without reason. He is not amoral as was Kirk-2 from the "mirror universe," merely our own Kirk without the love and compassion which makes him a complete being.

The "good" Kirk, on the other hand, is completely ineffectual in even day-to-day matters aboard ship without the ambitious and somewhat ruthless qualities absorbed into the double. He is weak, and in many ways, more of a danger to the ship than the "evil" Kirk. At least the "evil" Kirk could fight a battle, even though his tactics would most likely be reckless in the extreme and quite merciless.

The split, however, is much deeper than one would think. Kirk's feelings for Janice, which must have had an element of love, however slight, come to the surface as animalistic lust in his "evil" half. This is an indication of the basic difference between the two Kirks: The "good" Kirk, containing all of Jim Kirk's enormous capacities for love and compassion, offers that love. The "evil" Kirk, the creature of ambition and ruthlessness, *needs* love. It is this eternal joining of love offered and love needed which finally allows the two entities to be once again combined into a complete, fully functioning individual.

The events of these two episodes seem to have had a cathartic effect on Kirk. The doubts expressed by him while under the influence of the virus seem to have lessened, as has the ambition which had heretofore driven him in his career. Both would remain, of course, but each in its proper perspective. Kirk's love for the *Enterprise* grew even stronger, for freed from the obsessive need to command, Kirk could now appreciate her as the beautiful realization of his desires for freedom and exploration. The ship was transformed into a symbol of his love for space, not a focus for his obsession with it.

Lust, not love, was the primary motivation in "Mudd's Women." The Venus Drug, while obviously having the power to make women beautiful (as was graphically illustrated), must have also had the ability to make them desirable in the extreme. (This was not played up in the show, for the subject of working aphrodisiacs wasn't standard television fare in the late 1960s.) But is must have been so, for the highly trained, strictly disciplined men of the *Enterprise* crew simply went bonkers over these women—leering at their backsides (as did the camera), falling over each other, tongues literally hanging out. These are supposedly men who are surrounded daily by over a hundred intelligent, healthy, and beautiful women (many of whom are much better-looking than Mudd's trio), deep-space veterans who would have had the opportunity to sample the sexual fruits of dozens of planets. It is almost certain that the drug provided the women with something like Ilia's pheromones—either that, or the ladies on board the ship were engaging in *Lysistrata*-like behavior.

There was, naturally, the obligatory infatuation with the captain, but it seemed as if Eve's refusal to attempt to seduce Kirk stemmed more from general disgust with the whole scheme than from any strong feelings for Kirk. (For the first time, we hear the phrase that Kirk is "married to his ship," and from Harry Mudd of all people! Perhaps Harry strode the straight and narrow in his youth and had a love for a ship of his own.) Eve's feelings for Kirk, whatever form they took, slipped away pretty quickly and just as quickly attached themselves to Ben Childress. Even though her attachment to him begins as a sisterly chiding, we can see that it will soon blossom into a gentle, mutually caring, and mutually respectful love between them. Lord only knows what went on between Ruth, Magda, and the other two miners! If the men of the *Enterprise* went loony over the women, what then must have been the response of the poor miners who had been living in undesired celibacy for many months? Come to think of it . . . poor Ruth and Magda!

The concept of love was so all-pervasive in Star Trek that beings who were not generally considered to be "alive" were shown to feel it in one way or another. Apparently, we were being subtly told that love is a state of caring and involvement, which does not necessarily need to be physical in origin or intent. Even machines could feel it.

The first examples of this are seen in "What Are Little Girls Made Of?" The android Andrea, apparently constructed by Roger Korby, feels inklings of emotion awakened by the appearance of Kirk and the other humans. Kirk takes advantage of Andrea's newfound interest to gain information. Although he does not intend his action to harm the android, it eventually leads to her destruction when she transfers that affection to Korby, for whom she probably had unawakened love all along.

Korby's case is a bit different. Most likely he created Andrea to satisfy his need for female companionship, and perhaps his sexual needs as well. Again, because of the mores of television, this subject was nicely skirted (except for a lovely scene in which the appearance of Andrea gets a raised eyebrow from Chapel), and we have no information either way as to whether Korby's android body wanted or required sex. But the enticing face and figure of Andrea would suggest it did.

Korby, although his judgment seems to be impaired by the transfer into the android body, still appears to possess a full range of human emotions, giving doubt to Kirk's assertion that Korby can no longer feel. Korby displays anger, sadness, ambition, and, especially, love for Christine. Their embrace upon meeting is certainly not the sort of faked emotion one would expect from an unfeeling android. As we know that Kirk is neither a fool nor a liar, we can only assume that he is glossing over the realities of the situation to spare Christine's feelings.

By her faith that Korby would someday be found alive, Christine shows a fine and pure love, the kind that does not die just because circumstances say it should. We know that in a special place deep within her, she still loves and respects Roger Korby very, very much. And if nothing else, she has a good friend on the *Enterprise*. The touching scene where Uhura hugs Christine, sharing her happiness that Korby is alive, is the only time we see that these two are close. We'd have liked to see more of this friendship.

But what of Ruk? Although he is the last of his advanced android design, and he and his contemporaries were responsible for destroying the inhabitants of Exo III, he acts out of his own strange kind of love of logic and order. One suspects that the creators of Ruk went around killing each other just as Korby and the *Enterprise* crew do. He is more than willing to help Korby when things are peaceful, and it isn't until strong emotions begin swirling about him that he reverts to his former aggressive ways. The lesson of Ruk is overlooked by everyone involved, and it should not be.

The sweetly painful first love of adolescence is the heart of "Miri." The young woman of the title is beginning to enter puberty after a horrifyingly extended childhood, and who should appear just at the time she is beginning to feel the stirring of her sex but Jim Kirk, virile, sexy, totally *male* Jim Kirk. Like millions of viewers, Miri is immediately smitten.

Kirk is flattered, of course, and at first allows Miri to hang around mooning while the team works to find a cure for the viral infection. But when Miri sees him comforting Janice Rand—to our eyes a totally sexless scene, but to Miri, total disaster—she turns on him with all the force of a woman scorned. Poor Miri. She has two of the strongest adolescent burdens forced upon her at once, puppy love and jealousy. And she has to contend with her unfamiliar emotions without the benefit of adult example or advice. She has no mother to teach her or comfort her in her misery, and the only other woman around is her "rival."

To Kirk's credit, he does not take the tack of "If you really love me, you'd tell us" when trying to convince Miri to bring back the communicators. He instead appeals to her growing maturity and attempts to explain why the children turn into "Grups." He is successful in this, for Miri has the children return the tools when another child goes mad. Although Miri still admires Kirk, we can see that she's beginning to get over him—just as we all get over our first love.

Also in "Miri" is the first inkling of the love and devotion shared by the members of the *Enterprise* crew. When McCoy develops a serum for the disease, everyone insists on being the one to test it. McCoy, showing for the first time his lovable combination of compassionate man and curmudgeon, naturally uses himself as the guinea pig.

In "Dagger of the Mind," Kirk and Dr. Helen Noel are the victims of an artifically induced love thanks to Dr. Tristan Adams and his "neural neutralizer." Although Kirk feels passion for Helen (and has memories of a Christmas party that led to a night of love), he rather easily overcomes his feelings and goes about destroying Dr. Adams' operation. Again, his love for his ship and crew have proved stronger than the imprinted feelings for a woman. We suspect that however deep the "love" for Helen was implanted in Kirk's brain, to him that love was not so different from the many other infatuations he has had over the years. Now if the good doctor had used Spock as his guinea pig, it might have been a different story. . . .

In "The Corbomite Maneuver," we see Kirk show great compassion when he returns to aid the small First Federation ship, thereby proving the humans' worth to Balok. Balok (and presumably his race) is a bit more pragmatic, preferring to offer "brotherly love" to those who prove deserving of it—and to destroy those who fail the test. One can only hope that the association with the UFP has helped Balok's people to be a bit more open-minded. Perhaps not, for we haven't seen or heard from them since. Maybe they feel the United Federation of Planets, while an acceptable presence in the galaxy and no threat to them, is a little too liberal for their tastes.

"The Menagerie" is a feast for those looking for instances of love in Star Trek. We have the various sexually enticing forms of Vina that are offered to Pike; the unspoken feelings of both Number One and Yeoman Colt for Pike; Pike's own desires for peace, rest, and love; Kirk's feelings when he thinks that Spock has betrayed him; and, of course, the very great love that Spock shows for Christopher Pike by his dangerous and oh-so-wonderful actions. Each of these is deserving of discussion in detail.

Vina was the sole survivor of the crash of the SS *Columbia* on Talos IV, and although rescued by the Talosians, she was horribly disfigured. Living alone for many years with only the company of the intellectual and inward-directed Talosians, Vina must have suffered immense loneliness. The arrival of the Earthmen and the subsequent capture of Pike must have been like a dream come true for Vina. She was willing (at least in the beginning) to go to any lengths to keep Pike with her, even to the extent of allowing herself to "become" such a total sex object as a Green Orion Slave Girl. Vina only wanted Pike to love her and stay with her, but she soon found herself falling in love with him. In a reaction which must have completely astounded and dismayed her, that love took the form of helping Pike to escape.

Easier said than done, however. Vina spoke of the mental tortures which the Talosians could inflict on a human, and we could tell from the shudder that went through her that she was speaking from bitter experience. (Pike's brief taste of "hell" was frightening enough!) The Talosians, in their never-ending search for new experiences to mentally relive, must have found Vina's memories and subconscious fantasies a treasure trove. We can imagine only a mere fraction of the experiences they must have forced her to endure—experiences both pleasurable and painful. And like Pike, she would have found the mental images distressing because she would always *know* that they were not real, no matter how graphic or tactile they seemed. How would any of us like to spend eighteen years reliving our lives—and our fantasies and our nightmares—over and over and over again?

It has been suggested that Vina did not (thanks to the Talosians) see Pike as *Pike*, but rather as her "ideal dream man." Three things argue against this: First, Pike saw her as herself, admittedly a perfect, extremely beautiful image, but he stated that she was unknown to him, even as a fantasy image. The fact that she was a constant in each of the illusions was his first clue to their unreality. Second, because of the aforementioned enforced "reliving" of her life and fantasies, it is unlikely that Vina would be overly excited by her "ideal man," any image of which would have long since been pulled from her mind and placed into the illusions by the Talosians. Last, the need of the Talosians to draw Pike into their scheme required that he respond to Vina as a real woman, and having her see him the same way would heighten the intensity of the illusions. It was this that backfired against them.

Vina also displayed one other kind of love: self-love. Not unhealthy narcissism, but a self-respect and dignity that allowed her to reject the dream-existence of the Talosians to remain with Pike and the others and face death by phaser overload. It would have been very easy for her to slip back into the existence she had lived for so long, and it took a great deal of courage for her to choose not to. By so doing, Vina reclaimed her humanity and individual rights. Even though the Talosians gave the illusion of her beauty back to her (and the illusion that Pike was staying, in the original script), we can assume that they no longer "used" her for illusion-casting and that she was treated as much more of an equal.

When they discovered that their plan to have Pike respond to Vina was failing, the Talosians pulled Number One and Yeoman Colt from the ship. Figuring quite wrongly that all a human needed to be happy was a compatible mate, they cited health, youth, and intelligence as their criteria for choosing this new "breeding stock." But they carefully looked into the women's minds as well. In Yeoman Colt's mind, they found a natural and strong infatuation for the captain, one which could easily grow into love under the proper circumstances. They also mentioned her "strong female drives," which could mean a number of things, but probably referred to her desires for a home and children, as this is what the Talosians were hoping for a couple to develop. But we may suspect what they found in the mind of Number One was one heck of a lot more enticing for their parasitic urges (and one heck of a lot more interesting for us to speculate on): She had often had fantasies concerning Pike.

Christopher Pike's mind was on other things at the time, but you can bet he gave that little revelation quite a bit of thought when he returned to the *Enterprise*. Number One was as about as emotionless as a human could be, as well as coldly efficient to an almost robotic degree. It is highly unlikely that Pike ever had any fantasies concerning *her*, and it must have come as quite a surprise to him to discover that the reverse was true. Both were professionals, however, and we may assume that the incident was never mentioned again. Forgetting about it, however, was another matter, and it would be interesting to somehow see the reactions of the two when future command duties forced them together.

It must be noted in Number One's favor that when the Talosian made his pronouncement, she did not react with embarrassment (as did Yeoman Colt), but instead showed the same determination and defiance as did Pike.

Christopher Pike is one of the most complex individuals ever to appear on Star Trek. We learned more about him (and had more questions raised about him) in one hour than we ever did about many other characters who appeared far more often. Unlike Kirk, Pike did not seem to have an overwhelming need for command. He saw it more as a duty he had to take on simply because he was one of that "special breed." It was a job that needed doing, and he could do it better than anyone else. He yearned for relaxation, peace, comfort, and an end to tensions, decisions, and responsibility. In many ways, this makes him a better man than Jim Kirk; but in just as many ways, he is not a better starship commander than Kirk. We have seen how often Kirk is plagued by doubts. How much worse it must have been for Pike, a man who was not "born to be a starship commander," but had it "thrust upon him." Although he was an extremely successful commander (the respect he gained from Spock speaks for that), he probably was not a daring or imaginative one. He was not totally happy commanding the *Enterprise*, but as Dr. Boyce pointed out, he probably would have been unhappier doing anything else.

Unlike Kirk, Pike yearned for love. He would have liked nothing better than to share a life of quiet contemplation with a woman he loved. It is highly indicative that the most convincing fantasy presented him by the Talosians was just such a pedestrian, peaceful situation, drawn from his uppermost desires. When protecting Vina from the Rigellian warrior, he was performing his "duty"; when in the midst of the hedonistic slavers, he was out of place and disgusted with them and himself. It was only in the simple picnic setting that Pike looked at ease, however briefly.

Spock, although he did not appear to be close to Pike at the time of the Talosian incident, grew much closer to him in later years. His telepathic powers, always more sensitive to those he cared for, would have involuntarily "picked up" Pike's desires for love and the simple life. That knowledge probably played a major part in his decision to help the crippled Pike return to Talos. The Talosians could give Pike not only "freedom" from his injuries, but a perfect illusion of the peaceful life he so fondly desired and never found. Kirk, the fighter, would have received Spock's help in another form; perhaps by transference into an android body like those on Exo III, so that Kirk could once again roam the stars and command his beloved *Enterprise*. The illusions of Talos would not have pleased a crippled Kirk as they did Pike; they would have only served to magnify his distress at not really being in space.

Having responded to Spock's hesitantly proffered friendship, only shortly before these events, Kirk is quite devastated by the Vulcan's seeming mutiny. It is one of Kirk's worst dreams come true—to again have his friendship betrayed, as had been done by Gary Mitchell (and apparently several others). The vindictiveness Kirk shows briefly would have been caused by this hurt, although his natural sense of fairness and his affection for Spock soon return him to normal. When Kirk finally learns the truth, he is relieved not only because Spock will not have to face charges of mutiny, but because he is at last able to cast aside all doubts about the Vulcan's loyalty. His gentle chiding to Spock about "this distressing tendency toward emotionalism" is more than joshing; it is an affirmation that Spock is once again his trusted friend.

Spock is also Christopher Pike's trusted friend. There is no doubt of the great love Spock holds for Chris Pike; he shows it in the most graphic way possible. Spock risks his life, his friendship with Kirk, his career, and most important to a Vulcan, the chance of disgrace to help Pike. Had Spock been apprehended at the Starbase, he would most certainly not have offered to explain his actions, even under threat of court-martial and death. Such is not his way; Spock neither makes excuses nor speaks of his emotionally motivated actions. But his help to Pike is an emotional action, an action of completely selfless love, for Spock has absolutely nothing personally to gain, and very, very much to lose.

But, as always, his actions, no matter how emotionally motivated, are logically planned in infinite detail. How like Spock to do something absolutely quixotic, absolutely emotional, absolutely out of love, and then to compute not only each step of the process, but its eventual chance of success as well.

The only regrets we viewers must have over Spock's actions in "The Menagerie" is that we are never allowed to see any instances of the great friendship he and Pike shared. We must assume that it was Pike who was responsible for bringing Spock out of his totally Vulcan shell and introducing him—however reluctantly and grudgingly—to the value of experiencing and controlling his emotions rather than suppressing them. It is not too farfetched to feel that Spock is quoting some long-ago advice given to him by Chris Pike when he speaks so movingly of "this simple feeling" after his encounter with V'Ger in *Star Trek: The Motion Picture*.

Also in "The Menagerie," the concept of Star Trek is strongly restated in the realization of the Talosians that humanity so loves freedom that men and women would rather die than lose it. The yearning to be free, and to grant others freedom, is vital to the characters in Star Trek; one of the reasons why man first reached into deep space. Like the pioneers of old, they needed more "elbow room."

The Talosians also exhibit, if not love, at least compassion in their unwillingness to force the humans to remain on Talos IV, and in their action of granting Vina her illusion of beauty and of having Pike. More, they show that they truly care for the humans as a race, fearing that the secret of mental projection will spread beyond their world and destroy others as it had their own. Their help to Spock in returning Pike to Talos IV is an indication that they have become a more loving and understanding race.

In "The Conscience of the King," Lenore Karidian displays a great love for her father, Anton Karidian, also known as Kodos the Executioner. Her love is so great, in fact, that she slips over the edge of madness and resorts to murder to protect him. Her insanity becomes complete when she is the cause of his death. There was an unhealthy undercurrent of incest in Lenore's feelings and actions, subtly displayed by having her first seen playing Lady Macbeth to her father's Macbeth. Again, it was only a suggestion, for nothing could be overtly shown or stated on television.

Love culminates in marriage—almost—in "Balance of Terror" as Kirk is about to officiate at the wedding of Robert Tomlinson and Angela Martine. It is the only instance we were shown of crewmembers marrying or being married, although it would not be uncommon on the long voyages of a ship like the *Enterprise*. Perhaps while not forbidding the practice, Starfleet did not encourage it. The realism of Star Trek's world would have benefited by having a few married couples aboard the ship, and it would also have been an indication that things have changed greatly since our time. Angela's grief after Robert's death is realistically underplayed with the kind of dignity, even resignation, one would expect from a seasoned, professional Starfleet officer.

Then again, maybe she wasn't all that broken up. If Star Trek adventures happened in the sequence in which they were aired, Angela got over Robert's death pretty quickly, for in the following episode, "Shore Leave," Angela was happily flirting with Lieutenant Esteban Rodriguez and fantasizing about Don Juan. She also had a mysterious name change to Martine-Teller. If she was still grieving over Tomlinson, one would expect her to be more reserved, or for "Don Juan" to at least resemble poor old Robert, or for her to have changed her name to Martine-Tomlinson in his memory. Apparently Ms. Martine is a lady who quickly puts the past behind her and gets on with life. Kind of like a certain captain we all know.

Also in "Balance," we saw that the Romulans could share deep, loving friendships; the commander and the centurion are longtime friends. Their relationship is akin to that of Kirk and McCoy. We also see that the Romulans, as embodied by the commander, are occasionally men of great honor and character, assets which are often prerequisites for the ability to love.

We see Dr. McCoy work his Southern charm on a lady for the first time in "Shore Leave." The charmingly shy and genteel affair shared by Bones and Tonia Barrows is refreshing to watch, for it showed us a side of Star Trek (as well as the doctor) we hadn't seen before. Until this episode, love affairs in the series were the hinge upon which the plot swung, and therefore were played to the hilt with all the *Sturm and Drang* of bad theater. McCoy's spooning of his lady, on the other hand, was simply an enjoyable subplot to the show. (True, Tonia's "wish" for a White Knight led to McCoy's "death," but that could have been just as easily accomplished in any number of ways. At least it tied in with the plot better than the relationship of Martine and Tomlinson, which was included only to give us a look at some ship's personnel interacting, and to tug at our heartstrings when Tomlinson died.) It was fun to watch Bones work his winsome wiles on a totally willing young woman, and it's a shame we didn't get to see McCoy "romanticizin' " more often.

One of Kirk's old flames also pops up in the course of the episode, and their first meeting evokes a rare air of tenderness and nostalgia in Kirk. Ruth must have been very special indeed to Jim, for he pauses in his breathless chase of Finnegan to contemplate the flower that reminds him of her. What little we see of Ruth indicates that she was a gentle, quiet, and loving woman, one who was about Kirk's current age, and therefore most likely the "older woman" who gently and graciously introduced a young Jim Kirk to love in all its most sensitive and enjoyable forms. It is a part of Kirk's past we seldom get a glimpse of, and all the more pleasant for the sweetness of it.

Trelane, "The Squire of Gothos," flirts outrageously with Uhura and Yeoman Ross, but his behavior is based on his observations of eighteenth-century Earth, and like a child playing cowboy, he's imitating the actions of his heros. He makes no serious overtures toward them, and one suspects that if they'd made overtures toward him, Trelane would have fled in frightened confusion. Had Kirk, or one of the women, figured this out quickly, the crew would have most likely been given speedy leave to go ahead. Trelane, like most boys, probably wouldn't like that "mushy stuff." His desire for love is that of a child, to be made much of and flattered for his cleverness, admired, and feared. In that respect, Trelane was much like Charlie Evans. But unlike Charlie, Trelane has only been playing, and like all children who get too rambunctious with their toys, his loving but stern parents make him go to his room.

In "Courtmartial," Kirk not only suffers a bittersweet reunion with an old girlfriend, Areel Shaw (who is serving as his prosecutor), but he again meets with betrayal from an old friend. Finney's framing of Kirk is compounded by the bitterness of Jamie Finney, who blames Kirk for her father's death and professes hatred for him. Jamie's forgiveness when Finney is revealed to be alive doesn't help Kirk much. He has permanently lost another friend. Although they had not been close for years, Kirk would have overlooked Finney's resentment and still considered him a friend. Helping assuage the pain a bit was his relief at being cleared and a nostalgic kiss from Areel—with perhaps a promise of renewed closeness in the future.

The power of love to lead a person down the wrong path is examined in "Space Seed." Lieutenant Marla McGivers falls helplessly for Kahn's mesmerizing charisma and *macho* disdain. So captivated is Marla by this living example of everything she has always considered to be the "best" in a man that she almost worships him. In one repellant scene, Kahn grips her wrist painfully and forces her to her knees to prove her loyalty to him. After suffering such degradation, it is only a small step to betraying the *Enterprise* into his hands. Although Marla turns on Kahn when he intends to let Kirk die, she is still madly in love with him and is willing to suffer Starfleet's punishment if he can be spared. Kahn, impressed by her loyalty (and probably even more by the bravery she showed in defying him), "forgives" her and asks if she will accompany him in his enforced exile. She agrees, realizing that in his own chauvinistic way, Kahn loves her too.

(If, as rumored, the upcoming *Star Trek II* movie shows the civilization built by Kahn and his followers, perhaps we may see the changes wrought by Marla's influence, maybe a kind of turnabout "Taming of the Shrew.")

In "This Side of Paradise," we meet the Woman from Spock's Past (somehow we always *knew* there was one), and thanks to the intervention of the inhibition-loosening spores, we have the added treat of seeing Spock fall in love with her.

Not much is revealed about Leila Kalomi, save that she fell in love with Spock during his sojourn on Earth and tried her best to break down his Vulcan reserve. As Spock must have found the teeming millions of illogical humans on Earth trial enough for any Vulcan to bear, the appearance of a beautiful young woman who professed love for him would have just about driven him crazy, especially if he found himself beginning to reciprocate the feelings. Spock gently, but forcefully, told Leila that he was incapable of loving her, and he may have believed it at the time, but as we saw when he was under the influence of the spores, he was wrong.

It was not that Mr. Spock was incapable of loving Leila; it was that he was incapable of showing that love, or even of admitting it to himself. (Remember the surprise in his voice when he told her, "I *can* love you!" He was surprised—Leila wasn't.) Thanks to his strict Vulcan upbringing and his own natural shyness and reticence, Spock was disturbed by strong emotion . . . especially if those emotions were his own. To enter into a love affair, no matter how desirable the object of his affections might be, would be unthinkable for Spock. Unable to even consider the prospect, he put Leila out of his life completely. Shattered by his dismissal, Leila joined the mission to colonize Omnicron Ceti III, probably hoping to find a new life and new romance. But as she is still unattached when the *Enterprise* crew arrives, she obviously could not forget Spock.

Spock, his emotions now completely unfettered, leaps into a joyous love affair with Leila. He laughs, appreciates beauty and pleasure on an emotional level rather than an intellectual one, and is most happy to be sharing it all with Leila. If it were not for the fact that the spores' influence destroyed all ambition and drive, such a situation would be perfect for Spock.

It is interesting to speculate whether or not Spock would have remained in love with Leila if he had been forced to remain on Omnicron Ceti III. The first rush of emotional release, coupled with the proximity of a beautiful woman who already loved him, would certainly cause Spock to be smitten with her, especially since he had been strongly attracted to her on Earth. But it was truly first love that Spock was experiencing, and such love seldom lasts. It could have been that once his infatuation with Leila began to cool off, Spock would have acted like any normal human male and begun to play the field. It was not stated in the show, but one would suspect that a by-product of the spores' influence would have been the acceptance of free love within the colony group and its recent additions from the *Enterprise*. We shall never know.

It is enough for us to know that deep within Mr. Spock, no matter how carefully controlled and craftily hidden, there exists the capacity for joyful, sharing, and fulfilling love. Sadly for Spock (and for Leila), it was all too brief. But we can take comfort in the fact that for once in his life, Spock was happy. Perhaps the memory of that happiness will someday help him to break through the barriers of his training and tradition without the help of artificial influences and he will again share such a love.

"The Devil in the Dark" is the Horta, and the Horta is a mother. Like any loving mother, she acts in a most definite—and violent—manner to protect the lives of her young. It is again brotherly love which allows Kirk, Spock, and McCoy to save the Horta and her children from destruction and grant them the respect and rights they deserve as sentient beings.

The Organians in "Errand of Mercy" also practice brotherly love; but like Balok's First Federation, it is on their own terms. It is the second time (and will not be the last) that Kirk and his crew are presented with such an attitude from an advanced race, and one would think that the Federation and Starfleet would begin to consider the rightness or wrongness of such a policy. But again, beyond an occasional reference to the Organian Peace Treaty, nothing more is said of it.

James T. Kirk is the man who considered sacrificing a universe for the woman he loved.

That is the plot of "The City on the Edge of Forever" in a nutshell, but what a nutshell it is! It is our first glimpse of the kind of woman that Kirk would consider "perfect"—Edith Keeler. Edith is warm, loving, compassionate, and something of a visionary. She is also very lovely, but we can consider that to be beside the point. Kirk doesn't go out looking for a beautiful woman to spend a night with; he falls in love with Edith gradually, as he is forced to remain near her awaiting McCoy's arrival and is able to see her day-to-day activities. Seeing that she lives what she preaches, Kirk loves her for what is inside of her, not because she happens to be extremely lovely. (It is interesting to note that in his original teleplay for "City" Harlan Ellison stipulated that Edith Keeler not be beautiful, but possess a lively, fresh vibrancy that makes her lovely to behold.) It is testimony to the spirit of Edith that Kirk, involved as he is in trying to right his world, cannot help falling in love with her.

And fall he does. It is very plain that Kirk has *never before* felt this way about any woman. For the first time, he is willing to abandon his ship, his career, even his closest friends to remain with Edith. He almost abandons the future.

But Kirk's love for Edith is not the strongest love he displays in "City." The love that he has for unborn millions is greater. It is that love—not duty, not responsibility, not logic—that *love* that forces him to make the most difficult movement of his life and prevent Dr. McCoy from saving Edith's life. It takes a great love for a man to lay down his own life; how much greater then must a love be for a man to lay down the life of the only woman he has ever truly loved and at the same time sentence himself to an eternity of loneliness? That is the love story of "City" and it is a sad and beautiful one.

It is interesting to note that Spock could have erased the memory of Edith from Kirk's mind as he was later to erase the memory of Reena Kapec. Why didn't he? Because by removing Jim's memories of Edith, he would have also removed the memory of Kirk's sacrifice. Spock would have logically, and rightly, concluded that the pain of Edith's death would be lessened for Jim every time he considered the wonders and beauty of the twenty-third century. The existence of billions, the opening of the universe, the untold *good* that could be done—all of these and more would stand forever as a tribute to Edith in Kirk's mind. Removing the painful memories would have been a compassionate, loving act on Spock's part. Leaving them was an even greater one.

Kirk's love for his brother "Sam" and his sister-in-law was quite evident in "Operation Annihilate," but because of the urgency of the situation, he had little time or opportunity to express his grief. Coming so soon after his loss of Edith, this must have shattered Kirk, but he bravely managed to oversee the destruction of the cell-creatures. His control almost breaks when he thinks that Spock has been permanently blinded, and he takes out much of his anger and grief on McCoy, but he still goes on. The fact that his nephew survived (and that Spock's blindness was temporary) would have helped Kirk recover a little quicker, but so much emotional battering in so short a time would most certainly have left some very deep mental scars. Luckily for Kirk, some leave time was coming up, and he would have a chance to rest and recover.

He needed it. No sooner had the *Enterprise* set out on the second year of its mission when apparent tragedy again struck. Mr. Spock began to suffer the throes of *pon farr*, the inbred urge of a Vulcan male to return to his home planet and take a mate, or die. There was little love involved between Mr. Spock and his intended bride, T'Pring, but quite a bit of love was shown by Jim Kirk, who risked his career so that Spock would not perish. For a man like Kirk, this was much more of a personal sacrifice than risking his life—Kirk had risked his life for Spock and others of his crew many times, and would not hesitate to do so again—this Kirk was risking the loss of his ship and his position, another matter entirely. Without them, Jim Kirk might as well be dead. Yet, because Spock's life was in danger, and because he was Kirk's *friend*, Kirk unhesitatingly and willfully disobeyed a direct order from Starfleet and diverted the *Enterprise* to Vulcan.

And once there, he allowed himself to be drawn into a battle to the death against that same friend. True, Kirk thought he was protecting Spock by acting as T'Pring's champion, but he still placed himself in quite a bit of danger. The lust-maddened Spock could have easily killed or severely injured Kirk. And once Kirk discovered that he couldn't just spar around long enough to make it look good and then take a quick dive, he could have taken the safe way out and used his more rational thinking to quickly dispatch Spock. Instead, he chose to fight a defensive battle, hoping that somehow Spock would come to his senses. Had Dr. McCoy been a little more slow-witted or Kirk a little less nimble, we know that Kirk would have allowed Spock to kill him. Even knowing the agonies Spock would go through once he returned to normal and discovered he had killed him, Kirk couldn't have killed Spock. Death at the hands of his best friend wouldn't be the sort of death Jim would prefer, but as he said to McCoy, "I didn't bring Spock all the way to Vulcan to kill him."

McCoy showed love for both of his friends by managing to come up with the knockout plan under unbelievable pressure, then showed it again by emphasizing his anger to the point of seeming hatred when accusing Spock of murdering Kirk. We know that the doctor was only letting off some steam, but it also served the purpose of protecting Spock's honor and position. His was also the most profound joy at seeing Spock's emotional scene when the Vulcan learned that Kirk was alive, yet he chose to mask it in his usual cynical manner. It was his way of repaying Spock for the compliment of being invited to attend the ceremony (and the tacit acknowledgment it carried). Spock understood. His riposte was logical, calm, and quite warm and affectionate—*and* an open invitation for McCoy to have the last word. It was his way of saying, "Thanks, Bones!"

But what of the Vulcans, those coldly logical beings who disdain emotions such as love? Well, if ever a couple was in love, it was T'Pring and Stonn. He was willing to risk his life in battle to win her. She was willing to risk the shameful state of "chattel" to the victor to escape marrying Spock. Each of them had equal courage, and it is very difficult to determine whose love was the greater. Seemingly, it was Stonn, for we can't help but see T'Pring as a cold and calculating bitch, incapable of loving anyone or anything save power or position. Yet she chose Kirk to be her champion, not Stonn. Her reasons for doing so were so perfectly logical that even Spock congratulated her upon them, yet we can't help feeling that her primary motivation was to protect Stonn. Whatever the circumstances that threw them together and led them into the illicit affair, the love that grew out of it must have been a very deep and passionate one, for to keep it, they had to fly in the face of Vulcan tradition and law. While there's no arguing the fact that T'Pring was crazy, maybe we can amend it to "crazy in love," and hope that Spock's prediction did not come to pass, and that Stonn found the *having* of T'Pring just as satisfying as the wanting.

Apollo wanted not only to be loved, but to be worshiped. His race, having landed on Earth at the time of the ancient Greeks, were considered gods and worshiped as such. The feeling was, of course, narcotic, and Apollo demanded the same devotion from the *Enterprise* crew. In return, Apollo promised "love" to the humans, but it was not truly love he offered, but instead the kind of condescending protectiveness one would give to a likeable but not particularly important or intelligent pet. Man had changed much since the time of Apollo's sojourn on Earth, and Apollo was quite surprised at the adamant refusal of Kirk and his crew to bow to his superiority. When he finally realized that he could not longer have the worship he needed, he cast himself onto "the winds of time" and vanished. But it was the lack of love—blind, obedient, adoring love, the only kind Apollo could understand or accept—that destroyed him.

Although the attention and affection he showed her was never more than physical, Carolyn Palmas fell deeply in love with Apollo. Whether it was because of his charm and mighty mien, or because of some dim, half-remembered memory supplied by her Grecian ancestors, it was a strong love. Like Marla McGivers, she became so enthralled with an enemy that she temporarily forgot her allegiance to Starfleet and abetted him in actions against the crew. But also like Marla, Carolyn soon realized that helping Apollo to victory would serve to destroy everything she had devoted her life to, so she aided Kirk in defeating Apollo. Such loyalty, even in the face of overwhelming love, shows how deeply each of these women loved their fellows and the principles of the Federation. It is to be hoped that the same love resides within each of the crewmembers on the *Enterprise*. Carolyn had to make a choice between love and loyalty, and loyalty won. We can only hope that the tag to the original script (and in James Blish's adaptation) was true—that Carolyn bore the child of Apollo, and thereby had a living, loving memory of him throughout her life.

Carolyn loved Apollo—but Scotty loved Carolyn. For once, the master engineer placed his beloved *Enterprise* second to a woman. We were never told exactly what it was about Carolyn that attracted Scotty so. Yes, she was an extremely beautiful woman, and seemed vivacious, sexy, and intelligent, but so are many women on the *Enterprise* and we do not see Scotty constantly falling in love with them. Carolyn didn't even work in engineering, where a common interest and propinquity could have led to growing affection on Scotty's part. She also did not seem to care for Scotty over much. She was friendly and polite, but not at all loving in her actions toward him. We must assume that Scotty was—for whatever reasons—simply infatuated with Carolyn. Had the events on Pollux IV not happened, he probably would have tired of her indifference after a while, and forgotten about her completely when the next intriguing technical problem came along.

Her choice of Apollo over him, and her actions on Pollux IV, probably left him with more bitterness than he would have otherwise felt, but Scotty is that dour sort who looks at life cynically anyway, and he would have chalked it up as another in what is probably a long series of romantic disappointments. He probably drained a bottle of scotch, played a few mournful songs on his pipes, and immersed himself in his technical manuals. We can assume by the time the *Enterprise* made for its next port of call, Scotty was just about his old self again.

There is a distinct lack of love in the "mirror universe." The principles upon which the United Federation of Planets is founded would probably be a source of great amusement to the ruthless minions of the Imperial Starship *Enterprise*. But there was a smattering of love seen in "Mirror, Mirror." Most of it was simple lust: Sulu-2 wanted Uhura; Kirk-2 wanted a beautiful Captain's Woman. Yet the Captain's Woman, Marlena Moreau, did respond to Kirk's tenderness and probably would have fallen quite deeply in love with him given the chance. Surely, the (so she thought) uncharacteristic treatment he afford her was enough to soften her cynical attitudes. Spock-2 also displayed the beginnings of a love of freedom, not only for himself, but for all the peoples enslaved by the Empire. We can assume that he and Marlena would work from within to destroy the Empire—and their first objective would have been the conversion of Kirk-2, Spock-2 using his Vulcan logic, Marlena using her feminine wiles. (And in the matter of our own Kirk and the USS *Enterprise*'s version of Marlena Moreau—well, knowing Jim Kirk, we can guess that he had his *own* Captain's Woman, albeit temporarily.)

Love of principles was taken to the extreme by the Halkans of both universes. They were quite willing to die as a race for what they believed in. This is quite often the case with members of Starfleet as well, but men such as Kirk, Spock, and McCoy also recognize the value of compromise and the need to often make tough decisions about the relative rightness or wrongness of a situation. It is much easier to simply say no than it is to evaluate both sides of a question and choose one of them. For all their admirable qualities, the Halkans were obviously a stagnant and fearful race. They did not love peace, they worshiped it. And as Kirk realized in the case of Apollo, that which is worshiped is often a harsh and stultifying master.

Sex is more the question than love in "The Apple." The childlike inhabitants of Gamma Trianguli VI are complacent, simple, and extremely happy. They do not love, they simply peacefully coexist. It is not until the humans arrive and display affection to one another that the "people" begin to relate to each other as sexual beings. The tenderness with which they treat each other gives a seeming idyllic loveliness to their tentative advances, but there is no question that when their glands and instincts begin to work in full force, peace will be ended and jealousy, lust, and killing will begin. In freeing them from Vaal, the crew of the *Enterprise* condemned the "people" to thousands of years of strife and bloodshed, something the godlike computer was obviously designed to end in the first place. If a team of experts was not dispatched to Gamma Trianguli VI very quickly, Kirk and his men may very well have been guilty of genocide.

In "The Doomsday Machine," we saw how Commodore Matt Decker, a man very much like Jim Kirk, was completely shattered by the destruction of his ship and the deaths of his entire crew. It is an indication of how distraught Kirk would be in similar circumstances, but let us hope he would not go off the deep end, thanks to the friendship he shares with Spock and McCoy. Decker appeared to be a particularly friendless and insular man (much as his son, Will Decker, appears to be in *Star Trek: The Motion Picture*). Perhaps this is the curse of starship captains to lose close friends and loves in their quest to be the best. We know that Chris Pike became fast friends with Spock, as did Kirk. Such friends are apparently rare, and Kirk is probably one of the luckiest captains in Starfleet, for he has *two* of them. Their very presence increases his chance for survival.

Love, as Mr. Spock would be the first to point out, is an emotion, and when human emotions are suddenly thrust upon a being who has never experienced them, chaos can result. In "Catspaw," we see how the overwhelming sensations of Sylvia's newfound emotions drive her to acts which cause her mission to fail. She lusts for Kirk, tempting him with a variety of sensuous female personas, and like poor little Miri, becomes furious when Kirk spurns her advances. Her companion, Korob, seems to be somewhat less affected by taking on a human form; although he does show all-too-human uncertainty and fear. His help to the *Enterprise* crew does prove that his race can—if only under the influence of human form—feel compassion, and that bodes well for any future contact between the two races.

"Metamorphosis" is strictly a love story, *and* one of the few instances we saw in Star Trek of love between a human and a nonhuman. It is to be noted, however, that the Companion was a creature of force, without a physical body, and therefore nonthreatening in the sense of interbreeding. It is also female, a subtle indication of the double standard which has always pervaded television. When Zefram Cochrane learns that the creature is female, he is very upset, terming it "disgusting." It's difficult to rationalize his feelings, seeing as how he was completely satisfied to have a symbiotic relationship with the Companion while he believed it to be sexless. He's willing to have an "affair" with a sexless alien, but not a female one. Curious.

But the situation is quickly remedied when the Companion enters the dying body of Nancy Hereford, and becomes, for all intents and purposes, a human female. Now Cochrane is not disgusted; indeed, he seems more than anxious to have the relationship progress onward to the physical. He seems to ignore, or be ignorant of, the fact that it is the mental processes—the soul, if you will—that is the major distinguishing difference between all living beings. Cochrane is a chauvinist of the worst kind: He refuses to love a "female" Companion; he courts an equally alien "human" just because she now appears to be of the "right" race.

It is the Companion who is the truly sensitive and loving one in this relationship. She has cared for Cochrane for many years, met his every need (and probably demand) without question or complaint, and once in the vulnerable human form, would probably be willing to go with him back to Earth and an untimely death if he demanded. If nothing else, she has given up relative immortality for him. And all of this without any overt return of her affection by Cochrane through all those years—even after he professes disgust at her femininity. She is a beautiful example of love incarnate, and much, much too good for Cochrane. We can only hope that she is able to soften his attitudes as they live together—or failing that, the Nancy Hereford half of her personality becomes dominant, and that she is presently in the process of unmercifully nagging him to death.

In "Journey to Babel," we meet one of the most loving individuals ever presented in Star Trek: Spock's mother, Amanda. She is totally human, warm and smiling, obviously happy in her life with Sarek, yet just as obviously a sensitive and intelligent individual in her own right. She may defer to Sarek in public as a good Vulcan wife should, but we can be sure that she has her way in private. We got to see a little bit of it in "Journey," and that was outside the confines of their own home, in a milieu where Amanda would have constrained her feelings and comments even more than she usually did.

We shall probably never know the true story of how Sarek and Amanda came to fall in love and marry. Sarek will only say that it seemed like the logical thing to do at the time. Surely it was. Even an "emotionless" Vulcan would not be insensitive enough to let a treasure such as Amanda escape. Their love is shown poignantly in the small glances and gestures they share. It is a quiet love but a strong one; who would expect trumpets, bells, and fireworks from a Vulcan? This is mostly due to Amanda, we suspect. She would have patiently overlooked Sarek's reluctance to give of himself, while at the same time accepting and subtly encouraging such small indications as we saw in "Journey." That Sarek deeply loves her there is no doubt.

Amanda loves her son just as much as she loves her husband. Perhaps she treasures him even more. Spock must have inadvertently given his mother much pain during his childhood. She would have suffered with him through every rebuff, every insult, every setback. And it would have pained her as well to see him embracing and accepting the Vulcan way of life, with all of its constraints of behavior and denial of emotion. Emotion Amanda *knew* her husband felt; how much more then would the half-human Spock feel it?

Amanda treats Spock as an adult Vulcan male of accomplishment and position should be treated. Beyond a simple but extremely warm greeting, she does not fawn over her son, even though it has obviously been some time since she has seen him. Naturally, her first reaction is to find out whether or not he still insists on continuing the grudge situation with his father; it is the thing uppermost on her mind and has been for many years. As happy as Amanda's life with Sarek has been, her happiness has been marred by the breach between Spock and Sarek, and she wishes more than anything for it to be healed. But both of her men are stubborn, and loving them both as she does, she will not and cannot take sides.

Sarek and Spock love each other, but because of their pride, they refuse to acknowledge it. We know that Spock devoted his first two decades to the Vulcan life-style, but had to leave for Starfleet to gain any kind of measure of individuality. Sarek, expecting Spock to follow in his footsteps like a good Vulcan son, refused to give his blessing to Spock's plans. Neither would acknowledge that the other had a point; and being

Vulcans, neither would acknowledge that hurt feelings were the primary motivation for the split on both sides.

But Sarek is extremely proud of Spock, nonetheless. It can be seen in the way he gives a slight nod of approval when Spock speaks as a Starfleet officer. And when he feels that Amanda has belittled Spock in front of his peers, he lets her know in no uncertain terms that she is wrong. Thanks to the circumstances surrounding the voyage to Babel, Spock and his father are reunited. But one suspects that Sarek is more impressed by Spock's refusal to help him when in command of the ship than he is by the fact that Spock's blood helped him to survive the operation. Spock acted correctly, without undue emotion, and, above all, *logically* in Sarek's opinion, and that, more than anything, proved to Sarek that his son was correct and successful in his choice of career. Now it was possible for Sarek to display the respect and honor due a fellow Vulcan—and the small, almost indistinguishable indications of affection to a son.

Amanda, filled with relief that her husband and son both survived the crisis and that the break between them was finally healed, was aghast that they did not show more emotion. It was a warm moment, with all of the three enjoying a good "laugh," once again a complete and very loving family.

It is love for her unborn child in "Friday's Child" that causes Eleen to disobey the tribal command that she take her own life because she is carrying the child who would be the next chieftain. Dr. McCoy is instrumental in guiding Eleen to this decision, his own love for humanity showing her the wrongness of destroying an unborn innocent to satisfy custom.

The onset of extreme and debilitating age in "The Deadly Years" presents us with one of the strangest "love affairs" seen on Star Trek. Dr. Janet Wallace was attracted to Kirk, but seems to be even more so when he begins to age. Perhaps she only had a preference for older men, but it could also be that she saw Kirk as a father figure, an eventuality which would give her attraction to Kirk's "elderly" self an unhealthy tinge. Kirk seems to be put off by Janet's attentions, and although he has more important concerns on his mind, he cannot decide if she is attending him out of pity or affection. The impending loss of his virility would also have bothered Kirk quite a bit. It is interesting to note that Kirk is somewhat standoffish to Janet at the conclusion of the episode.

Kirk's affection for his former, late commander, Captain Garrovick, is the cause of his "Obsession." Feeling that as a junior officer his failure to blast the "cloud creature" quickly enough resulted in Garrovick's death, Kirk was consumed with both guilt and an overriding desire to destroy the creature. The presence of Garrovick's son, now an ensign on the

Enterprise, only serves to heighten Kirk's obsession, for he feels that young Garrovick blames him for his father's death. Although we are not told so, we can assume that young Garrovick has an uncanny resemblance to his father, which would have disturbed Kirk all the more. And although Kirk claims to be especially interested in and helpful to Ensign Garrovick, we don't see any indications of it in the episode. In truth, Kirk probably was even more standoffish to the ensign than he would have been to anyone else. With Kirk's history of losing those close to him, forming a close association with another Garrovick who could meet death at any time would not be something Jim would be eager to do. Garrovick disappears from the *Enterprise* soon after this episode, and we can suspect that he was as glad to get away from Kirk and the constant reminders of his father as Kirk was glad to get rid of him.

Kirk fears that Scotty has become a "Jack the Ripper" in "Wolf in the Fold" because of an injury to the engineer caused by a woman. We might also suspect that Kirk had some thoughts about Carolyn Palmas' affair with Apollo and the pain it caused Scotty, adding to his resentment of women. This was the only episode of Star Trek in which out-and-out murder was the problem faced by the crew; and sure enough, it *was* Jack the Ripper doing the killing—at least an immortal creature with the ability to possess bodies and feed off the fear instilled in the victim at the time of the murder. Much more interesting, but of course downplayed, is the hedonistic culture of Argelius II. A society based on pleasure and its gratification was pretty strong medicine for television in the sixties (and probably would be now, in this age of "let's talk about it, but never do anything" titillation shows). It's pretty tasty medicine for Kirk and McCoy, however, as they gleefully look forward to sampling the pleasures of Argelius II; McCoy even displays an expert's anticipation we would not have expected from him. The character of Morla of Cantaba Street is also fun to watch, for his is the unthinkable crime of jealousy and (gasp!) preferring a monogamous relationship with the dancer Kara.

Tribbles are the only love you can buy in the Star Trek universe (unless you can be satisfied with the varieties on Argelius II), but they are a royal pain in the turbolift if they get out of hand. It is nice to think that they are currently spreading love and affection throughout the Klingon Empire.

In "The Gamesters of Triskelion," Kirk not only introduces Shahna to physical love (however far it went off-camera), but to his own love of freedom and the unknown. It is this which helps to save his life when Shahna refuses to kill him, even at the risk of her own life, for she now knows that killing for the pleasure of the Providers is wrong, as is living in enforced slavery. Her action is taken as an individual; she is not trying to force the Providers' hand, she is merely taking a personal stand saying, "No more killing." It is a poignant echo of Kirk's avowal of what makes a person civilized: "We will not kill . . . today." She has become a thriving, growing person, and we feel that the various races on Triskelion will grow with her. For once, Kirk's use of a woman to achieve his own ends has a beneficial effect beyond that of ending his current crisis.

It's also amusing to look back at Chekov's distress at the overtures of the thrall Tamoon. But the question remains—was her deep voice and mannish demeanor what distressed him? Or was it the fact that he might be on the verge of losing his virginity?

Love is used wrongly in "A Private Little War" by Nona, the Witch Woman. She attempts to coerce her husband Tyree to war on the village people, threatening to withhold her sexual favors if he does not comply. Later, she saves Kirk's life, but the potion used is one which reputedly causes the recipient to fall helplessly in love with the one administering it. Kirk seems to be strongly attracted to her, but manages to overcome the witchery without too much effort. It would have perhaps worked better on someone with a little less practice at disengaging himself from love affairs. All Kirk had to do was operate on his well-honed instincts. Nona, of course, meets a bad end, killed by the very village people to whom she was attempting to betray Tyree.

It's interesting to note that in Star Trek, the punishment for misuse of love is swift and sure. Those who twist and corrupt love for their own nefarious purposes usually die, or at least end up suffering the fate they most fear. Because love is such an important and integral part of the series' premise, it apparently must be graphically illustrated that utilizing love as a tool of evil leads to destruction and ruin.

Sargon and Thalassa in "Return to Tomorrow" shared a very great love indeed. It endured throughout not only thousands of years, but also the alienation of having their consciousnesses trapped in globes of force. It is a very touching moment when they are reunited in the physical bodies of Dr. Anne Mulhall and Captain Kirk. One suspects that their love is all that has kept them alive while the others of their race have died. (Henoch, of course, stayed alive because of his hatred and ambition, but it is somewhat confusing as to how he managed to conceal this from Sargon, for they were both telepaths.) Perhaps Sargon realized all along that they would never again be able to exist with humans, and so allowed the plans for android bodies to be built—and the opportunity for Henoch's treachery—to go on, knowing that it was the only way he could convince Thalassa to give up her dreams of once again living in a physical body. In any case, he displayed a great love for humanity—"his children"— by sacrificing his and Thalassa's chance to live in android bodies because he feared their presence would ultimately prove harmful to the humans.

In "By Any Other Name," the Kelvans (like Sylvia) are undone by the onrush of sensation and accompanying emotional response caused by their newly acquired human forms. Love, or at least one of the signs of burgeoning love, jealousy, is felt by Rojan when he realizes that Kirk has been making advances toward Kelinda. While Kelinda handles her newfound emotions more successfully than Sylvia did, she is still quite willing to have Kirk teach her more about them. Kirk convinces Rojan that his own jealousy and anger, Kelinda's confusion, and the emotional responses of the other Kelvans are just the beginning of a full range of emotional sensations that will shortly cause them to become human in feeling as well as form, and virtual aliens to their own people by the time they reach Kelva. The Kelvans agree to abandon their quest, and allow Kirk to return them to the planet where they were discovered, where, we can assume, they remain to this day, happily experiencing and enjoying life as loving, laughing, fighting, emotional humans.

In "The Omega Glory," we have perhaps the strongest statement in Star Trek of man's desire for and love of freedom. The Yangs have spent many years, and countless lives, fighting to reconquer their homeland from the Köhms. The enormous respect and veneration with which they treat the "sacred documents" is indicative of the feelings which Gene Roddenberry holds for the Constitution and our other testimonials to democracy. Like so many of us today, the Yangs really didn't understand the words, but they knew very well what the documents stood for: freedom.

In "Assignment: Earth," we meet (for the only time, sadly) Gary Seven, an Earthman raised by mysterious alien beings and returned to Earth to assist in its survival and development. In the course of his efforts to prevent a disastrous rocket launch, Seven is both aided and encumbered by his secretary, Roberta Lincoln. Roberta is somewhat scatterbrained, but lovely and lovable. Seven is quite singleminded about his mission, and although his intelligence and skills are such that Spock would envy them, he has a range of human emotions, including a wry and well-developed sense of humor. We see a growing affection between the two; and although it is unlikely that Seven would desire to be drawn into an affair with Roberta, they are two healthy young humans, and between such, anything can happen. Complicating such an event, however, is Seven's other assistant, Isis. Isis, a beautiful black cat, sometimes appears as a sultry, dark-haired beauty of a woman. She also seems quite possessive about Gary and disinclined to let Roberta get too close to him. We would have liked to have their relationship—*whatever* it was—explained (as would Roberta!), but as this "pilot" show wasn't picked up by the networks, our imaginations will have to supply the details of this rather strange, but very interesting, triangle. It's hardly the classic one!

*   *   *

Editor's Note: In a future article (on page 207), we will examine the various forms of love in Star Trek's third season, the animated series, and Star Trek: The Motion Picture; *as well as in some selected Star Trek fiction, fan fiction, and comic books. The relationships of the various crewmembers will also be examined.*

NEW LIFE, NEW CREATION: STAR TREK AS MODERN MYTH

by Barbara Devereaux

We often hear that religion and theology have no place in the world today; that they are outmoded concepts unneedful of comment or concern. But it is not often we hear such pronouncements from a Star Trek fan. Fans seem to have an abiding interest in matters spiritual; this, coupled with the ever-present fan skepticism and a willingness to examine and accept all viewpoints, makes for some interesting opinions. Of course, philosophy and psychology are not forgotten; adding them into the mixture serves to spice up the result.

In the following article, Barbara Devereaux takes a few cues from earlier Trek *articles (especially those of Joyce Tullock), then adds a number of interesting thoughts of her own. Chances are you won't agree with her opinions or conclusions, but we guarantee you won't be able to ignore them.*

Once upon a time there was a very small planet, far, far away at the edge of the galaxy. The planet teemed with life of all kinds. One kind was intelligent, but the intelligent life form was sad, for the planet was dying. Its crystal-clear streams had grown dark and its atmosphere was filled with poisonous gases. Wars raged across the face of the planet; they were fought for power and land, religion and honor, freedom and peace. Thousands died and the intelligent life form was very sad indeed. Yes, great was the suffering on the planet. There were many who were very poor and many who were very hungry. They longed for bread and freedom, dignity and peace; above all, they hungered for hope. They watched in fear as the terrible weapons of war grew bigger and bigger and they wondered if there would be a tomorrow.

Then, one day, toward the close of a bloody, fearful century (as time was reckoned on the planet), an idea appeared. It took the form of a simple story that was a wondrous tale of courage, love, and a future filled with hope. The story went straight to the heart of the sad little life form, and it held the story tight and would not let it go. The story grew and grew until it penetrated every corner of the planet. The story revealed to the life form something of the truth of its own condition. In doing so, the story became a myth and the myth was called Star Trek.

There were many myths half-buried in the life form's consciousness. They were valiant attempts to bring order to a chaotic reality, to find logic and reason in an absurd and lonely existence, to transcend the limits of failure and death. Over and over again, the new myth explored the old, probing it gently, prodding it for signs of life. At a time when the life form feared for its dying planet, its eyes were turned to accounts of the planet's creation, to the beginnings called Genesis.

The life form had scorned the stories for many years, thinking them unscientific, tales for children or the very naive. Finally, the wisest of the life forms realized that truth has many faces and that a myth is not fantasy: It is truth in another guise.

"Eden," whispered the new myth, and proceeded to explore paradise. There were a few problems. . . .

To begin with, the mythic hero called Kirk didn't really like the idea of paradise. As Joyce Tullock explained in some detail in her article "Bridging the Gap: The Promethian Star Trek" *(Best of Trek #3)*, Kirk believed that to succumb to the temptations of paradise was to become stagnant. To accept Eden was to give up a fight—and Kirk believed life was a fight. Eden was for sissies. As he demonstrated in "The Way to Eden," Kirk had very little interest in pursuing mythological worlds and very little patience with people who were intent on doing so. Utopias should be made, not discovered.

But the mythic hero called Spock reacted to the idea of Eden in quite a different way (a fact that bothered Kirk not in the least). In "The Way to Eden," it was Spock who was sympathetic to the idea of finding paradise—so much so that he offered to assist in the search. Again, in "The Apple," it is Spock who suggests that the people of Vaal might have a viable society and that in tampering with it, Kirk gave them only pain, suffering, and death. Kirk's reply to Spock's concern ("Is there anyone on this ship who looks even remotely like Satan?") is a less than honest answer to Spock's question.

In "This Side of Paradise," it is Spock who discovers love (or thinks he does) on Omnicron Ceti III. It takes a great deal to tear him away from paradise, and eventually it is only his loyalty to Kirk that keeps him from returning. Joyce Tullock pointed out that a happy Spock is a boring Spock; however, as we shall see, *Star Trek II: The Wrath of Khan* demonstrated that this statement is not entirely true. Nor did the rest of the crew walk out of paradise as Kirk suggests—the captain, with Spock's help, quite literally dragged them away.

Finally, in *Wrath of Khan*, it is Spock who welcomes the Genesis Device. There are dangers, as the third mythic hero, McCoy, points out. The power to create is also the power to destroy. And (as McCoy neglected to point out, but as Spock was no doubt aware) creatures have a way of rebelling against their creators. To be alive, they must be free. The need to choose comes early, the ability to choose wisely comes much later. But still and all, Spock is willing to take the risk.

The idea of paradise is part and parcel of Kirk's heritage, but time after time, he rejects it. Maybe he's afraid of it. Spock, on the other hand, may be attracted to the idea for the simple reason that there never was a paradise in Vulcan mythology. It is truly an alien concept to Spock, and one that is enormously appealing to him. He is certainly not threatened by a myth that seems to contradict those of his own planet; rather, he is convinced that differences in themselves are good and eventually will combine to create something new and marvelous.

More intriguing than the question of paradise is the question of the Creator of paradises, God. His existence is rarely mentioned explicitly, yet the question of the Almighty hovers over the *Enterprise* like the biblical cloud by day and pillar of fire by night. Joyce Tullock has suggested that the heroes of Star Trek have outgrown the need for a god or supreme being. God was a handy theory to have around to fill in the gaps in our scientific knowledge, but once those gaps are filled, the need for him ceased. There are a number of points that argue against Joyce's position.

In "Who Mourns for Adonais?" a rather pathetic, lonely Greek "god" demands that his "subjects" (the crew of the *Enterprise*) worship him. Kirk calmly replies that they find one God quite sufficient. Now that is a remarkable accomplishment. To be able to recognize a false god and refuse to worship him is an accomplishment indeed. The sad little life form must have blinked his eyes in astonishment as he watched this episode, for the road through his century was littered with rusty idols that included everything from half-mad dictators to designer jeans. And the life form had worshiped every one of them. Kirk is so adept at recognizing false gods that he can even spot them in his own life. It took him a few years to walk away from the shrine of his own ambition, but he finally managed to do it.

However, there is an even more remarkable lesson to be learned from the new myth. In "Bread and Circuses," Uhura corrects Spock's false assumption that people with an advanced ethic of total love and brotherhood would worship the "sun." Her face was radiant as she explained that they worshiped the Son of God; obviously she was very pleased with the idea. The others on the bridge were equally pleased. Joyce dismisses this reaction as naive, saying that if the crew would remember that the history of Christianity included crusades and inquisitions, they might be less than enthusiastic. They're not naive. Certainly Spock, who seems so well acquainted with Earth history, would not be foolish enough to blind himself to the crimes committed in the name of religion. Vulcans are not known in the galaxy for their foolishness. Did our heros chicken out and decide that no one can knock religion? Star Trek is not known for cowardice in the face of tough issues. So what precisely is the crew's reaction to the possibility of a new Christianity?

Check this out:

There were 430 people on board the *Enterprise* on its first voyage. They were of different sexes (two, at least), different nationalities, different races, different species, and presumably different religions. They lived and worked together twenty-four hours a day (or however they measured time) on one ship for five years. Even a ship the size of the *Enterprise* can feel a little cramped after five years, but, miracle of miracles, they all got along. Better than that, they liked each other. Better than that, they learned to love each other. As Deanna Rafferty observed in her article "*Star Trek: The Motion Picture*—A Year Later" (*Best of Trek #4*), the crewpersons are comfortable with each other and their work (except in *STTMP*—an aberration from the norm). And because they are at peace with each other, they are at peace with their God.

Think about it.

Enterprise crewpersons are a feisty lot. They don't tolerate each other because a Starfleet regulation tells them to or because they are threatened with eternal damnation if they don't. They really believe in all that stuff about brotherhood, and when they find each other, they find God. They don't care if he is called Father or Christ or Allah or The One or The All any more than they care if a person is black or white or Vulcan or human. It's such a simple idea you'd think someone would have thought of it three hundred years earlier. Naive? Hardly.

There are 430 crewpersons, and on the *Enterprise*, God wears 430 faces. He is not a threat, he is not a weapon—maybe he is not even a "he." He is not the exclusive property of any one religion. He doesn't take sides in wars or football games. And the crew is neither frightened nor embarrassed by his presence in whatever form it takes.

Let us consider two of the 430 faces of God aboard the *Enterprise*: the God of the old myth, Genesis (because the new myth so often explores it), and the God of Vulcan (just because it's interesting).

Unlike other creation myths that were popular at the time (such as the Babylonian creation myth), the Genesis account is the story of an orderly creation. Step by step, the planet is filled with living beings; God approves of his creations, including those made in his own image, man and woman. What does the story tell us of the Hebrew God? He is reasonable, logical, gentle; he is a lover of all that is good; he is a God who can be trusted, perhaps even loved. *Star Trek: The Motion Picture* observed that we all make God after our own image. Not quite. The God of Genesis is not an image of what humans are, but of what they long to be.

Now, what of Vulcan? If you were God, how would you reveal yourself to Vulcans? Perhaps you would appeal to what is best in them, what is closest to your own heart. In a human, it is love; in a Vulcan, logic. The God of Vulcan is the eternal mind; the Cosmic Mind that flows through, with, and in the universe. Gene Roddenberry tells us in the novelization of *STTMP* (a point regrettably omitted from the film) that Vulcans are natural mystics. They are blessed with a *seventh* sense, which is like a window opening to the All. They are completely united with the All and yet they retain their individual sense of identity. For humans it takes years of prayer, fasting, discipline, and (in western traditions) the gift of grace to achieve mystic union with the One. A Vulcan does it by closing his eyes.

Let us return to the Genesis myth, for it is more than a description of God; it also describes the fall of man and raises the question of his subsequent redemption. In the second generation account in Genesis, Adam and Eve eat of the fruit of knowledge of good and evil, and suddenly become ashamed of who they are. Humanity loses sight of the fact that it is made in God's image, becomes afraid of God, and feels impelled to hide from God. In betraying their relationship with God, humans do not simply discover evil; rather, they forget their own intrinsic goodness—they no longer understand the meaning of their own humanity.

Joyce is correct that "The Empath" is Star Trek's story of redemption, its passion play, but she is off-target in thinking that the episode was a refutation of religion. It was certainly a refutation of bad theology and the false images of God that abound in religion. McCoy does become a Christ-figure in the episode; he offers his life for the others because he knows they are worth dying for. McCoy, more than anyone, knows their weaknesses, and knows that weaknesses don't matter. Kirk and Spock matter simply because they are Kirk and Spock.

There are any number of theories that attempt to explain the crucifixion— the area is even a specialty within the study of theology called soteriology (from the Greek *soter*, meaning "savior"). One theory (refuted by "The Empath") suggests that man was so evil that God surely would have destroyed him, except that Christ died to make up for that evil and to hold back the avenging hand of God. According to that theory, Christ died in order to change the Father's mind about destroying us—his death affected the Father, not us. Was it God who needed changing? Was God really intending to do us all in with some mighty cosmic blast? Doubtful. Look back at the creation myth. It was not that man became evil, but that he lost sight of his own goodness. To be freed from sin is to be freed from illusions, freed from our false selves and restored to our real selves who are made in the image of God. Christ died for us because we are worth dying for. He believed in our goodness, but most of the time, we don't. It is this second idea of salvation that "The Empath" affirms.

The fact that McCoy is an unlikely Christ-figure is not that surprising. Christ-figures are always the unexpected, least-likely persons . . . poor, uneducated carpenters or simple country doctors.

Although McCoy is often surprising and unpredictable, it is Kirk who is the most complex part of the triad. Joyce tells us he is "ambitious, lusty, bored with orthodoxy." At times he is all those things, but he is also a great deal more. Hedonism should not be equated with heroism, and we all know Kirk is an honest-to-goodness hero. There is a Promethean streak in him; he is a man who defies God and enjoys it. It is not a small coal he wishes to snatch away while God isn't looking, it's immortality. Courageous though he is, there are many things that frighten him: He is afraid of the peace of Eden (too much time to think?), enduring relationships, growing old, death. As he finally admits in *Wrath of Khan*, Kirk has never really faced death—he has tricked death, cheated it, but he has never faced it. Understandably, he takes a certain pride in his own unique solution to the *Kobayashi Maru* simulation; he did, after all, receive a commendation for original thinking. It is the same pride he takes in his other conquests.

Promethean theology assumes that God has created humans with the desire for divinity (or immortality), but if they dare draw close to God, they are punished. It's the kind of double bind that literally drives people crazy. Apollo might play that game if he's in the mood, but the sadistic God of Promethean theology hardly fits a description of the God of Genesis—or the God of Vulcan. The irony lies in the fact that Kirk wishes to steal what is already his.

The Trappist monk Thomas Merton wrote that one problem with the Promethean mentality is its basic assumption about ownership and conquest. Kirk has always had to own the things he most cares about—*my* command, *my* crew, *my* ship, *my* friends, *my* life. No wonder he can't face death; he is a man who has never learned to let go. The Promethean man assumes that God won't let go either.

Another aspect of the Promethean mentality is its obstacle-course theory of life. Life is not to be lived, it is to be conquered. Life is a fight, and Kirk was a scrapper from the word go. He fought his way into and through the Academy, fought to get and keep command. In "Friendship—in the Balance" (*Best of Trek #4*), Joyce Tullock comments that things happen *to* McCoy, but that they happen *for* Kirk. It is an excellent distinction; however, we can't overlook the fact that Kirk is very liable to *make* things happen. He is fiercely competitive, and his quiet comment "I don't like to lose" in *Wrath of Khan* is one of the great understatements in Star Trek annals.

The feeling extends to Kirk's explorations in deep space. Space is indeed the final frontier, and it is a frontier that Kirk intends to conquer. The conquest won't be military, of course—the Federation is beyond that—but very often the spirit of conquest is still there. It is Kirk who is first to ignore the Prime Directive, and we all know the man's not afraid of a fight.

Then there are the women—during the three-year series they seemed to average about one a week. Just watching the man was exhausting. In fairness to Kirk, most of the women were first-class featherbrains. (Despite Beth Carlson's defense of Rand in *Best of Trek #4*, Rand's still a featherbrain. Even Starfleet can make a mistake. Edith Keeler and Miramanee were notable exceptions; but Edith was an extraordinary woman and Kirk's involvement with Miramanee was equally extraordinary.)

It wasn't until *Wrath of Khan* that women were portrayed as intelligent individuals, as exemplified by Carol Marcus. Apparently, Kirk acceded to her wishes and stayed away: It was what she wanted—or was it what she wanted Kirk to believe she wanted? She never told him about David, but (as Vonda McIntyre says in the novelization), Kirk never asked.

Did the Promethean spirit of conquest in Kirk also extend to his friends? No one could doubt Kirk's affection for Spock and McCoy. They are old and dear friends and he cares for them deeply. No one would argue the point that the Triad works. However, when *Wrath of Khan* begins, Spock and McCoy are orbiting Kirk like two worried satellites. In the novelization of *Wrath of Khan*, we are told that Spock considers himself a caretaker for the *Enterprise* until Kirk is ready to assume command. He holds the ship in trust for Kirk. We are never really told what McCoy is doing with himself and why he just happens to be available to tag along with Kirk on a training cruise; Kirk seems to take his availability for granted. Both Spock and McCoy are aware that Kirk is unhappy, and both believe that part of the solution lies in his retaking command of the *Enterprise.*

It is easy to admire Kirk's fighting spirit, but the problem with the obstacle-course theory of life is that it doesn't work with those things that are most important. How does one win the love of a son or keep score in friendship? How does one conquer death? Fortunately, when Kirk must finally face up to those problems, Spock is around to help.

And what of Spock and the Vulcan God? (Surely, there's a Vulcan name for God, but like Spock's first name, we probably couldn't pronounce it.)

As pointed out earlier, there never was a Vulcan Eden, nor was there a fall from grace. Vulcans are inextricably linked with the One; it is not a matter of faith, but fact—biological fact, and it is a bit of Vulcan biology that would not be discussed with a non-Vulcan. The strength of the link varies with individual Vulcans and depends both on innate talent and fidelity to Vulcan disciplines. Although half-human, Spock was no doubt recognized very early on as being exceptionally gifted, and, trying to compensate for his "bad blood," he pursued the disciplines with grim determination.

In "The Savage Curtain" we learn that there was a specific moment in Vulcan history when its leaders chose peace over war, nonviolence over violence. It was probably at the same time that they determined emotion was the source of violence and that the complete repression of emotion was the price of peace. Vulcans perceived logic as being the opposite of emotion, and thus logic became the highest Vulcan ideal.

From earliest childhood, Vulcan children are taught that any emotional display is in extremely bad taste. If they know any parental affection at all, it is not affection that can be demonstrated in emotional terms. If a human were raised in an atmosphere of such stringent emotional repression, he would wind up becoming a psychopath. When a Vulcan child is raised in that atmosphere, he winds up like Spock. The difference lies in the Vulcan link with the One.

Even before a Vulcan child can walk, talk, or calculate decimals, he is aware of his link with the cosmos. In the most profound sense, the child is never and can never be alone. Later, the link is extended to other Vulcans, and occasionally to members of other species, in the form of the mind meld.

When a Vulcan talks about logic, he is not talking about two plus two equaling four. He is talking about the order and reason that permeate the very substance of the universe. A Vulcan can feel the pulse of the universe and knows that when an argument or action is logical, it is in harmony with the universe itself.

Although on a superficial level there is some competition in nature (the survival of the fittest), on a deeper level, there is a strong degree of cooperation and interdependence. Even on a subatomic level no particle can exist by itself. Vulcans, who were several centuries ahead of humans in their understanding of physics, realized that they themselves were part of a larger ecosystem. The thought of doing violence either to each other or to the environment was appalling; Spock's well-known vegetarianism is typical of the Vulcan attitude toward nature. Vulcans understand that it is not necessary to harm or destroy nature in order to preserve their own lives; rather, their lives depend on the continued preservation of the environment. Vulcan logic makes the preservation of one's environment imperative.

Thus, logic is not "cold reason," as McCoy and other humans often label it. In fact, it is the source of gentleness and sensitivity that is so characteristic of Vulcans in general and Spock in particular.

In "Requiem for Methuselah," McCoy tells Spock that he will never really understand what Kirk is experiencing because the word "love" isn't written in Spock's book. As is often the case when humans are dealing with Vulcans, McCoy was half right. The word "love" does not exist in the Vulcan vocabulary, and there is nothing that carries an equivalent connotation of emotion, romance, and sentiment. There is, however, a corollary to the principle of logic to which Vulcans would never attach the human word "love," although a few stubborn humans might insist that the term is appropriate.

From a Vulcan perspective, to act for the good of another is to enable the other to achieve an attitude of peace and harmony in the universe. It would never occur to a Vulcan to ask for anything in return. "Requiem for Methuselah" is a good example of the Vulcan corollary:

In the episode Kirk has unknowingly fallen in love with the android Reena; he and Flint come to blows over who will possess her. Spock, suspecting that Reena is not human, warns them several times to desist, knowing that the fragile humanity awakened in her by Kirk's love may be shattered in the face of violence. Kirk angrily tells Spock he doesn't understand what it means to fight for a woman (implying that Spock doesn't understand what it means to love). Unable to choose between the men, Reena dies (it is, presumably, a kind of heart failure). Spock then explains to the stricken Flint and Kirk that "the joy of love made her human, its agony destroyed her." In his adaptation of the episode, James Blish had Spock add, "The hand of God was duplicated. A life was created. But then—you demanded ideal response—for which God still waits."

After their return to the *Enterprise* and McCoy's lecture, Spock (apparently wearied by the whole thing) does not answer McCoy. However, after McCoy leaves, Spock uses the mind meld to attempt to alleviate some of Kirk's pain and remorse.

The events of the episode speak for themselves. We add only that Spock's analysis of the situation and his subsequent actions are perfectly logical and are consistent with the Vulcan corollary.

It is this understanding of logic which explains why we could never really accept the Spock of *Kolinahr* in *Star Trek: The Motion Picture*. We were, of course, fascinated by Leonard Nimoy's performance, but like so much of that film, it was another aberration from the norm. Logic and cruelty are not complementary; rather, they are contradictory. We could understand that Spock had failed to achieve the full mastery of emotion that is the goal of *Kolinahr*, and that he was venting his pain and frustration on his human friends (although even that is not truly in character), but we cannot accept the idea that Spock could sustain that position for a very long period of time. When one subtracts warmth, compassion, and understanding from a Vulcan, the result is a character that is merely disagreeably human.

How does Vulcan theology compare with Kirk's Promethean theology? In every instance, Spock's theology is the exact opposite of Kirk's. Kirk, for instance, is busy trying to steal immortality from God. Moral problems of thievery aside, Spock has no reason to steal, for all that is the One already belongs to Spock. Vulcans have never known anything but union with the One; Spock does not need to own what God possesses, nor does he need to own the things that Kirk seems to need. Although Spock is intensely loyal to the *Enterprise* and its crew, he has no need to possess them; he enjoys command but is quite willing to return command to Kirk without a second thought; he has "no ego to bruise." Spock's sense of identity has never been sustained by possessions, but there is one notable exception to his freedom in this regard—Kirk. That's what comes of being half human. In any case, Spock even manages to turn the friendship around: "I am your friend. I have been and always shall be."

Kirk is also busy conquering space; Spock has no need to conquer what is already his. In early Star Trek episodes (especially in "Journey to Babel") we are given the impression that Spock is in Starfleet because he cannot find a home on either Earth or Vulcan. However, the Spock of *Wrath of Khan* has grown and changed. This is a Spock who is at home anywhere; the universe is his. Unlike Kirk, Spock has never had to conquer the stars, for in some sense, he was always part of them.

In *Wrath of Khan*, Spock reminds Kirk that there are always possibilities; he does not add (perhaps he doesn't need to) that not everything is possible. No one can be all things, do all things, accomplish all things. It is not possible for both the *Enterprise* and Spock to survive, therefore Spock does what is logical. In such a situation, Spock would no more attempt to hold on to his own life than he would try to hold on to command when logic insists that Kirk is the better choice. And by letting go of his life, he—paradoxically in human terms, logically in Vulcan terms—gains everything.

At the end of *Wrath of Khan*, Kirk is a different person. When he tells David he should be on the bridge (admittedly a half-hearted ploy to avoid talking to his son), it has a ring of truth. He *should* be there, but it is probably the first time in Kirk's life that he *doesn't* want to be on the bridge, *doesn't* want to be in command. He no longer needs it, no longer has that hungry abyss of ambition to fill. He no longer must prove himself to God, to himself, or to anyone else. Kirk is finally free to command the *Enterprise* simply because he is the best and—as Spock said—anything less is a waste of Kirk's gifts. If Kirk commands, fewer people will die.

Of course he feels younger. The weight of a lifetime of struggle has been lifted from his shoulders, and he discovers in laying it aside that there remains a sense of honest accomplishment. He is even forced to let go of his closest friend and discovers, again as Spock promised, that the friendship has not been lost.

Dying and rising, death and rebirth are the theme of *Wrath of Khan* (and we all await the resurrection in *Star Trek III*), and one might be tempted to say that the new myth has replaced the old and that humans, in creating life, have become gods. Has the Promethean Gap been bridged? Has man become divine?

Perhaps it is not that the old myth has been replaced, but that it has been restored. Humans have not become divine, but they are rediscovering their own humanity. Kirk is becoming almost as human as Spock was all along. As Joyce Tullock said, man is no longer "standing, hands in pockets, toes kicking the dirt." But neither is he a defiant teenager out to prove he's his own person, shaking his fist and yelling "I'll show you" at God. In the twenty-third century, man is, at last, evolving into an adult. He no longer needs to own the stars, nor is he hell-bent on destroying what he loves. The author of new life can look into the face of his own Creator and know that he belongs.

And what of our sad little life form who searches for truth in the ruins of a dying planet? He brushes the dust of centuries away from the old myth and takes a new look at it. It is an incomplete work, an unfinished creation. For the life form, the new myth is not an answer at all, but a question.

THE WRATH OF KHAN —REVIEW AND COMMENTARY

by Walter Irwin

Walter is the first to admit that in his enthusiasm at seeing Star Trek on the big screen, he might have gone a little overboard with his superlatives in a review of Star Trek: The Motion Picture *a few years back. Promising to control himself "this time," Walter sat down immediately after seeing* Wrath of Khan *and typed out the following review. Yes, the superlatives are there, but this time Walter offers no apologies. And we think you'll agree he doesn't need to.*

The most telling moment of *Star Trek II: The Wrath of Khan* occurs during the first encounter with the Khan-commandeered *Reliant*, when Admiral Kirk offhandedly comments to Lieutenant Saavik: "You've got to understand how things work on a starship."

Kirk obviously understands very well how things work on a starship, and even more obviously, he has learned from his mistakes prior to *Star Trek: The Motion Picture* and done his homework.

Producer Harve Bennett and director Nicholas Meyer obviously did their homework as well. *Wrath of Khan* stands ably on its own, providing a tangible link to the series and its theatrical predecessor. (Although *Wrath of Khan* owes little or nothing in the way of character development or continuity to *Star Trek: The Motion Picture*; one could infer that Paramount prefers to pretend that the first film does not exist.)

Wrath of Khan is a wonderful movie . . . and it is also true Star Trek. One can easily see on the screen the sheer pleasure and dedication of everyone involved with the project; an aura of camaraderie and fun that has been missing from Star Trek since the earliest episodes of the first season. Much of this credit can be given to producer Bennett and screenwriter Jack Sowards, whose expressed desire to return Star Trek to its "roots" resulted in an exciting, literate, and witty script. But the bulk of the film's success is due to Nicholas Meyer, whose straightforward and unpretentious direction of the material and characters restored Star Trek to its former greatness.

The story is a simple one. Exploring various planets for a site suitable for testing Dr. Carol Marcus's experimental Genesis Device, Captain Terrell and Commander Chekov of the USS *Reliant* mistakenly beam down to Ceti Alpha V. There they are captured by Khan Noonian Singh and his remaining followers and forced to cooperate in the capture of the *Reliant*. Khan then flies off with the dual purpose of taking the Genesis Device and destroying his old nemesis, James T. Kirk.

A straightforward, exciting, and suspenseful premise—just the kind of thing Star Trek, the television series, excelled in. But, as in the series, we get more than just an adventure story. Along the way, we are given insights into the problems and psychological quirks that are always part of us: aging, death, vengeance, and, as always, friendship. The moral lessons and observations are gently and subtly worked into the plot—in many instances, they advance the plot—and never do the characters lapse into preaching or stridency. Remaining true to their original series archetypes, Kirk, Spock, McCoy, et al. render their opinions and beliefs in an honest and caring fashion. As a result, none of the strain which could occasionally be seen in the actors' performances in *Star Trek: The Motion Picture* is visable here; they not only enjoy what they're doing, they believe in it as well.

William Shatner is particularly good. His performance in *Wrath of Khan* is his best work in quite some time. (The only thing he's done lately even approaching it in quality is the controversial "good old days" scene in the *T.J. Hooker* pilot.) Although the James T. Kirk we first see in *Wrath of Khan* is an unhappy and confused man, still he is confident and competent, still very much the Jim Kirk we remember and admire from the series. Shatner limns this dichotomy of character very well; we totally believe that Jim Kirk is a man at midlife crisis, but we also immediately know that it is a crisis of circumstance, not confidence.

Once back in the center seat (this time by invitation!), however, it is as if the intervening years have not passed for Jim Kirk—or William Shatner. The familiar poise, the unconscious leaning forward in the seat as if to control the mighty starship by his own will, the sharp-eyed glances around the bridge, missing nothing, and the crisp, confident tone of voice tell us immediately that James T. Kirk is once again captain of the *Enterprise*. Although he makes an early error in judgment, it is Kirk's experience—and his bravado, bluffing, and careful planning—that allows them to escape destruction and bring an end to Khan's machinations.

Leonard Nimoy's Spock is, as always, excellent. It is a tribute to his acting skills that Nimoy is able to breathe new life into a character he has so often publicly expressed a reluctance to portray again. This time, however, he had help from the script—in *Wrath of Khan* Spock is again that appealing mixture of aloofness and warmth that so endeared him to the television audience. Thanks to his encounter with V'Ger, Spock has "loosened up" considerably, now freely able to express friendship and affection for Kirk, even able to permit himself a small joke about his lack of ego. (And didn't we, who have so often seen examples of the stubborn Vulcan pride, get a good laugh out of that one!) One of the most enjoyable things about *Wrath of Khan* is that it once again gives us a Spock that we can *like* . . . and, it is plain to see, a Spock that Leonard Nimoy can like as well.

Throughout the film, Nimoy easily and rather casually offers us a Spock who is very much a man happy with his lot. Nimoy even looks younger, a result perhaps of his having come to grips with the fact that he, regardless of protestations and denials, will always *be* Spock—just as Spock has finally come to grips with *his* dual nature. In both instances, the pleasure of this acceptance shows up onscreen.

We also see a new side of Mr. Spock in *Wrath of Khan*—the patient and caring, almost fatherly, mentor to Lieutenant Saavik. It is obvious that Saavik is Spock's "baby," the young and inexperienced officer who he hopes will someday prove his successor. It is his mission not only to teach her to be a competent and superior Starfleet officer, but to give her the gift of comfortably working and living with humans—something which Spock had to learn on his own. Because of this guidance and advice Spock has given her, Saavik will experience far less of the rejection and pain he suffered; her life will therefore be that much easier, happier, and productive. Such concern may have been logical, to be sure, but we can plainly see the emotion involved as well—Spock *cares* about Saavik very much.

Perhaps it is this involvement with Saavik which has brought Spock to total realization of himself. (We know from Vonda McIntyre's novelization of the film that Spock has been looking after her for some years.) "Fatherhood" may have been the final ingredient in the recipe for this content Spock we see in *Wrath of Khan*. For perhaps the first time since the events on Omnicron Ceti III, Spock is a happy man.

Thus, his death is all the more devastating. When we hear Scotty tell Kirk that the energizer chamber is flooded with radiation and that the warp drive cannot be restored until someone can get in and fix it, we *know* what's going to happen. Spock knows it as well. And if he had not been so busy and so involved in the battle with Khan, Kirk would have known it too. He certainly had no trouble figuring out what happened when he saw Spock's empty chair. . . .

The death scene is masterful. Shots of the newly aborning planet are sharply intercut with shots of Kirk racing along the corridors to engineering; new life intercut with impending death, a victory negated by the death of a loved one. By the time Kirk arrives in engineering, we are as apprehensive as he, and as devastated when he is held back by McCoy and Scotty, and we hear Bones's solemn "He's *already* dead, Jim."

For a moment, we are shocked. *Already dead*? Has Spock died offscreen, cheating us—and Kirk—out of the farewell that would be so difficult to watch and yet impossible not to look at?

No. Spock still lived. Kirk knew that Spock would hang on, would *refuse* to die until he was at his side. We knew it as well. Even in his agony, Spock forced himself to his feet and straightened his uniform. Straightened his uniform! What else could tell us more about Spock? On the verge of death, Spock paid his respects—to his captain and his friend, to his heritage and his dignity, to Starfleet and all it had given him—with this simple gesture. It is a subtly played, heartbreaking moment, one which forces us to be all the more affected when Spock's will finally fails him and he collapses against the Plexiglas wall. It is a shame and very disturbing that many members of the audience do not understand the significance of this gesture and break into sudden laughter.

Both Shatner and Nimoy play the death scene very well. It would have been all too easy to let the moment slip into scene-wrenching histrionics, but both men obviously appreciated the import of what was happening. It is also satisfying that the moment was used to reiterate the previous scene, wherein Spock professed his friendship for Jim, as well as the "logical" premise that "the good of the many outweighs the good of the few—or the one." This is, perhaps, one of the strongest statements of what Star Trek is all about that has ever been made. It is hardly original, hardly new, but all the more powerful because both men so evidently believe it.

The only complaint that can be made about the death scene is that Dr. McCoy was left in the background. It would have been nice to see Spock tell his friends goodbye at the same time; after having shared so much together, they deserved to have that final moment together as well as an affirmation of the Friendship. But fate—and, it could well be, Spock—had other plans. We didn't need to see a closeup of Bones's face to know he was weeping . . . weeping for Spock . . . and for Kirk.

As in many of the television episodes, DeForest Kelley didn't have nearly enough to do in *Wrath of Khan*, but he was a constantly visible and comforting presence throughout the film. (This is especially gratifying when one considers that early reports about the movie had the good doctor playing little more than a cameo role. Obviously, as Bennett and Meyer delved deeper into the Star Trek mythos and history, they realized the importance of Leonard McCoy—and DeForest Kelley—to the integrity of the concept. The movie simply would not have worked without him.)

It is no disparagement of Kelly's talents to say that he could play McCoy in his sleep—the doctor is part and parcel of his own personality, much more so than Kirk is of Shatner's or Spock is of Nimoy's. Unlike the other two, who portray vital and physically active characters, Kelley must use his voice, a wry twist of that marvelously expressive face, or his deep, soulful eyes to delineate his characterization. The laconic doctor is not an easier character to play than Kirk or Spock, just a different sort. And it is a character that DeForest Kelley is very comfortable with.

In *Wrath of Khan*, McCoy, like Spock, is a man happy with his life and station. He has finally accepted that his life is in space, and he has—at long last—left his ghosts behind him. His biggest worry seems to be about Kirk (Spock shares this concern: as we've always known, he and the doctor are more alike than either of them would ever admit), and he speaks his piece on the subject so bluntly that Kirk admonishingly teases him, "Say what's on your mind." McCoy is right, of course, and his concern causes him to lapse into repetitive needling—something we've rarely seen him do, even with Spock, for his insight into the human psyche (especially Kirk's) is usually unfailing, and he knows just how far he can go without crossing the line. His failure to see that line in regard to Kirk tells us just how concerned he was.

Fortunately (as in *Star Trek: The Motion Picture*), Kelley has some of the best lines in the script—including a few that *aren't* in the script. Apparently, some of those caustic comments like "*We* will" are pure DeForest Kelley. And it is only right and proper that the one comment that sums up the fans' feelings for Mr. Spock is delivered by the emotional and humanistic Dr. McCoy: "He's not really dead, you know . . . not as long as we remember him."

Speaking of scripts, the first draft of *Wrath of Khan* prominently featured a young Vulcan *male* named Saavik! Fortunately, somewhere along the line the decision was made to perform a quick sex change, and we are now blessed with the fascinating character of an enticing female Saavik, as excellently performed by newcomer Kirstie Alley. It is amazing that one as young and inexperienced as Ms. Alley can more than hold her own with such veteran scene-stealers as Shatner and Kelley, but Kirstie does just that. Saavik is a rarity in continuing fiction; she emerges as a full-blown characterization—a young woman who is sure of herself and her goals, but (as the young Spock must have been) very confused as to just how she will achieve those goals in a Starfleet rampant with illogical, emotional humans.

But, as we have learned, Saavik is not a full-blooded Vulcan—she is half Romulan. As such, she is not a hybrid *per se*, as is Spock—she would most likely be able to interbreed with either human, Vulcan, or Romulan— but she would still have many problems resulting from her dual heritage. Perhaps even prejudices . . . Romulans are, after all, the "enemy," and it is entirely likely that there are more humans in the mode of Mr. Stiles ("Balance of Terror") in and about Starfleet who will make life very difficult for Lieutenant Saavik in the future. But they had better be careful, for Saavik is not the type to take much of anything from anyone . . . even an admiral.

Immediately the film begins, we see that Saavik is no cold, emotionless robot; her muttered "Damn" when the *Kobayaski Maru* is shown to be carrying passengers is quite eloquent and revealing. But she has studied Vulcan techniques and has a certain amount of control over her emotions. We get a definite feeling that Saavik understands some human emotions more than others—and shares them as well—and it is primarily the more subtle emotions which escape her. She can't fathom teasing; camaraderie (as opposed to loyalty) is something new to her; and she obviously believes in that old wives' tale that Vulcans never bluff. But she is trying and she is learning. And it's no shame, for there are many humans, in our time and in Star Trek's, who will never even make that effort to grasp and enjoy those subtler emotions.

Besides her skillful acting, Kirstie Alley brings a smoldering sensuality to Saavik that is quite intriguing. (Not since Uhura crooned her blues to the accompaniment of Spock's harp has any female in Star Trek been so sexy.) One senses that Saavik would be quite a passionate lover—and on the other hand, she would be a vicious and tenacious fighter. Any male member of Starfleet desirous of checking out the former would be well advised to consider the latter!

Physically, Alley is perfect for the part. Her body movements and expressions are perfect; she has that same seemingly rigid yet curiously supple control of her body that Nimoy has. (It has been reported that Alley pretended to be a Vulcan during her girlhood, and sought to copy Spock's bearing. The Second Generation of Star Trek has truly come into being!) But it is the small things she does that round out the character so well. For instance, after she has grabbed David when the Genesis Device is beamed out by Khan, she releases him with a quick, almost repelled motion. It is as if she cannot bear to touch a human—or as if she cannot bear to touch *anyone*. Many mysteries are yet to be revealed about the enticing and exciting Saavik.

It is comforting to see that Saavik, as the first new continuing character to be added to the cast in many years, fits so well into the Star Trek universe. Like our other old friends on the bridge, we know that Saavik will never bore us. We will always be learning something new about her, and in the grand Star Trek tradition, in the process we will learn something about ourselves as well. Kirstie Alley's Saavik is a welcome and enriching addition to the cast.

Merritt Butrick, on the other hand, still remains a bit of a cipher to us. Although Butrick has a "dream role"—James T. Kirk's only son—we actually learn very little about David Marcus during the course of the film. Confined to mouthing dire warnings against "the military" for the most part, Butrick has scant opportunity to display his acting talents. Even in the finely written "reunion" scene, Merritt seems rather stiff and uninvolved, but we cannot lay total blame at his feet. For an actor to give a convincing performance, he must be able to get into the skin of his character, and Merritt Butrick was seemingly as perplexed by David Marcus as were we. Butrick may be a fine actor (surely he would not have been cast in a film such as *Wrath of Khan* if he did not impress the producers with talent and presence), but we had little opportunity to see indications of it in *Wrath of Khan*. We would like to know much more about David Marcus; we would like to see more of Merritt Butrick. But will we?

The role of David Marcus was a patent attempt to introduce a new character and give him immediate identification and acceptance with the audience—after all, how could any true-blue Star Trek fan *not* like Captain Kirk's son? But just dropping him in on us (and worse, dropping him in on Kirk!) was unfair; it was especially unfair to do so and then not provide us with sufficient background on his character or sufficient screen time to get to know him. We care about David Marcus because he's Kirk's son, but we've yet to see any good reason why we should care about him as an individual. It is possible that David will return in the next film (although the lukewarm reception to his character and Butrick's "Luke Spencerish" good looks makes it questionable at best), and if he does, the producers owe it to us to provide him with a larger, more interesting and involving, and more revealing part. Butrick is a likable fellow, but as one fan said recently, "Nobody's in love with him yet."

Because of the lack of involvement we felt with David Marcus, it is indeed fortunate that the planned romantic interest between him and Saavik was dropped during editing. It would not have worked in any case—Saavik was quickly, but firmly, established as being totally career-oriented, independent, and a bit of a shy recluse. She is also trying very hard to be a Vulcan and a Starfleet officer. None of this is conducive to romance; even less so when we realize that the David Marcus we saw in the movie didn't so much as cast a lingering look in Saavik's direction. Such a relationship is possible, of course, but not for a very, very long time. And it would have to have more of a basis than the desire of Paramount's publicity department to spew out stories luridly describing the "love affair" between Kirk's son and Spock's "daughter." That kind of nonsense we can very well do without!

Bibi Besch turned in a fine performance as the brilliant, but earthy, Carol Marcus. Now this is a character we would feel comfortable with; she would fit right into the *Enterprise* gang. If you ask where, then think again how natural she looked standing at Dr. McCoy's side during the film's final scenes. It wouldn't be such a bad idea to have a new doctor come aboard to fill Christine Chapel's shoes and give Bones a hand . . . and it would be nice to see Jim Kirk have a wife. At least it would rescue him from the position of being the Starship Stud.

It is strange that Carol Marcus was immediately acceptable to us whereas David Marcus was not. True, Ms. Besch is an accomplished actress, but her role was not that much more challenging or lengthy than Butrick's. Perhaps we fans can more easily believe that Jim Kirk would have an affair with this lovely, brilliant, and strong-willed woman than we can believe that he would go for many years without even hearing that she had a son—his son. True, Jim Kirk is notorious for loving-and-leaving, but in his position as chief of Starfleet Operations, he would, at one time or another, at least have come across Carol's name, and the fact that she and her son were involved in Starfleet research, however secret it may have been. But then, maybe Kirk was too concerned with the consequences of "opening old wounds." As with his total disregard of events on the *Enterprise* in the years preceding *Star Trek: The Motion Picture*, he may have closed his mind totally to any news of the one "true love" of his life. If Carol Marcus was truly that woman, Bibi Besch makes us believe it. Her Carol is one strong lady, able to stand toe to toe with James T. Kirk, give as good as she gets, and yet still remain completely feminine and appealing. Hers is one of the most complete female characters we have seen in Star Trek, and that simple fact may be why she is so readily acceptable to us.

New faces drop in during the course of *Wrath of Khan*, but so do old ones. Did you happen to notice our old friend Winston Kyle serving aboard the *Reliant*? It was certainly a pleasure to see John Winston again (even if only in profile), and he looked fit and well. (Which should certainly make reports of his death, like Mark Twain's, greatly exaggerated.) Let's hope now-Commander Kyle will be transferred back to the *Enterprise* by the time of the next movie, and we will once again see him at the transporter post where he served so well for so many years.

Other old faces include the crew. Unfortunately, Nichelle Nichols and George Takei as Uhura and Sulu had little to do. Competent professionals that they are, however, they manage to instill their small parts with the same charm and likability they had in the original series, and we are pleased to see them again. It is a shame, however, that the editing of the film cut the small scene wherein we learn that Sulu has been given a captaincy of his own.

Walter Koenig's Chekov fared much better. As the hapless first officer of the *Reliant*, Koenig got a chance to stretch his acting muscles a bit. He was especially effective in the scenes where he realizes the cargo containers they discover are part of the *Botany Bay*, and his reluctance to kill Kirk at Khan's command is also very well done. It was nice to see that Chekov has advanced and matured well beyond the callow navigator stage, and his reassignment to another ship was a believable and natural outgrowth of series "reality."

James Doohan turned in his usual competent performance as Scotty, but his part seemed strangely truncated. Also, no mention was made in the film of the fact that young Cadet Peter Preston was Scotty's nephew, as was stated in the script and early publicity. This omission effectively destroyed much of the pathos designed to be felt when Peter died. (Because of this, Ike Eisenmann's role of Peter was cut as well, leaving him little more to do than smile chipmunkishly and lie around covered with gore.) This little bit of insight into Scotty's family and background would have made us care a little more about the chief engineer, and it is a shame that it was excised. (We did, however, get to hear the "in joke" about Doohan's heart attack. Small favors.)

Rounding out the characterizations were Paul Winfield as Captain Terrell, and Judson Scott as Khan's henchman Joachim.

Winfield, a very fine actor with a great diversity of past roles, managed to give us a Clark Terrell who was almost completely realized in only a very few scenes. Terrell is one of the career officers, the backbone of Starfleet, and commanding the *Reliant* is probably as far as he will ever rise in the ranks. And he knows this. The mission to discover the suitable site for the Genesis Experiment is typical of the type of missions Terrell is given; we can see his resignation in the slump of his shoulders and the bored expression on his face. But Terrell has not allowed his ship to slacken; the bridge of the *Reliant* is clean and efficient, he and his men are competent at their posts, and Terrell still has that spark of independence that makes for a good starship commander. And his loyalty is without question—he kills himself rather than destroy an admiral, a man he has never even met! Winfield acted Clark Terrell with such skill and depth that one can only feel that he is a Star Trek fan himself. So it is all the more of a shame that his character did not survive the film, for he would have made a fine addition to the continuing cast . . . perhaps as that security chief/weapons officer who has always been so sorely needed to round out the bridge crew.

By the evidence, we can guess that Judson Scott is *not* a Star Trek fan. It was reported that he was unsatisfied with what remained of his role after the final cut, and asked that his name be removed from the credits. If this was the case, it was an unfortunate mistake, for not only has *Star Trek: The Wrath of Khan* made quite a bit of money worldwide (it never hurts an actor to be associated with a blockbuster movie), but his performance is very effective. As the rational Joachim, Scott more than holds his own against the flashy histrionics of Ricardo Montalban's Khan. Scott deserves to go on to bigger and better parts, but by disassociating himself from *Wrath of Khan*, he has made it more difficult for himself to do so. A shame.

And so to Khan. Khan Noonian Singh. Although he appeared in only one episode of the original series, he has lived fondly in our memories for these many years. It was a masterstroke on the part of the producers to bring him back as the villain in this film; not only is he an intriguing character, but he is perhaps the best example of the "anti-Kirk." Like our captain, Khan is powerful, intelligent, charming, and single-minded to the point of obsession, but unlike Kirk, Khan bends his powers toward personal gain and aggrandizement. Khan feels that the good of the one is more important than the good of the many. In his rage and grief, he becomes like unto the Satan of "Paradise Lost"; a man in battle with the forces of good, a man obsessed with destroying the individual he sees as the one thing blocking him from fulfilling his destiny. "He tasks me . . . he tasks me, and I shall have him!"

It is apparent that Ricardo Montalban, after so many years of smiling his way through episodes of *Fantasy Island* and shilling Cordobas, had the time of his life playing Khan again. In a performance that is overblown, but still splendidly controlled and built, Montalban rivets our attention each time he appears onscreen. So intense is Montalban's Khan that the viewer cannot help but become involved in his overwhelming hatred for Kirk and his lust for vengeance. Each of us felt a mixture of repulsion and admiration for Khan in "Space Seed"; he was so attractive and charming, so powerful and noble. But in *Wrath of Khan*, the charm is gone, the nobility besmirched. Khan is no longer attractive in the least, on the contrary, he has become a nightmarish figure of terror and death. Following the classical pattern, the once-noble figure has been twisted by forces beyond his control, warped by his own inner weaknesses. Montalban understood this, and he provides us with a Khan radically different from the one in "Space Seed." It is a brilliant example of the maturation—or, more accurately, the disintegration—of a character.

But, repugnant as he is, Khan is just plain old fun to watch. Montalban understood this as well—he provides us with an old-time villain, the kind we can gleefully boo and hiss; the kind of villain who chews the scenery unmercifully while mouthing poetry and thinly veiled threats. It has been many years since such an enjoyable nemesis appeared to be a thorn in Kirk's side, and the fact that we know and once appreciated the "superior mind" that has become so twisted by hatred makes him all the more interesting and exciting to watch. Montalban reportedly obtained a tape of "Space Seed" and watched it several times to reimmerse himself in the role of Khan, and his efforts were more than worth it.

Apparently someone at Paramount decided to bring *Star Trek II: The Wrath of Khan* into theaters at a running time of exactly one hour and forty-five minutes, come hell or high water. In several instances (such as those mentioned above) the film was harmed by this decision. It is never quite clear when David Marcus learns that Kirk is his father; it is also not clear exactly when Khan attacks Regulus I. It is always an advantage for a film to move quickly, but a few more minutes spent on characterization and exposition would have made *Wrath of Khan* a better movie.

Too, there are several discrepancies in the film. We wonder how Terrell and Chekov, trained and experienced spacegoers, can make the almost unbelievable mistake of landing on the wrong planet; even if that planet had shifted *exactly* into the orbit of Alpha Ceti VI, they should have noticed the absence of a planet in the system. This is sloppy scripting—coincidence and contrivance of the worst kind—and to make matters worse, there was not even the most flimsy or glib explanation given for the error.

The special effects in *Wrath of Khan* have been disparaged in some quarters, but this reviewer found them to be more than adequate, and in many instances very effective and realistic. Also helping the film were the varied types of special effects used. The computer animation of the Genesis Tape was particularly nice; it looked like something we would really see on a starship. Other effects, such as the creation of the Genesis Planet and the Mutara Nebula, combined animation, models, and "cloud tank" mattes to form more than adequate backgrounds.

The *Reliant* was lovely to see. Combining the best of the *Enterprise*'s classic features into an entirely new configuration, it was sleek and compact, a perfect example of the various kinds of starships the Federation would utilize. It was totally familiar, but strange at the same time, with its bright rear lighting, its unorthodox placement of engineering and phasers; it was a canny combination of the known and the unknown, serving perfectly as a vessel to convey the unpredictable Khan.

Effects reprised from the series and the first movie were phasers, photon torpedos, and the transporter. Yet, each of these effects was slightly different, again giving us a feeling of time having passed, of advances and changes being made. The new transporter effect, which allowed the characters to move and speak while in the midst of beaming, is a little hard to get used to, but it allows for more freedom of action and gets rid of the distracting "freezing" of the characters that often marred the series. The gradual disintegration of Terrell when he used his phaser on himself was far more frightening than the flare effect used in the series; and the effect of the large ship's phasers slicing into the hulls of the ships was also exciting and realistic-looking. (The destruction of the *Reliant*'s nacelle and the resulting shower of debris, electric arcs, and static charges was much more effective than the cheap "sparklers" or blaze of animation utilized in the original episodes.) The photon torpedos still look a bit "cartoony," but it was a nice touch to see that one of them could miss its target and fly on by to expend its energy elsewhere.

The engine room, a standing set from the first film, was made more interesting by the addition of several more control consoles and the deadly radiation chamber. The effect of the radiation from the warp-drive bypass upon Spock was also quite good; it was accomplished by the use of simple lighting and a wind machine.

New to *Wrath of Khan* was the torpedo room, a redress of the docking port from *Star Trek: The Motion Picture*. The tracking shot along the torpedo launching track as the crewmen lifted away the protective grids and the sleek, deadly torpedo was lowered into place was one of the most exciting of the film. It gave an immediacy to the proceedings that no amount of shots of fingers pressing buttons or flashing lights could have.

The *Enterprise*, the drydock, and the redressed and inverted space station were all miniatures from *Star Trek: The Motion Picture*, but each was used to good effect in this film. Several shots of the *Enterprise* in Earth orbit and in drydock were stock footage, but this too was used effectively and sparingly. The "warp effect" was changed somewhat; the "boom" when the ship entered warp space was eliminated, and we saw no shots of the ship leaving warp space; but the addition of the effect to give an impression of constant acceleration when the ship was escaping the Mutara Nebula was most welcome, and served to heighten relief at the narrow escape. Also reinstalled in *Wrath of Khan* was the dull roar the mighty warp engines make as the ship moves through space. Used only in the earliest episodes, the noise was forgotten very quickly; the official explanation was that there is no noise in space, but in actuality, the dubbing in of the roar was an additional expense of time and money, one of the many small touches dropped as the series progressed and the expected high ratings failed to appear, causing the network and Desilu to spend less money on each episode. Having that roar in the background as the *Enterprise* makes a flyby enhances the "reality" of the scene and increases our enjoyment.

The battle of the two starships was exciting and superbly choreographed. The only complaint that can be made about these scenes is that they sometimes looked a bit too two-dimensional, but every effort was made to avoid (or at least disguise) this, including front-projected lighting effects within the nebula and the use of a constant perspective. It was not a problem at all when the ships were seen in orbit or passing through space; such shots were also enhanced by the new, "deeper" starfields.

The only disappointing effects shot in the film were those inside the Genesis Cave. It is difficult to understand why these failed; they are simple matte shots, the kind used with great success for many years. Perhaps too much was attempted in too little time; no one part of the cave (with the exception of the rocky cave entrance where Kirk and party camped) was clearly visible, and the long shots were murky, giving little indication of the vastness we were told about. A potentially fine effect, the one cavern wall covered with cascading waterfalls, was almost completely lost because of lack of color definition and contrast. It is probably not the fault of the effects people—they did a fine job on the rest of the film. But the Genesis Cave was so important to the plot, a tangible demonstration of the power of the Genesis Device, that more time should have been spent showing it to us.

Mention the new uniforms to a Star Trek fan and you are likely to find yourself in an argument. Oh, not about whether or not they look good, but what they may symbolize to that fan. The uniforms are soundly condemned by many as being "too militaristic." Well, Starfleet, like it or not, *is* the military. However benign and altruistic its mission, Starfleet is a peace-keeping and exploratory force with military chain of command and traditions. To complain that the uniforms worn by members of this force are "militaristic" is silly—it's like complaining that William Shatner's uniform in *T.J. Hooker* makes him look too much like a cop. Those who complain that the uniforms are not within the spirit and intent of the original series are wrong. As Carol Marcus said, "Starfleet's kept the peace for a hundred years." It is ridiculous to assume that any organization could operate so effectively if it denied its military backgrounds and mission. For Starfleet or any member of it to pretend that it is not a military organization—or for us to pretend that it is not—would be totally untrue and a great disservice to the enduring concept so carefully and lovingly crafted by Gene Roddenberry and Gene L. Coon so many years ago. And what does it matter anyway? We like Kirk, Spock, McCoy, and the rest regardless of what they're wearing—we like them for what they *are*, not for what they look like. Contrary to legend (and contrary to what many fans seem to think), clothes do *not* make the man.

Whatever connotations you choose to place on the cut of the cloth, it cannot be denied that the new uniforms are very effective. The primary rust-brown color does not clash with the starship interiors (and certainly does not blend into the background like the uniforms worn in *Star Trek: The Motion Picture*). Too, the design is flattering to almost every figure. A bit of variety is seen in the cut of various uniforms: the nifty landing-party jackets, the "pullovers" worn by the cadets and supporting personnel, and the revamped and more colorful engineering and security armor. Made from natural materials and having just enough differentiation in design and accouterments, the uniforms work splendidly as something we can definitely "believe" in.

Other clothing worn in the film worked quite well, although we got to see all too little of it. Kirk's and McCoy's suits looked comfortable and expensive, just the kind of thing two mature and unself-conscious senior officers would wear when off duty. Saavik's loungewear was a nice touch: the functional but feminine cut perfectly reflects her personality. And it was nice to see that Spock still owns and wears his traditional Vulcan robes. These were the same ones that appeared in the first movie, but he certainly looked more comfortable in them this time! Perhaps in the next film we'll get a look at the off-duty wear of some of the supporting characters. What do you want to bet that Sulu's favorite clothing is more than a little reminiscent of an eighteenth-century swashbuckler?

Take them as you will—the uniforms, the off-duty clothing, the weaponry, the sets—*everything* in *Wrath of Khan* has a purpose. Nicholas Meyer was speaking of the plot when he said that "this film is of a piece," but everything in *Wrath of Khan* is carefully constructed to return Star Trek to its origins; to recapture the spirit of the glory days of the first seasons, but yet with a new freshness and vitality. It worked, but it was mostly the characterizations that made it work. Each and every person in *Wrath of Khan*—yes, even including Khan himself—had a mission, a purpose, a sense of worth. We saw, for the first time in many years, men and women doing something because they believed in it, because it was *right*.

As always, the success or failure of a Star Trek tale rests on Kirk and Spock. It is inescapable; they are the movers and shakers and how they act and react determines the course of the story. Fortunately, Spock and Kirk were both quite different men in *Wrath of Khan* than they were in the first movie. They were both forceful and capable, Spock in particular. A few years ago, it would have been inconceivable to have Spock commanding a training cruise—almost as inconceivable as it would have been to have Jim Kirk admit, confront, and accept the fact of his own mortality. The solid, reassuring presence of both men added immeasurably to the film. Not for many years have we seen Spock, Kirk, and McCoy so sure of themselves, so at home on the bridge and with each other. This is why the movie succeeds—this is why fans are proclaiming it as "true Star Trek." Everything we love and admire about the series was included and enhanced in *Wrath of Khan*; everything we cherish about the characters was expanded and reaffirmed. Harve Bennett, Nicholas Meyer, and the cast and crew achieved something beyond their wildest plans and imaginings—and, to be honest, beyond ours as well: *Star Trek II: The Wrath of Khan* is an excellent movie, and more important, it is excellent Star Trek. It is an honor to Gene Roddenberry that the series he created has finally become such a rich and alive entity that it can go on without him; it can reach new heights and achieve new growth without his personal guidance. Star Trek has achieved a life of its own, and we *know* that no one is more pleased than Gene Roddenberry!

But what of the future, now that Star Trek has reached this landmark? What next? And the question that everyone wants answered: What is going to happen to Spock? He will return, that much is certain. It was practically flashed on the screen in the mode of the James Bond films—"This is the end of *The Wrath of Khan*, but Spock will return in . . ." And Kirk's musings, the long, lingering, loving scenes of new life on the Genesis Planet, and McCoy's unintentionally prophetic statements practically chart out the course of the next movie. (Which will, according to Paramount, be somewhat unsubtly titled *In Search of Spock*.)

All of the elements for a logical revival of Spock were carefully planted *throughout* the movie; we can only hope that they will be brought into play and were not just red herrings. Such continuity would be pleasing, for we have been told that an entire series of Star Trek movies is planned, each one to lead logically and chronologically into the next. It is only by establishing such continuity and credibility that Paramount can ever hope to bring in the "new generation" of Star Trek characters and events. If this is done with care and sensitivity, if it is done within the spirit and framework of the original concept, and if it is done with consideration and appreciation for those whose efforts have made Star Trek such an enduring success, then, and only then, will we fans accept changes and departures and not be angry at the "loss" of our beloved series regulars. Instead, we will have the pleasure of watching them move on to other things, other careers, and look back on their tenure on Star Trek fondly, without any rancor or bitterness to spoil our memories.

Thank you, Harve Bennett, Nicholas Meyer, and the production crew, for a great movie! Thank you, Gene Roddenberry, for getting it all started! Goodbye, Spock—for a little while. Welcome, Saavik—stay awhile. And to Kirk, McCoy, Scotty, Sulu, Uhura, Chekov, and Kyle—good to have you back home, guys!

SPOCK RESURRECTUS—OR, NOW THAT *THEY'VE* KILLED HIM, HOW DO *WE* GET HIM BACK?

by Pat Mooney

Pat Mooney (better known as "Wheelchair") has been a devout Star Trek *fan from Day One—yet he had never written a word about the series until a series of discussions with Walter and G.B. bestirred him to do so. The result is the article you are about to read, and we think it's one of the finest first efforts we've ever seen. And we say that even though Pat has craftily taken all of our logical, rational and carefully wrought arguments and ripped them to shreds. Oh, well. . . .*

To paraphrase the ancient dirge, "The Vulcan is dead! Long live the Vulcan!" For those of us who hold the Star Trek mythos just a little bit closer to our hearts than we would like to admit, the death of Mr. Spock is hard to accept. And if the sun shone a little bit dimmer as we left the theaters, well, we have put that behind us and are eagerly looking forward to *Star Trek III*, with its working title of *In Search of Spock*. For apparently Spock *will* return, the only questions being, "How?" and "When?" Almost as if in answer to these questions, Kirk quotes Spock in *Wrath of Khan*: "There are always . . . possibilities." Naturally, the most likely possibility involves the use of the Genesis Effect (the script made that more obvious than necessary at the end of *Wrath of Khan*), but there are several other methods by which Mr. Spock might be revived, each consistent with previous episodes and the Star Trek universe. But each of these methods (including Genesis) also has problems.

First, we must uncategorically reject the idea of Spock's existing on a higher plane of consciousness. Fans will not stand for the illogic of Mr. Spock shimmering into view during a crisis situation and telling Captain Kirk to trust the Force and let his feelings go. That's fine and quite effective within the universe for which it was created, but it won't hold up in Star Trek's "reality." The less said about this "possibility" the better.

Having gotten that out of the way, let's consider the possibility of utilizing time travel as a means of preventing Spock from ever dying and thus neatly avoiding the question of how to bring him back.

The *Enterprise* crew have time-hopped several times, the most famous instance being the events in "City on the Edge of Forever." So we can have dreams about Captain Kirk determinedly leading a party of volunteers through the Guardian of Forever to arrive, say, on the bridge of the *Reliant* with phasers blasting.

This won't do, however. Not only is it out of character for Kirk, but there is no guarantee that such a commando raid would ever reach its target. Getting to the Time Portal itself is no problem, but the Guardian was made to offer its destinations at a given rate, which, in terms of the original episode, was "Perhaps a month, a week if we are fortunate." That's just not precise enough for the purpose at hand: A week too soon and Captain Terrell is still in command of a calm ship; a week too late, and there's no *Reliant* to land on. And all of those calculations assume the bridge of the *Reliant* is even offered as a potential destination by the Guardian!

In an earlier episode, "Tomorrow Is Yesterday," the *Enterprise* inadvertently went back in time because of a "slingshot effect." Even if Kirk and Scotty decided to utilize a handy star and duplicate this effect (as they did on Starfleet orders in "Assignment: Earth"), the *Enterprise* would then find itself in a time where it existed in two places at once. This is theoretically impossible, although the paradox was ignored in the animated episode "Yesteryear," in which Spock goes back into Vulcan's recent past to save his own life when a boy. (One rationale for this is that the adult Spock could coexist with his younger self only because he was trying to correct a flaw in time lines which he and the other members of the landing party knew to have occurred *since* their arrival on the Guardian's planet—perhaps even *because* of that arrival.)

Of course, the *Enterprise* could avoid the problem of being in two places at one time by simply returning to the time of the Eugenics Wars, where a couple of well-placed photon torpedos would remove the threat of the *Botany Bay* before she even reached deep space.

The main problem with such a long-range jaunt is that old bugaboo about the effects of time travel increasing geometrically the farther back ones goes. Beyond saving Spock's life, what effects would destroying the *Botany Bay* in the past have on the present as the crew of the *Enterprise* knows it? In fact, the ripple effect of Spock's death begins with that death, and any attempt to alter the time line created by it will have some effect—perhaps minor, perhaps major.

Also, what if the past cannot actually be changed? An action that saves Spock from death in the reactor room might set in motion a chain of events that would lead to his death on the bridge. Whether or not the past can actually be changed is a question which has never been satisfactorily answered on Star Trek: Do the actions of Gary Seven and the personnel of the *Enterprise* in "Assignment: Earth" fulfill history or change it? Could Dr. McCoy have affected the past in "City" if Spock and Kirk had not been present to set things right?

In any case, we can assume that Kirk would reject all time-travel options to save Spock as being too risky (although not without much soul-searching). Neither would the Federation order or authorize such a gamble; Spock was a valuable asset, but not an irreplaceable one. Besides, the two instances we can draw on as authorized time missions ("Assignment: Earth" and "Yesteryear") were for observation purposes only, and even then both almost led to disruption of the time flow known to the men and women of the *Enterprise*.

The second possibility to resurrect Spock is cloning. Cloning, though in reality little more than a primitive form of Genesis, has the added dramatic bonus of irony: The same forbidden science that gave us Khan would return Spock to us.

To clone, all one needs is the method and a tissue sample with which to begin the cloning process. Presumably, the procedural information would be an almost everyday facet of Federation science (any science which can construct Genesis has probably long since perfected cloning; it is likely that most of the Federation's food animals are cloned, for example), but obtaining permission from the Federation to clone a living being might prove difficult, as the horrors of the Eugenics Wars would have instilled stringent taboos. Tissue samples of Spock would probably be available in a number of places; if nothing else, McCoy would have taken them when he had to operate on Sarek and cross-matched Spock's blood in "Journey to Babel." If no one at the Federation can or will oversee the process, Kirk and company could return to Phylos to seek the expertise of Dr. Keniclius 5 and his giant Spock clone, "The Infinite Vulcan." These two had solved the thorniest problem of cloning—duplication of the subject's memory.

For without this methodology, a Spock clone—any clone—would not be unlike the Spock body in "Spock's Brain," the difference being that instead of a body with no brain, a cloned Spock would have a body possessing a brain with nothing in it. Were Spock regenerated in this way, he would have to be reeducated *à la* Uhura in "The Changeling." This is certainly feasible, and would doubtless delight Dr. McCoy, but the cloned Spock, no matter how skillfully retaught, would miss out on the millions of nuances a sentient being picks up just by living day to day. (Unlike Uhura, whose original personality remained beneath Nomad's overlaid "erasure"; as she regained factual knowledge, her prelearned experience and nuances returned, restoring her to normalcy.)

A Spock clone, however, would have no prelearned anything on which to draw. For example, McCoy could and would tell the new Spock that Kirk and McCoy are his best friends. Spock would accept this—he'd have no reason to doubt it—but he would have no memory of the friendship, no depth of shared experiences, the kind of thing that develops only with the passage of time. Even the knowledge the clone received might be colored by the memory of the teacher.

Because of the unique hybrid nature of Mr. Spock, another problem comes to mind. Let's assume that Dr. McCoy tried to train the Spock clone. Ultimately, McCoy would come to a point—probably rather quickly—where he would realize that for this new Spock to have any chance to resemble the original, he must be trained on Vulcan to have full exposure of the Vulcan Way. As the clone received this Vulcan training, however, he would assimilate it as an adult rather than in the ongoing, maturing way a growing child receives his education. Thus, the Spock who would eventually return to Starfleet would in effect have been raised in an environment "different" from the original and would necessarily be a different person.

In fact, the entire cloning procedure might backfire because of this reeducation. Remember, the original Mr. Spock did indeed have emotions. His lifelong struggle was to control them, to suppress them in favor of the logical intellect. Spock's clone would have been told of these emotions, but deprived of the influence of a human mother through years of normal growth, he would feel them in only the most clinical sense, if at all. As he trained on Vulcan, it might thus be easier for the Spock clone to attain *Kolinahr,* in which case he would logically not wish to return to the *Enterprise.*

Obviously, then, cloning is unacceptable because it gives us the form but not the substance of Mr. Spock. An individual is the sum of his entire life—his knowledge, experiences, environment—and, more important, the simple action of day-to-day living. Such cannot be duplicated, even in the abstract. Even the loss of childhood would profoundly alter a clone's personality from that of the original; to lose an entire lifetime would produce a vastly different being. It is *Spock* we care about—the proverbial reasonable facsimile will not do.

However, there *is* just such a reasonable facsimile available; he exists in the universe of "Mirror, Mirror." Spock-M, we'll call him, is a true Mr. Spock. He is half human, half Vulcan, and as such would have been subject to the normal span of growing up in two cultures where neither really accepted him. In short, all of the developmental deficiencies of a Spock clone would not exist because Spock-M would have grown into what he is—nurtured rather than hatched, as it were.

Spock-M would still miss the brass ring in a crucial sense if he were tapped as a replacement for our Spock: There would be no relationship between him and his new captain, despite the fact that at least some of the fireworks between him and McCoy would soon develop. Spock-M might even be incapable of developing the ties of friendship, since the culture from which he came did not encourage friendship and trust. In any case, because of the vast differences in the societies of the two universes, Spock-M would be quite unlike our Mr. Spock, however similar their childhood struggles might have been. For example, you'll recall Spock-M didn't seem to have any moral objections to the Empire, he just felt it illogical to preserve a system doomed to self-destruct. It is very doubtful that Spock-M could fit into our scheme of things.

But the most important reason Spock-M could not be considered as a replacement for our Mr. Spock is also the simplest: Why would he want to be a replacement? This is, after all, not his universe. Between the time we last saw him and the proposed visit by the *Enterprise* to sign him as Spock's replacement, he may have effected enough change to make his universe a better place for his purposes. Even if he hasn't, why would he want to change universes to become a surrogate friend to a man he had met only briefly? Logically, he would not, and therefore is unavailable to replace Spock.

We cannot believe that Jim Kirk would accept—or even want—such a surrogate, be it Spock-M, clone, or something else. To Kirk and McCoy, Spock was a friend, a very special individual, so why should they wish to replace him? But they might, however, try very hard to *revive* him. . . .

Which finally brings us to Genesis—which is probably where those who are behind Star Trek wanted us in the first place.

Sherlock Holmes, another beloved fictional character who would not die, might well have been speaking of Genesis when he said, "When you have eliminated the impossible, whatever remains, however improbable, must be the truth." That truth is "improbable" because, in terms of the film itself and in Vonda McIntyre's excellent novelization of *Wrath of Khan*, the detonation of the Genesis Device by Khan *cannot* result in the rebirth of Mr. Spock. That isn't to say we cannot use Genesis, but we aren't that far along yet.

When we last saw Mr. Spock, he had just saved the *Enterprise* from the effects of the expanding Genesis Wave. In doing this, however, he absorbed lethal doses of radiation from the ship's warp engines and died following one of the most moving farewells possible. Presumably, he was placed in the photon torpedo casing—as effective a coffin as any—and launched into space, finally coming to rest on the newly created Genesis World.

Here's where the problems arise. At this point, his body *must* be lifeless—even on a cellular level. If it is not—if, say, Mr. Spock had slowed his bodily processes to their absolute minimum—the Gensis Wave will destroy that living matter in favor of its preprogrammed matrix. At the beginning of the film, Dr. Carol Marcus is insistent that not even proto-life can exist on the test world, so all-consuming is the effect of Genesis. And even if the body is lifeless, the Genesis Wave will touch the casing and convert the inanimate matter both inside and out into fuel for its matrix. There might thus be a tree or a rock with pointed ears somewhere on the planet (!), but no trace of Spock's body should remain.

It is marginally possible that the Genesis effect had spent itself by the time the burial capsule made planetfall. Carol Marcus says that the Phase II (the Genesis Cave) matrix took a day to develop, but that vegetation and other life forms took longer, though still at an accelerated rate. This indicates that Genesis is an ongoing effect which continues at least until its program is fulfilled. One must assume that the larger the device, the longer the effect will continue, and the device set off by Khan was designed to terraform a world. Such an extensive program might take weeks, or even longer, to execute.

Nor is there any basis to assume that Mr. Spock will be reborn on the planet's surface as part of the Genesis process. There would have been no reason for any genetic information relevant to Spock to have been programmed into the test, nor any need to do so. Spock was, after all, completely healthy until three minutes before detonation, let alone matrix programming.

In fact, we don't have any idea what the programming was—or, ominously, what it might have become. Suppose Khan cracked the code for the matrix—considering his origin, he must have had more than a passing interest in eugenics—and reprogrammed it to suit his own ends? Presumably those ends would not have included Mr. Spock. Until we have evidence to the contrary, however, we must assume that Khan did not have either the time or the opportunity to reprogram the Genesis Device.

Since we were shown the torpedo casing resting undisturbed on the planet's surface, we must accept that there is a body inside, albeit one ravaged by radiation poisoning. Once presented with that coffin, we can grant an exception to the cold logic of Genesis and postulate that the interaction of the radiation in Spock's body with the brand-new kind of radiation created by and for Genesis caused the body to be preserved intact and with all damage repaired, but still inert and lifeless.

But Genesis provides an even simpler way of restoring Spock that does not require any stretch of logic. Nothing could be simpler than for Dr. Marcus to study Spock's genetic code and devise a small, completely insulated matrix dedicated solely to restoring the Vulcan. Spock's genetic code is probably on file in any number of places; a captain of a starship, he would have need for certain kinds of information, access to which could only be obtained through the use of retinal scan (like the one Kirk used early in *Wrath of Khan* to view the Genesis Tape). Retinas have cells and cells have genetic codes; once the Genesis scientists have that, the result is preordained.

As we have seen, however, a physical duplicate which is little more than an animated mannequin is insufficient for our—or Kirk's—purpose. We need the essence of a man—or, in this case, a Vulcan—that usually perishes with death.

Usually, yes, but perhaps not in the case of one who is the acknowledged master of both the Vulcan nerve pinch and the Vulcan mind meld. It should be relatively simple for such a one to transfer "himself" into the body of another, all the while maintaining mental control of his own body in order to direct it to the task at hand. There is plenty of precedent for this within the series. "Return to Tomorrow" features Spock's essence residing in the body of Christine Chapel until his body is safe-guarded and ready for his return. In "Requiem for Methuselah," Spock uses his linking ability to rob his great friend Kirk of the unbearable memory of his impossible love for Reena. And now, in *Wrath of Khan*, he has obviously arranged for McCoy to remember something, although we can only guess what that "something" is.

One thing for sure is that McCoy does not remember it *now*. We will, however, for if Spock has set up the means for his own revival, he would also specify a set of conditions which would trigger the memory in McCoy whenever it was needful for him to produce this information. Since Spock would realize that the scientific community would never tire of studying the Genesis World, he might couple this knowledge with an evaluation of human character to surmise that Kirk would one day be drawn to the scene of his friend's death, probably with McCoy in tow. At that point, the trigger for McCoy's heretofore suppressed memories would be pulled, and Spock's essence would be available for introduction into a newly available Spock body. (This scenario is particularly attractive if we adhere to the lenient exemption of allowing Spock's body to remain intact on the Genesis World.)

There are variations possible on this—for instance, McCoy might suddenly develop distinctly Vulcan mannerisms, causing Kirk to suspect enough to return to the Genesis World—but all in all, the "Spock body restored by Genesis and his consciousness in McCoy's body" scenario is probably what the people behind Star Trek are aiming for.

We should also speculate briefly on what role Saavik might play in all of this. Much of our information about and insight into Saavik comes from Vonda McIntyre's novelization of *Wrath of Khan*, and although there are some inconsistencies between the novel and the film, enough threads remain in the film to weave an intriguing fabric of speculation. In the novel, Saavik's protége-mentor relationship with Spock is richer, and it is she who has the first glimmer that all is not as it seems in regard to his death. She is also probably most responsible for the body of Spock being on the Genesis World at all, for in the novel, Kirk orders that the casket be sent into a decaying orbit to burn up when it enters the newly formed atmosphere. Saavik, however, programs a course into the launching system that results in landing the torpedo casing on the planet's surface.

One could easily argue that the Spock-consciousness residing in McCoy's body made mental contact with Saavik's subconscious and ordered her to reprogram the guidance system in order that his body might survive for future occupancy. In any case, the mind link with McCoy must become an integral part of any revival of Spock—else the use of Genesis opens a Pandora's Box that would soon destroy Star Trek's illusion of reality.

Consider: If Genesis alone can be used to recreate Spock, what limits has it? Why not reanimate Mirimanee? Or Edith Keeler? Or even Kirk's boyhood idol Abraham Lincoln?

Theoretically, once word of Genesis reaches the Federation at large, whoever has access to Genesis could live forever, continually recreating new, healthy bodies after the old one has aged or died. In fact, every defect in the human condition—or in creation, for that matter—could conceivably be corrected by Genesis . . . probably altruistically (with Federation approval), but at least potentially "for a price" in unscrupulous hands. And let us never forget its horrifying potential for destruction; were it to be used on a wide scale to solve problems, sooner or later it would be used to *eliminate* other problems. Certainly, stringent controls and orders would be passed regulating its use, but rules are made to be broken, and someone who felt strongly enough that his use of Genesis was justified would not hesitate.

Clearly, a limit is called for, and it would be logical to establish at the earliest opportunity that observation has determined that Genesis cannot reproduce sentient forms. Since the original intent of Genesis was stated as being to reform worlds with a view to accepting and nurturing life forms the Federation *might later choose to introduce*, this limit would be right in line. Arguably, of course, the film has already gone slightly beyond this limit by showing a fawn in the Genesis Cave, but unless one considers Bambi, deer are not known for their sentience. Anyway, the fawn and any other life form in the cave could have been placed there after Genesis.

But the importance of this limit on Genesis cannot be overstated, for in addition to tying up some monstrously loose plot ends, it also demonstrated the relevance—make that *necessity*—of the essence safely tucked away in what Spock would not hesitate to point out are vast unused areas of his brain, then the reversal of the mind link at the appropriate time would provide the unique spark which would allow the Genesis Effect to succeed in creating this one particular instance of sentient life.

Nor could the process be successfully repeated unless one party to the effect knew the mind-melding technique, but there are several races, such as Vulcans and Medusans, who can mind-meld. They do not do it casually (remember Spock's ethical and cultural bias against melding mentioned in "Dagger of the Mind"?), but the revival of a deceased loved one or very important person might be enough incentive to overcome any reluctance. So the potential for abuse (or altruism) is still there, with the selective stirring of consciousness becoming a powerful weapon in the hands of anyone with knowledge of how to duplicate Genesis, the mind-melding and shifting process, and the means to place particular "essences" in selected life forms.

The implications are frightening, so frightening in fact that Dr. Marcus (or the Federation) might even refuse to employ Genesis to restructure Spock (should we go that route) without a much more compelling reason than we have produced so far. Even Spock himself realized there were a plethora of ethical considerations surrounding the use of Genesis, although he would not debate the issue with McCoy.

In fact, in any of the scenarios we have postulated so far, McCoy would probably be constantly at Kirk's elbow to remind him of the ethical impropriety of what they were trying to do. For all of his friendship with Spock, he would definitely not approve, and like Dr. Marcus, might not participate—consciously, that is. Remember, he appears to have forces at work within him that he is unaware of, forces that may override every veto and lead to the return of Mr. Spock.

Even with all the problems inherent in every means described for the return of Spock, we can certainly accomplish it. That we want him back is without question—but should we bring him back? Maybe not.

Of all the "possibilities" raised by Mr. Spock's death, the possibility that he should remain dead is the most distasteful. And perhaps the most important. Viewed on one level, *The Wrath of Khan* is a grand action piece, arising out of one of the most popular episodes of the series, and proceeding beyond the limits of the small screen of television to take movie technology with all its scope into the Star Trek universe. But if it were *just* that, we might as well watch *Forbidden Planet* or *Destination: Moon* or any of hundreds of science fiction movies.

But *Wrath of Khan* is a Star Trek movie. Those of us who loved the series come to the film to see the characters we care for face whatever situation is dreamed up for them. In this case, the entire film is about change and how the characters react to it. Saavik has trouble understanding *Kobayashi Maru*; Kirk understands it, but avoids it by changing the rules of the game—"I don't like to lose." He cheats death at every turn and, as the hero of countless battles on behalf of the Federation, he should do no less. Finally, however, he faces a no-win situation which is beyond his ability to fix and survives only through the self-sacrifice of his dearest friend. The *Enterprise* is saved—but at a price. "The needs of the many outweigh the needs of the few. Or the one."

The characters in Star Trek have always, for the most part, been treated with intelligence and so drawn as to react realistically to a given situation (dramatic license aside, of course). William Shatner recently reinforced this in an interview. He said that he believes the enduring popularity of Kirk is due in part to the fact that Shatner the actor has Kirk the character react in a way that Shatner the person would like to think he would react in an idealized situation. And, with the passing of the years, as Shatner's reactions to a given situation have changed, so too have Kirk's. Realism is the key, and Kirk must react realistically to the death of Mr. Spock. In *Wrath of Khan*, Kirk is finally forced to acknowledge that "the way one faces death is at least as important as how one faces life." Having accepted that, what will be the effect on Kirk if and when his friend returns? Perhaps a tiny speck of his character will be weakened as he says, probably on a level which he doesn't even consciously recognize, "Well, I won again."

Granted, the milieu of Star Trek is fictional; nevertheless, the reactions of the characters should be, and always have been, *real*. In our "real" world, the first reaction to the death of a loved one—and there's no sense in saying that Mr. Spock is anything but that to thousands upon thousands of fans—is one of rejection. There is a feeling of "this can't be happening," a period of worrying over what might have been, what should have been, and "if only . . ." But ultimately, the living get on with the business of living. Ought we to expect any less or respond any differently when the death involves one who we have insisted for fifteen years should react realistically, and who has been treated, in a sense, like a living being?

No, for the bitter lesson which Kirk learns with the death of his friend really applies to all of us who see the movie. After all, Star Trek may sail the galaxies for years to come, but the people who are in it will change and will be replaced by others who, if the transitions are handled with taste and skill, will come to merit our admiration, respect, and maybe even love as the films roll on. Who would have thought in 1965 that these particular characters would so capture the hearts of fans?

Although these questions are posed in all sincerity, we *know* in all certainty that Mr. Spock, "dead" though he is, has joined a very select company. He sits at the left hand of Sherlock Holmes in that fine limbo where beloved characters never die, but merely wait for the next adventure. And, again to paraphrase, "There are always . . . adventures."

ANSWER YOUR BEEPER, YOU DREAMER!

by Jacqueline Gilkey

We receive many articles which try to express the inner turmoil that being a Star Trek fan can sometimes cause. Friends, family, and co-workers don't always understand or appreciate our hobby or our devotion to it, so it is understandable if once in a while we tend to start talking to ourselves . . . or, once in a great while, to Kirk, Spock, and various others of the Enterprise *crew. The following—ah—discourse is among the best we've ever seen in describing that mental mixture of frustration, rhapsody, and plain old wishful thinking that makes up a* Star Trek *fan.*

Why are you smiling? Look, just because your beeper goes off, it doesn't mean the *Enterprise* is trying to contact you. Come on, now! You're in the real world, remember? A respiratory therapist!

Why it is that every time I walk down the hallway at work, I think I'm walking the corridors of the Starship *Enterprise*? Huh? Every time I write in a patient's chart, my mind is off pretending that I am a young medical officer in Dr. McCoy's Sickbay. What's happening to me?

Since we're on the subject of work, should you dare to torment your coworkers with one more, "Ahead, warp factor three!" as you go off to do your breathing treatments, well, you're sure to drive them to the point of avoiding you. So, dreamer, go into the workroom where it says "Mr. Spock is on the ventilator" (suffering from radiation poisoning, no less!) and erase it. And, dammit, take off that stupid "Beam me up" button you constantly wear. How many people have asked you what it means? Then you're disappointed because they don't share your enthusiasm. It really surprises you when a few of them tell you that they've never even *heard* of Star Trek!

But no. That's hardly the case with you. You spend so much time thinking about Star Trek that your personality continually reflects serious obsessive components. You're even beginning to show signs of delusions of grandeur. Ha! Imagine believing that you are talented enough to write the script for *Star Trek IV*! I see trouble brewing down the road for you.

Actually, if you'd take the time to notice, people at work are beginning to get sick and tired of your constant attack upon the typewriter. Give them a break, won't you? Haven't you noticed that even your own typewriter at home has had enough of this silliness? Your fingers are rebelling against you. Look at them! They're hardly able to stand yet another pounding from that overworked manual typewriter. The poor pathetic thing should break down for good.

I guess that once I get home from work today I could force myself to go outside for a walk. Perhaps I might call up my scuba-diving friends or . . . I might even get back on my motorcycle and go for a ride. But gee . . . what's the use? Sitting on Max, the wind whistling through my helmet, just does not satisfy me anymore. It feels so, well . . . unstable. Hmm . . . maybe it's me who's the unstable one. I just can't get my mind off Star Trek!

Look girl, tonight when you go home, I demand you immediately take down that poster of Spock. And really, that *Enterprise* poster? It's just that, only a poster! How can you stare at that thing and honestly believe it could ever get off the ground?

Grow up! Get rid of those *Enterprise* crew pictures which intervene between you and the living-room wall. Reminds me of something you'd see in the post office. The infamous Starship Seven strike again. Especially the one with the nickname. What is it? . . . "Bones"! The reason for your blind devotion to him escapes me. After all, you have a more accessible male friend. Have you forgotten him? Aren't you a wee bit cognizant of his existence? If so, I suggest you diversify your energies in pursuit of a relationship more tangible than those conjured up by the sight of a picture or those described by a book!

*   *   *

You know, you're beginning to sound a little like Mr. Spock. Which reminds me. I need to steer clear of bookstores for a while. Why, however in the world could I have asked that overweight salesgirl about ordering some Star Trek books? That look on her face! She was angry with me! All she had to do was spend twenty minutes of her time searching through the microfilms. I remember how happy she looked while telling me that all the books I had requested were out of print. Except one. *"I Am Not Spock,"* she said. She sure as hell wasn't!

I can see that any further discussion attempting to dissuade you from continuing with this Star Trek thing would be worthless, but hear me out! As you attend the next Star Trek convention, remember exactly how ludicrous you must appear to the nonbelivers as you stroll through the convention center in your black pants, boots, and blue shirt. Let me be the one to remind you that those few days alone are the only time when public display of such a shirt, with its gold braid on the sleeves and the insignia whose meaning is known only to a privileged few, is looked upon with equivocal interest. Then, after it's all over, take note of how your stomach growls because you've gone and spent all of your hard-earned money to buy Star Trek memorabilia, and now there's nothing left with which to buy groceries to stock an empty refrigerator!

Still, knowing you as I do, I imagine you'll just pass it all off as the price paid for being given the opportunity to participate in such an exhilarating event. That would be just like you. You've been so . . . irresponsible lately!

Now answer your beeper, you dreamer!

"Answer your beeper, you dreamer," says Ben, gently nudging my arm.

Detached, I rise. A familiar hand moves to the phone. The fingers punch out the numbers 2-1-3-5. There is a ringing in my ears, and then a voice that says:

"Hello, intensive care. May I help you?"

"Hi," a distant voice answers back. "This is sickbay . . . er, respiratory therapy!"

Ben's mouth drops open. He is beginning to fear for my sanity. My unseeing eyes fall upon him.

"Ben to space cadet," he says.

Oh, Ben, I think. If only those puppy-dog eyes of yours were blue mirror images of this planet of ours, why, I could be staring at Dr. McCoy.

"What's up, Jax?"

"Ventilator changes in ICU."

Ben points to the blackboard. "On Mr. Spock, I presume?"

"Very funny, Ben!" He knows better than to mess with me when I am attempting to unite the real world.

"Come on," I say, dragging him out of the workroom toward intensive care.

Halfway down the hallway, a resident passes us muttering, "Beam me up?"

Ben whips out his beeper-communicator and attempts to flip up the invisible grid. With synchronous precision, the little black box beeps back at him.

"Ben to *Enterprise*," he says. "Two to beam up, Mr. Scott."

Stopping dead in his tracks, the resident veers around to evaluate our behavior. He fears for our sanity. Ben and I manage to conjure up our most pathetic expressions in an attempt to excuse our eccentricity. Disgruntled and impatient, the resident turns from us and walks quickly away. Ben and I enjoy a fit of hysterics.

"Boy," says Ben, "I hope that wasn't a psych resident!"

"Who cares?" I respond, laughing. Then off we go toward the intensive care unit, the look of disbelief on the resident's face pleasantly stored away in our memory banks.

"You'll get me hooked yet!" Ben tempts.

To Ben and me, intensive care appears to be a cavern of imminent disaster. Beeping, humming, and unsettled tension fill the air. A nurse barks at a half-dazed patient lying in one of the beds.

"Take a deep breath!" (Mr. Spock?)

The patient writhes in pain.

Ben and I walk to the purring ventilator and make the appropriate changes.

"Gases in an hour!" the nurse shouts after us.

Over at bed three, the situation looks grim. We peer at the medical scanner.

"Heart rate, two hundred ten. Blood pressure, eighty over thirty-two. Respiratory rate, forty-five," reports Ben. A dwindling cardiac output causes the patient to gurgle like a baby.

"Gee, if this keeps up much longer, we'll have a code on our hands," I reply. "Someone had better call Dr. McCoy!"

As the tension level within the intensive care unit continues to rise, Ben and I decide it's time to retreat back to the safety of our own department—before all hell breaks loose!

Later that evening, after the code, we sit in the lounge. For weeks now, Ben has been witness to my zealous attempts at story writing. He stares at me in amazement as I scribble on a piece of paper.

Curiosity overcomes him and he asks, "What in the world are you writing?"

Biting on the tip of my pen, I look up.

"Ben," I begin, "what would you say if someone said to you, 'Is that the reason?' "

"The reason for what?"

He's confused. I know what I mean—why doesn't he? I explain it to him.

I trace back through the thoughts and feelings of the characters in my story. Ben becomes intensely absorbed; he makes a gesture showing he comprehends their motivations.

"So, Ben," I ask again, "what would be your reply if someone said to you, 'Is that the reason?' "

Ben paces the floor reflectively. Instead of the profound response I expected, all I get is, "Well, what do you think?"

Honestly, Ben, what kind of an answer is that?

The next shift arrives for duty and report begins. Anyone unfamiliar with the bizarre vernacular might think the ongoing conversation of extraterrestrial origin. IPPB, PEEP, ABG, and IMV dot the conversation. Someone points to the blackboard and asks, "What about Spock?"

Questioning fascination fills the faces of the next shift.

"Vital signs stable," I begin seriously. "Heart rate, two hundred forty-two. Blood pressure, eighty over forty. Respiratory rate, sixty-one. Give him a few cc's of Benjisidrine, and he should be extubated by this time tomorrow."

"That's stable?" someone observes sagely.

Ben winks at me. "It is if you're a Vulcan!"

I leap into the front seat of my car. Engaging aft thrusters one quarter impulse power, I cautiously proceed through the maze commonly known as the parking garage. Once outside its confines, I advance into warp drive.

"Out there. Thataway!"

The tape player in my car enthusiastically devours the cassette with the score of *Star Trek: The Motion Picture*. Harmoniously intertwining melodies tear my heart apart with an insatiable yearning for my own chance at interstellar travel. I am . . . inspired!

"Home, the final frontier.
These are the voyages of the Street Vehicle *Valiant*.
Its thirty-five-minute mission,
To explore strange new road surfaces.
To seek out and discover new potholes and unclearly defined detour routes.
To boldly go where no car has gone before!"
(Rattle, hesitate, SWISH!)

*   *   *

I continue listening to the STTMP soundtrack with devotion. Suddenly, as if from nowhere, my scanners detect a Thunderbird of Prey.

"Damn those Romulans! First the cloaking device, and now this!"

The vessel bears down on me, provoking attack.

"Deflector shields up!" cries my mind. "Standby photon torpedos!"

"Shields up, sir. Torpedos ready for fire on signal."

"FIRE!"

HOOOOONNNNNKKKK!!!!

Inevitably, the Bird of Prey draws in closer.

"Photon torpedos ineffective, sir!" I choke out, noticing that my heart has repositioned itself at the back of my throat. I envision *Valiant*'s demise.

"Evasive starboard!" I scream, taking over the comm. Swerving to the right, I punch the gas pedal to the floor. Valiant dances nimbly away from the Thunderbird.

"You did it!" congratulates my mind.

"I did nothing! Except almost get myself killed!"

To my relief, the remaining twenty minutes of my journey home prove uneventful. I finally reach my destination. Why, if a man's home is his castle, then surely a girl's apartment is . . .

"Really a mess."

Partially written scaps of paper lie all over the floor. I begin to gather them up. In the process I spill a bottle of correction fluid left open on the coffee table. Tossing the papers aside, I sit and begin to type.

The ribbon in my typewriter has become frayed with use. It revolts against another impulsive creative session. I stop to hunt for my Merriam-Webster dictionary, *Roget's Thesaurus,* and Stewart Bronfeld's *Writing for Film and Television.* I remember quite distinctly placing them in one corner of the living room or on the kitchen table or . . . somewhere? Passing by the record player, I notice *Inside Star Trek* still spinning there from the night before.

"Hey! Where are my rubber Spock ears?"

I search frantically for them, tripping over the stack of *Trek* magazines also lying haphazardly askew on the floor.

"What's this? My phaser!"

My senses detect a strange life form. I spin around to face the alien. Crouched down, with both hands gripped tightly onto the butt of the phaser, I await its approach.

"There it is!"

Covered with fine fur, it is approximately twenty-six centimeters in height, excluding the long bristling tail which flicks from side to side. Back arched, the creature stands on four erect legs. I catch a glimpse of razor-sharp fangs as the furred life form ever so slightly opens its oral cavity.

"Preowit!"

Unable as I am to understand this foreign tongue, I engage the universal translator. The creature assumes an even more aggressive position. Pointed ears press close to its head. I set my phaser on stun. Again the creature speaks.

"Preowit!"

The translator interprets "preowit" into "You have neglected me!"

I reply, "My cause is just."

Without further warning, the alien creature leaps at me, hissing and growling, surgically sharp needles protruding from its footpads. With the phaser still locked on target, I drop to the ground to avoid contact.

"Where in the blazes is *Enterprise*?"

Like Dr. McCoy, I too am not fond of the idea of having my molecular structure scattered throughout the vacuum of space but at this point I am desperate. For what seems like an eternity the creature and I wait, each pondering the other's next move.

Enterprise finally comes into view, but she is not functioning under her own power. Her destination is controlled by the alien. Highly intelligent, it is capable of determining how best to inflict intense suffering upon my sensitive form. The starship is flung headlong into the wall; it explodes into four separate pieces. My phaser tumbles from my hand and I struggle to avenge *Enterprise*. The furred creature, possessing great agility, slips gracefully away from my enraged grasp.

Snapped back into reality, I walk to the fragmented starship. Gathering her pieces into my arms, I carry them gently to the coffee table. A tear rolls down my face. With stoic courage recall her once majestic form, then human emotion overcomes me and I begin to cry. I think of *The Wrath of Khan*.

"Lock phasers on target."

"Locking phasers."

"Phaser bank one, fire! Evasive action!" (Oh, too late.)

"Begging the admiral's pardon, sir, but don't you think we should have raised the shields?"

Enterprise doesn't look much like the pride of the fleet anymore. Sacrilegiously, my mind envisions me playing frisbee with her primary hull.

"Look sharp, mister!" I say out loud.

Regaining my composure, I being making repairs on her. She *will* fly the skies of my living room again!

The telephone rings. From under the sofa peers a frightened Marvlin Marie, her eyes as large and black as the twin moons of Asteroidus. Before it can reverberate through my senses again, the telephone is swatted on a journey toward the floor.

"Me—ouch!" says my feline sidekick as she scampers toward the kitchen.

The call seems . . . unimportant to me. I no longer seem to be able to respond to something someone says about this or that, or the inevitable.

"Maybe we can get together for lunch sometime?"

"Maybe . . ." I manage weakly as my mind begins to wander. "Gee," I think, "what if this were a call from Starfleet Headquarters? Now that would be important!"

I stand before the admiral.

"Mr. Gilkey, it has been my observation that you have chosen to isolate yourself from the others around you. On what premise is this behavior based?"

"Sir, I regret the alternative life-style I have taken up is due to an obsession of unusual nature."

"Oh?"

"Yes sir. It occurred during my last assignment when I was transported to the Earth colony Omaha, Nebraska, for the Love of Trek convention."

"Go on."

"As I'm sure you'll recall, sir, the purpose of the assignment was to make contact with 'the Star Trek fan.' "

"And what were your observations, Mr. Gilkey?"

"I found them an intelligent, vibrant people, and quite loyal in their own right, sir!"

"Explain."

"At one time this particular life form could be found in great abundance at these briefings—er—conventions. And their numbers spanned the continent! Yet, sir, there were times when the species seemed on the verge of discontinuity."

"And why is that?"

"I don't know. But observing them elicited my own diligent belief in their cause."

"Which is, Mr. Gilkey?"

"Why, to promote the concepts of unity, peace, and brotherhood, as it is propagandized by the Star Trek philosophy."

"And how many Earth inhabitants profess to pursue the Prime Directive?"

"Unknown, sir! Outside of these . . . conventions, it is difficult to ascertain their loyalties. It is positive that some of them are quite conspicuous in their outright devotion to the cause, but for the most part, sir, they are subdued. Example: I have offered numerous communiqués to those of the group with . . . status. I have received no reply."

"And what are your intentions at this time, Mr. Gilkey?"

"I wait. It's only a matter of time before the Great Bird of the Galaxy—"

"Great Bird of the Galaxy! Surely you are not attempting to credit this devotion to the Prime Directive to Romulan intervention?"

"No, sir, I . . ."

"Jax? Did you hear me?" says the person on the other end of the phone line. I make my apologies and concentrate on the real conversation at hand.

"So call me sometime, okay? I was really beginning to think that you had fallen off the face of the Earth!"

"Beamed up . . ." I respond dreamily.

"What?"

"Oh, nothing."

Anxious to return to my work, I bid the proper farewells and hang up. Walking to the record player, I replace *Inside Star Trek* with *Star Trek Bloopers*. I sit and listen once, just for fun.

Scotty says, "We'll havta do thot again."

Okay, I'm easy enough to get along with. The blooper record spins around again. It sounds a bit scratchy. Well, I guess the needle *is* long overdue for replacement, but, gee, I haven't bought anything lately. Except of course those Star Trek pins, patches, posters, fan magazines, paperback books, comics, dolls, games, puzzles, records, video discs, viewfinder, and . . . A doleful expression emerges upon my face in lament of the now broken *Enterprise* model.

"You're not going to buy anything?" Dad asked incredulously of me one day when we were down at the New Jersey shore. I sensed the beginning of yet another of those "You should save your money as you might need some of it someday" lectures coming on.

"Nope!" I replied, trying to avoid an argument. I just had to add, however, "Not unless it's something Star Trek!"

Dad laughed. "You've got to stop living in the future."

"Doctor McCoy, will you please beam down with the medicine?"

What? Did I hear McCoy's name mentioned?

I perk up, listen closer. "Bones" forgets where to exit the bridge. Maybe *he* needs some medicine? No, I decide McCoy just needs to be beamed directly into the center of my living room. Well, I guess that wouldn't be wise. This place is really a mess, and besides, there's nothing in the refrigerator. Certainly he wouldn't be interested in moldly bagels. But then again, he might just want to analyze my home-grown version of penicillin. Hmmm?

On the blooper record, De Kelley is laughing. I smile and gaze fondly at his picture hanging on the wall. The wheels in my mind begin to turn again. The blooper record strikes at the core of my motivation as I hear:

"Fifty-five apples, one."

Bill, De, and Leonard run through their lines.

Suddenly I'm standing with Gene on the set of *Star Trek IV*. The production is evolving before my proud eyes. Yes, the human adventure continues with the introduction of this new character, so vital to Leonard McCoy's existence. . . .

FADE IN
EXTERIOR SPACE—*Enterprise* zooming by on starry field
KIRK'S VOICE
Captain's Log Stardate 8301.20. . . .

The doors of the elevator (turbolift) swish open. I enter, presenting myself as company to one of Abington Memorial Hospital's most prominent physicians. He smiles at me, noticing the "Beam Me Up" button I proudly wear.

"Beam me up, heh?" he asks.

"Yeah . . ." I reply in defensive readiness. "I love it!"

"Aye lass, me too!" he responds in mimicry of Montgomery Scott. "Just gae me thae word and I'll blast thaem damned Klingons ri' ow o' thae sky. . . ."

Come on now. For the sake of a dreamer's sanity, please . . .

"Beam me up, Mr. Scott!!!"

LOVE IN STAR TREK— PART TWO

by Walter Irwin

As stated in the first half of this article (on page 132), *Star Trek showed us in many ways that love is a universal constant. This concept was carried on and further developed in the two feature films. But, as is ever true with Star Trek, such development did not always go in the direction that we expected it to. In this concluding part of his article, Walter examines these further examples of love in Star Trek and explains what the differences are and what they mean.*

Love in Star Trek, as in life, takes many forms. Throughout the course of the series' run, almost every type of love which one sentient being may feel for another was presented. The need and desire for love was presented as an everyday, natural part of the characters' lives, just as it is of our own. Sometimes love was the focus of an episode, as in "Requiem for Methusulah"; other times the tug of conflicting loves was the focus, as in "City on the Edge of Forever." Other types of love than the romantic were also pivotal to many episodes: brotherly love ("The Empath"), love of freedom ("The Menagerie"), paternal love ("The Conscience of the King"), and even love for inanimate objects ("This Side of Paradise").

Star Trek is, of course, based on love. The underlying theme of the series is the assurance that man will one day overcome his own humanity and learn to live in peace and brotherly love not only with his own kind, but with myriad other sentient beings throughout the universe. The love of freedom is also a very important part of the Star Trek concept. Each person is allowed the right to be free and desires that that same right be extended to all others. It naturally follows that love of individuality is the one theme which ties both of these together. This is embodied in the Vulcan philosophy of IDIC (Infinite Diversity in Infinite Combinations), which states that it is the differences between beings which must be revered, not the sameness, and that tolerance and understanding between all life forms can only result in love. Stated as it is in such terms, we can see that the Star Trek concept was an extremely optimistic one—especially when we consider the turbulent times in which the series was first developed and introduced to the viewing public. In order to make his message of tolerance and love more palatable to a public which had so often heard the word "love" bandied about in conjunction with everything from antiwar protests to tennybopper cosmetics that it had become virtually meaningless, Gene Roddenberry wisely incorporated healthy doses of adventure, exploration, mystery, danger, and the lure of the unknown into the Star Trek format—a form of "sugar-coating" the messages, as it were.

(It must be noted, of course, that these same elements are prerequisites for any successful television series, and Roddenberry did not coldly and cynically include them simply to trick viewers into watching his programs. When speaking of love, it must be remembered that the average human loves nothing more than excitement, danger, mystery, and the scary unknown—especially if all of these can be experienced in the comfort of his living room.)

Even though Gene Roddenberry's firm guiding hand was absent from the third-season episodes, and a number of the philosophical elements which had made the series so rich in texture and depth were sadly absent, both the concept and practice of love permeated many of these third-season programs. Indeed, although many of the basic plotlines in this season are generally acknowledged to be among the series' weakest, many of the strongest affirmations of the concepts about love were presented in third-season episodes. It was the only season during which Kirk, Spock, McCoy, and Scotty *all* enjoyed brief encounters with love.

Spock was the first. In the second episode of the season, he became involved with one of the most fascinating and mysterious characters ever seen in Star Trek—the Romulan commander. (Yes, she has a name. It is rare and beautiful and incongruous when spoken by a soldier. And we never learn it.) Nor do we learn much of anything about the commander. She is undoubtedly one of the most complex and conflicted characters appearing in Star Trek, and that is probably even more of a reason for her lasting popularity with fans than her involvement with Spock. But we must not forget that any woman who can so intrigue Spock is also irresistibly intriguing to us. . . .

From one standpoint, the commander can be seen as the archetype of woman as presented in film and television—the cold, seemingly emotionless "female executive" who finds that her intrusion into "the man's world" has left her lonely, frustrated, and vaguely unhappy. She doesn't realize *why* she's unhappy, of course. It isn't until a dominant, virile male comes along and sweeps her off her feet into the bedroom—or kitchen—that she discovers all she ever *really* wanted was to be a complacent and compliant hausfrau. (You've seen it a zillion times in Doris Day movies.) It's very easy to view the commander as a lonely, frustrated, and vaguely unhappy Romulan warrior who doesn't discover the True Meaning of Life until Mr. Spock comes along and sweeps her off her feet. She then discovers that all she ever really wanted to be is a good little Vulcan wife.

But, as always, Star Trek adds a little twist. The commander is no spinster pining away in lonely isolation at the top, compensating for the lack of Mr. Right through power and ambition. She is a vital, willful, and highly intelligent woman who has risen to her present position by being *more* vital, willful, and highly intelligent than the men around her. She, like her male counterpart in Starfleet, Kirk, is obviously smitten with a desire and need for command, and she is highly proficient at her job. After all, her ship was chosen as the vessel to test the cloaking device and Federation defenses, so the Romulan High Command must have confidence in her. Her position is not compensation for a lack of love in her life; it is a result of her intelligence, skill, and ambition. She likes to command, she likes being a warrior.

We can only surmise the details, but judging by the take-charge manner in which she becomes intimate with Spock, the commander has an active and satisfactory sex life. In this, as in her position as a commander, she is complete. There is no question of compensation or sublimation of her desires in any area. So why does she seemingly go ga-ga over Spock?

Simple . . . she doesn't. At all times during their "affair," *she* is the one who is in control, the partner who is dominant. If there was any seducing done in those scenes we didn't see, it was *she* who did the seducing. In a coolly calculated manner which would draw a whistle of admiration from Kirk, the commander leads Spock into her boudoir and into her arms. Spock, as we all know, was acting out of duty—playing along for the purpose of buying time. But he certainly didn't look unhappy with his duty. In fact, we get the distinct impression that he was downright enjoying it. Although the commander was understandably upset and unhappy when Spock's true motives were revealed, she didn't moan and groan . . . she quickly and efficiently ordered his immediate execution. However much he may have touched that soft, sensitive, and feminine part of her (and that is not a repressed part, by any means; she revealed it quite willingly and naturally), Spock wasn't nearly as important to the commander as was her career. Or her revenge.

If she wasn't in love with Spock, however, then why did she beam aboard the *Enterprise* with him? It was an act completely out of character for her. She wasn't afraid or panicky—she is much too haughty and controlled for that—and surely she didn't have a wild desire to remain with Spock "under any circumstances." The only possible explanation for her action is that she couldn't bear the thought of Spock's getting away without her being on hand to prove to Kirk that Spock's deception was not totally successful. Kirk (and in her mind, Spock) might be able to gloat about stealing the cloaking device, but she was going to make damned certain that they wouldn't be able to gloat about Spock's putting one over on her. It was pride, pure and simple, that sent her to the *Enterprise*.

Spock *was* affected by the commander to a certain degree, but it was probably most likely the unaccustomed physical closeness to a female that affected him. (It has been suggested that the wily commander slipped an aphrodisiac into Spock's drink. Romulan fly, most likely.) Spock would probably have reacted to any Vulcanoid female under similar circumstances, and the results would have been the same. It was an uncomfortable and somewhat unnerving experience for him, but his control of his emotions (and presumably his libido) and his loyalty to Starfleet completely obliterated any chance that he would become the least bit involved with the commander. It is more likely that the reverse is true—the commander would have been drawn to Spock's integrity (an attribute highly prized among Romulans) and perhaps by the challenge of "unfreezing" a Vulcan. There was respect between them, yes, perhaps even admiration. But not love.

We can only assume that that wily commander managed to convince her superiors that her journey to the *Enterprise* justified her "capture" and that she was restored to her command. Chances are she's out there somewhere today, fighting battles, advancing her career, and helping to spread the many good things that are part of the Romulan Way.

Miramanee, the Amerind maiden of "The Paradise Syndrome," was one of the most charming and appealing women to have graced Star Trek. It is little wonder that Kirk/Kirok fell in love with her at first sight. Although he had suffered an almost complete loss of memory, Kirk still retained his basic personality and knowledge, as well as his sharp eye for a shapely female and his recently expressed yen for a life of peace and quiet. In Miramanee and her people, Kirk found both, and while he remained ignorant of his true self, he was more happy than we had before or since seen him. He loved Miramanee totally, but even that love was not enough to keep his dynamic personality in check for long. Unable to be content with the simple life-style of the Indians, Kirk suffered from "strange" dreams and urges; by the time the asteroid arrived, he was pushing the Indians into civilization. Miramanee instinctively knew that their love couldn't survive a resurgence of the suppressed memories represented by the dreams of "the lodge that flies through the sky"; once Kirok's satisfaction with the simple life turned to boredom, his satisfaction with his and Miramanee's idyllic marriage would end as well.

Unfortunately, it ended in tragedy. Although Kirk was saddened by the death of Miramanee and their child, it is doubtful that he felt any regret for the loss of their life together. His love for Miramanee was deep, but it could not, under any circumstances have lasted once he regained his memory. As Kirk or Kirok, the captain simply could not be satisfied (at that period in his life and career) with the simple pleasures of a wife and family.

Other examples of love are seen in this episode: Salish, the ousted medicine chief, loved Miramanee, and his jealousy led him to attempt murder; another example of how twisted love invariably leads to evil in Star Trek. Spock, on the other hand, remained completely in control of his emotions, even to the point of suppressing his worry about Kirk, and concentrated totally on the problem at hand. To Spock's logical mind, love was the necessity of saving as many beings as possible from the threat of the asteroid, even though that meant abandoning Kirk temporarily to an unknown fate. It must be noted, however, that both Spock and McCoy felt that Kirk was still alive on the Amerind planet, and that much of the cause of Spock's obsession with halting the asteroid could have been prompted by his knowledge that Kirk would surely die if the asteroid struck the planet. McCoy, naturally, misunderstood Spock's logic and fretted unendingly about Kirk.

In "All the Children Shall Lead" the evil "angel" Gorgon twists the affection of children to his own ends. As the love of children is a pure, innocent love, such manipulation is a definite no-no in Star Trek. Gorgon's powers of illusion force the children to forget the deaths of their parents, and they naturally transfer all their boundless love to the most convenient and kindliest-seeming adult figure available—Gorgon. His hold on them was probably strengthened by his illusory powers; he could have appeared as one of their parents or any other beloved figure, or he could have supplied them with the fulfillment of their childish fantasies. It is only when Kirk and Spock remind the children of the true love they shared with their parents that the children can see Gorgon for the evil being he really is and are freed of his influence. As is always true in Star Trek, real, natural love is more powerful than artificial, unnatural love. It is interesting to note that (again) it is Kirk's love for the *Enterprise* and his command and his fear of losing them that provide the key to defeat Gorgon.

Another love triangle appears in "Is There in Truth No Beauty?" but this time it is a slightly different one: Larry Marvick loves blind telepath Miranda Jones, but she is deeply involved with Kollos, an alien so hideously ugly—or beautiful—that to see him will drive a human insane. The question that lingers from this episode is, of course, if Kollos and Miranda actually shared love. Marvick thought so, but he was unbalanced to begin with (again, jealousy is condemned and punished), and we get a definite feeling that Miranda, for her part, wanted to love Kollos. It was her uncertainty about this that led her to fear and resent Spock's ability to mind-link with Kollos—and his ability to actually *see* Kollos. It is this which bothered Miranda the most, for she was unable to see the object of her affections, and Spock—her rival in a sense—could. It was not so much jealousy that prompted Miranda's resentment of Spock, but instead her fear that Kollos would find her lacking—and therefore undeserving of his love—after melding with the intellectual Spock. Not only was Miranda reluctant to help Spock, but in an indirect way, she was also responsible for Marvick's madness, because she saw the error of her ways and performed heroically to help restore Spock's sanity. It is interesting to note that it is only *after* she helps Spock that she is able to form a permanent link with Kollos, leaving us with the impression that Kollos desired to share love with her, but required that she relieve herself of her irrational behavior and attitudes before he would commit himself. One could even suspect that Kollos took the opportunity provided by Marvick's attack on him to place the ship deep into the energy zone and force a situation wherein Miranda would be forced to face herself.

"Spectre of the Gun" reaffirms Star Trek's dictum "Love thy fellow being"; that peace and the refusal to kill are values highly prized by superior beings and that our acceptance of this philosophy is a first step in the maturation of our species. An interesting sidelight in this episode is Chekov's instant and somewhat overanxious attentions to the dancehall girl, Sylvia. Looks as if Chekov was overdue for shore leave.

Again, love for others was the lesson in "Day of the Dove," but in this instance we saw a more tangible and horrifying result of hatred—the alien entity that "fed" off of enmity and violence. Here, we see Chekov's inner demons take the form of a sexual attack on Mara . . . the boy was *way* overdue for shore leave!

It was, in the minds of many Star Trek fans, high time for Leonard McCoy to have a true love affair. In "For the World Is Hollow and I Have Touched the Sky," he not only had his affair, he ended up married! True, in Star Trek fashion, McCoy was not truly "himself" during this period. Suffering from xenopolycythemia, McCoy wasn't functioning mentally on his usual level. So when he discovered a mutual attraction with the beautiful Natira, McCoy decided to grab what happiness he could and agreed to stay with her on Yonada. In his mind, a few months of wedded bliss was a fair trade for the million-to-one chance of finding a cure in space. This seems like a rational decision, but had McCoy been acting normally, he would never have agreed to remain with Natira; regardless of his illness, he would not have given up so easily. We've seen him work many sleepless hours to discover cures for literally dozens of diseases, and he knew he would have the full support of Spock and Kirk in his search. Too, McCoy would not normally have been so callous as to marry a woman knowing that he would shortly die and leave her bereaved. He had seen too much pain to so casually inflict it upon another.

All of these considerations aside, McCoy *did* choose to remain with Natira, so we may assume that the shock of discovering he was doomed seriously affected both his judgment and his consideration for others. If nothing else, a normal McCoy would have been drawn to her beauty and gentle mien, but he would surely have balked at the first sign of her iron will. (As a matter of fact, the moment he was cured, he jumped back aboard the *Enterprise* and flew away without so much as a quickie divorce!) To be fair, McCoy would certainly have realized that a marriage between himself and Natira could never work, and he used the excuse of her duty to break it off quickly and cleanly. Bones is basically a decent and straightforward man, and he would never have asked her to marry him (no matter *what* the circumstances) if he hadn't truly felt something for her. We can only hope that Bones someday finds Yonada again, and that he and Natira have a lingering and mutually satisfactory reunion.

"The Tholian Web" is notable for its reaffirmation of the Friendship. Kirk, via prerecorded computer cassette, instructs Spock and McCoy to look to each other for strength, guidance, and friendship. It is the first time we are given any indication from any of the Big Three that they are mortal and can die—but that their friendship can continue even if one of them dies. Thus, the Friendship is elevated into the realm of love, for love does not require the presence or interaction of the loved one, and love remains, can even grow, after death.

Also in "The Tholian Web," we get an interesting glimpse into the psyche of Uhura. It has long been conjectured by fans that Uhura is deeply in love with Kirk (and perhaps vice versa). During the time that

Kirk is trapped in the interphase, it is Uhura who seems to feel the loss most deeply when he is presumed dead. It is also she who first sees the phantomlike visage of Kirk. It is left up to the reader to decide if Uhura's love for Kirk enabled him to partially return from the interphase dimension and thereby be saved. Or was it just coincidence? Was Uhura only mourning the loss of a good friend and her captain—or was it very much more?

Well, in "Plato's Stepchildren" we get a little more evidence. When the Platonians cause two women to be beamed down to participate in the "entertainments" with Kirk and Spock, it is Uhura and Chapel who are summoned. So we have something more to add to our conjecture: Were the women picked because they were the most handy? Or were the thoughts of Kirk and Spock somehow scanned and the most suitable partners chosen for them? More likely, however, because of the presence of Christine, it was the thoughts of the *women* that were scanned—and, again, it was Uhura who showed the greatest affinity for Kirk. When she and Jim are forced to kiss, Uhura is almost on the verge of tears . . . but are they tears of humiliation or are they caused by the fact that she has longed for such a moment (as did Christine with Spock) but is shamed by having it forced upon Kirk? Again, we can only speculate.

The Platonians, because of their mental powers, had lost the capacity to truly love; they instead turned their passions toward decadent and humiliating entertainment. Here we see another tenet of Star Trek. Love cannot survive within a stagnant society; it is only when man continues to strive, to better himself and his fellows, that love may flourish. Of all the Platonians, it is only the dwarf Alexander who shows any compassion or affection for the *Enterprise* crewmembers; it is only he who has not gained the telekenetic power; it is only he who has remained active and growing throughout the years.

Deela, queen of the Scalosians in "Wink of an Eye," wants only to have Kirk (or any suitable male, for that matter) impregnate her. In the process, however, she succumbs to Jim's charms as so many others have done, and although she truly loves Rael, she develops quite a liking for Kirk. It is unfortunate the mores of the time prevented full exploration of the desperate existence the Scalosians were forced to endure, for the interplay between Deela and Rael only hinted at the pain and embarrassment they suffered. It is quite amazing that Star Trek was able to get away with as frank an exploration of sexual matters as is seen in this episode. Male sterility was hardly acknowledged to exist within the world of network television in the 1960s, much less a sterility which forced the females of the species to mate with any being they could, literally, "get." Even more shocking is the concept that these females were acting with

the full knowledge and approval (however grudging) of their male counterparts. The thought of being impotent is horrifying enough to the
average male viewer. The further thought of having to sit helplessly by
while another male, a healthy, virile male, makes love to his woman . . .
It's a wonder the plotline didn't give the network boys the screaming
willies and cause them to quash the show while it was still in script. This
was extremely strong stuff for television in the '60s and another indication
of how Roddenberry's science fiction format allowed discussion and examination of themes which would be completely taboo in an everyday
dramatic presentation. It is a shame that this ability—this power, if you
will—was so often misused or frittered away by silly plots and endless
moralizing.

Self-sacrifice is the greatest expression of love, and its undying importance was constantly reaffirmed in Star Trek in many ways. But never
more so than in "The Empath." It is only through an act of self-sacrifice
that the beautiful mute empath Gem can save her people, but (according
to the Vians) such an act is completely alien and unknown to her race.
(One can only wonder how a people can even begin to approach the
fringes of civilization without such behavior as a working part of their
value system; perhaps Gem's race had some sort of religious or social
taboos against self-sacrifice.) In order to meet the Vians' specifications
for survival and have her people rescued (a goal Gem probably does not
even know she is seeking), Gem must not just sacrifice her life, she must
learn to do so. This she has been unable to do until the arrival of Kirk,
Spock, and McCoy. It is through their example, their willingness to die
for each other if need be, that Gem learns the value of friendship and
love, and she is finally able to make such a choice by and for herself. She
has not been able to learn this from the Vians, who (in true Star Trek
"villain" tradition) are a stagnant, inbred race no longer capable of
feeling or loving. (Gem has also obviously been incapable of learning
from the researchers, but we don't know if they were unwilling to exhibit
self-sacrifice, or if they simply didn't last long enough under the Vians'
tender mercies to teach her anything.) Gem learns her lesson very well
and as a reward is spared. Her race, through her, will be deemed
deserving by the Vians and thus rescued. Perhaps too the Vians will
reconsider their life-style and morality, and if they are able, will try to
imbue their race with a little more compassion and understanding . . .
which, if they are successful, will eventually restore their ability to know
love.

Also in "The Empath" the Friendship is again affirmed, this time
through the example of each man's love for the others. Each is quite
willing to die (or worse) to spare his friends, and the other two, together

and separately, are equally as adamant that their friend will not make such a sacrifice. It must also be remembered that Gem learned from these three about the joys of *living* and gained that spark of human spirit and will which keeps humans from surrendering. Gem was taught not only how to sacrifice herself for her fellow man, but, more important, how to *live* for her fellow man. It was this which allowed her to live after healing McCoy; it is this which will allow her people to begin again after the traumatic shock of being transplanted from one planet to another by the Vians. The program is a warm example of all that is best in man, and a solid and visible example of the love and respect underlying the characterizations of Kirk, Spock, and McCoy.

Kirk falls in love with the haughty and volatile "Ellan of Troyius," but he does so because of a strange psychophysical "love potion" contained within her tears. Ellan is hardly the lovable type under any circumstances, and it is not hard for us to believe that Kirk could so easily throw off the effects of the tears. Spock, however, in his usual perceptive way, offers another explanation: Kirk's antidote for Ellan's "magic" is the *Enterprise* . . . and in his particular instance, there is no cure.

Also in "Ellan of Troyius" we saw a rarity in Star Trek—the use of marriage as diplomacy. It is not hard to imagine that arranged marriages exist on many worlds in the galaxy (it seems to be the practice on Vulcan, for example), and it is one easy step from that to arranging marriages between members of two races or two planets or even two species. Even so, Star Trek seemed to shy away from portraying love and/or sex as a tool to be used in such a fashion—which is, when you think about it, a curious thing, for sex was portrayed as being an integral part of life in every other area, affecting the outcome of many battles, personal problems, captivity situations, etc. Apparently when dealing with political issues, Star Trek preferred to use such broad strokes, such elusive and nonidentifiable allegorical mirroring of our society that the question of sex would be of minor import. According to Freud, sex is the root of every human action. According to the Network, however, sex is the root of everything except business and government.

Marta, the Green Orion slave girl in "Whom the Gods Destroy," has an unusual hang-up: She must kill those she loves . . . and the lady falls in love *very* easily. She is, of course, quite insane, but we can see in her character a restatement of the Star Trek position that love must be pure—i.e., untouched by insanity or loss of control, without perversion—to be true love. The case of Garth of Izar is a curious one, for he received his injuries and subsequent madness because of an action taken to help others. Perhaps Garth was unstable to begin with and his actions were prompted more by reasons of personal aggrandizement than by altruistic motives.

Although Star Trek lauded self-sacrifice as a viable and sometimes desirable course of action, we saw the occasional instance wherein self-sacrifice was represented as being unnecessary and meaningless. Nowhere was this more strongly stated than in "The Mark of Gideon," wherein the beautiful Odona is to become a casualty of Vegan choriomeningitis (a culture of which is taken from Kirk's blood) and will die as an example to her people that voluntary death is a solution to Gideon's horrifying population problem. It is not, of course, necessary for Odona to die—any more than it is necessary for *any* of Gideon's inhabitants to die. Only their bizarre prejudice against birth control keeps them from stabilizing their population. And if they felt that custom must be preserved at all costs, many of the inhabitants could simply leave Gideon and colonize new worlds. The introduction of a deadly plague to a world where death is unknown would not be inspiring to its populace. Instead, there would probably be mass panic, leading to the eventual destruction of Gideon society. Even if the people were conditioned to accept this solution, it is entirely possible that the epidemic could get out of control, and soon destroy everyone in the planet. This episode tells us that altruism, like love, can sometimes be carried to ridiculous lengths.

Losira ("That Which Survives") must have been a wonderfully warm and loving woman. So much so that her computer replica feels regret and pain at being forced to kill, causing the hesitation that eventually enables Kirk and Co. to defeat the computer. We saw how Kirk and McCoy reacted to the replica (and even Spock to an extent), and it would be interesting to see how they would have responded to a flesh-and-blood Losira.

Because of his disappointing experience with Carolyn Palamas, it wasn't any surprise that it was quite a while before Scotty let himself feel anything for a woman again. (Indeed, his shattered, one-sided affair with Carolyn probably contributed to his temporary distrust of females as seen in "Wolf in the Fold.") So it was nice to see him once again interested in a lady in "The Lights of Zetar." Mira Romaine, the new object of Scotty's tender affections, seemed to be much more his type: She's intelligent and somewhat technical-minded, and unlike the glamorous Carolyn, Mira is a woman of mature and gentle loveliness. Although she wasn't head over heels in love with Montgomery, she did care about him and returned his affection in a tender manner that indicated she could grow to love him very much. Indeed, her greatest fear about the aliens was not that they were invading her mind and body, but that they might prove harmful to Scotty. If you read between the lines of Alan Dean Foster's *Log* series of adaptations of the animated series, you get the impression that he believes Mira and Scotty eventually married, and share an open marriage which allows both of them to pursue their respective careers. We can only hope that this is true, for if anyone deserves happiness, it is Scotty.

Throughout the course of Star Trek, we saw Captain Kirk fall in love many times, but always under unusual circumstances or when his reasoning faculties were impaired: He had a false memory of love for Helen Noel impressed upon his mind by the neural neutralizer; he was misplaced in time when he fell in love with Edith Keeler; his dependence on Dr. Janet Wallace was caused by his loss of confidence when he grew unnaturally old; he was suffering from amnesia when he wooed and wed Miramanee; and his passion for Ellan was caused by the "magic" of her tears. Not once did we see Jim Kirk fall naturally and completely in love with any woman while in his normal state of mind under normal circumstances. This has, naturally, given rise to speculation that Kirk is unwilling—or unable—to fall in love in the normal, everyday manner. He must, many fans say, have to be "out of his mind"—or at least have extraordinary circumstances as an excuse—to bind himself to a woman.

We know that this is not true. We were told of several instances in Jim's past when he was very much in love with certain women, and none of those instances could be described as unusual. It's just that during the particular time of his life that is portrayed in the series, he didn't happen to meet the "right woman"—in this case, the term being applied to a woman with whom Kirk would be willing to share a long-term relationship and not necessarily a marriage partner or a "true love." And who knows what happened offscreen?

Kirk is a warm, loving, compassionate, virile human male, and whatever his failings may be in affairs of the heart, being unwilling to love is not one of them. It may very well be that he is often *too* willing to fall in love . . . and under "normal" circumstances, guards against it.

But we have a quandary presented to us in "Requiem for Methusulah": Kirk, while seemingly himself and in control of his emotions, fell deeply in love with Reena Kapec. She was, unbeknownst to him, an android, which might seem to be the "unusual circumstance" seen in every other case, but Kirk didn't discover this fact until well after he had acknowledged and declared his love. It didn't make any difference in any case, for he continued to respond to her as a "real" woman even after he learned the truth. So why did this happen? Was Reena the right "woman" after all?

Probably not. Kirk fell in love with her too quickly, too totally. While apparently a warm, innocent, and undeniably beautiful girl, Reena simply would not be the type to whom Kirk would be irresistibly attracted. As we have seen, it is always the strong-willed dynamic female that catches Jim's fancy, and Reena, while highly intelligent and versed in many talents, had all the personality of a doormat. Kirk might have found her naiveté charming in small doses, and probably lusted after her lush form, but he wouldn't fall in love with her.

Yet he did. So there must have been a reason, an outside influence which caused Kirk to succumb so quickly. It could have been that Flint used some sort of "love potion" to affect Kirk, causing him to fall in love and (hopefully) arouse the corresponding passion and emotions in Reena that he, Flint, had been unable to awaken. (Some fans have speculated that Flint speedily programmed Reena to "match" Kirk's psychological profile so completely that he couldn't help but fall for her, but this is highly unlikely. Flint had no knowledge of Kirk's psyche, and besides, Reena was to be *his* "ideal woman." He would hardly have wanted her to be a "love match" for another man.) Flint could have introduced the drug/elixir/potion in any number of ways (most likely in the drink he served Kirk), or Reena herself could have exuded some sort of artificial pheromone that affected Kirk.

Flint would not have capriciously selected Kirk. Spock is a Vulcan, which automatically eliminated him, and McCoy was a bit too old. He would have been a bit too much of a father figure in the mold of Flint. And don't for a minute think that Flint didn't know that Reena loved and respected him as a father; he was too experienced in love and life to have made that kind of mistake. Reena's earth-based education would have provided her with an intellectual aversion to incest, which is why she never had any kind of passionate feelings for Flint, and he knew that the only chance he had of overcoming her prejudice was to have Kirk awaken her sexuality. Then, once Reena had become a fully functioning and sexually active woman and Kirk was gone . . .

Spock must have suspected the artificial source of Kirk's feelings; it would otherwise have been unthinkable for him to delve into Kirk's mind without permission and pull out memories in such a wholesale fashion. Spock is no stranger to emotion, even love, and he would know that even in an unhappy love affair, part of the human need is to hold on to the memory, even if the majority of memories are sad ones.

Flint, on the other hand, tried to create love. As Star Trek often showed us, the only kind of love which is acceptable is that which is natural and mutually shared. It cannot be created, forced, or bargained for. The greatest irony is that Flint had already gained Reena's love—the love of a daughter for her father, the love of a student for her teacher, the love of a friend for a friend—but in his single-minded quest for an immortal sexual partner, he was blinded to the virtue and value of a loving and devoted daughter. Flint paid for his aberration with the death of Reena and, eventually, his own.

Spock is strangley drawn to the nonviolent principles (but not practices) and the "free love" of the space hippies in "The Way to Eden." His experiences on Omnicron Ceti III probably caused him to feel a little nostalgic at the mention of an "Eden"; he probably also sympathized with the youngsters' alienation. Kirk, on the other hand, dismisses it all as sheer nonsense; he has little use for an Eden, as his actions on both Omnicron Ceti and the Amerind planet showed. Regardless of the interests of the principals involved, Star Trek again used an episode to illustrate the folly of meaningless, and ultimately loveless, existence.

The Vulcan embodiment of "love," Surak, makes an appearance in "The Savage Curtain." Hailed by Spock as the father of all that Vulcans are, Surak is completely nonviolent, preaching the value of brotherly love and sharing over the self-defeating practices of fighting and distrust. As in our own civilization, the principles of nonviolence are fine until the time comes when men must fight to preserve freedom. This is something Spock understands (and most other modern Vulcans as well; Vulcan is a full participant in Starfleet), and he disappoints Surak when he chooses to remain with Kirk and fight the villains. The difference in the attitudes toward their respective idols shown by Kirk and Spock is revealing: Kirk considers Lincoln a great man, someone to be admired and emulated; Spock seems to feel that Surak is almost a god, someone to be worshiped. While both replicates die bravely, it seems to be Kirk who is less disappointed by meeting his idol "in the flesh." Spock, while he still reveres Surak for what he was and what he accomplished, is forced to admit to himself that Surak's principles are not always correct or reasonable. This was perhaps Spock's first great revelation: The Vulcan Way is not always the right way.

Spock, like Kirk, never fell in love while "himself"—although that would, in any case, be a heck of a lot less likely to happen with Spock than it would be with Kirk. But in "All Our Yesterdays" the circumstances were such that Spock *was* himself—at least the self he would be if all psychological and social restraints were removed; the Spock he would have been had he been born thousands of years in Vulcan's past. As a result of not having been "prepared" by Mr. Atoz's atavachron, Spock reverted to the psychic demeanor of his ancestors (or his contemporaries; it's all in how you look at it) and began to fall victim to temptations of the flesh. And succulent temptation indeed was the enticing Zarabeth. Freed of his emotional constraints, Spock was able to eat and enjoy meat, became angry to the point of violence with Dr. McCoy, and fell in love with Zarabeth.

Which wouldn't be too hard for any normal, healthy male, be he human or Vulcan. Zarabeth was a beautiful, intelligent, and self-sufficient young woman, just the type that Spock would approve of as an excellent example of her species. Once Spock had reverted, however, all he cared about was that Zarabeth was a woman. (It is interesting to speculate why Dr. McCoy did not revert to a more savage mien as well. Perhaps he, as a human, was *already* acting as savagely and emotionally as were his counterparts on ancient Earth.) Although Zarabeth was lonely to the point of madness and desperation, still she was a warm and bright individual, completely lacking in the coyness and martyrdom that flawed Leila Kalomi's personality. She and Spock, even in the throes of his artificial passion, made an attractive and well-matched couple. We cannot help but get the feeling that he would have had an interest in her even under normal circumstances—and we also get the feeling that he will not forget her as easily as he would like to have Dr. McCoy think. We can only trust that nine months or so after her visitors from the future departed, Zarabeth had a pointed-eared little toddler to ease her loneliness.

Was Kirk once in love with Janice Lester? Surely she was in love with him to the point of becoming quite insane when they split up. Perhaps they were too much alike. Janice, in her madness, reflects in a warped and unhealthy manner many of the qualities that we find in Kirk: ambition, obsession with command, vanity, ruthlessness. Or maybe she just aped these things in her insane desire to *be* Kirk, taking them to extremes because of hatred and illness. Revenge, not love, was Janice's motive, but the root cause of all her trouble was her unrequited love for Kirk. We can't blame him, of course; he was very young and didn't desire to remain in an affair that would have destroyed them both. He was also too young and inexperienced in true human emotions to realize how deeply Janice was hurt; a more mature Kirk could perhaps have found a way to end the affair without such bitterness and rancor. In any case, he could not have predicted that Janice would be so disastrously affected by the breakup.

Dr. Coleman loved Janice. Yes, it doesn't make sense for a man to help the woman he loves become another man, but love often doesn't make sense. Probably Coleman felt that once Janice had achieved her wish to be Kirk, she would realize that she was happier as a woman being loved by Coleman, and would reverse the mindswap. Coleman seriously misread both Janice's degree of insanity and her intentions, but then he wasn't the most stable of personalities himself. He allowed Janice to use him at every opportunity, worrying only about the consequences of their actions, never about the morality of them. As we said, love in Star Trek takes many forms—and not all of them are logical or healthy.

The animated Star Trek episodes, while well done within the budgetary and time limitations imposed upon them, were nonetheless sorely lacking in character development and exposition. Thus many of Star Trek's attitudes (both stated and implicit) about love and examples of the same were absent from the animated shows. However, several episodes did manage to sneak in a few instances, and those are worth mentioning in this article.

"Yesteryear" showed us a young Spock who had great respect and affection for his parents, but a lovely and purely innocent love for his pet *sehlat*, I'Chaya. Thus we learn that Spock was no different from little boys everywhere: He felt misunderstood by his parents, he fought with his friends, he ran away from home, and he had a "dog." But it is when I'Chaya is severely wounded and young Spock makes the decision to have him put to sleep rather than suffer constant pain that we see the beginnings of the adult love and compassion our Mr. Spock displays in abundance.

In adapting the form of Carter Winston, the Vendorian shape-changer also assimilated many of Winston's characteristics, including Winston's love for Anne Nored. The more he is around her, the more he is drawn to her—a combination of Winston's memories and feelings, and the alien's own need for acceptance and affection. When he finally reveals himself and admits to his treachery, he is surprised to find that Anne is willing to accept him as Winston and he eagerly agrees to her suggestion that they "talk it over."

"Mudd's Passion" introduced a love potion onboard the *Enterprise*, and naturally it was poor old Spock who got the biggest dose of it. (Most of the other crewmembers got to share in the fun as well when the potion got swept into the ship's ventilation system.) Of course, Christine would never have agreed to mess with Mudd and his schemes if she thought the potion would actually work; when it does, she is more surprised and aghast than anyone. An amusing side effect of the potion is that it causes the folks who fall in love because of it to hate each other violently for several hours afterward . . . kind of the same feelings this episode engendered in most fans.

The longtime love of Robert April and his wife, Sarah, is one of the few instances of a successful, mutually enhancing marriage we saw in Star Trek. No greater indication of the happiness of their union can be thought of than their decision to revert to their true ages, and their reason for doing so: The only life worth living over is one which has left you unfulfilled. As Robert and Sarah are very happy indeed with the lives they've led together, they do not require "a second chance." It is a nice affirmation of what love should be and one of the finest moments in animated Star Trek.

Of course, many other animated episodes contained instances of love at its best as postulated by Star Trek. Kirk's unwillingness to kill the cosmic cloud creature in "One of Our Ships Is Missing" and its corresponding reluctance to harm the *Enterprise* crew; Dr. Keniclius 5's desire to bring peace to the galaxy ("The Infinite Vulcan"); and the examples of acceptance of difference seen in "Magicks of Megas-Tu," "The Terratin Incident," "Time Trap," and "BEM."

So we may see that although the limitations of the animated form did prevent the series from achieving the richness of characterization and interaction that made the original series so involving, the concepts of Star Trek were so overridingly *right* that even the kid-vid mentality of Saturday-morning cartoons couldn't destroy them.

Star Trek: The Motion Picture contained many examples of love, some of them quite startlingly different from the kinds of love previously displayed in the Star Trek universe. Many fans have commented that Gene Roddenberry's view of Star Trek and its universe seemed to somehow change during the years-long layoff, seemed somehow to have become cynical and embittered, seeing the *Enterprise* as a harsh mistress rather than as the demanding and unforgiving, but ultimately supremely rewarding, lover than she was in the series. This, of course, resulted in a drastic change in the characterization of Kirk (who, as always may be seen as Roddenberry's alter ego); changes in Kirk's character resulted, not unsurprisingly, in changes in supporting characters. Most important of these was the change in Spock. The changes in Spock were valid and logical within the emotional framework which had been built over the course of the series (these changes will be discussed in depth later), but it may be simply stated for the purposes of this argument that Spock's characterization changes and actions were performed so as to completely alienate Kirk, allowing his total aloneness to be the core around which the film's plot was built. A Kirk deprived of the three things he loves most—his command, his ship, his best friend—is a Kirk lost, a Kirk unlike any other we have ever seen. In causing this to happen, Roddenberry immediately supplied himself with a plot premise guaranteed to grab the emotions of every fan, and he also enriched and furthered the characterization of Spock and Kirk (and, resultingly, those around them) to a degree which would have otherwise been unthinkable.

Kirk, as we were shown innumerable times during the course of the series, coveted the *Enterprise* and the power and prestige afforded to him as her captain. This was, except in times of mental distress or, rarer, total honesty, expressed as "love" for the ship. This is quite an unusual way for Kirk to feel, especially toward an inanimate object. Kirk seldom, if ever, displayed the type of personality which would attach feelings to (or attribute them from) an inanimate object. On the contrary, from what we learn of and can see in Kirk's personality, he is a man who encumbers himself with as few possessions as possible, denoting a distinctive lack of sentiment. Aside from a few ancient books, his medals and awards (which he does not display), and some works of art, Kirk's cabin is almost spartanly bare. One cannot help but feel that his soul is in similar shape. So why, then, do fans so insistently declare that Kirk passionately loves the physical being, the nuts and bolts, the "stem to stern" reality of the *Enterprise*? It is simply not logical and is certainly not backed up by fact or statement.

There is sentiment involved, of course—fan sentiment. Not wanting to admit that their beloved Kirk can be less than perfect, they choose instead to cloak his perfectly natural and understandable passion for command in a more romantic desire for "a tall ship and a star to sail her by." This fiction is harmless enough—one even suspects that Kirk himself has used it to good effect now and then during the course of a love affair or two—but it must have particularly rankled Roddenberry, who originally conceived Kirk as a Horatio Hornblower surrogate; not a romantic or a dreamer, but instead a hardheaded, professional spacefarer who was tempered by compassion, love, and dreams, not ruled by them. When preparing *Star Trek: The Motion Picture,* Roddenberry could have seen this new film as the opportunity to rectify this misapprehension of his main character in a most dramatic and detailed manner. The result: the harsh, demanding, almost obsessed Kirk we saw throughout much of the film.

This was not a "new" Kirk by any means—we had seen him a number of times previously acting in just such a roughshod and domineering manner. The difference in *Star Trek: The Motion Picture* was that Kirk was, for the first time in our experience, acting from a position of weakness, not a position of strength. Deprived of the confidence and authority of legitimate command, the very worst side of Kirk's passions revealed itself. No, this was nothing like the sneering, brutal "evil side" of Kirk we saw in "The Enemy Within" . . . the Kirk in *STTMP* was a man floundering, desperately grasping for a last chance at—what? Life? Love? Freedom? Perhaps all of these.

But it is love which is our consideration here, and it was through an act of love that Kirk regained his self, his true identity. But Roddenberry wasn't going to be that obvious. It would have been easy to allow Kirk to suit up and go after Spock, unconscious from his encounter with V'Ger. (Indeed, we are teased with a shot of Kirk donning the EVA suit.) Spock, however, was sent back to the ship by V'Ger, depriving Kirk of a "typical Kirk self-sacrificing scene" in this film. There would be no easy catharsis, no simple heroics to put things aright. Kirk would have to face his own humanity and failings in the face of his friend Spock. It was obviously not only the Vulcan who was experiencing the joy of that "simple feeling"—as Spock felt, for the first time, what it meant to *know* that loved ones care, so too was Kirk's own self-worth reaffirmed in the love that Spock shared with him.

Spock formed a new link with humanity, and through his humanness, Kirk reformed his broken link. Thus, we learn that the power of love and friendship enables men to transcend doubts and fears. In sharing feelings, they are able to become more than the sum of their parts.

Spock's actions at the end of the original five-year mission are almost incomprehensible to most fans. Denying all that he had learned about himself and his own humanity, he left his human friends and Starfleet and thrust himself into the harsh Vulcan *Kolinahr* discipline. We may assume that this was a case in which love was not enough—Spock felt so incomplete and so dissatisfied with his life that the love and respect of his friends was unfulfilling. Eventually, however, the love Spock held for them, especially Kirk, betrayed his ambitions to achieve a state of total absence of emotion. The dullest schoolchild could have told Spock that you can't forget those you love, no matter what kind of mental disciplines you use. Those you love are too much a part of yourself to deny.

One of the most charming and/or exasperating things about Spock, however, has always been his stubbornness about admitting the extent to which emotions affect him. Once again, he denies their strength, and upon arriving on the *Enterprise,* affects a mantle of cold aloofness which fools no one, but exasperates everybody. This time, however, Spock is not simply standing back and remaining uninvolved. He must, for the sake of his own sanity, keep the onrushing emotions from taking control. Having for so long attempted to eradicate these emotions, he must have found it devastating to find out how completely he had failed. Any lesser man would have been crushed. The cold logic of V'Ger is, Spock feels, his last hope. If he can only discover what the secret is, how the entity can be so free of emotion, then perhaps he can salvage something of his ambitions.

Of course, Spock ultimately learns that the very logic of V'Ger's mind causes it to be barren of hope and beauty and faith and all of the other million-and-one intangible things that make human life so interesting and exciting. Or so Spock says.

Consider this: V'Ger was compared, by Spock, to a child . . . questioning, seeking, wondering who it was and where it was going. These are not cold, logical concerns. They are the stuff of self-awareness, of burgeoning humanity. If V'Ger could seek something greater than itself, then it could at least understand the concept of faith, even if it could not accept it.

Spock, in his abortive meld with V'Ger, would have seen all this and more. It probably was more like a look into his own mind than anything else, and it could have been this realization which led him to an appreciation of the "simple feeling" of shared human love and friendship. Spock, being Spock, still could not bring himself to simply admit he had been wrong. So he sort of colored the situation a bit in his own favor. And that is more than enough proof that he accepted and embraced his humanity.

Love in *Star Trek: The Motion Picture* is seen, above all, as a healing force. Not only are Kirk and Spock flawed, Decker and Ilia are also. Separated by the dual demons of duty and honor, they are each incomplete without the other.

(It is a curious statement that Star Trek makes in regard to "mixed" love between partners of different planetary species: in every example seen, the love shared is unusually strong and pure, as if the very action of overcoming the taboos and strictures against interspecies romance forms stronger, more passionate bonds.)

Ilia is incomplete simply by virtue of the fact that she must (by oath!) refrain from sexual contact while serving in Starfleet. For a being as sexually oriented as are the Deltans, such abstinence must be as debilitating as the lack of proper sleep or food would be to us. One cannot help but feel that Ilia is punishing herself in some way by agreeing to such an existence. The most natural supposition, of course, is that she joined Starfleet both to forget Decker and to serve penance for having committed the crime of falling in love with him. If so, then her choice of career was a rather strange one, for chances were that she would eventually come across him again; a classic case of self-fulfilling disaster.

Decker, on the other hand, is more of a "young Kirk" than is at first evident. At the time of his unconsummated affair with Ilia on Delta, he was more concerned with his career than with his happiness. Or, rather, he made the same mistake as did Kirk of confusing ambition with gaining happiness. Will tells Ilia that had he attempted to tell her goodbye, he would have been unable to leave. This, too, evokes echoes of Kirk, who also often seemed to be at a loss when ending an affair—probably because, like Decker, he feared that he would be unable to say a meaningful goodbye. By the time of *Star Trek: The Motion Picture*, Will has achieved his desire: captaincy of a starship. But he is probably not totally happy, no more than was Kirk when commanding the *Enterprise*. He, perhaps unconsciously, yearns for something more, to be a part of something greater. We may assume that Ilia was inextricably wound up in this desire; it may even have centered around her. In any case, when they again met aboard the *Enterprise*, Decker's decision to remain with her, in whatever fashion, became a certainty. Neither of them would have been able to bear parting again. Indeed, so strong was Decker's love for Ilia that he transferred it to the V'Ger-created simulacrum. So strong was her love for him that it survived even within the circuitry of that being and kept it from becoming totally a machine and a creature of V'Ger.

Decker and Ilia, like almost every major character in *STTMP*, are seriously flawed, and it is only when they are literally merged with each other that we see them as complete beings. We are never flat-out told that they are "two halves of a whole," that would be too easy, too much a cliché. But it is a definite impression we gain through their actions, their scenes together. The two of them, together with the "soul" of V'Ger, come together to forge a new life form, one which must, of necessity in this Star Trek universe, contain the best—and worst—of each of them. Even though unthinkably advanced, it will still be a living, conscious, loving being . . . one with the galaxy and with all things.

Star Trek II: The Wrath of Khan presented us with an abundance of love, not only through our old friends, but through the introduction of new characters and situations.

Once again the story revolves around Kirk, and once again he is unhappy. This time, however, his unhappiness is caused by the fact that he feels that life is passing him by. He would much rather be back in space, in command of the *Enterprise*, but we get the impression that it is not so much the ship and the power of command that he covets, but instead any opportunity to do something meaningful with his life. His overweening concern with age is caused more by a surplus of time in which to sit around and think about it than by any physical symptoms. He is bored and lonely. He feels old and useless. He feels unloved.

For Kirk, love has always been inextricably tied up with his career and the resulting respect and admiration gained from it. He has rarely, if ever, entered into a one-on-one relationship with a lover or a friend on a basis of equality. Even when he lost his memory and fell in love with the Indian maiden, Miramanee, Kirk was considered a god by her and the members of her tribe. And now that he is more or less stalled in his career, "flying a desk," his status is no longer a bulwark to his confidence. Although he holds high position and has achieved great honor, Kirk obviously feels that he is little more than a civil servant. And when confronted by his friends, he feels out of things, hopelessly left on the sidelines as they, and life, pass him by. For the first time, we see Kirk surrounded by *things*, albeit beautiful, meaningful things, but inanimate objects nonetheless. It is the mark of how much Kirk has changed, of how he considers his life to be forever set upon a single path. Kirk's antiques and souvenirs tell us that he expects to spend the rest of his life in those rooms, eventually becoming, as McCoy warns, one of the antiques himself.

This is not strictly true, of course. The chiding that McCoy gives him as a kind of backhanded birthday present lets us know that it is still possible for Kirk to get a deep-space command simply by asking for it. Why he does not is the deepest mystery of the film. We can casually assume that he would not feel comfortable unless he captained the *Enterprise* and was surrounded by his old crew, but that would be wrong. As much as Kirk respected and admired and depended upon these people, he could, and would, successfully serve without them. No, the reason why Kirk would not obtain another ship is a mystery which will only be solved when we learn the story (or stories) relating what happened during the years between the films.

In any case, once Kirk is forced by circumstance to take command of the *Enterprise*, he soon becomes his old self—rusty to the point of danger, perhaps, but still *Captain* Kirk. It is important to note that Kirk did not actively desire to wrest command from Spock—regulations required that he do so. And when he went to the Vulcan's quarters to inform him, Kirk sounded genuinely regretful and apologetic. Spock, as usual, had the perfect response and we saw immediately that their friendship, so painfully affirmed in *Star Trek: The Motion Picture*, remained intact and stronger than ever.

There are no problems between Kirk and Spock (and McCoy) in *Wrath of Khan*. They are close friends and associates; McCoy even serves on the *Enterprise* under Spock! The triad is complete—but somehow a little less interesting than before. . . . Perhaps the loss of the tension caused by Spock's adamant refusals to admit to his human side is more debilitating than we ever thought it would be; perhaps each of them is just a little older and a little more sedate and less interesting. In any case, we see three men who have aged well, each growing richer through the others. Except for Kirk's dissatisfaction, we could say that they had reached a kind of Star Trek nirvana.

Even if Kirk were not feeling old, he still is actually growing old. And the one inevitable fact of life is that by living it, we leave a trail behind us, an unalterable past, full of our follies and wisdoms. If we are lucky, our pasts will never catch up with us. James Kirk, although it would be inaccurate to call him unlucky, *is* something of a magnet for trouble. And in *Wrath of Khan*, we basically see the story of what happens when several large chunks of Jim Kirk's past present themselves to him all in a few days. . . .

We may assume that Kirk loved Carol Marcus and that they spent quite a bit of time together, they may even have had a short-term marriage contract. But we get the distinct impression that their parting was not as amicable as their present behavior would lead us to believe. Kirk speaks bitterly to McCoy of "reopening old wounds"; we do not know if this refers to the circumstances of their parting or Carol's insistence that David be raised free from Kirk's influence. In any case, Kirk's feelings for her have survived relatively intact through the years, as his comment to McCoy and his tender mien to her unmistakably display. It might be too strong a statement to say that he still loves her, but he definitely still has a soft spot for Carol, and probably easily could fall in love with her again.

Of course, Kirk's feelings for Carol are inextricably tied up with his rather ambivalent feelings for David. Kirk says flat out in the film that he stayed away because she wanted him to; it is possible that he transferred some of the resentment he felt toward Carol to the child, a perfectly natural response, and one which would allow him to justify the fact that he was not around when his son was growing up. (It's interesting that in her novelization of *Wrath of Khan*, Vonda McIntyre softens Kirk's position, leaving a question in our minds as to whether or not he knew of David's birth.) Deep in his heart, Kirk probably knows that he would have made a lousy father, what with being absent most of the time and not possessing the temperament for home life anyway. What is rather amazing is that Kirk did not attempt to keep track of David. Knowing how possessive and obsessive Kirk could become under certain circumstances, it is hard to believe that he could so totally divorce himself from the life of his child. We would expect Kirk to gain information, in one way or another, about David and even, in whatever ways possible, to influence his upbringing. Either Kirk so loved Carol that his agreement to stay away was inviolable to him, or else he was so hurt that he literally blocked thoughts of David from his mind. The latter is probably the most likely, for we never got even a hint, in word or deed, that Kirk knew or even cared that he had a son growing up somewhere.

Now, however, Kirk's overriding desire is to have David's respect. Jim probably believes that it is too late to ever have the kind of love from David that he could have had as a true father, but it would not be too much to hope to gain the boy's respect—even though David philosophically despises much that Kirk stands for.

David, on the other hand, does not even know Kirk, except as "that Boy Scout type" that his mother used to see. (David obviously learned from Carol or, more likely, another family member that she was once involved with Kirk, as he would not have seen Kirk in the flesh.) We do not know for sure when David learns that Kirk is his biological father. We can only assume it is sometime after Spock's death, for there would not have been time for Carol to have told him previously. (Unless, knowing that they could all soon die, and wanting David to know that Kirk was his father, she informed him just before he came to the bridge during the battle in the Mutara Nebula.) It would have been interesting to know exactly how David reacted to this news. Was he shocked, or did he already suspect, having seen his mother and Kirk together? Did he decide to tell Kirk of his regret for Spock's death and his pride before or after he learned the truth? It wouldn't make much difference to Kirk, but it does in the context of David's mindset. If he had gained a new respect for Kirk, and Starfleet, before discovering that they were related, it would indicate that he was admitting to the necessity and value of men such as Kirk and the job that they do. If he was only expressing his pleasure at being Kirk's son, then he may not have learned anything of real value from the situation at all. We shall have to wait until future adventures to see.

The other new kid on the block, Saavik, also piques our curiosity, especially in the matter of her parentage. True, we are given no overt evidence that she is Spock's biological daughter, but we cannot avoid the feeling that she *is* a part of Spock, a larger part than can be explained by just respect and affection. There is that between them, oh yes, respect and affection in an amount and of an unshamed evidence that we never saw between even Spock and Kirk. (In the "old days," that is . . . now, nothing could be plainer or more obvious than the existence of their friendship.) Spock, without doubt, has allowed himself, on the one hand, and Saavik, on the other, to move their relationship far beyond that of teacher and student. In perhaps everything but name, she is his daughter and the spiritual heir of all that he stands for.

Having been raised as an outcast among the harsh Romulan colonies, Saavik probably did not see, or even perhaps feel, any love or affection during her entire childhood. Chances are that she was an embittered and completely recalcitrant child when discovered by Spock and his team. That she has developed into an intelligent and caring person is nothing short of a miracle, and we can only assume that Spock himself was responsible for it. Chances are that he did not, himself, see to her upbringing; an educated guess would have him giving Saavik to Sarek and Amanda to raise. She would have been taught Vulcan lore and educated in the sciences by Sarek; Amanda would have taught her how to act as a civilized Vulcan woman. And also, with or without Sarek's permission, what it means to be a human woman as well, for Spock would have surely explained the difficulties Saavik's dual heritage would cause her in the future. And while human feelings and emotions are not like those of Romulans, they are certainly closer than anything Vulcan ritual could offer. Also, in the loving, safe warmth of Spock's home, Saavik could learn what it means to have a family and a heritage. It worked, for she now thinks of herself as "Vulcan" —but, as Spock undoubtedly told her, thinking of yourself as something and actually being it are two different things.

If the above is true, then it would be more proper to consider Saavik as Spock's "little sister" rather than as his daughter. This is less romantic, but more realistic. Saavik's anger at David for suggesting she is Spock's daughter in the novelization of *Wrath of Khan* pretty much puts that possibility right out of the window. One would have to invent such unlikely scenarios as the Romulan commander's self-fertilization with Spock's semen to otherwise explain his parentage of Saavik. No, Spock, having mellowed and accepted his humanity, responded to the need of a child who must have, almost unbearably, reminded him of himself. And, like any compassionate, caring being, he helped her. Having helped her once, he continued to do so, until he had virtually adopted her. In the sense that he took it upon himself to accept responsibility for a child and to offer her encouragement, training, and even love, then, yes, Spock is Saavik's father.

Now, what of David and Saavik? They exchanged a few bickering lines in the film, but most of the exchanges between them which were to indicate that they were becoming interested in each other were cut out. We are then left with the impression that although they respected and liked each other to a certain extent, they did not immediately fall head over heels in love. Many fans expressed disappointment at this, feeling that a match between Kirk's son and Spock's "daughter" was such a natural outgrowth of the Kirk/Spock relationship that to not allow it to happen would almost be sacrilege. Upon reflection, however, even the most rabid fan would have to agree that such a relationship, while still entirely possible and not disagreeable, *must* grow from within the characters themselves, and not be arbitrarily forced upon them just to satisfy our sense of continuity. As of yet, we know virtually nothing of Saavik's and David's true personalities, and without the kind of week-by-week exposure to them that we had with Spock and Kirk, we never will. Would you expect to introduce two strangers and have them fall in love almost immediately? It is the stuff of bad fiction, and although Star Trek has had its share of bad fiction, it has yet to stoop to such soap-opera tactics.

It is not a new Spock we see in *Wrath of Khan*, simply a Spock who has exorcised his demons and is now free to give and accept friendship and love. He learned, and learned well, from his experience with V'Ger and has successfully applied those lessons to his life. We can expect not only that Spock can now openly and unashamedly call Kirk "friend," but that he also found the words to tell his mother and father of his love for them. The fact that he willingly sacrificed himself is nothing less that we would have ever expected of Spock, but his action affected us all the more because he had now become a richer, more accepted, and, surely, a happier person.

One would hardly expect to find the Khan of *Star Trek II: The Wrath of Khan* discussed in an article about love, but it is Khan who is probably the perfect example Star Trek gives us of how love may be warped and perverted to evil ends. Not since the original series has Star Trek made such a forceful and eloquent statement about love in all of its forms.

Khan, once the noble, if flawed, prince of millions, has been reduced to the leader of a ragtag group of survivors, living in almost subhuman conditions. It is little wonder that he goes quite mad. He still, however, manages to instill in his followers the same fanatical loyalty that he did in the past. Some of them, such as the hapless Joachim, obviously loved him. And Khan has not forgotten his beloved Marla McGivers. Not only does he speak in sadness and anger of her death, he wears a medallion modeled upon the *Enterprise* emblem she wore on her uniform. (It is possible that Marla fashioned this medallion herself in order to remind her—and Khan—of all that she had sacrificed to remain with him.)

Khan, however, represents more: He is the embodiment of all that can go wrong when the aims of science, government, religion, and even love miss the mark, go somehow terribly wrong. Man, as postulated by Star Trek, is a fallible being who does his best to overcome the destructive urges of his humanity, all the while constantly striving to become something more through the acquisition of knowledge. In simple terms, life is a constant struggle to better oneself.

At one time, it was thought that genetic engineering would be the solution to man's problems and faults. Simply design a better man, the scientists must have said, and he will guide the rest of us to paradise. But, Star Trek tells us, the end result of taking human powers to their limit is a being whose failures and faults are also taken to their limits . . . and you end up with a superbeing who is completely amoral, so completely *human* as to be, in a civilized society, inhuman. The first and the most powerful of these beings was Khan. He was the first ultimate male, and, inevitably, the first ultimate failure.

Khan, perversely, is the product of hope and love. Man, utilizing the hard-won knowledge of millions of years, decided he could improve upon nature in a benign fashion and that nature would not object. Nature, however, is an unforgiving force. It cares nothing for high hopes or altruism. Nature simply *is*. And so nature did not cooperate in the experiment. Unconcerned, nature gave the supermen the same animalistic urges and selfishness that she gives the rest of us.

In the case of Khan and the other supermen, love and good intentions were not enough. Yet, in their own smug, superior-minded way, the supermen craved and needed love—not only from each other, but from normal humans as well. Khan's domination of Marla McGivers in "Space Seed" was a means to an end—escape—but there was also a feeling of desperation in it, as if he felt that unless he was loved, even worshiped by someone, he did not exist. And, as mentioned above, Khan, at least, was quite capable of feeling love.

Yet loving individuals is quite a different thing from the kind of love that makes us more than ourselves—love of others, love of freedom, love of diversity. It was this kind of love which Khan and his followers were incapable of feeling, for it requires that one look beyond oneself. Like animals, the "superior" humans could not do this, and thus they were less than human, not more.

With the arrival of Genesis, not only does man now have the power to create not only "superior" humans, but entire worlds may be manipulated and created or recreated to specification. Or whim. Like nature, it matters not to Genesis. *Wrath of Khan* leaves us with the question of Spock's return. Will the power of Genesis revive the Vulcan? But the question is greater than that, yet more subtle. Will the power of Genesis revive humanity's basest urges? McCoy certainly thinks so, and he's always been a pretty good judge of human nature.

Ultimately, however, it comes down to the statement which Kirk made so many years ago: "We are not going to kill today." Mankind can, and must, control itself, its animalistic urges. Any madman could gain control of Genesis and wipe out perhaps dozens of planets before he was stopped, or a would-be dictator would find Genesis a most tempting weapon. Such is the risk of any new technology, whether it be the bow-and-arrow, gunpowder, or nuclear weapons. It is the control of man as a society which must concern us. When the society decides to use Genesis, or any weapon or technology, for sheer destruction and to further its own ends, then the tenets and beliefs of Kirk, of Spock, of Star Trek will have been abandoned.

As stated in the first half of this article (on page 132), Star Trek is based on love. The underlying theme of the series and the films is that man will someday overcome his own humanity and learn to live in peace and brotherly love not only with his own kind, but with myriad other sentient beings throughout the universe. By following Kirk's advice, by admitting to our own humanity and controlling our own inhumanity, we can make that day come all the sooner.

INDIANA SKYWALKER MEETS THE SON OF STAR TREK

by Kyle Holland

Not everyone liked Star Trek II: The Wrath of Khan. *In fact, a number of our readers expressed extreme dislike for the film, for a wide range of reasons. In the following article, Kyle Holland explains why he didn't care for* Wrath of Khan *as a Star Trek story; he further examines factors underlying the film and its success which he feels do not bode well for the future of Star Trek. Is he right? Judge for yourself.*

Movie reviewers, television reviewers, and Star Trek fans seem to be in general agreement: *The Wrath of Khan* successfully translated Star Trek to the big screen, just as its precedessor, *Star Trek: The Motion Picture*, failed to do so. In conventional terms, *Wrath of Khan* is certainly a better "movie" than *STTMP*. But the spirit of Star Trek has always been to keep ahead of convention (suffering a bit for doing so, if necessary) and to pave the way for new and better standards. If one follows such logic, then *Star Trek: The Motion Picture* was a more authentic contribution to the shaping of Star Trek than was *Wrath of Khan*.

Wrath of Khan has a dramatic structure calculated to please the masses: An insane, bloodthirsty menace of a man has vowed his vengeance upon the good crew, and you may be sure that there will be plenty of torpedos and flying guts before Good triumphs. *STTMP* offered no such dramatic handle to the viewer. If you weren't content to experience the journey toward, near annihilation by, and ultimate reconciliation with V'Ger, you didn't get your money's worth. This is why so many have commented that *STTMP* improves with multiple viewings: You watch it for a second time (or more) only if you are willing to experience it. You are open in a way that few who watch the film for the first time are.

Star Trek: The Motion Picture can best be appreciated by repeated viewings. *Wrath of Khan*, on the other hand, is a shoot-'em-up in the style of *Star Wars* and *Raiders of the Lost Ark*—very thrilling the first time you see it, but not much left for a second viewing. In essence, *Wrath of Khan* is indeed a "movie," relying on suspense, which is exhausted once the action is run through. *STTMP*, on the other hand, is a film novel, revealing new patterns and nuances, new poetry, as it becomes more familiar.

If, as the Star Trek constituency, we claim to cultivate a sense of the future, we *must* recognize *Wrath of Khan* as part of a contemporary phenomenon—the one-time, pay-for-thrills motion-picture show—that cannot last. In future, films will be integrated into home technologies as disks, cassettes, etc. and will be purchased on the basis of their multiple-viewing merits. Under these standards, *STTMP* will easily qualify for inclusion in home libraries; it will, in its way, be a forerunner of future "good movies." This is the Star Trek tradition.

Beyond the sheer commercialism it embodies, the structure of *Wrath of Khan* raises philosophical questions to which we should be sensitive. The format is ironclad: Khan is evil, pure evil, and cannot be redeemed. Now just think back over all seventy-eight television episodes, and even the professional and fan fiction. When did you see a villain like this? An antagonist with whom meaningful communication is impossible, whose viewpoint cannot be comprehended by the *Enterprise* crew (or vice versa), an antagonist who can never be enlightened and with whom there can be no rapprochement, or even a truce? There was no villain like this in the series, but Khan is like this in the movie, because the premise of the plot would collapse if he were not. This is the first Star Trek in which there is a real alien: Khan himself.

The dramatic structure of *Star Trek: The Motion Picture* is purely within the developmental trends established by the series—so much so that many have repudiated it as a rehash of "The Changeling." Decrying the allusiveness of the film is something like giving demerits to Tolstoy or Faulkner because some of their novels depended upon characters or plot lines (or even whole passages) from earlier short stories. The themes of mistaken identities and intentions, evolution in both human and nonhuman spectra, and the longing for identity through confrontation with one's creator are central Star Trek themes, and we should consider them seriously whenever they are offered to us. "The Changeling" was indeed the sketch upon which the "novel" *Star Trek: The Motion Picture* was based, and that sums up the relationship between the two.

Many, many people (including Leonard Nimoy) have said that there is more of "the character" in *Wrath of Khan*. Nimoy's comments clearly were directed toward the *potential* movie in the unedited footage, which did indeed include characteristic exchanges: much of this was ultimately edited out, since as an action film *Wrath of Khan* could not afford to linger over the development of characters who should, ideally, be interchangeable with Luke Skywalker and Indiana Jones. What about the movie to which we now have access? In peculiar ways, real violence was done to the characters. As the old proverb says, you should be wary of wishes, for they may come true. . . . If you want a lot of "the characters" in a movie, you should be prepared for things to happen to them.

On television, when things happened to characters, it usually meant that they were hurt or captured, worried over, then rescued or healed; or they were struck dead, mourned, then revived. Deep emotional experiences were usually caused by aberrant conditions of one sort or another—meaningful enough while they lasted, but you knew that by next episode all traces of trauma would be gone. For all that, the series was not shallow for a very fundamental reason: Each character had a set of built-in and unresolvable conflicts which both animated and limited his or her actions, regardless of plot. These inner dynamics, it must be recognized, were primarily crafted by the actors themselves, with cooperation from Roddenberry and Fontana. One can only admire the stamina of this group in attempting (often without success) to fend off the attacks of bad writing which plagued the series. In the end, they won: After many bizarre diversions, the characters they created stood as vivid, integrated, and consistent.

A movie, even a Star Trek movie, cannot consist of two hours of injuries, rescues, fistfights, resurrections, and counterlogical assaults on arrogant computers; and if you want something to "happen" to the characters, it has to be something that will not wear off in five minutes, and—one hopes—that is consistent with the characterization itself.

Before discussing each film's handling of five pivotal Star Trek "characters"—the Federation, the *Enterprise*, Kirk, Spock, and McCoy—it must be noted that we are not told the chronological relationship between the two films. In real time, there was about a ten-year lapse between the last television episode and *STTMP*, although we are informed that the events of the film take place (almost unbelievably) about two years after the *Enterprise*'s return from its "five-year-mission." *Wrath of Khan* followed about two years later in real time, and *Star Trek III* is apparently scheduled to follow about two years after that. But (reasons to be discussed) internal evidence suggests that the events of *Wrath of Khan* happen at least five years, perhaps more, after the events of *STTMP*.

The Federation

This was a valid presence in the series. With its Prime Directive and the *Enterprise*'s peaceful mission of exploration (Kirk explained patiently to Garth that he was no longer a combatant, but now an "explorer"), its purposes were clear. But there was not only idealism behind the Federation's nonmilitaristic attitude. We saw many instances in which the amicable reputation of the Federation brought it lucrative trading contracts or access to natural resources (usually at the expense of the aggressive Klingons); in addition, this policy seems to have been the key to political stability. Think of Kirk's lecture to Spock-2 on the longevity of the Empire (several hundred years) compared to that of the Federation (several thousand years).

We recognized the ranks and uniforms (casual togs, unsuitable for combat, certainly), and we knew something of Federation procedures. We knew, too, that they could fight, and fight effectively—but only if and when other alternatives did not exist.

It is not very surprising that in *Star Trek: The Motion Picture* this Federation is headquartered in a very beautiful San Francisco. We get glimpses of its shuttle platforms and logos, and its staff bustling about; we find out that Star Fleet Command is headed by Admiral Nogura, who is apparently a tough guy (in the novelization of *STTMP* he is actually exploitive of Kirk—for the greater good, of course). Basically, we see the Federation going about the business we expect of it, and the physical details are pleasing and familiar.

By the time of *Wrath of Khan*, it appears that the Federation has been overwhelmed and drastically altered by some cataclysm—possibly revolution. The jumpsuits of *STTMP* are replaced by highly militaristic get-ups; if they had high bearskin hats they would look exactly like the guardsmen at Buckingham Palace. You can hear the psychological sabers rattling when they walk. The only aspect of training we glimpse is a simulated battle scenario, and the grimness with which it is taken by both Kirk and Saavik suggests that this is not a peripheral aspect of the curriculum. The assertion that Kirk underwent the same simulation as a cadet is intended to suggest that this is part of Federation tradition. But the actors have wisely suggested that in earlier days *Kobayashi Maru* could hardly have had the same significance: The gleeful mugging of Sulu and McCoy as they "die," together with Kirk's reluctance to admit that he "passed" the test by cheating, assure us that the test is a bigger deal now than when they were young. We also have to swallow the extraordinary attitude of the scientists of Regula I toward the Federation. Carol Marcus, for her own reasons, is merely less than confident that the Federation will not corrupt Genesis into a weapon; the rest of her team are frankly suspicious, and her son openly paranoid. Is this the way the scientists of Memory Alpha felt?

The Enterprise

The transformation of an inanimate (in fact, nonexistent inanimate) object into a living presence was a special achievement of *STTMP*. The long approach of Scott and Kirk to the ship in the shuttle was a crucial step in this transformation, and this sequence may be taken as a study in the creative application of modern special-effects technology: The intent is not to startle, frighten, or thrill the viewer, but to create a reality that did not exist before. The effect is reinforced in the many flank and distance shots of the ship in transport, in jeopardy, in release. The interior of the ship is believable. Clearly, the *Enterprise* has undergone some interior redecoration since its return. Its pale blues are suitable for extended habitation—much more so than the reds and oranges that were part of the old decor. The officer's quarters are efficient but not spartan—very much in the style of the voyaging *Enterprise*, but more moody, comfortable. Indeed, like a living entity (the *very* "living machine" that V'Ger considers it to be), the *Enterprise* has a mood of its own, a patient, contemplative, yet inquiring spirit.

In *Wrath of Khan*, the *Enterprise* has become, for all practical purposes, a battleship. The sickbay is no longer a chamber of wonder and discovery; it is full of bloody boys, many dying. Now the site of ship detail is the torpedo run (in a bit of heavy-handed theme-mongering, we are forced to note that Spock's coffin is actually one of these instruments of death). Kirk's quarters are fitted with oak and antique weapons as befits a man of war; in fact it is merely because of the threat of combat that he has assumed command of the ship. And in its visual representation, the *Enterprise* has no independent existence. It is merely a part of the battle panorama, dodging, shooting and rolling.

Kirk

We used to know Kirk. He was that prickly individual always trying to overcome his temper, that physical guy trying to become gentle, that fighter trying to become peaceful, an infant trying to become wise. Enlightenment and backsliding were the constants of his experience, since, as he was proud of saying, he was "human." Love and companionship he viewed as necessary to life, but unattainable in their absolute forms; when he and Spock nodded to each other at the end of "The Naked Time," their meaning was clear enough. And finally Kirk was the victim of that peculiar emotional projection whereby the *Enterprise* became the symbol of his own origin and his own destiny.

This Kirk fits very naturally into *Star Trek: The Motion Picture.* Two years behind a desk, a pawn for the Admiralty, has made him childishly ruthless in his determination to "get back" the *Enterprise*; his claim that it is merely the exigencies of the moment which prompt him to assume command fools no one. His return to the *Enterprise* is the first of the "capturing God" coils in the film's complex structure. Slowly he learns to handle the ship and himself. With his old stubborness he tries to reassume his role as human sounding board to Spock. Above all, we recognize him for his openness to V'Ger and his fearlessness, his confidence in the success of communication and compassion when approaching it.

Shatner's splendid performance in *Wrath of Khan* is the only means of recognizing the erstwhile captain. Somehow, he has again given up the *Enterprise* (Spock tells him bluntly that for him to do other than command the ship is a "waste"—apparently he saw *STTMP*, which is more than can be said for Admiral Kirk). He has no passion for getting her back; he seems to spend a lot of time mooning around his apartment, where he is told by McCoy (who also saw *STTMP*) to get back his command. This Kirk is marvelously blasé and mature. He doesn't stop himself on the verge of temper outbursts, he doesn't muse aloud about how much wiser he is now than an hour ago. He doesn't look for and try to cultivate evidences of warmth and communicativeness in Spock, he doesn't have any eyeballing sessions with McCoy. We are told, as if this were a new "fact," that this Kirk is still incomplete, but what is this mysterious something he is missing? Why, a wife and child, of course, who are promptly produced (literally out of thin air), providing him with new (and boring) preoccupations. It is probably because of these new problems that Kirk gives not a moment's consideration to the misfortunes (for which he was indeed partly responsible) that drove the egomaniacal Khan to madness.

Spock

He is, of course, the center of *Star Trek: The Motion Picture,* and those who claim that they can't get enough of "the characters" from the movie should consider this. When McCoy says, only half sarcastically, "Lucky for you we just happen to be going your way," he is speaking for all of us; the search for V'Ger is Spock's own. The visual subtlety and power of the *Enterprise* interiors are, it may be suggested, inspired by Spock and the relationship of the physical journey of the ship to Spock's spiritual journey. The view of Vulcan included early in the film is fully consistent with the series, yet surpasses anything we have seen. And the Vulcan scenes contribute to the integrity of the film as a freestanding entity, establishing Spock's condition at the beginning of his search, and the nature of his calling. The brittle Spock who appears on the *Enterprise* bridge is more complex than any Spock we have met before, yet fully recognizable; he is fresh from a major disappointment, a failure (of the sort only Spock could experience), and this is indeed how he should behave. The discussion with Kirk and McCoy is authentic Star Trek: Spock's unexpressed (but evident) anguish, McCoy's baiting sarcasm, Kirk's willingness (and inability) to understand his resentment of rebuff, his tenacious loyalty. This scene is right. The same can be said, surprisingly, of the sickbay scene. Think of creating a scene in which Spock is supposed to squeeze Kirk's hand, profess that this "simple feeling" (of what? hand-squeezing? human contact? friendship? love?) is superior to anything else in the whole universe. Suppose you hadn't seen it, you just had to create it, and it had better not be soppy or bizarre, or invite whistles from the audience. It would not be easy—unless you left the execution to the instincts of the creators and actors of Star Trek. And this scene works, against all odds. It is something that happens to Spock; and if you didn't think it showed, you missed the warm, meaningful looks he was giving his friend, the wisdoms he was speaking about V'Ger (himself), the new directness of his speech.

You probably missed them in *Wrath of Khan* too, because they weren't there. The emotional premises of *Wrath of Khan* are not clear. Both Spock and McCoy apparently decided to stay with Starfleet (why?). Only Spock, it seems, is actually attached to the *Enterprise* under normal conditions. Nevertheless it appears that the three are used to spending time together, possibly even seeing each other on a daily basis. Kirk does not take the wry pleasure in the Spock-McCoy debate that he would after a separation—he just considers it annoying and cuts it off. They are three old friends who know each other thoroughly. And this is as it must be, since this movie will not allow a drama to develop among the three, as did *Star Trek: The Motion Picture*. Kirk's drama is to come from the materialization of an old lover and a son. Spock's is to come from a heroic death.

The treatment of Spock in *Wrath of Khan* is so insipid that it is actually insulting to the audience. Those who are not familiar with Star Trek must wonder who the guy with the funny ears is; those who *are* familiar with Star Trek must also wonder who the guy with the funny ears is. Fortunately it is common cultural knowledge that he is half-human, half-Vulcan—you won't find this out in the film. Since we must surmise that he is in daily contact with Kirk, meaningful stares would probably be out of place, but why should Spock act like a cold fish? During the five-year mission, Spock at his Vulcan worst was never like this; in fact, the Spock who got off the *Surak* and fixed the *Enterprise* engines in *STTMP* was considerably more soulful. We can only conclude that the revolution which militarized the Federation has left Spock drained of enthusiasm for life.

No wonder! For the first time, Nimoy has been miscast as Spock. Spock, a scientist whose previous experiences as a commander so often came near to disaster, is now inexplicably commander of the *Enterprise*. Spock, with his respect for authority, has now *become* the authority, as commander and teacher—no duller prospect could loom for the character's creator. The mentor/student, father/daughter relationship with Saavik is not believable: The last we saw of Spock, he was still an emotional child, and said so. In fact, it is part of his destiny to always be an emotional child, but to keep up with Kirk he is supposed to assume the role of "parent." In total, the film allowed Spock exactly one authentic word (as opposed to whole scenes in *Star Trek: The Motion Picture*): On his way to the reactor room, Spock short-circuited McCoy's objections with a nerve pinch and, lowering him, touched his temple for mental contact, saying, "Remember." For about twenty seconds, we see Star Trek: First the nerve pinch (beggars can't be choosers), Nimoy's own creation, then the one-word (and rather effective) allusion to the tag scenes from "Requiem for Methuselah." We are not surprised to discover that even this meager offering was not in the original script.

McCoy

Supporting actors can hardly be inconsistent, and since the doctor is only allowed to support, we recognize him always and everywhere. But as a support, his role fluctuates according to what is happening to Kirk and Spock. In *Star Trek: The Motion Picture*, the man shines. He has left the Federation—that sounds right—and he has been "drafted" back. His objections are all authentic; we don't have to hear the explanations to believe it. His blunt talk to Kirk about his *Enterprise* complex pushes us several steps forward; we couldn't go on the way we were, and this is the first time Kirk's problem has been stated out loud for him. For Spock, the doctor does as much as he ever could—a little effusion, a little sarcasm, a little huffing and puffing, and a lot of waiting. If things are "happening" to Kirk and Spock, as they are in *STTMP*, McCoy must be there.

Only the artificial and ridiculous happens to the two in *Wrath of Khan*; inside them there are no events, and so the doctor is just hanging around. Why is he mucking about with the command crew in the *Kobayashi*

Maru? Why is he standing around on the bridge or on the Genesis Planet, hands behind his back? Nothing to do. Nobody to talk to. When the doctor has nothing to say, you know you are far from the heart of Star Trek.

Wrath of Khan is an entertaining movie masquerading as a Star Trek adventure. "Space Seed" was pillaged of the Khan character to create a facade of continuity; the earlier Khan was much more interesting than the devil (no offense to Milton) we are confronted with in the movie. The Star Trek figures, as scripted, are unrecognizable. How did this happen?

One could point to individuals; producers and writers with other than the best integrity of the entire Star Trek phenomenon at heart; a director who, in his novels, has been doing for years to Sherlock Holmes what he is commencing to do to Star Trek; and so on. But these people are only doing what they are supposed to do: make popular movies—and *Wrath of Khan* was a *very* popular movie.

The real problem, perhaps, is that we have not recognized that Star Trek has taken on a bilevel existence, and we must develop bilevel standards of appreciation. Space movies and action movies are the current trend. What smarter move could there be than to make a popular space movie based upon cult heroes who have a broad and enduring constituency? You'll grab the best from both worlds. If, in the process, you maul, distort, and kill those very heroes—so what? The object is to sell tickets. It will never be in the spirit of Star Trek to wish for a closed, esoteric stratum into which popular and commercial values do not enter; on the other hand, let's recognize the cynicism of *Wrath of Khan* for what it is. It is a kind of parallel universe, not our own.

The final argument for this point is the overall visual treatment of the figures in the two films. Remember that in two years they couldn't have changed all that much. In *Star Trek: The Motion Picture*, the pale hues of the ship and the uniforms serve to emphasize the human presence. Faces are as important here as they were in the series. You see people when they speak, you understand more than their words. The camera was interested in the beauty of the individual faces and figures: Kirk standing still as the tinted door of the briefing room drew closed before him; the trim doctor in full beard; Spock telling with childlike intensity of his Vulcan contact with V'Ger. The crew has reached a point of mature beauty to which the camera is open and sensitive, and these images are themselves an advancement of the legend.

Compare this to the brutal lighting schemes of *Wrath of Khan*. The bridge of the *Enterprise* is bathed in an ugly red haze (a cheap and convenient solution to the perennial problems of screen visibility), and everybody on it looks ninety-two and unshaven (women included). The ravages inflicted upon the images of the "heroes" themselves were not, obviously, a major consideration. The same can be said for the uniforms. They have a certain dash. Unfortunately they also make Spock look extra-gangly and Kirk extra-dumpy. Not important. Add to this the terrible chopping of Spock's hair and the conclusion is inevitable: No respect for these characters as characters was operating here. If, in the overall interests of a flashy production, the heroes had to be uglified, so be it.

The Wrath of Khan notwithstanding, the human adventure is still just beginning.

THE TREK "FAN ON THE STREET" POLL

by G. B. Love

Several years ago we ran a filler page which was a simple series of questions about our readers' major likes, dislikes, and attitudes about Star Trek. We expected enough of a response to this poll to fill another page or two, providing our readers with some insight into how their peers felt about the same things. Were we surprised when literally hundreds of responses to our poll began pouring in! We were forced to devote a full-length article to the results of the poll (Best of Trek #1), and it itself drew almost as much mail as did the poll.

Several years have passed since then, and readers have continually asked if we were ever going to take another poll. Well, we already did. Earlier this year, we pulled out the list of questions from the first poll, added a few new ones, and set out with clipboards and tape recorders to talk to the general public about Star Trek. We talked to people in shopping malls, theaters, schools, etc., and our only criterion was that they know a little something more about Star Trek than just "a TV show" and "pointed ears." We were not surprised at the number of people who did have a fairly intimate knowledge of the show, along with (naturally) strong opinions about it, for it's long been our contention that the Star Trek characters are about to enter (if they haven't already) that shadowy realm of folk heroes. In any case, here's what the average person thinks about Star Trek. And if you think you know what's coming, well, think again. . . .

The questions in this poll were asked of people halted at random and asked: "Are you familiar with Star Trek?" "Do you like it very much?" "Can you remember any of the shows?" If an affirmative answer was given to these questions, then the subject was led into the poll questions. Each question was stated in a conversational manner, and while every effort was made to keep answers specific, it was not always possible to do so. The results of this poll, then, are quite unscientific, but damned revealing and a lot of fun.

All of the responses are given in percentages, with the exception of the most-liked and most-disliked shows, which were given weighted point values . . . again, unscientifically. If the subject gave several responses, they were put in order of like or dislike; if only one was given, the fervor of the like or dislike was considered. Also, as most of the general public does not know and would not recognize the titles of the episodes, we always accepted a brief, but fairly accurate, description of the episode instead. For instance, if someone said that he really loved the show "where Mr. Spock's parents came on the ship and Spock and his dad argued," we put "Journey to Babel" as his response. However when the subject obviously was confused, we overlooked his response. For example, if that same person had said, "I really liked that show where Spock went home to get married and saw his father and mother," we put no response at all. As the average viewer remembers only a few episodes with any clarity at all, whether liking or disliking them, the listing of ten "favorite" and "most disliked" episodes are listed in the order in which they were the most mentioned.

A bit dissimilarly, because all of the characters on the series are so familiar to viewers, we accepted such responses as "the engineer" or "the black communications lady" or "the guy with the pills that made women beautiful" for questions asking about favorites. We feel that to have insisted upon proper names would have defeated the spirit of the poll, for, again, the average person is not nearly as involved or interested in Star Trek as we are.

Several questions were discarded from the poll. They were judged as being either too esoteric for the average person (for instance, "Who is your favorite Star Trek writer?") or else no longer valid or of interest (such as "Do you think that Arex and M'Ress should be included in the Star Trek movie?")

We also decided to have a little fun and start the poll off with a rather unusual question:

1. What do you think of immediately when you hear the words "Star Trek"?

Overwhelmingly (87%), the respondents answered, "Mr. Spock." Captain Kirk accounted for a minuscule 3%, and the remaining 10% was broken up among such responses as "the Starship *Enterprise*," "space travel," "Khan," "pointed ears" (which was not accepted as Spock), and "the future."

2. Name your favorite episodes in the order of your preference.

1. "Space Seed"
2. "City on the Edge of Forever"
3. "Journey to Babel"
4. "Arena"
5. "Mirror, Mirror"
6. "Charlie X"
7. "Balance of Terror"
8. "Shore Leave"
9. "The Menagerie"
10. "Amok Time"

We found this result very interesting. Seven of the episodes which made this "top ten" were in our readers' poll ten favorites, and the remaining three are all excellent episodes. This should not be surprising, for excellent shows should be, and often are, viewers' favorites. The fact that "Space Seed" tops the list is also not surprising, for it may be assumed that many viewers' memories of it were refreshed by *Star Trek II: The Wrath of Khan*, and most of those who named "Space Seed" their favorite admitted they'd watched it again since the movie premiered.

What makes this list so notable (and somewhat different from our readers' poll list) is that each episode named is a particularly memorable one: One has a Gorn; Spock dies in one; Spock's parents appear in one; a boy with superpowers is in one; etc. We feel that it is these striking images, as much as the quality of the episodes themselves, which have made them fondly remembered favorites of the average viewer.

3. Who is your favorite Star Trek character?

Sorry, Spock fans, but Captain Kirk won this one overwhelmingly with a whopping 73% of the vote. Spock did, however, finish second with 20% of the vote, leaving a scant 6% for Dr. McCoy, and a vote of 1% for Uhura, the only other crewmember mentioned.

Why this result would be so lopsided is a mystery to us. Perhaps the average viewer, who is not as involved with the mythos and inner workings of the show as is the dedicated fan, finds it harder to relate to the Vulcan. It could also be simple chauvinism, a reluctance on the part of people to express a preference for an "alien." Upon reflection, however, we feel that it boils down to the simple fact that the average viewer does, and wants to, identify more with Kirk than with any other member of the crew. Kirk is a hero in the classic mold, a spiritual and dramatic descendant from years of hard-jawed, fast-talking film and TV heroes—private eyes, soldiers, adventurers, and so on. Add to this the fact that William Shatner is by far the most recognizable and prolific of all the Star Trek actors, and the result seems almost inevitable.

Spock had his followers, as always, and they were indeed vehement: "Star Trek would be just another show without Mr. Spock" was a typical comment. Just as supportive were those who chose Dr. McCoy as their favorite. Not only were we treated to cherished snippets of McCoy dialogue from several of his supporters, his was the only instance in which *everyone* who picked him remembered his name and at least one episode in which the good doctor had a pivotal role.

4. Which actor is your favorite? Which do you think contributed the most to the show?

William Shatner won the first half of this question by a margin only slightly smaller than that by which his characterization of Kirk won "favorite character," 65%. Leonard Nimoy finished with 30%, and DeForest Kelley got the remaining 5%. Again, the familiarity of Shatner and the popularity of Kirk probably accounts for the large lead.

More interesting, however, was the response to which actor contributed the most. Here the results were more even between the two leads: 51% for Shatner and 47% for Nimoy, with 2% for Kelley. Apparently, even many of those who prefer Shatner as an actor appreciate the contributions of Nimoy's Spock to the success and popularity of the series. This is due, we feel, primarily to the immense amount of media coverage which the Spock character and Nimoy have received (you'll remember the overwhelming response to our first question), causing the average viewer to appreciate a little more the difficulty of creating and maintaining such a character.

5. Which villain from Star Trek do you remember best?

As would be expected from the first-place of "Space Seed" in the "favorite episode" category, Khan Noonian Singh finished well beyond any of the other villains. What surprised us the most, however, was the sheer number of villains recalled fondly by the respondents to our poll. We expected, at most, four or five, including Khan and Harry Mudd, but the eventual number was sixteen. (This would have been seventeen, but several people named *T'Pring* as their best-remembered villain, and we just can't bring ourselves to put her in such company. T'Pring was misguided, yes, but hardly evil.)

Harry Mudd, as one would expect, finished second with 18% of the vote, followed by the Gorn captain with 3% and 1% (or less) each for Charlie X, the Mugato, the Tholians, the Ultimate Computer, Trelane of Gothos, the Horta, Kor and/or Kang, the Talosians, Gary Mitchell, the Salt Creature, Janice Lester, and both the male and female Romulan commanders.

6. Which male guest star do you remember best?

Again, Khan came most to mind, and almost every respondent mentioned Ricardo Montalban by name. So overwhelming was the response for Montalban, in fact, that just about every respondent was asked to name a second guest. It is these which are listed below, with the understanding that the majority of them were second choices to Montalban.

William Campbell was mentioned by most of those polled for his portrayal of Trelane. He got a substantial 31%. Second was Mark Lenard, with 21%, mentioned for both his roles, the Romulan commander and Spock's father. (It is interesting to note that many of those polled did not realize that Lenard played both parts.) Third in the balloting was Roger C. Carmel with 13%; it seems that although his portrayal of Harry Mudd was loved and remembered by quite a few respondents, he himself was not as popular. Finishing with 8% was Jeffrey Hunter, a number substantially higher than his finish in our strictly fan poll. The remaining 23% was divided among a long list of male guest stars, including David Soul, Robert Lansing, William Windom, John Colicos, Gary Lockwood, and Robert Walker, Jr. Weirdly, we found that a number of respondents had somehow gotten the impression that Henry Winkler had guest-starred in a Star Trek episode, and that many firmly believed that the fellow in the Gorn suit was a very young Tom Selleck. How in the world do these rumors get started?

7. Which female guest star do you remember best?

As she did in our fan poll, Joan Collins led the pack by a wide margin. We feel that this is due not only to Miss Collins's fine performance in "City on the Edge of Forever," but also to her current scintillating appearances as the evil Alexis in *Dynasty* (not to mention her even more scintillating appearances in *Playboy*—part of this poll was taken in the month that Joan's photo layout appeared in that magazine). Miss Collins garnered a hefty 58% of the vote, and no one else was even close.

What is most interesting about Miss Collins's votes is that the percentage of those who voted for her as "the woman who played Edith Keeler" or "the woman that Kirk fell in love with back in time," etc. came out to just about 20% of the total . . . which is uncannily close to the 21% which Miss Collins got as favorite guest actress in our fan poll.

Finishing second with 23% of the vote was Mariette Hartley, who has also become considerably more well known since her appearance on Star Trek, thanks to the popular series of ads for Polaroid cameras she did with James Garner. Third-place finisher, with 11%, was Arlene Martel, memorable for her role as T'Pring. Sharing almost equally the remaining percentages were Teri Garr, Susan Oliver, Joanne Linville, and Madlyn Rhue, who didn't receive any votes in our fan poll, but apparently rode in on Khan's coattails in this one. One somewhat startling result was that the lovely Jane Wyatt did not receive even one vote for her performance as Spock's mother, Amada. In our fan poll, she finished second.

8. What do you think was the most believable piece of equipment aboard the *Enterprise*?

The overwhelming favorite, 57%, was the phaser. Most respondents pointed out the phaser's similarity to a laser beam (or simply believed they were the same thing), and noted that we have laser beams now, which are doing more and more things every day. Several respondents actually have had laser surgery performed upon them; many others have had skills or services performed for them by lasers, and realize that the devices are coming into everyday use in many fields.

The shipboard computer was also a favorite choice, getting 22% of the total. We had suspected, with the recent rise in popularity of the personal home computer, that more respondents would choose this device, but perhaps computers have become a little *too* familiar.

The communicator, which tied for first place in our fan poll, perhaps also now seems rather a commonplace device, and this time around it got only 6% of the vote. Tying for that 6% was the warp drive; quite a few respondents also mentioned it as their second choice. Apparently the average viewer fully expects science to someday break the light barrier. Finishing with only a minuscule 2% was the transporter . . . apparently the average person is not as convinced of the feasibility of matter transport as he is of the warp drive or other Star Trek devices. Also mentioned were the shuttlecraft and the various sick-bay devices.

9. Which kind of Star Trek episodes do you like best, those which are primarily action or those which lean more toward ideas?

Surprisingly enough, "idea" shows finished way ahead, with 61% of the vote. Many of those who expressed a preference for such shows said that they were "tired of chases and cops" and found many such shows boring, making a Star Trek "think" episode a refreshing change. Even those who picked action shows as their favorites said they liked the fact that Star Trek "always had something in it to make you think."

10. Name your least favorite episodes in the order that you dislike them.

1. "Spectre of the Gun"
2. "For the World Is Hollow and I Have Touched the Sky"
3. "The Way to Eden"
4. "And the Children Shall Lead"
5. "The Cloud Minders"

A couple of surprises here. "For the World Is Hollow" certainly would not appear on a fan "worst episodes" list; especially not on that of a McCoy fan. And "The Cloud Minders," while not generally acknowledged to be among the best episodes, is certainly not considered by fans to be one of the worst, either.

The terms used most often to describe those episodes chosen were "silly," "boring," and "unbelievable." Only the top five vote-getters are mentioned above, but the range of least-liked shows was much greater than that of most-liked shows. Apparently, *any* Star Trek episode can contain something which just rubs somebody the wrong way, for many of the best-liked and most famous episodes were mentioned as least-favorites, and a couple were even vehemently derided as "real stinkers."

11. Would you rather Paramount keep making Star Trek movies or would you rather have Star Trek return as a series on TV?

The majority of those polled (76%) would prefer that Star Trek return as a weekly series, but only "if they could keep the quality high." Several suggested that a monthly, or even semimonthly schedule might be the best, allowing more time for special effects and the like; a similar number thought that cable television could do the best job, providing us with four to six Star Trek movies each year.

Of those who wanted to continue with the practice of having Star Trek as an ongoing series of theatrically released motion pictures, most thought that the greater amount of time and money that could be allotted to a theatrical film made enough difference in quality to make up for a lack of quantity. Several also felt that it would be impossible to get the original actors to return to a weekly series, and rather than eventually have replacements in the roles, they would live with the biannual schedule. Just about everyone who favored feature films thought that they could be made and released at least once a year without any loss of quality or box-office appeal. Only a tiny number felt that quality would drop if the films were made more often. One respondent, however, was adamantly opposed to speeding up the schedule, claiming that the public would get "burned out on Star Trek" if the films appeared any oftener than every two years or so.

12. Would you go to a Star Trek movie or watch the series on TV if different people played the parts of Kirk, Spock, etc.? Do you think you would like the show any less?

Most of those polled (89%) said they probably would give Star Trek a try if other actors took the major roles, but that percentage dropped sharply at the second part of the question. Only 41% of the respondents said they thought Star Trek would be just as good with new actors; 27% thought it would be better ("depending on who they were" or "if it was somebody I really liked"); and something less than 30% thought Star Trek would be totally unsuccessful without the original cast. A few respondents had absolutely no opinion at all.

In general, however, most of those polled did not find the prospect of having new actors take over the roles to be repugnant. Several mentioned characters like Sherlock Holmes or Charlie Chan who had been played by various actors over the years; others bluntly pointed out the undeniable fact that the original cast members aren't getting any younger.

13. Do you think that the producers should start bringing in younger people, playing new characters, who can take over Star Trek when the original cast retires?

Surprisingly, this suggestion found less favor with most of our respondents than did the previous one: 65% of those polled thought that bringing in new people was a bad idea; 31% thought that it would improve the series, as well as be smart planning for the future. (The remaining percentage, again, had no opinion.)

Those who were against new characters cited disappointing experiences with new characters being introduced into favorite television shows. They felt in most cases, such replacement characters were only pallid copies of the originals, and that the same thing would happen with any new characters brought into Star Trek. Those in favor of the practice pointed to the popularity and presence of Kirstie Alley's Saavik and Merritt Butrick's David as evidence that it could, and should, be done.

14. Do you think that it was a good idea for Spock to die in *Wrath of Khan*?

Respondents were about evenly split on this question at 46% on each side, with the remaining percentage having no opinion. Those who felt that it was a good idea for Spock to die thought that the act provided some needed realism to the series. "After all," said one person, "people die in real life. It's kind of silly to have us believe that none of the officers would die in [a voyage of] ten or fifteen years."

A smaller number of those favoring the death stated that it made for a natural progression of making room for new people and plots.

Those who opposed Spock's death were more mixed in their opinions. Many felt that it had been done as "a cheap publicity stunt" and had hurt the series' overall credibility. Others felt that Spock was a symbol of the series (again, see question 1), and to kill him off was to kill off a part of the series itself. Still others thought that Leonard Nimoy was at fault, and blame him for callously disregarding the wishes of fans. And a tiny number blame William Shatner, claiming that he "pulled strings" to get rid of the Spock character and grab all the glory for himself.

Most of those opposed, however, simply felt that Star Trek just would not be the same without Mr. Spock. Not as a symbol, but as a beloved and admired character.

15. Do you think Spock should be brought back to life?

Again, the voting was about evenly split on this one: 52% felt that, yes, Spock should be brought back to life in the next film. (This question was asked several months before the release of *The Search for Spock*.) Most of those voting yes felt that the Star Trek series would benefit from having Spock back; again, many cited a simple belief that Star Trek would not be the same without Spock, and they were willing to overlook just about any breach of film logic to have him return. One respondent said, "Sure they can bring him back. It's science fiction, isn't it?" Indeed it is.

Several others, while in favor of bringing Spock back, made sure to put a caveat on their yes vote. Most of them felt that if the resurrection was not logical and dramatically effective, it should not be done at all. Said one lady, "If they bring him back the Start Trek way, all right. If they do it like some of those other movies, I won't like it." We agree; "the Star Trek way" it should be.

Those opposing the return of Spock were more adamant. "No way!" was a typical reaction. The great majority of the 45% who felt that Spock should rest in peace said that they thought having him revived would stretch the bounds of credibility a little too far. Many also believed that the Spock death storyline was such a strong and effective one that to effectively negate it by having Spock brought back to life would be a shame. "Spock died a hero," said one respondent, "why not leave it at that?"

A vociferous few took the position that it would be "a cheat" to revive Spock, both from the standpoint of invalidating the series' integrity and as a somewhat sleazy way to get patrons into the theaters. "If Spock can die, then come back, anybody on the show can. So who cares if they die?" said one person polled. Another took the other tack: "First the big deal was to see him die. Now the big deal is to see him come back. What's next . . . a sex change?"

16. If you could change any one thing about Star Trek, what would it be?

This question, of course, cannot be expressed in percentages, nor can a consensus of opinion be reached. Many respondents to our poll had no answer to give to this question; most simply said they had never thought about such a thing. Those that did have an answer, however, were most definite—they know what they'd do with Star Trek if they were in charge:

"I'd put in more laser-beam battles and action like that."

"Kirk and Spock should retire from the service and go off in a ship of their own. Be explorers or something."

"I'd like to see everybody in the crew have a chance at running things; Kirk does too much himself."

"I'd like to see Saavik and Uhura do nude scenes."

"I'd hire Michael Jackson to be the new captain."

"The show should be more accurate. The captain wouldn't go on missions, he'd send people. And ships would go out in bunches, convoys if you will. Make the show more like the real navy."

"If I was in charge, I'd have Kirk and his people quit the Federation and steal the ship and go off and be soldiers-of-fortune."

"Kirk, McCoy, and Spock should retire."

"I'd have more aliens on the ship, and have everything look more futuristic, weirder."

"Uhura should get a chance at being captain."

"I'd redesign the *Enterprise*; it's been the same for too long. And I'd show more of Earth and Vulcan."

"The main thing that Star Trek needs is new blood. Why not bring in a second crew, on a second ship, and kind of cut back and forth between them? As a matter of fact, you could have movies about Captain Kirk and the *Enterprise*, and a television show about this new ship and captain and crew. Every once in a while they could meet or fight the same villains. That would be neat."

"I'd like to see some pets aboard the *Enterprise*. I think Spock would be a cat person."

"Give everybody a drink from the Fountain of Youth."

"I'd go way back to the original premise of the show. Let Kirk and the ship be out there all alone, cut off from everybody and having to make decisions and deal with things without help or interference from the government."

"Have more romances."

"Have more comedies."

"Have more action."

"Have more drama."

"Don't dare change a single thing!"

And, finally, our demented favorite:

"I'd kill everybody off and start all over again with trained monkeys."

So what does it all mean? When all of these responses are put together, what have we learned about how the average "fan on the street" feels about Star Trek?

Well, we see it like this:

The average viewer most clearly recalls with fondness those episodes which had a strong, active villain or overt threat to the *Enterprise* crew, contained a goodly measure of action and suspense, and put the crew or a particular member of the crew in an unusual situation, while also being colorful, visually exciting and fast-paced. All of the episodes which made it to the top ten favorites contain one or more of these elements, and every one of them is noted as a particularly memorable episode by the average viewer and hard-core fan alike.

The average viewer did not seem as concerned with the moral viewpoint or message of an episode as were fans, but it's interesting to note that every episode in the top ten is a show with a strong moral viewpoint, and each carries an extremely strong and effective message. Many respondents made it a point (either at this question or when naming least-liked episodes) to give an example of how a particular episode had a bearing on their lives, and how real life experiences helped them relate to Star Trek. In several instances, we were told how a Star Trek episode helped that person relate to something in his or her real life. The magic of Star Trek can, apparently, work both ways.

We quickly learned in the course of taking this poll to ask the "favorite episode" question again about three quarters of the way through; invariably, the questioning and the respondent's own growing enthusiasm had led to his remembering more and more about the show, which occasionally led to a change or addition to the "best shows" list. (As the average viewer can hardly be expected to remember every Star Trek episode, we felt this was quite fair.)

The average viewer is far more partial to Captain Kirk than to Mr. Spock (or to any other member of the crew, for that matter); but although respondents followed in this vein and chose William Shatner as their favorite actor, they feel that Leonard Nimoy's portrayal of Spock is the most important contribution to the series. As we stated above, we feel (and several respondents came right out and said so) that they felt more comfortable liking a human character with whom they could identify more easily. The most intriguing thing about this question, however, was the number of people who, later in the poll, changed their mind and switched from Captain Kirk to Mr. Spock (or William Shatner to Leonard Nimoy). Frankly, just about *everybody* leaned toward Kirk when the question was first asked—typically: "Well, I guess the captain . . . no . . . it'd be okay if I said Mr. Spock, wouldn't it?"—and only chose Spock somewhat reluctantly and, we were amused and amazed to see somewhat embarrassedly.

Those who favored other characters and other actors had no such qualms of conscience—they (especially the McCoy/Kelley fans) came right out and said so, loud and clear. Perhaps they feel part of a small and somewhat persecuted minority, and proudly and unashamedly bear the banner of their favorite. One young man told us, "I just like that little devil Sulu. . . . Most people like the captain or Spock, and they look at you kind of funny when you give Sulu as your favorite. Lots of people don't even remember him right off."

As stated above, there's no mystery why Khan finished so far ahead of everyone else in the "favorite villain" category; the immense popularity of *Star Trek II: The Wrath of Khan* and the subsequent flood of rebroadcasts of "Space Seed" made the Eugenic Prince a certain winner, as it did Ricardo Montalban in the "favorite male guest star" category.

What's most notable about the villains chosen by our average viewers is that each of them is colorful and bizarre, definitely memorable. Harry Mudd, thanks to Roger C. Carmel's fun-filled, larger-than-life portrayals, is always a favorite, and we feel that he'd have won this category easily if not for the influence of *Wrath of Khan*. The relatively high finishes of such creatures as the Gorn captain and the gorillalike Mugato tells us that the average viewer remembers monsters clearly; but the presence of Janice Lester and Gary Mitchell tells us that the average viewer will remember and appreciate a strong character as well. It was a pleasant surprise to find Jeffrey Hunter finishing fourth in the guest star balloting. We feel that this fine actor is being sadly forgotten, even by Star Trek fans to an extent, and we were heartened to see that a number of viewers remembered him as "the first captain" of the *Enterprise*.

Joan Collins's victory was no surprise. What interested us most was seeing who would finish second. Sad to say, most viewers don't remember female guest stars as clearly as they do male guest stars. The nature of the medium has a lot to do with this, as, unfortunately, a female guest star is often relegated to playing "the girlfriend of the week" or a victim or a walk-on yeoman. Star Trek offered more strong female roles than most series of its time (and of today, sad to say), but there really weren't that many of them. The three top finishers in the poll, Miss Collins, Miss Hartley, and Miss Martel, had perhaps the three strongest and most developed female roles on Star Trek. It is heartening, however, that the average viewer remembered each of them with fondness, and many expressed a desire to see similar roles for women in programs made in the future.

As we stated, it was a surprise to us that viewers expressed a preference for "think" shows over "action" shows. What is strange, however is that *all* of the shows which made the top five on the "most disliked" list are "think" shows. Maybe it's just that they're *bad* think shows, for fans aren't overly fond of a few of them, either. What we thought of when we looked at this short list is that in none of these shows "Spectre of the Gun," "For the World Is Hollow and I Have Touched the Sky," "The Way to Eden," "And the Children Shall Lead," and "The Cloud Minders"—is there a particularly strong and colorful villain; indeed, in none of them can a particularly strong performance be found from anyone, including the regular cast. As these elements are invariably found in those episodes named as favorites by our respondents, we can only assume that the absence of a strong central character or villain and/or an outstanding performance will not make for a memorable show—unless, of course, it is remembered as a *bad* show.

As do fans, the respondents to our poll feel that you can't get enough of a good thing, and they overwhelmingly want Star Trek returned as some kind of television series, even if it appears on pay cable. The movies, while extremely popular, don't seem to be satisfying enough for the average viewer, especially at the present rate of release. As we saw, even those who prefer feature films over a new television series feel that they should be released more often, preferably at the rate of two a year.

A majority of those polled thought it would be a good idea for the producers of the Star Trek films to start bringing in new, younger actors, but not to replace the original actors in the original roles. This seems pretty clear-cut. Fans have always been divided in their opinions about whether or not new actors would be acceptable as Kirk, Spock, etc., but the average viewer, probably because he is less involved with the mythos and background of the series, feels such substitutions would be a major mistake, although a majority of them say they'd give a new series and new stars a chance anyway.

Respondents were just about evenly split when asked whether or not Spock should have been allowed to die; and they were evenly split again when asked if he should be brought back to life. The most interesting aspect about these questions when considered in tandem is that there is not a one-for-one overlap in opinion. In other words, those that felt it a bad move to kill Spock are not always those in favor of bringing him back, and those who thought it a good idea to have Spock die didn't automatically feel it would be a mistake to bring him back. We found this not so curious as one would think upon first consideration, for the resurrection of Spock is an event which would prove so dramatic in intent and form that it really has little bearing on his death or the intent behind that death. Mostly, respondents' feelings about whether or not Spock should come back were colored by their expectations of how such an event would take place, and not by how they were affected (or not affected) by his death.

The opinions expressed about if and how to change Star Trek ranged from the ridiculous to the sublime, but most of those questioned simply wanted to see more shows of quality similar to that of those they enjoyed and remembered from the past. One typical comment was, "If they can keep making shows as good as those I remember, then they don't have to change anything." A good many subjects stated that the best thing a new series could do is to "get away" from the "garbage," "preaching," and "crappy junk" of the third season, and return, in spirit and practice, to "the neat kind of shows" Star Trek presented during its first season. (This seems like a good place to note that in conversation, many fans admitted that they stopped watching Star Trek during its final season, and if they can recognize one as such, they still refuse to watch most third-season episodes in reruns.)

It seems to us that the average viewer knows what he wants and likes from Star Trek: He likes fast-moving, involving episodes with a strong storyline and a colorful villain. He likes lots of action and strong, involving characters (and does not mind if they are women). He dislikes shows which offer an overly obvious or awkward message or viewpoint. He prefers and identifies with Kirk, as a rule, but appreciates the contributions of Spock and the rest of the cast. He'd like to see Star Trek return to television, but only if the quality returned to the high standards of the first season. He is not opposed to change, even supports the introduction of new characters, but doesn't want to see new actors play the main characters.

All in all the average viewer, who watches Star Trek only occasionally but harbors many fine memories of the series and individual episodes, feels much the same as we hard-core fans do. We all want the same thing and it's really very simple: We want good, enjoyable, involving Star Trek, and we want it just as often as we can get it!

Now you didn't think that we'd publish this article without giving you readers a chance to speak your piece, did you?

Yep, here it is, your chance to participate in our brand-spanking-new Trek Fan Poll #2! You'll notice the questions are somewhat different from those asked of the "Fan on the Street"; we feel that you readers are more involved in Star Trek and therefore more willing to talk about it.

1. Please list your name, address, age, marital status, profession, and sex. (All of these except your name are optional; we just want to get a statistical overview, and the information will be kept confidential if you choose to include it.)

2. Please list, in order of preference, your ten favorite episodes.

3. Please list, in order of dislike, your five least-favorite episodes.

4. Who is your favorite Star Trek character?

5. Who is your favorite Star Trek actor?

6. Which character do you feel is the most important to Star Trek?

7. Which actor do you feel contributed the most to Star Trek?

8. Who is your favorite villain?

9. Who is your favorite male guest star?

10. Who is your favorite female guest star?

11. Which do you think is the most believable piece of equipment aboard the *Enterprise*?

12. Whom do you consider the best writer of televised episodes?

13. Do you prefer "action" shows or "think" shows?

14. Do you think that the major characters should die, marry, or otherwise undergo major changes?

15. Would you prefer to have Paramount keep making Star Trek movies or would you prefer to have Star Trek return to television (commercial or cable) as a regular series?

16. Would you go to a Star Trek movie or watch a television series if new actors played the parts of Kirk, Spock, etc.?

17. Do you think the producers should start bringing in new, young actors, playing new characters, who can take over when the original cast members retire or move on to other things?

18. If you could change any *one* thing about Star Trek, what would it be?

19. Who is your favorite Star Trek writer?

20. Which is your single favorite episode?

21. Which is your favorite Star Trek movie?

22. In which episode do you think each of the major actors gives his or her best performance?

23. Which episode do you consider to be the best-written?
24. Which episode was the very first you saw?
25. Which episode so interested you that you became a Star Trek fan?
26. Which Star Trek novel is your favorite?
27. Who is your favorite Star Trek fiction writer?
28. Which is your favorite Star Trek merchandising tie-in (posters, toys, comics, etc.)?
29. Give a brief (very brief, please!) description of your "dream episode" —the Star Trek show *you'd* make if you had the chance.

Please don't worry if some of your answers seem to contradict one another. This isn't a test, and we probably won't even read them in sequence anyway. We'd appreciate having your response typed or at least written as neatly as possible, for we'll be reading lots of them. We'll try to have the totals and comments in our next *Best of Trek*, so if you're going to respond, please do so as quickly as possible. Send your responses to:

Trek Fan Poll
P.O. Box 408
Simonton, TX 77476

Thanks, and we'll be looking forward to hearing from you very soon.

BENEATH THE SURFACE: THE SURREALISTIC STAR TREK

by James H. Devon

James Devon, a newcomer to Trek, *surprised us with this submission; seldom have we seen a first-time effort so well thought out and skillfully written as is this article. James took a look at Star Trek from a new angle—surrealism—and found that the series manages to stand up even under that offbeat and demanding discipline's scrutiny. We're awfully proud of this article, for it supports our contention that if you look hard enough, you can always find something new in Star Trek. And after you finish reading James's article, we think you'll want to go back and watch some of the episodes again, from a new and slightly different viewpoint.*

There's a stranger within the man. He looks out cautiously, secretively, curiously . . . impatient with the intellect and trained personality which rules him. He's angry, yet respectful of those strict limitations which are the sign of civilized man, and looking out, he wonders about a way to speak, longs to express his own undefinable presence.

The subconscious is the alien in every man or woman; the truest, deepest part which desires so strongly to speak of matters for which his conscious being has no precise words. That subconscious can be wild, untrained, amoral, inventive, undefined, and, in its own way, extremely beautiful. It has been called many things and *is* many things: the subconscious, the id, the sex drive, the creative unconscious. It's the powerful raw material of personality, and as such is a fit topic for science fiction.

It has always played a large part in the work of the genre's best authors, but it is difficult to put a label on just what these writers are referring to. Their material deals with something beyond the consciously evident, beyond the practical and recognizable, and consequently splits the audience into two halves: Those who simply shrug and turn away, complaining that there's "no plot, it makes no sense"; and those who read or watch, entranced, mystified, as they receive a message which is not transferred so much through the trained intellect as it is by a sort of logical/emotional creative subconscious. To this second audience, the work becomes something *more*, something very personal. It is no longer something which can be cleanly converted into words of definition.

Undoubtedly, the finest accomplishment of science fiction is the explicit portrayal of that mysterious part of man known as the subconscious. Science fiction, at its best, is the art of revelation of the creative subconscious. Using dialogue, story, and special effects, it expresses symbolically the workings of the subconscious mind. It is surrealism.

And this is the point at which Star Trek fans and general science fiction fans often take up arms against one another. Those who consider themselves sophisticated, well-rounded science fiction fans might point to Star Trek, their lips curled in disgust, and say "Space opera." And the avid Star Trek fan, always ready to defend his old friends, Kirk, Spock, and McCoy, will, just as rudely, point to some fine piece of surrealistic science fiction and mutter, "It doesn't even tell a story." He would then go on about how Star Trek is, after all, a series which tells stories about people and "the human adventure," about things of the human heart.

So, like the two Lazaruses of "The Alternative Factor," our polarized fans will battle eternally, each defending his own little corner of his own little self-defined world. And all for nothing, because they're not only missing the point of it all, they're missing much, much more.

Like the legendary prophet without honor in his own land, Gene Roddenberry has come under a great deal of criticism for his work and for some of the things he "said" through that work. Yet that very work, Star Trek, helped to make science fiction a popular medium, bringing it and its surrealistic themes out of the dusty back corners of the library and into the living rooms of not just the United States, but the entire free world. And if his episodes lacked the finely tuned sophistication of the best science fiction, they did tell lively science and futuristic stories with all the love and subtle grandeur of a Heinlein. You just can't *sell* the tough surrealism of a Clarke to a meat-and-potatoes audience.

But Roddenberry did his best to retain science fiction's surrealism in Star Trek. Again and again we find episodes containing themes which deal with some aspect of the subconscious mind: "Man Trap," "The Enemy Within," "The Menagerie," "Shore Leave," "The Return of the Archons," "This Side of Paradise," "Amok Time," "Mirror, Mirror," "Charlie X," and "Catspaw," to name just a few. These are stories which can and *should* be viewed on many levels, levels which would often prove complex and self-revealing in nature. These episodes speak of the mysteries and power of the human mind, sometimes glorying in that mind's ability to reach beyond the mundane, oftentimes in awe of the mind's dualistic power to create and destroy. Often, this subconscious or surrealistic motif deals with the most powerful, driving force in and of the human mind—sexuality.

Even the good ship *Enterprise* is generally thought to have been designed in a fashion which would bring to mind symbols of male and female sexuality. The ship's round, feminine hull, and her accompanying oblong, phallic warp engine nacelles are representative enough of the shapes which stir the sexual subconscious ever so slightly. Done laughing? Now consider the psychosexual themes of such episodes as "Amok Time," "Metamorphosis," "Elaan of Troyius," and "The Empath." These episodes deal more with human sensuality than with sex, and range from the agonizing, logic-ripping sex drive of the Vulcan *pon farr* in "Amok Time" to the gentle, very feminine and healing tenderness of Gem in "The Empath." We're not talking about sex here any more than we're talking about sex when describing the shape of the *Enterprise* . . . we *are* talking about that aspect of sensuality which exists in a given episode and which might be speaking directly to our subconscious. Its only relation to sex is as a catalyst that touches or even awakens the deepest, most powerful areas of the human subconscious. Such episodes *use* sensuality to draw our attention to the story and its message—nothing more. A story like "Amok Time" cuts through the barriers of sexual/emotional taboos by presenting us with a being who is not human and whose sex drive need not be embarrassing to us for that reason. It's damned interesting, but not threatening. So considered, "Amok Time" is probably Star Trek's single most sexually powerful episode, and yet its passionate story is "safe," not an overt threat to a non-Vulcan audience.

It would be narrow-minded to claim that surrealism or the surrealistic mood of science fiction deals with only the sexual subconscious. In "The Empath," an episode which is more theater than television, something entirely new is added to Star Trek. Yes, the show certainly has undercurrents of sex and sadism. There is the stripped, tortured Kirk, the brutalized but not defeated McCoy, the lovely, innocent Gem. But the story itself does not have a sadomasochistic theme. Quite the opposite, it is a

story of simple humanitarianism and human devotion, bringing the friendship of the Three the closest it ever comes to spirituality. It reveals
something of the good and evil, the negative and the positive of the
human subconscious, calling to mind the depths of man's cruelty, and,
more important, the powerful force of his compassion. In this sense, of all
the Star Trek *television* episodes, "The Empath" is the most progressive
and daring statement about the personal destiny of man. But it relates its
message quietly, not so much by word or deed, but by the craftsmanship
of the artists involved.

Whenever you are dealing with "good" science fiction, especially in the
surrealistic sense, you are also dealing with the theme of the destiny of
man. Roddenberry, most of his actors, and at least some of the directors
and producers knew that. But only so much can be done on television, so
it was not until Star Trek took to the big screen that the Big Story
happened.

And when it did, Star Trek fandom split right down the middle.

The Movie. It is to the discredit of the science fiction motif of Star Trek
that many fans disinherited Paramount and Roddenberry at the film's
release. *Star Trek: The Motion Picture* is one of the finest *science fiction*
films ever made. The fact that a good number of fans resent the movie
will not change that fact. But if many fans were turned off by the fact that
it wasn't the soap opera or action-adventure that they had expected,
others were awed by the scope of the film.

Yes, there were flaws. Poor editing, for one, rectified too late when the
movie finally aired on network TV. A certain amount of nepotism: too
many friends and relatives—and, most especially, too many fans—were
involved in the film . . . some of whom turned on Roddenberry when a
new producer and new "opportunities" came along. This hurt the necessary overall look and "feel" of professionalism in the film. Then there
was some plain, ordinary bad acting. To make things worse, someone
seemed to have forgotten that there *is* no single star in Star Trek—
resulting in a show "over-Kirked" (as were most in the third season).
Most unforgivably, William Shatner forgot that he was acting on the
movie screen, not the TV screen, and so came across as overblown and
uneasy.

But despite it all, *Star Trek: The Motion Picture* held to a powerful,
hard-core science fiction theme: the evolution of mankind. The story uses
a multiplicity of themes and subplots to work its way to a masterfully
orchestrated, unifying climax. And Nimoy and Kelley, whose strong
affection for their characters was evident, held the friendship together at
its darkest hour.

But first and foremost, of course, is Kirk and his tragically wonderful
headstrong determination, not only to face the alien V'Ger, but to once

again command his beloved *Enterprise*. Thus the continuing all-important symbolism of the masculine sex drive is established at the outset. Kirk's courageous determination is, at times, almost blind, driven—and one might even say that on the subconscious level it matches the desire to reproduce, to rule, to *live*. Kirk *is* very much acting out of instinct here, and on a larger scale it is that primitive instinct of his that ultimately leads to the confrontation with V'Ger and the saving of planet Earth. So while some fans seem unfairly annoyed with Kirk's masculine sex drive—and perhaps even turned off by it—it's clear enough that this facet of man is extremely important to the part he is to play in the surrealistic Star Trek.

As if to mirror the masculine and sometimes virtually out-of-control passion of Admiral Kirk, we are introduced to Lieutenant Ilia, the Deltan navigator. She is beautiful; she is very, very feminine, evoking completely the idea of sensuality—but she is also very much in control of her sexual "self." She has to be, as she is Kirk's (and all other humans') sexual superior. Her calm sense of sexual identity and security gives her maturity and emotional well-being that contrasts perfectly with Kirk's almost child-like need to "prove himself" through command.

Persis Khambatta, as Ilia, is certainly one of the unsung heroines of *Star Trek: The Motion Picture*. She is to be commended for her insightful portrayal of the alien, achieving the delicate balance of eroticism and innocence so necessary to this being who is pivotal to both the overt and the symbolic storylines of the movie. Ilia is, after all, the mother of a new race in which the feminine is to be combined with the masculine, the emotional to be combined with the logical, flesh and blood with the living mechanical. Because of her great passion, she is the connecting line between Decker and V'Ger, ultimately to lead the human Decker (symbolic of the god/man/creator) and the alien V'Ger to *understand*. Even though the machine entity has *destroyed* her actual carbon-based body, it is not able to erase that superior aptitude for passion and love. Thus, she becomes both the enticer and the savior/mediator (memories of Gem?) and the mother—as well as the child—of a new life form.

In *Star Trek: The Motion Picture*, Kirk and Decker are, on a symbolic level, the same man. Or at least Decker *represents* the same kind of man as Kirk. He is ambitious, determined, strong, and sexually impulsive and has a great genuine love for people, human or otherwise. The admiration he holds for Mr. Spock matches Kirk's, although, of course, it is backed up by legend, not years of personal friendship. Figuratively, he steps in for Kirk at the end of the story, sacrificing his life despite Kirk's pleadings, because—through his very sexually oriented communication with Ilia—he feels it is his duty, his destiny, even his *right* to join with V'Ger. Decker, symbolic of the evolving human race, takes over where the more primitive form of mankind, represented in Kirk, cannot. It's almost as if the personality represented in Kirk takes over in the new, younger, and perhaps a bit more emotionally advanced figure of Decker to take that next step in human evolution.

It's been said before, but it cannot be said enough: Emotion/Imagination/Logic = Ilia/Decker/V'Ger = McCoy/Kirk/Spock. These combinations are really one combination, read on many different levels. To some, it is simply the Friendship. To the science fiction fan, it is the evolution of man to something greater. To the lucky person who allows himself to fit into both categories, it is a great deal more: It is the achievement of something that is very difficult to put into words. But if examples help, it might be apt to point out here that the thing that happens with/through the Friendship in *Star Trek: The Motion Picture* is the same sort of thing which goes on throughout the series. What occurs in the movie is, on the subconscious, symbolic level, the same thing which occurs in "The Empath": the preservation and even advancement of a race through the qualities exemplified in the friendship of McCoy, Spock, and Kirk.

And the best part of it is, it doesn't matter *who* makes the sacrifice. In "The Empath," it is McCoy. In *Star Trek: The Motion Picture*, it is Decker. It seems, in Star Trek, that it is not the individual who makes the sacrifice who is alone responsible for what that sacrifice achieves. The value of his "gift" is measured ultimately in the way in which these personalities who are closest to him respond and contribute. In this way, the very surrealistic quality of the Friendship is made apparent. The great value to the viewer on a subconscious level is that McCoy/Kirk/Spock are, as Roddenberry himself has explained, representative of one man. The qualities they display as a team are the qualities which go into the making of any man. That, in itself, might be one explanation for the phenomenal charm the Friendship holds for fans. Like all such phenomena, it cannot be explained in simpler terms. So we might say here that we like McCoy and Kirk and Spock because they show us our own potential. Never has there been a more positive, more compelling team of characters. And never before has a group of actors combined so cleverly to portray a theme which is essentially surrealistic in nature.

It is ironic that *Star Trek: The Motion Picture* fell short for many of us because of its failure to present the Friendship the way we were used to seeing it on the series. The reeditied TV version is much better than the original release print. This second edition of the film makes it obvious that in the first release, the characters of Spock and McCoy were shorted for the sake of Kirk. The only explanation for this is that those with editorial power had absolutely *no* instinct for the surrealistic nature of the Friendship and the importance of the balance contribution of the three leads. Someone obviously thought that Star Trek was, or is, Kirk's story. It is, as we all know, the story of all three . . . the Three. And it takes place on such a sublime, surrealistic level that to change or tamper with or ignore that fact leaves us with something that is not Star Trek at all. Paramount may someday be able to get away with putting new characters on the bridge of the *Enterprise*, but they will never be able to continue the magic of Star Trek without the same kind of combination which McCoy, Kirk, and Spock represent to the subconscious mind.

But while the Friendship is the ultimate key to the underlying mood and success of Star Trek, it is not all. In *Star Trek: The Motion Picture*, we have the achievement of something that goes even beyond discussing the personality of man. It is, after all, through the qualities of the Friendship that a *new being* emerges. Cosmically evolved from the rudiments of man's logic, V'Ger, the machine/entity, comes in search of its creator. V'Ger is an emotionless entity—at "heart" still only a machine, after all—and unmoved by those things which touch man. It knows neither beauty nor ugliness. It only follows its creator's command: to learn all that is learnable. But by the time it returns to earth, it has, through its achievement of so much, reached a crisis point: It has come, through the process of its own evolution, to know that it is alone. Rather than a monster, it is, as Spock tells us, "a child," terrified in the night and on that brink of self-awareness and questioning we all reach during childhood. And, on an even deeper, symbolic level, we might say that it is not even really a child, but that still, powerful, pre-life, "nothingness" which exists even before infancy. The prime, untouched, unmoved force of life.

The special-effects genius of Doug Trumbull takes over to give the audience the subliminal sexual/intellectual message of V'Ger; a surrealistically erotic journey through the curling labyrinth of V'Ger's protective cloud membrane—the very womblike core of the machine entity. There, the Voyager probe waits with an eerie kind of patience, symbolic of the egg waiting for fertilization. Throughout the special-effects journey, in fact, the viewer is treated to a number of subliminally erotic scenes, from the first mystically swirling entry into the cloud, with its rich, hypnotic blend of blues, pinks, and grays, always soft and beckoning—to the mutedly devilish features which peer at us from the cerebral psychosexual "landscape" of V'Ger's surface. It is, none too subtly, a mind-enlivened imaginary journey to the sexual center of the subconscious of man. The *Enterprise*, commanded by the virile Admiral Kirk, penetrates the V'Ger "orifice" (take that allusion as you will; for as each individual member of the audience takes it, so it was meant to be received) and drives onward through the deep, ovarial recesses of V'Ger proper. In the erotic vastness of V'Ger, the *Enterprise* becomes tiny, fragile, seedlike, as the sperm would appear as it makes it long, mystical/biological journey to the ovum. And as if to reinforce this subliminal message in the minds of viewers, the scientific symbols for the male and female are portrayed clearly just outside the orifice . . . as if to say, "This way, folks! Proceed with caution!"

Could it be that V'Ger has unknowingly developed a sexual subconsciousness of its own, and that its cerebral/mechanical landscape is portraying it for us? We are, after all, now deep within V'Ger's most secret places. And if, as Spock tells us, V'Ger has achieved consciousness, would it follow that it would also have achieved its own unique form of a subconscious? And it is just as possible that some form of its creator's subconscious sexual symbolism would have found its way into the programming and building of the Voyager probe itself. The basic sex drive is, after all, sublimely evident in all we do, certainly in art, mechanics, or any such creative design. Man is first and foremost a sexual creature, so it stands to reason that he leaves that mark on all he touches. It is no different with the V'Ger probe, and no less likely that it would have picked up on those strange, compelling seemingly unnecessary points of design (with the curiosity of a child?) and, as it evolved, would have programmed and transcribed them in a logical, technical way. In short, V'Ger, as it matured, contrived a technical map of its own sexual subconscious. It was too innocent to know what else to do with the curious, seemingly impractical "knowledge" of sexual identity.

V'Ger's original command and purpose, to go into the unknown and bring something back for the benefit of man, can also be interpreted on a deeper level (if a more organically basic one). V'Ger was designed for the benefit and survival of the race which was its creator. As a mental probe of man, it was a mechanical extension of the sexual urge. And the human sex urge must be recognized (as portrayed in Kirk) as the primitive basis of man's need to discover the secrets of the universe, to venture into the dark unknown for the sake of extending mankind. It's a matter of growth and plain evolution. In Star Trek, it is instinct.

The sexual experience has often been equated with a kind of death. In the final V'Ger scene, we have the powerful, all-giving/all-receiving orgasmic union of Decker/Ilia/V'Ger. Is it a death or a rebirth? Kirk reports Decker and Ilia as "missing." McCoy gloats like a new father as he pronounces the "birth" of a new life form. One thing is for sure, the Friendship of Kirk/Spock/McCoy is very, very happy. The race of man has been saved, has evolved. It was perhaps the most satisfying and rewarding of all their missions together. They have a right to be proud.

If *Star Trek: The Motion Picture* has fallen out of grace with the fans, it is only a temporary thing, very likely due to the vast popularity of that charming shoot-'em-up *Wrath of Khan*. Unlike *Wrath of Khan*, the first movie is just too complex, too intense and sincere in ambition, with its intricately interwoven themes of positive/negative, virility/barrenness, emotion/logic, man/machine. From its celebration of IDIC to its insistence that man can accomplish more through understanding than through fighting, it was just too completely "Star Trek." Too much mental work, not enough phaser fire. Paramount has since learned the hard lesson we fans taught it—thus, the death of Spock. Don't blame Paramount for giving the public what it wants.

Nevertheless, *Star Trek: The Motion Picture*, as a whole, is not a story about good versus evil. It is a story of the evolution of human values and worth. It is, perhaps, too powerful, too threatening a story for the average viewer. It is one of those science fiction stories which, like *2001: A Space Odyssey*, must sit on the back burner of American consciousness for a time before it is truly and honestly appreciated.

But Star Trek, from "The Cage," to *The Search for Spock*, has always dealt at its deepest level with the inner growth of man. Of course, this growth is often portrayed in a psycho-sexual sense—it is the way of the art, the way of legitimate science fiction, the way of man. From what we have discovered about the underlying themes of some of the episodes (including the movies), from what we have seen of the Friendship—probably the cleverest combination ever to be achieved on film—and from what we know to be the basis of man's subconscious self, it's certainly fair to say that Star Trek does indeed speak with the charming, surrealistic tongue of true science fiction. And through the magic of its science fiction, special effects, and symbolism, the "alien" within each of us is allowed its brief, beautiful, and very revealing hour in the sun.

KIRK AND DUTY

by William Trigg and Dawson "Hank" Hawes

G.B. Love's article "Captain Kirk's Duties" (Best of Trek #2) gave us a fine overview of what the day-to-day duties and responsibilities of a starship captain are. Mr. Love's article was admittedly written in a rush to meet a deadline, and he is the first to admit that it is not nearly as comprehensive as it should be. With his permission, this article will expand upon his final original (in some instances using his phrasings), as well as update it to contain information in the Star Trek films. Moreover, we will attempt to show the ways in which duty and the necessity for obeying orders has affected Kirk personally and professionally—how a lifetime of adherence to duty, honor and the rules, regulations and traditions of Starfleet and the Federation have molded Jim Kirk into what he is today.

James T. Kirk is undoubtedly one of the finest and continuously successful officers ever produced by Starfleet. Surely, if nothing else is considered, he is one of the most experienced in terms of dealing with the unknown and unexpected, and probably the only starship commander to have returned from promotion and a ground assignment to retake command of the same ship from which he "retired" . . . and Kirk performed this small miracle not once, but *twice*. There is little doubt that Starfleet Command considered Kirk to be their number one line officer, for he is allowed to get away with things for which other captains would be court-martialed on the spot.

We know that much of Kirk's success comes from his willingness—indeed, even his need—to take chances, to bend the rules, to do it his way and no other. We also know that even with the edge offered by his innate skills and the famous "Kirk luck," he many times would have suffered defeat or disgrace without the help and support of his friends and subordinates, especially Spock, McCoy, and Scotty.

Throughout much of his career, however, Kirk was pretty much on his own, both personally and professionally. He was not a loner in the ordinary sense, for he had many friends and quite a few affairs, and we can assume that he was fairly popular in a quiet, respectable way. He also would have to have gotten along well with his co-workers and superiors, for no military man, no matter how gifted, can expect command to come his way if he is not able to work with people and both obey and command them. But from the time he made up his mind to attend Starfleet Academy to the present, James Kirk was and is his own man.

A person as independent and diligent as Kirk instinctually understands the necessity of duty. He feels dutiful not only to his country and his service, but to himself as well. Kirk knows that only by doing the very best that he can, only by doing a job as well as it can be done, can one feel satisfied and self-assured.

Although we know little about Kirk's early years, we do know that he is essentially a self-made man. This inner need to pull himself up by his bootstraps, if you will, and the greater, more pressing need to get into space, caused him to become the grimly determined, often unsmiling underclassman so many of his contemporaries remember. But the lack of smile would've been caused by distraction and determination, not through any grudge against those classmates who did not share his overriding desire to command. Kirk simply would not have had time for them; if they didn't want to get on with their careers, it wasn't his worry . . . he had too much to do.

We may assume that Kirk understood and accepted the concept and necessity of duty when he was still quite young, so the strictness of military life and the constant hazing by upperclassmen would have been much less surprising and disheartening to him than to a young man less prepared.

The unsmiling, determined young cadet was immediately targeted as a scapegoat by one Cadet Corporal Finnegan. Finnegan and his cohorts (such bullies always have sycophantic followers) made Kirk's life a living hell for the first two years at the Academy, but although he wanted nothing more than to lash out at the sneering Irishman's face, Kirk managed to hold his temper and channel his hatred and aggression into constructive areas. Thanks to Finnegan, Kirk became the most unflappable cadet at the Academy, able to think quickly and coolly under extreme stress (and occasionally under extreme pain, as well). Both of these qualities—controlling his temper and staying cool—would later help to make Kirk a successful commander, but at the time the future seemed far away. It was only strict adherence to duty which kept Kirk from retaliating overtly—for although he could have convinced himself that ignoring Finnegan was the best way to get along, just part of the process, Kirk was too stubborn to allow himself this mental "out." Finnegan was a superior officer, and even if he ordered Kirk to wallow in the mud, wallow Kirk would. For it was his duty to follow orders.

Kirk, of course, had other things to do at the Academy besides jump whenever Finnegan said "frog." He, like all cadets, was required to attend all scheduled classes and to keep over a minimum grade point average in those classes. He also had to go through rigorous physical training and a rating of his skills. Besides the curriculum, cadets were expected to stand guard duty, serve KP in the kitchens and dining halls, serve as functionaries for visiting dignitaries and civilian guests, act as aide-de-camp or secretary for instructors and officers, assist in routine maintenance and cleaning, and go through continuing and constantly varying military training and exercises ranging from the erection of a pup tent to starship maintenance.

It was a killing schedule, designed to weed out those whose strength and determination were not equal to the demands of serving as an officer in deep space. Fully half of Kirk's entering class was gone by the end of the first year, and something more than two-thirds by the end of the second year. Kirk, despite Finnegan, thrived on it, gradually loosening up as he became more self-assured. Now that Finnegan was gone and he was no longer subject to the onerous chores and humiliations of an underclassman, Kirk was able to concentrate solely on his studies and his self-improvement. As part of that self-improvement, he naturally sought out and gladly accepted a greater amount of duties. Kirk had been, from the very first, recognized by his superior officers and instructors as a cadet of promise, and now their hopes were fulfilled. Kirk was taking on unassigned duties and responsibilities—the mark of a dedicated and ambitious officer. Kirk was too sharp not to have very soon realized how this pleased his superiors, and although he was pleased at their approval, such favor really did not matter to him. He was only doing what he thought was right and proper, and although he was vain enough to enjoy the attention and perks which eventually came his way because of his hard work, he did not attempt to use his superiors' liking for him to curry easy assignments or promotion. If he deserved it and did his duty, promotion and credit would come his way.

As an upperclassman, Kirk found himself even busier than before. While his new duties were more pleasant than washing garbage cans or digging trenches, they were no less difficult or time-consuming. And they were considerably more important.

Kirk was now acting as an instructor in military history and basic tactics, the two classes in which he had obtained the highest marks in Academy history. He was also in charge of a crack phaser company, acting as both instructor and drill master. While completely uninterested in sports, Kirk found time to join teams which he thought would serve as invaluable experience. He belonged to the unarmed combat team, and although he placed in several tournaments in his weight division, he was never of championship caliber. He could never quite believe that skill alone could best a larger, tougher opponent and so tended more toward an eclectic roughhouse style which was not popular with judges . . . or with battered opponents. Kirk also joined the shooting team and the fencing squad. Through constant practice, he eventually obtained an expert rating on the range, and although he was not naturally proficient with the phaser, he did develop an unbelievably quick concealed-weapon fast draw. He was never more than a fair fencer; he simply could not relate to the mystique of edged weapons.

All of these duties and extracurricular activities Kirk performed with his usual skill and determination. This was in addition to his normal schedule of Academy duties which included, still, classes, drill, and physical training, plus running a squad of underclassmen (and necessarily hazing them, although Finnegan had planted a distaste for the practice within his mind), serving as officer of the guard, day officer, etc., and overseeing groups of cadets at work and study. By now, however, Kirk and his fellow classmates were more than used to the punishing schedule; indeed, they thrived on it, Kirk more so than most. Now he became almost the exact opposite of the solemn-faced, obsessively dutiful cadet he had been for the last two years. He easily commanded his cadet charges, winning their respect by his firmness and fairness; he made friends among classmates who until now had only been acquaintances. Again, however, Kirk was not trying to win any popularity contests. It was simply that he now felt that he was going to make it, and he could relax a little bit, enjoy life a little more. The thing which had concerned him the most, that he would not be able to rein in his independence and stubbornness and fit himself into the tight strictures of military life, was no longer a worry. He was not only surviving the Academy, he was conquering it.

Kirk's duty load increased dramatically during his senior year, but he took it in stride. Now added to his burden was yet another teaching assignment, plus the extra classes needed to qualify for Command School. Kirk had decided that he did indeed have "the right stuff" (as it had been called for uncounted years) and felt he could be one of those very few who were allowed to command starships. Most cadets by now realized either that they did not have within themselves the necessary tools to make it as a starship commander or that the responsibility of starship command was more than they were willing to accept. Even so, a larger number of cadets announced (as they were required to do) their intention to try for acceptance to Command School.

Kirk did not graduate from the Academy with highest honors, but he was in the upper 10 percent of his class and, more important to him, was accepted for Command. The only disheartening thing about the honor was that he would be required to spend two more years at the Academy while his former classmates would be out in space. Those accepted for Command, would, however, get "out there" first though they wouldn't stay long, for in lieu of a summer vacation they would take their first training cruise into deep space.

It was on this cruise that the first weeding-out process was begun. Cadets were required to serve duty watches for sixteen to twenty hours straight, then to rise and attend classes after only a few hours' sleep. They had to swab the decks, anti-frictionize the engines, cook the captain's dinner. Although full-fledged Academy graduates technically holding the rank of ensign, they were for all intents and purposes the lowest of the low on this cruise, subject to the same living and working conditions as the average crewmember—ordered around by every noncom, treated as deadheads and dunces by the regular crew.

The annual Command training cruise was known among Starfleet veterans as the "baby run," and it was considered privileged and very cushy duty. For when and where else could an able shipman give a good ranking-out to a fresh-faced ensign? Starfleet did not have the Command cadets treated this way just for the enjoyment of the crewmembers (although the practice was common knowledge throughout Starfleet and helped to boost overall morale), but rather to give them some practical experience in what it feels like to be a common crewmember in the service. The theory was (and Kirk agreed with it) that a man could not lead those whom he did not understand, nor order work done which he had not himself experienced.

Kirk saw the value of this and so uncomplainingly performed the onerous chores and good-naturedly endured the sometimes less than good-natured razzing from the enlisted crewmembers. He immediately saw the value of the plan, however, for the varied "scut" duties took the Command cadets to every part of the giant starship, and working with the crewmen, he learned things which he would not have learned in years of classroom simulation. Mostly, however, the cadets learned about themselves. Some who had breezed through the worst hazings and tensions which the Academy could offer them found themselves lacking the same poise or patience in real-life day-to-day contact with working crewmen. Others realized that there was just too much to learn, too much to be responsible for, when commanding a ship, and they too fell by the wayside. Although the attrition rate was not as dramatic as that of Kirk's first year at the Academy, a fairly large percentage of his classmates decided that Command School was not for them after all.

When the three-month cruise finally came to an end, Kirk and his mates immediately disembarked to a schedule of classes and training which tested them, mentally and physically, as they had never been tested before. Menial work and harassment were now forgotten; they had proved themselves as officers and gentlemen on the cruise . . . now it was time to begin molding them into commanders, and as such they were treated with the utmost respect and expected to comport themselves accordingly.

Each person was now on his own more than ever. Command cadets were expected to keep to a rigid schedule of classes and duty watches, just as they would aboard ship, but no one stood over their shoulders to see that their assigned work was performed properly—indeed, if it was performed at all. Cadets now stood watches in command of groups of enlisted personnel and civilian workers, and they were responsible for the results attained by their groups.

Such an environment was, of course, exhilarating to Kirk. Duty was now not a question only of obeying orders, but of taking charge of himself and his men to get a job done well. Kirk realized that if he could not command himself under such conditions, he could never hope to command others. So it was himself that he gave the roughest discipline, assigned the hardest, dirtiest chores, gave the most critical evaluations. It was not, to Kirk, a question of whether or not he would make it—he knew he would—it was a question of whether he would make it according to his own harsh inner guidelines.

As the months passed, the cadets' schedules became somewhat less hectic, but they were assigned accordingly more important duties. Many of these duties, somewhat surprisingly to Kirk, were at various locations on and around Earth. Thanks to the transporter and other high-speed people movers, Command cadets could report for duty to any Starfleet Earth station, any space-docked ship, any moon base, and so on. This not only gave them experience in an amazingly varied number of duties, it removed them from the somewhat cloistered confines of the Academy. With all of this experience, it seemed almost an anticlimax to make a second deep space cruise at the end of the first year.

This cruise, however, was quite different from the first. This time the class was not dumped aboard one ship, but broken into smaller groups and sent to a number of different ships going to different areas. Too, the cadets were now treated as officers, with the respect due their rank of ensign. Ensigns didn't rate all that much respect, Kirk soon found, but when serving midnight watches on the bridge, he consoled himself with the thought that at least he wasn't swabbing the poop deck.

As he did on Earth, Kirk thrived on this duty. Moreover, now that he occasionally had a little time of his own, he discovered that he was developing quite an affection for space and space travel. He knew that in time he would come to love space, and eventually, when given command of just the right ship, he would come to love it as well. More important, he also discovered that he loved command. Looking into himself as objectively as he could, Kirk decided that it was not the simple power to order men and machinery about that attracted him, but rather the continuing process of self-testing and self-assurance, the thrill of making a decision quickly and coolly, the satisfaction of having the respect of subordinates and a job well done.

To Kirk, duty was becoming life itself. Although he had to admit to himself, somewhat ruefully, that his ego was often larger than necessary, he was seized by a growing conviction that he could do just about any job, command any ship, better than anyone else. This conceit did not go unnoticed by his fellow cadets and superiors, but it was not only understood, it was expected. Each of them felt a similar conceit to one degree or another; how could a person in good conscience command a starship when he felt that someone else could do a better job? What it was necessary to instill in the cadets was acceptance of the knowledge that although perhaps no one could do the job better, there were many others who could do it just as well.

During the second year of Command School, Kirk and his mates were given more of the same duties as in the first year, the only difference being that they spent more time aboard starships and their classroom time was increasingly devoted to lectures and demonstrations by captains and first officers on or recently returned from space duty. Much of the time, these men simply sat and talked with the cadets, answering questions and relating incidents having to do with the cadets' current studies. Kirk, as cadets were intended to do, found these sessions to be overall more informative about what made certain people good commanders than technically rewarding. Some of the speakers were defensive about their work, others offhand. But those who impressed Kirk the most were those who obviously considered it to be nothing more than their duty. These commanders invariably gave credit for successes to their crews; just as invariably they took the blame for failures upon themselves. Also in each of them was a fierce pride, a determination to succeed, which Kirk found perfectly mirrored within himself.

It was under one such captain that Kirk gratefully found himself serving when he graduated from Command School. Charles Garrovick was one of the "old line" of starship commanders, having served in the United Earth Forces which were only now slowly coming completely under Federation and Starfleet command. He was considered something of a maverick by

Headquarters, and generally ignored when it came time for promotion and assignment to the newer ships, but no one could fault his ability.

In Garrovick, Kirk found a mixture of adherence to duty and dogged independence which more than matched his own. Garrovick might gripe and rail and call Starfleet Command names that made even his grizzled old engineer blush, but he never hesitated one second to follow orders and perform his duty to the best of his, and this crew's, ability. Only once did Kirk see Garrovick disobey an order: He refused to leave an area where space mines were being tested until he'd succeeded in rescuing a crewman with a malfunctioning spacesuit.

What surprised Kirk more than Garrovick's disobeying the order was the fact that his bridge crew seemed to expect him to do so—nobody but Kirk so much as raised an eyebrow when Garrovick ignored the group admiral's order to leave the area. They also, Kirk discovered in later conversations, seemed unconcerned that the reprimand that Garrovick would surely receive would also be mentioned in their own permanent records.

Kirk, of course, understood Garrovick's reluctance to abandon a crewperson—he too would do the same thing for a person under his command, a person who was his responsibility—but what he didn't understand was how Garrovick and his crew could treat the whole thing so blithely. Duty was duty and orders were orders, and to ignore them, even for sufficient reason, even though he would have unhesitatingly done so himself, was not something to be proud of, certainly nothing to treat as an everyday occurrence.

Garrovick noticed the stiffness with which Kirk faced him for several days after the affair, and rightly surmised what was going on in the ensign's head. He called Kirk in for a talk and led the young man into opening up. In response to Kirk's questions, Garrovick explained that in his opinion, a commander held as much allegiance to his men as he did to his command. Duty, therefore, became a balancing act: what was best for the service versus what was best for the members of his crew. Garrovick always liked to tip the scales to the side of his men, but this was often not possible or prudent. Kirk would have to set limits within his own mind, his own conscience, and decide when he would and would not cross those limits.

It was the first good look Kirk had gotten into the head of a starship commander. He had heard other commanders talk about the occasional need to disobey orders—some of them had paid dearly for doing so—but this was the first time that he had been able to relate to it on a personal level. He knew that he would have made the same choice as Garrovick under the circumstances, but what of other times, other circumstances? He knew that he should do as his captain suggested and define within his own mind some limits, but he also knew that to set such limits now and cement them into permanency would be ultimately self-defeating. He decided that he would, as long as possible, simply "wing it," and take each situation as it came. He trusted his ability to think fast on his feet and knew that his subconscious would now be working constantly on the problem and would suggest the proper course of action to him at the proper time.

Of course, quick decisions and making choices are two of the most—if not *the* most important—aspects of command. They often go hand in hand, and more often than any commander would like, human lives are involved. Even if a person is as self-assured as was young Ensign Kirk, one split second of indecisiveness, or one wrong choice, can lead to a lifetime of recrimination and regret.

Kirk discovered this sad fact when Captain Garrovick was killed by a mysterious, malevolent "cloud creature" because—Kirk believed—Kirk "froze" and failed to shoot his phaser quickly enough. Kirk had enough self-awareness to know that he had not failed to shoot because of coward-ice, and, indeed, he was not given any sort of reprimand, official or unofficial, by Starfleet, but Kirk did blame himself for not acting quickly enough. He saw it as a failure of will, of determination. The effects were devastating enough to cause Kirk to doubt his qualification for command for some while, but the assurances of his shipmates and superior officers that he still had "the right stuff," plus his natural self-confidence and desire to command, soon brought him out of his depression.

In fact, Kirk became a better leader after the untimely death of Garrovick. He steeled himself with the determination to never again "freeze" in a crisis, but more important, he began to see the importance of careful planning ahead. Kirk reluctantly admitted to himself that if the maverick Garrovick had taken a full security team of experienced veterans down to the planet with him rather than just raw ensign Kirk, he would probably still be alive. Preparation and following the rules were two things which Kirk, enamored of his ability to think on his feet, had previously given little attention to either at the Academy or on shipboard. He now knew why rules were rules, and why it was important to follow regulations. Duty, Kirk realized, was more than just leading men. It was leading them in the proper fashion, utilizing the accumulated knowledge and experi-ence of an entire history of military chain of command.

This lesson didn't stick all that well. Kirk was too much of a maverick himself to keep to the ordered, regimented style of doing things, but the knowledge that these seemingly stultified, outdated, hopelessly stiff-necked rules were often *right* had been permanently branded into his subcon-scious. Now the military history which Kirk had always so loved to read and study meant more to him than just battle plans and adventure. He developed an understanding of the problems of discipline, of supply, or ordnance. He now had the potential to become a better officer than Garrovick had been, a more rounded, better-informed officer whose maverick streak would be tempered by an appreciation of the necessity of military hierarchy.

Kirk's next assignment was to the *Exeter*, where the newly promoted Lieutenant Kirk served as relief helmsman. On this, his first full-time duty post, Kirk had drilled into him the necessity for keeping to a minutely detailed schedule, one infinitely more complex and demanding than those he had followed as duty officer or other such "watch" posts. He also learned to train himself to instantly obey any command from his captain or first officer. Helm was one of the most sensitive and demanding positions aboard a starship, and one to which promising young officers were often assigned to test their mettle. In times of battle or emergency, a helmsman had to instantly translate his captain's verbal orders into commands to the controls of the ship. A moment's hesitation or uncertainty could result in the destruction of the ship. Although the active Kirk found it stifling to be sitting in one place for hours at a time, he learned to love the way in which the mighty ship responded immediately and smoothly to his slightest touch on the controls. For the first time, he felt in touch with a ship, almost part of it. (It was felt in the service that no person could be fit for command without experiencing this feeling, another reason why promising young officers were assigned to helm.) A real feeling of communion grew between him and the *Exeter*, and he was reluctant to leave the helm position when his captain decided he should have some firsthand experience in dealing with diplomats, semihostile aliens, and the bureaucracy, and took Kirk along as his orderly to the Axanar Peace Mission.

Diplomacy was one of the duties of a starship captain which Kirk had not yet experienced, and, to to truthful, had little desire to experience. He knew that he was too impatient, too unforgiving of duplicity, and too straightforward in speech and action to be a good diplomatic negotiator. He quickly changed his mind, however, for the negotiations which took place on Axanar were nothing like the soft-voiced, polite ramblings he had seen on occasions in the Federation Council or the world Government on Earth. These negotiations were a series of hotly contested bargaining sessions in which several parties vied for advantage or leverage. Occasionally things got a little loud, and once or twice diplomats from the opposing sides came close to blows.

Kirk realized that here were beings fighting—with words rather than weapons, but fighting none the less—for what could eventually be the very survival of their respective cultures. It was enthralling, it was exciting, it was the education of a lifetime. Kirk's captain, Chester Pao Ng, was there to represent Starfleet, whose constant threat of intervention in the Axanar crisis had brought the opponents to the bargaining table in the first place, and when the conference quickly bogged down under the leadership of a Federation diplomat, Ng made it plain that he was not just going to sit idly by and watch the opponents wrangle and waste everybody's time while a ruinous war still went on. He quickly took over, backed up by his own forceful personality and by the unstated but ever-present knowledge that his powerful starship was parked, guns ready, just a few thousand kilometers away. He intended to run the conference in, he snapped in his incongruous British accent, "Bristol fashion." This action, at first greatly resented by the parties at hand, later admired when Ng proved himself fair and firm, made more work for Lieutenant Kirk than he expected.

In fact, the work load was almost too much for one man: Kirk not only had to keep track of the computer notes and records of what was said, proposed, rejected, etc., but he was responsible for overseeing the lodgings, feeding, etc. of the diplomats and their large and often unpleasant staffs. Kirk also was in charge of security, a constant headache, for there was not yet peace, and the threat of terrorist activity or even Klingon intervention was always present. In addition to all of this, Kirk was constantly at loggerheads with the staff of the official Federation Diplomatic Corps, who (rightly) resented Ng's intervention in a mission which was expected to be their show. With them, however, Kirk did not have to be polite, and he made it plain that he backed up his captain to the hilt and if the Diplomatic Corps couldn't run the show, then they should get out of the way and let someone who could do so get the job done. Kirk's bluntness made him many enemies among the younger members of the legation, who did not have the experience or aplomb, as did their elders, to overlook internecine rivalries and bickering, and with the eventual success of the mission, all of the resentment felt against Ng and Starfleet focused on Kirk. He gained a reputation of being "antidiplomat," a reputation which he did little or nothing to destroy in the ensuing years.

Starfleet, with the grudging concurrence of the Diplomatic Corps, awarded specially struck medals to Ng, Kirk, and their staff for their efforts at the Axanar Peace Mission. More valuable to Kirk were the lessons in diplomacy he had learned, and the ways in which those lessons tied into starship command.

Diplomacy, Kirk discovered, was as much a part of the duties of a starship captain as was the day-to-day running of a ship. Often during a lull in the negotiations, Ng would take the time to point out to Kirk similarities to other disputes and disagreements he had had to settle in his role as Federation representative in deep space. A starship captain, Ng explained, *is* the Federation when venturing into unknown and unexplored territory. A starship captain is automatically appointed military governor of any colonies, outposts, or expeditions in his space sector. In this capacity, he is the final arbiter of the disbursement of materials, persons, or facilities to and from these outposts, etc. He is also authorized to settle any disputes over claims or territorial rights. If he feels the need is dire enough, a captain may severely restrict the activities of these outposts, etc., or even go so far as to completely shut them down.

Kirk, of course, had learned all of this at the Academy, but it took on more meaning now that he had experienced first-hand just how difficult it could be to deal with fiercely independent beings fighting to retain their rights and property, especially since those beings often felt their fight was right and just. He also gained an appreciation of just how hard it could be to be fair to all sides involved in a dispute. The truth or the right was not always clear-cut, and Kirk realized that diplomacy, like command, was a series of tradeoffs, a balancing act between duty and immediacy.

This would be more and more of a problem in the coming years, Ng pointed out, for space travel was growing at almost a geometric rate. By the time that Kirk and others of his generation became starship commanders, there would be literally hundreds of thousands of vessels, outposts, colonies, etc. spread all over the galaxy. Space was becoming less and less the property of the military, and as a larger number of private citizens made their way into space in one way or another, a feeling of resentment and an attitude of "So who needs you anymore?" would inevitably rise against Starfleet.

Too, each newly discovered inhabited planet would bring problems of its own. Some would prove resolutely hostile, others unbendingly resolved to have nothing to do with outsiders. Many would fall under the protection of the Prime Directive, and as such would have to be policed against interference by Klingons, other alien races, and unscrupulous citizens. Inevitably, a starship captain would find himself in the middle of disputes, sometimes even open war, between newly discovered planets or systems, and in each of these cases, a captain was under standing orders to make his best effort to bring hostilities to an end and offer the good offices of the Federation to settle disagreements peaceably.

Each captain had to decide for himself how best to carry out such duties. Many captains went strictly "by the book," but Ng had discovered that although the book was generally right in a given situation, he was rarely given that particular situation. Often a captain had to make decisions quickly, without time to give a fair hearing to all sides of the question. This is where instinct, experience, and plain old-fashioned luck came into play. Ng had given Kirk a start on the experience, and he believed that the junior officer's instincts were good as well—but was he lucky?

Kirk felt he was; in fact, he had always counted on his luck to aid him to a certain extent throughout his career. But what Ng was telling him now was that any officer who trusts solely to luck is courting disaster—there is no substitute for intelligence and knowledge. Kirk had to remember that "chance favors the prepared," but also, "fortune is always on the side of the largest battalions."

So impressed was Starfleet Command with the record Kirk had so far compiled and with the glowing recommendation Captain Ng had given him that he was jumped several grades and made first officer aboard the pocket destroyer *Chesty Puller*. Once again, Kirk was confronted with an entirely new set of duties. As first officer, he was responsible for the smooth running and maintenance of the ship; in other words, for the thousand and one details with which a captain cannot be bothered. Now more than ever, Kirk had to learn to deal with subordinates and crewmembers in shipboard routine. He quickly learned that such routine is deeply ingrained, and even ambitious, young, spanking-new first officers find such routine almost impossible to change.

Frustrated at first by his inability to implement what he saw as badly needed reforms in the operation of the ship, Kirk began to resent the people under him who, seemingly, were either too stubborn or too stupid to understand what he was trying to do. He became especially frustrated with the endless necessity of following the chain of command with every order he gave. When he wanted something as simple as a new kind of cleanser in the toilet areas, he found that just calling down and ordering the steward to change cleansers was impossible. The man could not act without approval from his chief, who could not approve the request without orders from his section head, and so on. And this, moaned Kirk, was on a relatively small destroyer. What must things be like on a starship?

More frustrating, however, were the reams and reams of paperwork which confronted Kirk as first officer. He knew that much of his duty involved relieving the captain from such mundane chores, but it seemed to him that the captain handled just as many papers as he did. (The term "paperwork," of course, does not refer to actual sheets of paper, for such had long since been replaced by computer-terminal and hand-held displays, but rather to the flood of often meaningless and endlessly repetitive *words* with which Kirk had to deal each day.)

Most irritating to Kirk were the everpresent fuel consumption reports, an archaic practice which nobody ever seemed to be able to stop. On the *Chesty Puller*, there were thirteen different computer stations which monitored fuel consumption, and a readout of fuel used, remaining, etc. was continually available on the main screen. But still yeomen came up from belowdecks every hour on the hour with the official report, which had to be signed by the officer holding the conn. None of the other paperwork was as omnipresent or as irritating as the fuel reports, but a never-ending stream of relatively useless facts, data, and trivia crossed Kirk's desk each working day.

This, then, was the dull, repetitive side of command which Kirk had been warned about by many commanders, a surprising number of whom had been burned out not by the responsibility or pressure, but simply by the never-ending routine. Kirk, confident as ever, thought that he could change things once he was in charge—streamlining, cutting red tape, eliminating the endless rounds of duplication and rubber-stamping which needlessly complicated any order or request. Like so many others before him, he failed.

What he learned from his experience with onboard bureaucracy and paperwork was not the kind of thing of which Starfleet officially approved; Kirk decided that whenever possible, he would simply skip the inner workings and do things himself. This decision did much to negate his earlier vow to work through channels and "by the book," but it served to make him a more independent and efficient officer. Of course, by doing so he took upon himself an immeasurably greater amount of personal responsibility, but he figured that ultimate responsibility came with command anyway, so what was the difference?

This final phase in the battle of rules versus independence which had been going on in Kirk's mind since his Academy days marked his maturation as an officer. He now spent less time worrying about whether or not he was doing the right thing and instead did what he *thought* was right. If he was wrong, he would find out soon enough; if he was right, then it was one less problem to worry about, leaving him available to go on to the next chore or problem. Kirk began in this way to see facets of command separately, and learned the necessary trick of compartmentalizing his mind and organizing problems in order of their importance and urgency.

All of this Kirk had known before, or had been lectured about it at the Academy, but now he was beginning to do it easily, instinctively. He was beginning to think like a captain, and, as a result, he began to act like one as well. A certain maturation took place in Kirk about this time: He no longer let his impatience with things beyond his control affect his work; he became less critical of others who were less gifted or less dedicated than he; he became somewhat more introspective and broadened his reading habits to include philosophers, poets, and novelists, for whom he had previously not found time. Mostly, however, he learned how to relax, rather than play hard. Without realizing it, Kirk was responding to his broadening experience which had taught him that a good commander is more than just a great tactician or crackling disciplinarian. A good commander realizes that duty flows both ways, up and down the chain of command, and a commander must be as responsible *to* his ship and crew as he is responsible for them.

Kirk got his first taste of actual battle not long afterward when a Klingon cruiser launched a sneak attack against the *Chesty Puller*. Badly outgunned, the ship suffered massive damage from the first blast, including the complete destruction of the bridge with all hands. Kirk fortunately had been on the way to the bridge at the time, and although suffering from a serious head wound taken when his turbolift shuddered with the impact, he managed to make his way to auxiliary control. With only two crewmen available, Kirk had to man the helm himself while issuing orders to the rest of the ship. Kirk brilliantly managed to evade the Klingon ship (and another which arrived thereafter), and succeeded in getting his badly wounded ship into Federation space without further incident. He was rewarded with the Medal of Honor and command of his own ship for his gallantry and quick thinking.

While recovering from his wound at a Starbase, Kirk was offered a chance at which any ambitious young officer would normally jump: to participate in an experimental officer-exchange program with the Klingons. Kirk, however, was having none of if. Klingons had just killed his captain, ruined his ship, and put him in the hospital. Now Starfleet wanted him to delay his promised command to live and work with a Klingon. Kirk adamantly refused.

A com-link "visit" from the widow of Captain Garrovick caused Kirk to change his mind. It was his duty to join the exchange program, she insisted. Not only could he perhaps learn something about the Klingon mind and personality which might someday help to preserve lives, it was possible that this program could be the beginning of a rapprochement between the Federation and the Klingon Empire which would end forever the possibility of war between them. She lashed out at Kirk. How dare he refuse when his duty was clear and the stakes were so high? Still, Kirk would not commit himself.

Kirk did not really believe that the program would have any lasting benefits. They would learn nothing about the Klingons which the Klingons did not want them to learn; on the contrary, the Klingons would probably learn more about the Federation and Starfleet and the people in it than would be advisable or prudent. Kirk also believed that any real peace between the Federation and the Klingons was a long way away, and would come only after the Klingons had decided they'd been beaten often and thoroughly enough. They understood fighting, not talking.

Mostly, however, Kirk was instinctively distrustful of any project which was fueled more by goodwill than good sense. It seemed to him that mankind would never learn that good intentions and high hopes were no substitute for fair and firm resolve. If anything, he believed that his duty not only compelled him not to participate in a program which he believed to be foolhardy, but to actively speak out against it.

Kirk was not out to destroy his career by becoming another Billy Mitchell, however, and he refrained from making public statements, instead confining his comments and objections to interservice memos and letters to friends and associates. Many of the higher-ups in Starfleet agreed with Kirk—the project had been instigated and insisted upon by the Federation Council—and they admired the courage with which he voiced his convictions. The program had to go through, however; major funding for the next few years was inextricably tied to it. But it was now also a must that Kirk join in the program. He had become a rallying point for opponents, and continuing criticism of the project could only be stifled by his active participation.

It was left up to Captain Ng to convince Kirk. The *Exeter* was "coincidently" rerouted to the starbase where Kirk was just about to be released from hospital, and Ng paid him a visit. He pointed out that no one, not even Kirk, was more philosophically opposed to the program than he, but that they must, as soldiers, follow orders and make the best of it. If the program had not been publicly announced as voluntary from the start, Kirk would have been ordered to participate, objections or no. Now, because of the furor he'd stirred up, he had to take part, or the long-term effects could be much worse than anything the program could cause.

Kirk ruefully had to agree. His stand was beginning to hurt the service; if that wasn't enough of a consideration (and it was), the service would soon lash back at Kirk and his career would be over. Kirk had to swallow his pride and agree to participate. A bargain of sorts was struck, however, before he would finally agree. He would not have to travel to a Klingonese planet, nor would he promise to remain silent if he thought the program was a complete fiasco. Starfleet Command agreed, and Kirk signed on.

Kirk's time spent in the exchange program was not as bad as he feared it would be. He was assigned a charming young Klingon officer named Kumara as a roommate, and while they never became friends, they developed a grudging respect for each other. The main benefit of the program to Kirk was the acceptance of his book-length report on the program (and the events preceding it) as required reading at the Academy, as well as the attention and respect which the entire affair, and his behavior during it, gained for him among the Starfleet hierarchy. For diplomatic reasons the exchange program was termed "a complete success," but Starfleet knew it for a failure and it was never repeated.

For Kirk, the affair had marked the first time that he had felt strongly enough about something to be willing to put his career on the line, and take on all of Starfleet if necessary. He knew that it would probably not be the last, but he also realized that the action had made him a stronger, better officer. He also had a new conception of duty: His loyalty would be given unquestioningly, as he had sworn, but he would reserve to himself the right to question and even protest against Starfleet and Federation policy when he thought it wrong. He'd follow orders, yes, but he would also resign rather than violate his conscience and his convictions. As the goals and beliefs of Starfleet and the Federation generally paralleled his own, Kirk saw little chance for conflict, but he had learned that both people and governments change. Kirk would go a long way before he would allow things to reach a point at which a line must be drawn, and he believed Starfleet would as well, but he mentally prepared himself for a possible time when he would have to resign his commission.

This decision marked the final maturation of Kirk as an officer and a creature of duty and honor. To simply, unthinkingly obey orders, any orders, Kirk believed, is not what makes a good officer. Indeed, it makes a very bad officer indeed. Kirk had finally learned that what was required of an officer in the performance of his duty was the intelligent carrying out of orders. With foresight, planning, reliance on skills and procedures, and a little bit of luck, it would never come to a pass where he would have to refuse to follow orders. He must be a thinking captain, not one who simply reacts to events and depends on "the book" to get him out of trouble when in over his head.

Kirk was given his first command shortly after the completion of the exchange program, and he proudly and prudently began to apply all that he had learned. Now it was his responsibility to represent Starfleet and the Federation when venturing into new, uncharted space. Kirk took on his duties as commander, administrator, lawmaker, and diplomat. As he took his vessel deeper into almost unimaginable reaches of space and became responsible for more crewmembers and more colonists, miners, explorers, etc., Kirk was often called upon to exercise his almost unrestrained powers in areas of dispute, conflict and even war. It was a mark of the highest confidence in Kirk as a commander that he was continually advanced in grade and assignment, eventually reaching command of a Constitution-class starship, the *Enterprise*. For above all others, a starship *is* the Federation in the minds of many and the practical experience of a few.

In his years of command, Kirk made mistakes, but he also, often by making those mistakes, discovered new things about command, himself, the ship, his enemies, and his men. He learned how to accept victory graciously and defeat unblinkingly; he learned to accept death—and the threat of death—as an everpresent companion. Mostly, he learned what it means to be alone.

James T. Kirk has the hardest job in Starfleet, and the loneliest—a job which has literally destroyed many good and brave men. But it is a job that he believes in, loves, and performs exceptionally well. It is somewhat wondrous, then, that when we realize the sheer number and weight of his responsibilities, we still think of him most for his humanity. Although it is James Kirk the captain we admire, it is Jim Kirk the man we love. That is why James Kirk has touched, and will continue to touch, our lives in so many ways.

IN SEARCH OF SPOCK: A PSYCHOANALYTIC INQUIRY

by Harvey R. Greenberg

Want a good laugh? Close your eyes and picture Spock lying on a psychiatrist's couch. Yet the longer you keep that image in your head, the less funny it becomes. Spock undoubtedly has problems, so why shouldn't he (or any of the Enterprise *crew) seek professional help? And how is it that we know this character so well that we can understand and emphathize with his problems?*

Few characters in fiction have been so finely drawn as those in Star Trek; we know their strengths, weaknesses, foibles, and inconsistencies perhaps even better than our own. The greater part of this information was naturally developed during the course of the series and in the films, although fan writings have done much in the way of examination and explanation.

Working from such information, Dr. Harvey Greenberg took a clinical look at Mr. Spock and his world. What did he discover? Read on. . . .

Star Trek was launched by the National Broadcasting Company during the fall season of 1966. The series immediately received an enthusiastic reception from science fiction readers. It offered the pleasures of the best speculative literature: plausible characters in a plausible future, searching out new life forms throughout the galaxy. A second season followed, but then ratings wobbled and rumors of cancellation spread. At the eleventh hour, Star Trek was rescued by an incredible grass-roots write-in campaign. It did not survive its third season, mostly because of inexplicable unpopularity with NBC executives.

During its later airings, episodes were moved from 7:30 p.m. on Monday evenings to Fridays at 10:00 p.m., a sure "kiss of death" slot. Network pundits thus demonstrated a perverse disregard for many of Star Trek's staunchest advocates—adolescents and preteenagers. But when Star Trek went into syndication, canny local station managers screened it between 5:00 and 7:00 p.m., prime time for the adolescent viewer, including flocks of youngsters who had never seen the series before. (Late-adolescent college students were hooked—or rehooked—by post-midnight showings.) David Gerrold writes in *The World of Star Trek* that "it was the same thrill of discovery that the first generation of 'trekkies' had experienced only three years before, and it was happening all over again. . . ."

Week after week, Star Trek still continues to savage every kind of competition across America. Its incredible popularity reaches throughout the world, and even beyond the Iron Curtain. It has generated three successful feature films, innumerable novels, and "fanzines." At national conventions, Star Trek actors receive the veneration ordinarily accorded rock idols and Hollywood superstars. Scraps purloined from outtakes are hawked at galactic prices, while over five million copies of *Enterprise* blueprints have been sold.

This article focuses on the character universally nominated as a major source of Star Trek's enduring appeal: Mr. Spock, the elfin-eared science officer of the *Enterprise*. To date, Spock's psyche has been plumbed most extensively by Karin Blair in *Meaning in Star Trek*. She views him from a Jungian perspective as an archetypal hybrid, a healing mediator between clashing polarities. She believes Spock has a particular impact on female fans because identification enables them to contact their "animus-selves." Lichtenberg et al. (*Star Trek Lives!*) write from a similar feminist viewpoint.

My theories about Spock and Star Trek derive from my work as an adolescent psychotherapist, as well as from a passion for speculative fiction and cinema that reaches back to my own teens. For two decades, adolescent clients, children of friends, and two sons have told me why they found Spock compelling. Their observations lead me to conclude that he embodies the central virtues and dilemmas of puberty. His noble, flawed figure recapitulates in outer space many a Terran youngster's search for a viable identity. I will also show that the series entire, as a late-1960s creation, is informed by a curious political torsion, an "adolescent" wrenching between conservative (even prejudicial) values and libertarian ideals.

Beyond the following brief outline, the reader will require at least a nodding acquaintance with Star Trek's milieu. Star Trek postulates that by the twenty-third century, mankind will conquer its earthbound evils, explore the solar system, and make first contacts with other civilizations of the galaxy. A loosely knit "United Federation of Planets" is formed to promote amity, trade, and exchange of scientific data. Starfleet Command comprises the Federation's military and exploratory arm. The reach of Starfleet's authority is epitomized by its starship class vessels. The *U.S.S. (United Space Ship) Enterprise* possesses awesome weaponry and research capacities; its almost completely human crew is balanced according to the democratic principles demonstrators marched for in the 1960s. (Other starships are crewed by aliens from their own home planets, supposedly in aid of greater efficiency. Note the "back of the bus" table of organization.)

VULCAN AND THE VULCANS

Spock's role was relatively minor in early Star Trek episodes. His background was never presented systematically, but was sketched in as interest grew. Although some guidlines existed, it was left to the writers to interpret Spock's persona as each saw fit. The result was an inconsistent mélange, a fascinating quick study of popular myth in the making.

Spock hails from Vulcan, a deep-red planet in a far-off solar system with a hot, harsh environment similar to that of Mars. While some episodes suggest that the Vulcans originated there, one implies that Vulcan was seeded by vastly intelligent beings from outside the galaxy (shades of *2001*); they probably conducted similar applied anthropology on Earth, the planets of what was to become the Klingon and Romulan empires, and the other "M-type" worlds with humanoid life, explored by the *Enterprise* during her five-year mission.

Vulcans are slender, attractive, with upswept eyebrows, a chloritic complexion, and large elfin ears; stronger than humans, they also possess more acute senses and limited telepathic ability. Their sexuality and aggression are intimately wedded. Every seven years, the adult Vulcan male goes into "rut"; he must then return to his home territory, mate, or die. Any impediment—particularly by another male—arouses murderous rage. Between cycles, both sexes seem to eschew copulation, cherishing "mind melding" instead.

The ancient Vulcans were a virulently militaristic race. Several times they forged mighty empires, only to nearly annihilate themselves through civil war. Finally, the philosopher Surak persuaded them to renounce anger and be guided by reason alone. Down through the millennia, their conscious suppression of aggression somehow evolved into repression of every affect (emotional mood). In *Civilization and Its Discontents*, Freud likened acculturation to the imposition of an obsessional state. He was not sanguine about its ultimate success, believing that the collective superego would ultimately be unable to restrain aggression. While our world seems daily to fulfill his bleak vision, the Vulcans have fared better; their sublimations have held due to the steely Vulcan will or some other fortunate accident of alien metapsychology.

Contemporary Vulcan mores include altruism, industry, and stringent observation of the proprieties, particularly personal privacy. The Vulcans are respected throughout the Federation for their achievements in art, science, and diplomacy. They have also become an intensely spiritual people. Although women hold high political and religious office, the father still rules the Vulcan home. With its valorization of the obsessional virtues and the patriarchal family, Vulcan bears an uncanny resemblance to Victorian England, happily without the latter's undercurrent of hypocrisy and vice.

The excesses of the rut cycle have long been mitigated by arranged mindlock between prepubescent children. When the Vulcan youth goes into definitive heat after several nonfatal cycles, he is quickly married to his childhood intended. (Vulcan women apparently are not affected.) Thereafter, Vulcans are monogamous to a fault. Both sexes put the highest premium on an enduring partnership and stable family life.

SPOCK'S HISTORY

Spock is the only offspring of a rare interspecies marriage. His father, Sarek, descends from one of the most illustrious Vulcan families; he is a noted astrophysicist and statesman like his father before him. He is about a hundred years old (late middle age) and cuts an austere yet charismatic figure, the very personification of Vulcan *gravitas*. Spock's mother, Amanda, is an Earthwoman. By profession a teacher, she met Sarek while he was assigned to the Vulcan embassy on Terra. We do not know how he managed to elude child betrothal and win her hand. She was not welcomed easily into his family; the Vulcans, despite conscious disavowal of prejudice, harbor an unconscious sense of superiority verging on xenophobia. Eventually her own considerable diplomatic powers prevailed. She and Sarek have remained devotedly together for forty years.

Although Vulcan in appearance, Spock was taunted throughout his childhood because of his mixed birth; possibly he betrayed too much affect on the playground. At length, he resolved to become more Vulcan than the Vulcans in suppressing emotion.

(Vulcan emotiveness receives the widest interpretation from Star Trek's writers. In some scripts, the Vulcans appear to have an inborn absence of affect—subtly implying that the ancient teachings engendered genetic modifications. Other episodes suggest that Vulcans learn to suppress feelings at some unspecified point in their development. Spock's hazing by his classmates seems to indicate that Vulcan children indulge in irrational abuse as readily as their human counterparts.)

At the appropriate time, Spock was affianced to T'Pring, the daughter of an equally noble family. His academic career was brilliant. Sarek hoped his son would follow in his footsteps on Vulcan. Instead, Spock enrolled in officer candidate training with Starfleet Command. His decision was as hurtful to his father as his childhood withdrawal of affection was to his mother. Consequently, Sarek and Spock became virtual strangers.

After graduation, Spock entered active duty and served aboard starships with brief respites (including one painful visit home). As the series opens, he has lived aboard *Enterprise* for fifteen years. He is regarded highly throughout Starfleet, and has become something of a legend on Vulcan. During his first decade, he was Captain Christopher Pike's science officer. Following Pike's transfer, he continued in the same capacity under Captain James Kirk until the death of Gary Mitchell, Kirk's exec and close friend. Spock then accepted Kirk's offer to Mitchell's post in addition to his regular duties. He inherited the mantle of Mitchell's affection for Kirk as well.

SPOCK'S ADOLESCENT QUALITIES AND CONFLICTS (OR KEEPING THE LID ON THE ID)

Joe, a fifteen-year-old client, affectionately calls Spock a "reformed nerd," and thinks of himself as grossly unreformed. He entered therapy because of depression, which began after his first "girlfriend" (1.5 dates) threw him over for the class jock. Joe's teachers rate him a genius in math and computer science, like his idol. He's been a rabid Trekkie since he was eleven. His parents, more modestly endowed in brains and ambition, find him pretty much of a mystery. His orderliness and nitpicking drive them to distraction. Behind his weisenheimer facade, he is painfully shy, fearful of aggression. He frequently provokes his peers with brash displays of intellect, then morbidly anticipates attack or rejection.

It is easy to see why compulsive overachievers like Joe admire Spock, but less cerebral youngsters identify with the sublimatory, obsessional cast of his defenses, too. For Spock's battle to control his passions accurately reflects the consuming struggle of the early adolescent to master biological turmoil and integrate a radically new body image. The transforming body of the adolescent is mirrored in Spock's physique, with its incredible strength and adaptability, its uncanny blend of the familiar and strange. His ears are the most visible signets of change, lovely, unsettling phallic metaphors. He owns the appealing grace and awkwardness of many adolescents before they have settled comfortably into their expanded dimensions. (Frankenstein's movie monster, whom I have elsewhere analyzed as the incarnation of his master's disavowed adolescent self, shows a more exaggerated stiffness.)

Spock's ancestors nearly perished because their intemperate aggressiveness was melded to a savage reproductive cycle. Their ancient barbarism resonates with the adolescent's worst fears of unleashed aggression and sexuality. But centuries of logical praxis have all but eliminated the clamor of instinct from Vulcan puberty. The rut cycle's disruptions have been all but neutralized by encrusted ritual. Compared with the stormy course of Terran adolescence, an orderly ripening marks the Vulcan child's maturation. In humans, the downside risk of an uneventful pubertal progress can be an unquestioning attitude toward the status quo in adulthood. Vulcans do not seem to view this resolution amiss.

Thus, hybrids like Spock are possibly Vulcan's only true adolescents; they are understandably rare. Throughout childhood, Spock's emotive human half rendered him an object of scorn and distrust to his fellows and himself. Besides displaying detestable weakness, he could be forced into angry retaliation, just as serious as a threat to Vulcan self-esteem. Within Spock's bosom was resurrected the murderous potential of the entire Vulcan past. Even more than his peers, Spock prevailed through denial, suppression, repression, reaction formation, intellectualization, and sublimation. The adolescent ego summons these defensive strategies to tame and redirect rebellious instinct—putting the lid on the id, so to speak.

Spock's endearing attributes bloom in the adolescent, but are inevitably alloyed with a large dose of narcissism and insensitivity. Spock's "adolescent" virtues, his loyalty, altruism, and idealism, are purely manifested, defying external incitement or intrapsychic muddle. Where lesser men would lust or rage, he calmly saves the day, offering a helpful example to his colleagues and to viewers. The following example is but one of many.

In "Balance of Terror," the *Enterprise* is attacked by a vessel crewed by Romulans, a race which had battled the Federation to a truce a century before without making visual contact. Now on viewscreen, they appear Vulcan, leading Spock to theorize Romulus was a colony that lost touch with the mother culture millennia ago and kept its warlike ways. Lieutenant Stiles, whose family was slaughtered in the old conflict, sneeringly insinuates that Spock is a spy, a summary offense to Vulcan probity. In the climactic engagement, Stiles is overcome by a coolant leak and cannot respond when Kirk orders him to engage the phaser banks. At mortal risk, Spock fires the weapons and drags Stiles to safety. After the

Romulans are destroyed, Stiles apologizes. Spock demurs; he could hardly be offended since Stile's behavior was so patently "illogical."

Exasperated parents of youngsters like Joe will readily recognize Spock's maddening exactitude; fellow crewmembers find it equally aggravating, especially when he insists on announcing their imminent destruction to the nanosecond. But adolescents know that Spock's nerdy precision is the less adaptive side of his "cool," making him fallible and even more endearing. Joe figures if Spock can act like a wimp and still come off as a hero in the end, perhaps he has a shot, too.

Were Spock always in control of his emotions, he would simply be too perfect for teenagers to identify with. During several of Star Trek's most popular episodes, emotional upheaval fractures Spock's cool facade. Through typical dream-factory rationales, his dyscontrol is never seen to arise from brittle defenses, but from some outside agency; often, it afflicts humans even more painfully, legitimizing Spock's "breakdown."

In "The Naked Time," the *Enterprise* is infected by a virus that causes loss of inhibitions. Spock suffers exquisite torment from the eruption of his feelings, which is cured by Kirk forcibly confronting him with his duty, and by his empathy with the captain's unmasked loneliness. "This Side of Paradise" has the settlers of Omicron Ceti III expose the crew to spores that transform them into placid pod-people and Spock into a goofy romantic. Kirk discovers that violent emotions reverse the pod's effects. He hurls racist epithets at Spock, provoking a vicious attack that returns the horrified Vulcan to his senses.

Eros, not Mars, rules such transformations. When Spock's psychic redoubts go down, tenderness rather than aggression emerges from his human half, albeit transiently. Lelia Kalomi, a beautiful botanist who had once wooed him unsuccessfully, deploys the spores of Omicron Ceti III to win his heart. The virus of "Naked Time" turns sober Nurse Chapel into a vamp; Spock is profoundly shaken when she reveals longings for him, and for the first time acknowledges the psychic scars caused by his hybrid birth. He becomes so ashamed that he locks himself away from his companions like a mortified teenager. When he recovers, his love for Chapel vanishes. Poignantly, hers endures.

"Amok Time" (*vide infra*) is the only episode where the agency that unleashes Spock's affect originates within him, provoking violence rather than midsummer madness. Here, of course, Spock's savagery is clearly intrinsic to the Vulcan rut cycle, no part of the tender humanity which, according to Star Trek's unconscious agenda, constitutes his "genuine" core. Adolescents may thus sympathize with his unruliness, while maintaining comfortable ego distance.

SPOCK AS ADOLESCENT MEDIATOR

Every adolescent is a hybrid, a fascinating blend of what has been and what is yet to come. Adolescence regularly spurs inquiry into the status of the status quo. Hence, teenagers admire Spock's ability to confront novel situations with a fresh outlook, unencumbered by preconception. Confronted with inexplicable phenomena, the very rationality called up in the service of Spock's repressions paradoxically opens the world to his lucid understanding. When his shipmates are revolted by the appearance of alien life or baffled by the customs of some distant race, Spock's unbiased perception prevails. Kirk also has excellent intuition about extraterrestrials, but Spock's native alienation and telepathic power give him an intuitive edge Kirk prizes.

In "The Devil in the Dark," the pergium miners of Janus VI are being incinerated by a monster in their tunnels. Cornered, it resembles a mobile slag heap. Nevertheless, Spock guesses it is sentient and stops its extermination. His mind meld shows that the creature is a mother "Horta," a gentle being with a silicon biochemistry, capable of liquefying rock. It killed when its eggs were destroyed during the excavations. The angry miners are mollified. Through Spock, they apologize and contract a symbiotic arrangement: The newly hatched Horta will fulfill their biological imperative by digging for the costly pergium while the humans grow rich.

"The Way to Eden" is of particular interest because Spock mediates between the crew and a group of human youths revolting against the arid mechanization of twenty-third-century life. From a hijacked, crippled vessel, the *Enterprise* rescues an unlikely assortment of dropouts and bohemians who are seeking a bucolic existence on the mythical planet of Eden. Their leader, the brilliant renegade Dr. Sevrin, is unmasked as a charismatic paranoid who blames technology because he carries a potentially fatal germ. He steals the shuttlecraft and flies his acolytes to Eden, where the lush soil proves highly toxic. With their paradise exposed as a poisonous delusion, the young people quietly return to the *Enterprise* and home (Sevrin's bacteria would have killed them if Eden's environment did not). Sevrin defiantly bites into a fruit and dies.

The episode's apparent "liberated" text conceals a rightish critique of 1960s counterculture. Sevrin is a Leary-like narcissist, his project fueled not by revolutionary ardor, but by narrow resentment over his health. Spock's receptivity to the dissidents is balanced by a subtle conservatism, ambiguously deployed here (and elsewhere) to defend the established order. Although he sympathizes with the "space hippies," he never joins them; nor is he happy to have been the the agency that brought them to their fatal Eden. One must live in the real world, the text seems to say, not in the fool's or knave's paradise of Sevrin's cracked ambition—a conclusion sadly echoing the facile advice heaped upon "political" youth by their parents, their government, and, all too often, their therapists.

(One notes that, without explanation, the Terran Sevrin bears huge scalloped ears, emphasizing his negative doubling of Spock, his intriguing *sequestration* of Spock's potential disruptiveness throughout the episode. Exiled from humanity much like Spock, Sevrin plays Mephistophelean fomenter of adolescent revolt, the harbinger of chaos instead of the healing mediator.)

SPOCK AND MCCOY: BRIDGING THE GALACTIC GENERATION GAP

Embattled adults rarely accept adolescent re-vision gracefully. The perennial struggle across the generations is nicely captured in the prickly relationship between Spock and Dr. Leonard "Bones" McCoy, the *Enterprise*'s cantankerous senior surgeon. McCoy's exasperation with Spock is a staple of Star Trek's humor. McCoy frequently seethes with indignation over Spock's bloodless *modus operandi*. When he demands that Spock forsake the head for the heart, one may be sure that Spock's irritating precision will escalate. McCoy's congenial humanism is balanced by a chronic rigidity of disposition. He is an inherent conservative, not always in the best sense of the word; under pressure, he often invokes unhelpful "commonsense" explanations for uncommon phenomena or "practical" solutions that are not daring enough to succeed. Thus, Spock's challenges to the quotidian incite him even more than the iciness of Vulcan logic.

Fired by the rationality McCoy deplores, Spock's imagination soars aloft while McCoy's limps behind. The two are natural foils: Spock plays adolescent *agent provocateur* to McCoy's stodgy parent. In Leonard Nimoy's reading, Spock is much more conscious of his provocation than a deadpan demeanor betrays, which is not lost on amused teenage viewers. The duo's rapprochement, frequently mediated by Kirk, proves to the adolescent that conflict between the generations can be fruitfully resolved. Equally pleasing is the support each character finds in the other. Despite his bluster, McCoy genuinely values Spock's intellect and uncompromising honor, while Spock garners secret comfort from McCoy's tough-minded compassion. It is a testament of Spock's respect that he consigns his *katra*—the Vulcan immortal spirit—to McCoy's unconscious, shortly before sacrificing his life in *Star Trek II: The Wrath of Khan*.

OEDIPUS IN SPACE

Humanity's ancient myths often portray the adolescent boy as hero/outcast, wrestling with a contested patrimony to forge his identity. Taken together, the two episodes "Amok Time" and "Journey to Babel" comprise a futuristic reinvention of this primal drama; its obvious Oedipal theme, the resolution of Spock's prolonged adolescent identity crisis, which largely stems from his struggle with his father and the repressive Vulcan tradition Sarek incarnates.

It is a clinical commonplace that a charismatic father like Sarek may engender intense competition in his son, the original object of which is the woman both love; *mutatis mutandis*, a father whose Oedipal problems remain unresolved (often a function of competitive anxiety toward his own father) may secretly tremble before the son's majority. In either case, the result is likely to be an escalation of the son's Oedipal conflict, with delays in psychological maturation and often far-reaching effects upon choices in love and work.

Oedipus was rescued from his father's reprisals by strangers and became a youthful wanderer. When we first meet Spock, he has long since quit the scene of Sarek's wrath to live as an exile in Starfleet. He seems to have reintegrated well within his new "family." His talents are widely recognized; first Captain Pike's support, then Captain Kirk's warmth appear to have supplanted Sarek's dissatisfaction (McCoy remains an ambivalent surrogate in his chronic criticism—Sarek's nearest human replicant).

But, in fact, Spock is profoundly unhappy. He has never been comfortable in Terran company, even with Kirk. He has shunned the limelight, denied himself promotion, and excluded the love of women. He has especially avoided home because he dreads confronting Sarek's displeasure and the yoke of Vulcan custom. In "Amok Time," he can elude his instincts and their social consequences no longer; if he does not mate with T'Pring, his childhood betrothed, he will surely die. To save him, Kirk flagrantly disobeys orders and reroutes to Vulcan.

During Spock's absence, T'Pring has turned to Stonn, a thoroughly unprepossessing type she no doubt selected because he is more pliable material. Vulcan law dictates that if she refuses the contracted marriage, her fiancé must battle a male of her choice to the death. She becomes the winner's chattel. When Kirk and McCoy beam down with Spock, the wily T'Pring chooses the captain to fight Spock rather than Stonn. Kirk only discovers the lethal implications of the challenge after accepting it as a favor to his distressed friend.

According to T'Pring's devious logic, if Spock triumphs he will gladly put her aside. In the unlikely event Kirk prevails, he will just as surely refuse the dubious honor of her hand. Either way, she gets the negligible Stonn. The subsequent "marriage-or-death" ceremony fuses wedding with adolescent *rite de passage*. The combat unfolds in the ambiance of an Achaean dream. The setting is spare and surreal: bare rocks against angry red horizon, hieratic costumes culled from a Martha Graham Atrean ballet. The Oedipal thrust of the proceedings is underscored by a piece of simultaneous negation/affirmation. Sarek does not attend and, instead of a fellow Vulcan, Spock contends with an obvious father surrogate. The absence of Sarek—indeed, of any relative—highlights the triangulation between Kirk, Spock, and T'Pring (Stonn is such a nonentity that he fades into the rocks).

(Although the lack of kin is probably due to a writer's oversight, one may speculate from what is known of the Vulcans that family members are excluded because it would be exceptionally painful for them to watch combat should it occur, and no less mortifying for the bridegroom later. It is also not unlikely that a couple would be married quickly and privately, reserving a large public wedding for a later time when the groom, safely out of heat, could behave with proper Vulcan decorum.)

After being thoroughly mauled, Kirk is pronounced dead by McCoy. Spock rejects T'Pring—true to her scenario—and beams back to the ship with Kirk's corpse, which miraculously revives. McCoy reveals that a stimulant he gave Kirk to buffer the Vulcan climate was actually a delayed-action depressant mimicking death. Spock's enormous joy at seeing his friend alive somehow acts as an antidote to the rut cycle's perturbations for the remainder of the series. He is liberated from the chemistry that would have killed for lack of a suitable sexual outlet, or had him dwindle down to a dutiful slave of Vulcan custom—death, either way.

(In *Star Trek III: The Search for Spock*, Spock's mindless body evolves rapidly on the Genesis Planet and undergoes several rut cycles. The beautiful Vulcan/Romulan Lieutenant Saavik guides him through the ordeals. While they touch fingers ritually, it is left unclear whether they have mated or whether Spock will be afflicted anew with rut once his corpus and spirit have been rejoined.)

The latent patricidal motif of "Amok Time" emerges undisguised in "Journey to Babel." Sarek appears in the episode with Amanda for the first and only time. (He figures briefly without her in *The Search for Spock*.) In this episode, the *Enterprise* ferries Federation ambassadors to a conference considering admission of the mineral-rich Coridan system. An unusually tangled narrative has Sarek inadvertently fingered by Spock for a murder he did not commit; Sarek's collapse from a heart ailment during Kirk's interrogation; cardiac surgery by McCoy, requiring that Spock undergo dangerous marrow stimulation to provide blood for his father; a seriously wounded Kirk forced to quit the bridge while the ship is being attacked by the assassin's confederates (smugglers seeking to protect their interests on the Coridan planets); Spock halting the operation to assume command; Amanda furious with her son for putting his and her husband's life in jeopardy; Kirk's return, feigning good health, so that Spock can rejoin the surgery; the invader's defeat; and, finally, Spock's reconciliation with Sarek after McCoy's efforts succeed.

In this convoluted tale, sinister outsiders disrupt the Federation's adoption of a new "child," the Coridan system. The surface text echoes a deeper theme: the disruption of Spock's relationship with his father by the latter's implacable ire. Its "realistic" basis is Spock's disavowal of his heritage and Sarek's misgivings about Starfleet military aims. But the psychoanalyst intuits another wellspring of Sarek's hostility, an atavistic contradiction to millennia of Vulcan logic. Lest the following seem too anthropomorphic, let us remember that Vulcans were, after all, created out of the fantasies of Earthmen.

Ample clues indicate that Sarek's aggressive and erotic drives are fiercer than the average Vulcan's (or his controls more tenuous). His romance with an Earthwoman points to a singularly passionate disposition. As for his aggression, Spock states with chilling certainty: "If there were a reason, my father is quite capable of killing . . . logically . . . and efficiently. . . ."

Amanda speaks of her profound love for her son and her distress over Spock's torment by his playmates. Given the generosity of her nature, she undoubtedly comforted him by word and touch throughout his childhood, try as she may have to restrain herself. Her affection must have been enormously unsettling for Sarek, given Vulcan abstemiousness in physical matters. It is likely that Sarek's undemonstrativeness stimulated Spock's human mother's demonstrativeness. Here we have an atypical, needy Vulcan father who watched his wife lavish inordinate attention upon his son. This, I submit, kindled the flames of an ancient, deadly Oedipal rivalry.

Nota bene: Sarek's father was a "competitor" at least as illustrious as himself. It is legitimate to inquire if he might have been as disapproving. Exogamous object choice is a well-known resolution of Oedipal conflict; one assuages incestuous anxiety by marrying a partner of a different religion, class, or race—or, in Sarek's case, of a different species.

Of course, Sarek would have found murderous rivalry with his own child even more reprehensible than a human father in similar circumstances, the zenith of unreason. Despite rigorous repression, his unconscious jealousy escalated the normal austerity between Vulcan father and son. Sarek became an even more frightening and removed figure throughout Spock's childhood. It was then tragically inevitable that Spock should distance himself even further from Sarek during adolescence. Being semihuman, his Oedipal strivings were closer to consciousness, even more frightening than his father's; the means to control them were faultier. Terrified of his resurrected jealousy, dreading Sarek's imagined retaliation, ever hoping to preserve a vestige of his father's love, Spock executed the characteristic defensive maneuver of puberty: identification with the aggressor. He identified with Sarek's *aloofness*.

He had already turned away from Amanda during latency, forswearing the object of Oedipal competition, placating the internalized father, and demonstrating to his peers he could be as Spartan as the next Vulcan kid on the block. For further protection of father and embattled self, he quit Vulcan altogether. Spock repudiated Sarek's provenance to make common cause with the Terrans of Starfleet. The gesture was ambiguous. Oedipal combat, instead of being negated, was merely relocated to a different arena. Joining his mother's people was a potent signet of Spock's revolt against Vulcan patriarchy. It recapitulated the intense affiliation between Spock and Amanda which Sarek had earlier found so painful, and from which he had exiled himself.

Sarek dealt with his suppressed rage, savaged pride, ambivalent but genuine love for Spock the only way he knew—with more culturally sanctioned withdrawal. The punishing quality of his stoic stance is grasped when, with barely a trace of disdain, Sarek acknowledges Spock's presence upon his arrival on the bridge. Amanda has endured Sarek's frosty despair for nearly two decades; that she still loves him is a testament to his virtues, his charisma, and quite possibly a schizoid thrust in her own disposition.

Spock outdoes his father's coldness with his own obsessional withdrawal during "Journey to Babel"; his behavior toward human and Vulcan alike is as mechanized as his computers. But rage will out: a plot replete with menaced fathers and their substitutes repeatedly implicates, then exonerates him of patricidal motive. His "artless" revelation of the Vulcan execution method used to murder one of the ambassadors and his appalling candor about Sarek's aggression put his father under suspicion. Kirk's interrogation of Sarek nearly induces a fatal cardiac seizure—once more, Spock nearly breaks his poor parent's heart! After undergoing perilous marrow stimulation, he abandons Sarek at the eleventh hour to supplant a gravely wounded Kirk, Sarek's surrogate. As in "Amok Time," his human friends rescue him from his racking between intolerable alternatives through guile, self-sacrifice, and medical art. Kirk disguises his wounds, allowing Spock to retire with honor, so McCoy can heal Sarek.

While Sarek and Spock never discuss their differences, they do reach a mild *rapprochement* by the episode's conclusion. The surface plot contrives to discharge their mutual rancor safely. Spock can pursue his career with a lighter heart, while Sarek returns to Vulcan with a mended one. But it is poignantly evident that Spock will never experience the communion with Sarek his humanity craves. Their antagonisms—and similarities—run too deep.

SPOCK AND THE INFERNAL FEMININE

Spock's chronic isolation from his mother remains unchanged at the end of "Journey to Babel." While her feelings toward him have warmed again, he is, if anything, more glacial toward her. After she expresses pleasure to Kirk about seeing her husband and son reconciled, Spock says to his father: "Emotional, isn't she?"

Sarek: "She has always been that way."

Spock: "Indeed . . . I have often wondered why you married her."

Sarek: "At the time, it seemed the logical thing to do."

Amanda smiles, consenting unwittingly to their derogation.

Spock has asked a summary question of his existence: Why her? Why the outsider, this labile creature with her unseemly emotions? Why not a good, cold Vulcan wife who would not trouble us with her tears, her smiles, her touch? Sarek's ironic answer implies he was so infatuated that he did not realize the trouble he was buying when he sought to warm his obsessional spirit at Amanda's hearth. For him, the reward has been worth the jangle.

Unfortunately, Spock's hybrid nature and the undefendedness of childhood rendered him far more vulnerable to the anxiety of her comforts. It is a reasonable speculation that Spock was chronically overstimulated by his mother through no fault of hers, *de rerum naturae*. The pleasure of her nurturing was always countered by the fear of flooding from tidal waves of unmastered affect. Consequently, he withdrew first from her, then from all women behind a schizoid carapace. In the adult Spock's psyche, Amanda's representation still remains deeply split between the Good and the Bad. His love for her is tainted not only with the fear of Oedipal reprisal, but with far weightier pre-Oedipal dread. In similar clinical cases, fantasies derived from this primal *angst* range from mere exploitation by the Bad Mother, to being engulfed, devoured by her.

"Amok Time" incarnates Amanda's Bad Mother persona both in the cold schemer T'Pring, and in T'Pau, the matriarch-priestess of the marriage-or-death ritual, who dominates a rut-maddened Spock and a diminished Kirk. But even women unambivalently devoted to Spock own a malevolent aspect. Their passive presence is fraught with peril or they actively pursue devious, hurtful means to win his heart. In either case, the toll exacted by their intimacy is unendurable. To cite only one example, the spores released by Leila Kalomi on Omicron Ceti III reduce him to a witless buffoon.

Spock's dilemma reinvents the misogyny of the early adolescent boy. Like Amanda, many contemporary mothers must endure contemptuous avoidance by the pubertal son who a few years before seemed the sweetest fellow imaginable. From the son's perspective, she has been transformed into the forbidden Oedipal object and the awful Bad Mother's signifier of childhood dependency. His scornful withdrawal rapidly extends to sisters, their friends, and the entire feminine tribe. Until his independence is more assured, he will probably take comfort in groups of like-minded misogynists.

Spock's ambivalence toward women further identifies him with Kirk and McCoy. They too have a penchant for ladies with dangerous tendencies. For McCoy, the Bad Mother's vampiric menace surfaces blatantly in "The Man Trap." An old flame of McCoy's, the archaeologist Nancy Crater, has been killed for the salt content of her body by an intelligent shape-shifter, the last survivor of its race. It joins her husband in a malignant symbiosis, sustaining the illusion of her presence in return for the salt of his body. When the *Enterprise* arrives at the Craters' dig, the creature preys upon the crew, dispatches Crater, and even assumes the moonstruck McCoy's identity. Finally cornered as Nancy, it is phasered down by the anguished doctor when it attacks Kirk. As it dies, it changes back to its true form, a loathsome thing of tentacles and suckers.

Kirk is more romantically inclined than Spock or McCoy, but his affairs come to no better end. Many temptations are strewn in his path, but his ruling passion for the *Enterprise* invariably triumphs.

Occasionally, Kirk's amours bear the Bad Mother's obvious harpy imprint; the worst of these is Dr. Janice Lester of "Turnabout Intruder," whose jilting by Kirk many years before precipitates fulminating para-noia. Delusionally certain his success has caused her lack of advance-ment, she engineers a punishment fit for his "crime" by switching their bodies.

Even Kirk's numerous wholesome loves, like Spock's, regularly threaten to deprive him of identity, life, or prestige, albeit through "circum-stances" rather than malicious practice. In "Court-Martial," he stands wrongfully accused of manslaughter over the death of a fellow officer. Starfleet compels another old flame, the brilliant attorney Areel Shaw, to prosecute him.

Kirk's deepest affection of the series is stirred by a woman harboring titanic destructive potential for the entire human race in "The City on the Edge of Forever." Another tangled scenario sends Kirk, Spock, and McCoy back in time to Depression-era New York, where the captain becomes infatuated with a charismatic social worker, Edith Keeler. The episode concludes as Kirk stands by helplessly while she is killed by a truck. Were she to survive, she would lead a pacifist movement that would inadvertently enable Germany to win World War II, precipitating an Armageddon from which the future of the Federation could not evolve.

These are only a few of a disproportionate number of Star Trek episodes where the *Enterprise* is threatened by disruptive alien females, troublesome past or present lovers. The subsequent narrative recaptures the *Status quo ante* for the ship and, usually, one of our three heroes. At the end, the galactic trek is resumed—shades of Shane clopping off into the sunset or Rick Blaine and Inspector Louis Renault embarking on their journey to Brazzaville in *Casablanca*.

In such adventures, Star Trek's main protagonists are seen to share a common estrangement from women, as intense as their bonding with each other and their dedication to the missions that keep them far from Mother Earth. Spock's avoidance obviously springs from intrapsychic conflict; McCoy's is ascribed to the hurtful divorce which made him leave a lucrative private practice to enlist in Starfleet. Kirk's shrinking from commitment is chalked up to the exigencies of duty, a familiar pass of the cinematic commander. These are dramatic plausibilities, but also rationales for an overarching vision of the feminine as a seductive menace. The final fault for fleeing intimacy is never ascribed to masculine *angst* of being unmanned, humiliated, having one's ego absorbed in foul fusion, or merely being brought to ground or bored to death. Instead, it is *woman* who stands accused as prime disturber of the (male) peace.

In the Star Trek universe, one approaches woman with exceptional caution, frequently to contend with her for survival. Given the inevitability of her presence on a liberated vessel, one might try domesticating her; indeed, the *Enterprise*'s female crew, unlike the legion of bumptious feminine intruders, are a generally placid lot, passively observing the action or servicing male endeavor. One might try doing without women altogether, like Spock. Whatever the *modus vivendi*, it is strongly implied that life would be easier and the work at hand would proceed more efficiently in trustworthy male company.

Similar figurations of adolescent misogyny, including the woman-hating companionability of the male pubertal gang, pervade film genres enjoyed by adolescents of all ages—the Saturday serials of my youth, private-eye capers, Westerns, horror and science fiction cinema, sundry epics of the road, the air, the sea, the jungle or mining camp. The masterbuilders of the adventures are "men's men" like Hawkes, Huston, and Walsh. Siegel and Peckinpah are their direct inheritors; recently the mantle has passed to Milius, Schroeder, Scorsese, Coppola, Lucas, Spielberg, Kotcheff, Eastwood, and Stallone.

The scenarios of these luminaries and other less worthy repeatedly summon up the same conservative, partriarchal ethos: a lonely hero or male group undertakes dangerous military or professional challenges, uncovers sinister plots, faces down a multitude of evils with exemplary valor and skill. Woman may be the occulted villain of the piece—the spider at the center of the web entangling the private eye, the symbiotic menace improbably toothed and clawed in weird cinema. In the "task-oriented" adventure film, she is kept essentially peripheral to the action as the hero's adoring girlfriend, the group's den mother, or raucous mascot. At best, she gains entry into the charmed circle by proving herself a diminished buddy. In another variation of the theme, a worthy female enemy is won over by the hero's character or sexuality—*viz.* the bondage of Pussy Galore in *Goldfinger*.

Star Trek evolves out of these "macho" genres into a decade of turbulent social and political change. The sexism, racism, and "rightism" of its antecedents do not usually jar within their social context or filmic text. However, the collision of genre conservatism with the jaunty liberalism of Star Trek's day does generate textual "uneasiness." Star Trek's illiberalisms often mix poorly with the overall progressive thrust of many episodes. One analogizes to the adolescent's struggle between outworn parental values and newer adaptive possibilities.

The internal wrenching with each Star Trek adventure varies, I suspect, according to the ideological bent of the individual writer. Scripts like "The Way to Eden" are virtual conservative apologias. In others, the influence of rightish or prejudicial tendencies is negligible. "Devil in the Dark," for instance, portrays a repellent alien who possesses strong sympathetic qualities once Terran xenophobia can be transcended.

Star Trek's sexism and misogyny constitute its most thoroughly reactionary problem, an egregious example of which is Shatner's hysterical portrayal of the feminized Kirk/Janet Lester in "Turnabout Intruder." Nevertheless, a few competent and attractive women do appear. The Romulan commander of "The Enterprise Incident," whom Spock stolidly romances during the rather unsavory theft of her ship's cloaking device, is quite admirable. (Beyond a shared ancestry, the two have much in common, are obviously drawn to each other, and would make excellent partners were it not for the fact that she is also the Federation's avowed enemy.) *Star Trek II: The Wrath of Khan* and *Star Trek III: The Search for Spock*, produced after a generation of advances in women's rights, contain several unambivalently likable, capable female characters: Dr. Carol Marcus, another former love of Kirk's who mothers his illegitimate child as well as the Genesis Project, and Lieutenant Saavik, the feisty Vulcan navigator.

SPOCK IN THE SPIRIT

Tales of exploration like Star Trek have always delighted adolescents. The teenager's thirst for new outer horizons often is matched by an inner quest for meaning. Beyond wondering what vocational path to follow or which friends to choose on life's journey, many youngsters ponder the agency which set them on the road and the fate awaiting them at its terminus. Star Trek rarely inquires after the Big Questions; no chaplain services the *Enterprise*. While Kirk occasionally waxes eloquent about the insatiable curiosity that drives man to the stars, his rhetoric, deconstructed, reads as a materialistic panegyric to the American Pioneering Spirit. Only Spock seems to hunger after ontological truth. In his search resides the final locus of adolescent identification I will address.

Spock's spirituality is firmly grounded in his heritage. Vulcan mysticism is a fascinating enigma to the Federation's other races. Though we know little of their beliefs, there appears to be much Zen in the Vulcans. They perceive unceasing change as a central aspect of existence. According to Spock, the universe's "infinite diversity in infinite combinations" is an abiding focus of their daily meditation. Their impressive achievements in art and science may be taken as a continuous realization of their contemplation. They have the kind of massive speculative intelligence that inclines one to seek a transcendent figure in the elegant tracery of mathematical logic. Under obscure circumstances, their *katra*—a psychic organ akin to an immortal soul—can be reincarnated.

Suffering may spur a spiritual vocation as decisively as one's own theological or intellectual antecedents. The void created by Spock's estrangement from parents, home, and self have intensified the normative anguish of adolescent alienation. His exile, the inherent spirituality of his temperament and race, all impart a special religious quality to his quest for a new belonging. Human companions and Starfleet duties cannot afford a final resting place for his perturbed soul; these are necessary but provisional attachments in the phenomenal realm. Like Terran mystics of East and West, Spock pursues a union more profound, with an ineffable ground of immanent reality.

Spock's philosophical and spiritual beliefs were to have been a major focus of Star Trek's canceled fourth season. Instead, they were developed in *Star Trek: The Motion Picture*, and to a lesser extent in *The Search for Spock*.

In *Star Trek: The Motion Picture*, Spock has retired to Vulcan for several years. Rigorous mental discipline prepares him for the supreme Vulcan test of *Kolinahr*—shedding all emotions. But he fails at the last moment: His human feelings are stirred by telepathic contact with a vastly intelligent entity sweeping through deep space. Sensing its purpose may be linked to his quest, he rejoins the *Enterprise*.

The entity, which calls itself V'Ger, is a megalithic living computer, crafted by a machine race from an ancient NASA Voyager satellite which fell through a black hole on the other side of the galaxy. The machine beings programmed it to wander the universe, learn all it could, then return to its "Creator" and yield up its data. After three centuries, V'Ger now travels back to its Terran origins. Unfortunately, it has conceived that the Creator is a mightier machine, and humans mere "carbon-based" infestations interfering with its mission. Hence, it destroys every living thing on its path back to Earth, until it receives the Enterprise's messages of friendship. Then it swallows the starship whole.

Spock's nearly fatal mind meld reveals that despite its awesome technology, V'Ger is an empty vessel, incapable of understanding the simplest emotion of friendship. "In all this magnificence, V'Ger finds no awe, no delight . . . no meaning . . . no answers." A short time later, Kirk discovers his friend on the bridge, a single tear coursing down his cheek, the only time Spock cries while in full possession of his faculties. "I weep for V'Ger as I would a brother," he tells the captain. "As I was when I came aboard, so is V'Ger now, empty, uncomplete, searching. Logic and knowledge are not enough . . . each of us, at some time in our lives, turns to someone, a father, a brother, a God, and asks, why am I here? What was I meant to be? V'Ger hopes to touch its Creator, to find its answers. . . ."

(This crucial scene was inexcusably cut when *Star Trek: The Motion Picture* was first shown; it was later restored in the televised and videotape versions.)

To study the crew, V'Ger vaporizes Ilia, a beautiful Deltan officer, and resurrects her as an android probe. Captain Will Decker, Kirk's protégé, had loved her when she was alive and now awakens the affection embedded in the Ilia-android's circuitry. As V'Ger enters Earth orbit, Kirk and his officers are taken to V'Ger's core, where the ancient satellite is enshrined. It is ready to transmit its enormous store of data but does not respond to the old NASA trigger code. Spock finds the antennae leads have been fused so that it can only be triggered manually: V'Ger wants the Creator's personal touch. Decker hurls himself forward to complete the code, embraces the Ilia-android, and both are engulfed in swirling plasmas of light. The entire V'Ger complex dissolves, leaving ship and crew unharmed. Afterward, Spock elects to remain onboard—"My task on Vulcan is completed."

The film's conclusion implies that V'Ger has discovered the meaning it sought through the infusion of human love; analogously, Spock will find the meaning of his existence by allowing himself access to his own tender feelings. Such materialist/humanist texts commonly assert that the heterosexual union is as much an intimation of the Divine as any being can reasonably expect. Since numerous conflicts bar him from woman's love, Spock must settle for the sublimations of male friendship.

An alternate reading rescues him from the bathos Spock occassionally seems to provoke in his narrators. It hinges upon a single question: Why, having come so far in his quest, does not *Spock* complete the trigger code and merge with V'Ger? Is he so surprised that he lets Decker slip under his guard? Hardly, for his reflexes are quicker than a human's. And even if Decker does catch him off balance, he is still powerful enough to push him away from V'Ger's control panel. Danger cannot stay his hand, for he repeatedly rushes against orders into the very teeth of death. I submit that his decision springs from a flash of altruism and insight. Mystic union cannot easily be prefigured by woman's affection for Spock given his chronic schizoid position. Furthermore, he knows Decker still loves Ilia, whatever her form. Nor can enlightenment come through fusion with V'Ger. All his life, Spock has been tormented by obsessional self-manipulation. He says, in effect, that even with its awesome power V'Ger still bears a peculiar taint of cog and wheels for him; it cannot possess this deadened connotation for Decker.

V'Ger, therefore, represents a tantalizing but rejected expedient, of which there are many along the seeker's path. Spock must employ less artificial means. Other Vulcans may dwell comfortably at home while they shed the constraints of ego desire and dualistic thought. His *Kolinahr* lies elsewhere, in far-off galaxies, in selfless service to the Federation with Kirk and McCoy at his side, in continued meditation on the eternally unchanging, unchanged source of his divided self. Through these expedients may he touch and be reborn into that profound emptiness that engenders, moment by moment, the universe's "infinite diversity in infinite combinations."

Personal death holds no qualms for this seeker. The ultimate ace of adolescent altruism—laying down his life for his friends in *Star Trek II: The Wrath of Khan*—is merely another minute metamorphosis in the ceaseless ebb and flow of creation. We shall leave him now, incompletely resurrected at the end of *The Search for Spock*. Unlike television's recycled heroes, Spock has served as a durable ideal for adolescents of all ages during the past twenty years. There is every reason to believe he will continue in the same capacity for generations to come.

It is utterly unimaginable that any actor other than Leonard Nimoy could play Spock. In the Star Trek pilot, Spock seemed like a gangly teenager. Nimoy grew palpably into the role to convey Spock's lucid intelligence, somber dignity, quirkiness, and wit. Offstage, Nimoy persistently refuses exploitation of Spock for commercial gain. He has avoided becoming permanently identified with his avatar, pursuing a remarkable variety of unrelated roles and work in other fields. One likes to think that Spock would have found him admirably "in character" on every score.

Harvey Roy Greenberg, M.D., is in private practice of psychiatry and psychoanalysis in New York City. He is also associate clinical professor of psychiatry at Albert Einstein Medical College. He has published frequently on both adolescence and cinema. The author expresses his appreciation to Mr. Alan Pakalns for furnishing invaluable research data.

BROTHER, MY SOUL: SPOCK, McCOY, AND THE MAN IN THE MIRROR

by Joyce Tullock

We've found that we really don't have to say much in these introductions to Joyce Tullock's articles. In fact, we kind of suspect that most fans just skip over them in their rush to read the article itself. Joyce is back again with an intense look at the eternal but ever-changing relationship between Spock and McCoy. Sound like the same old thing? If you think so, then you're not familiar with Joyce Tullock's work.

Star Trek is a saga of contraries. From its most obvious episodes to its most subtle, it consistently deals with the problems of our universe in a dual perspective. It's as if it were the very personality of man himself. It won't let us rest, in fact, for the very nature of the series (including the movies) has been a desire to face the positive/negative aspects of life and find a central ground. Even its main three characters are a kind of diplomatic equation; Spock and McCoy, the opposing natures of man, Kirk that "central ground." But in Star Trek's desire to take us along on the five-year mission—to discover not only the universe of space, but the universe of inner man—it has taken us on a very complete adventure in the greatest contrary of all: the logical and emotional mind of man.

In all the discussions of contraries, opposite viewpoints, and differing perspectives, we see a running theme. We see aliens who seek to be understood, we see evil that might not be so evil if viewed from another perspective, we see monsters who turn out to be more beautiful than beastly. Finally, we see difference and try to understand it. That's the magic and the heart of Star Trek, or any good science fiction.

And for many, the best of Star Trek involves the discussion of difference—sometimes referred to as "the unknown." But good science fiction always strives to make a human point by employing a somewhat nonhuman perspective. An attempt, perhaps, to discover the "unknown" within each man by taking the view outside of himself. In Star Trek, the very heart of this science fiction theme lies in the Spock/McCoy relationship. An unusual relationship which Leonard Nimoy once short-sightedly referred to as being the same as the Doc/Festus friendship of television's long-running *Gunsmoke* series. Nimoy came close, but he now himself admits that there is much more to the Spock/McCoy relationship than meets the eye. It is the perfect starting point, too, for a discussion of the way Star Trek deals with the complexities of the human mind.

Spock the alien is the aloof, quiet-minded sophisticate. Raised in a tradition of order and aestheticism, Spock grew up to be very much his father's son, a scientist dedicated to the concept of logic as a way of life. But it also fits into Star Trek's theme of contraries that Spock should choose to rebel, and against his father's wishes, join Starfleet. His reasons for this decision are, on the surface, unknown. In all other ways Spock seems to admire his father, and in "Journey to Babel," he struggles in his own way to gain his father's approval by choosing the course of greater logic over the feelings of a son for his father. He resists McCoy's pleas that he provide blood for his father during heart surgery, maintaining that to do so would take him away from his task as acting commander of the *Enterprise*. (Kirk has been wounded by a spy, and is temporarily unable to captain the ship, which is in danger of attack.)

Of course, this episode gives us some good Spock/McCoy stuff. We see the doctor, the "mere" human, openly feeling inferior and inadequate for the task he must undertake (more of that Spock/McCoy "man in the mirror" stuff). Sarek is dying, and McCoy, who has never performed heart surgery on a Vulcan, must now do so. There is an irony in this episode involving the emotion/logic theme in the Spock/McCoy relationship. At first, McCoy refuses to operate because he feels his lack of skill might endanger the patient. Then, when he gets his emotional, very "human" feelings of inferiority in hand, he knows he must operate and is willing to go ahead, but Spock refuses to take part, claiming (on behalf of logic) that he has more important duties. Oh well, it's probably really quite in character that the two are out of synch!

In this particular episode the Spock/McCoy conflict is reinforced by the presence on the ship of Amanda, Spock's all-too-human mother. She backs up McCoy's point of view where Spock's resentment of emotion is concerned. She reminds her son, not only in words, but by her very presence, that he too possesses the qualities of being human. And by giving the audience a flesh-and-blood Spock's mom to look at, Star Trek accomplishes a mighty task. It gives Spock's conflict and his half-humanness a very real backdrop on which to build the character as a whole. Spock was, of course, a well-established character in Star Trek by this time. Nevertheless, Amanda and Sarek have continued to play a very important, even magnificent part in the Star Trek mythology ever since, even to the point of becoming well developed in the amateur fan literature which began some time after the series' demise. Jean Lorrah's works on Sarek and Amanda are especially fine examples of what could be done with characters who had appeared so briefly in the series. And when we finally see Sarek again in *The Search for Spock*, Mark Lenard's portrayal of him is so huge and powerful that his short part in the film seems somehow larger, overshadowing even the performance of William Shatner.

Sarek and Amanda's marriage is a natural example of Star Trek's tendency to seek a consolidation of differences and understandings between peoples. Here we have two beings who, by tradition, ethnic background, and even genetics, are diametrically opposed—and yet they find a haven and a life in one another's company. It is beautiful—a marriage which defies all the rules of Sarek's logic, of Amanda's human desire for overt sentiment. They have obviously found a place which is neither of logic nor of emotion. It is likely that neither has compromised beliefs to find that place. They have simply grown together so closely, so trustingly, that they have learned that there is another way to be.

In this way, Star Trek has provided a first step in a long journey, toward an idea which must indeed take form in the real world: the idea that great differences can be resolved to the benefit and betterment of all involved.

But what of Spock? What did the marriage of Sarek and Amanda do for him? Was it all good? It demanded, for one thing, that he, evidently the first Vulcan/human, be born into a world which was not entirely his. He quite literally was an experiment in the consolidation of opposites and the unbiased blending in differences. Born of an important Vulcan sophisticate and his Terran wife, Spock no doubt started out in life as an oddity, rejected (so Amanda implies in "Journey to Babel") by his classmates and peers, probably not totally trusted or accepted by his father's friends and associates. As if Vulcan life was not lonely enough, Spock was an alien in his own world.

So Spock had to prove himself. It is too bad, in a way, that McCoy could not have known him as a child. (And remember, the original series plans called for Spock to be about a hundred years old. Strange to think, isn't it, that McCoy and Kirk could have been over fifty years his junior? But perhaps we should here dismiss the original concepts of Spock's age. Star Trek's writers and producers seemed to have abandoned it way, way back. And surely if Spock were really about a hundred by the time he joined the crew of the *Enterprise*, he would have already had enough life experience to have "found himself" as he finally does in *Star Trek: The Motion Picture*.) McCoy, had he known the young Spock, would no doubt have interfered enough in his upbringing to give him a clear example of the glories of being human. But to be fair, it is unlikely that a young Leonard McCoy would have been a good example. Even as a mature adult, the devil sparkles from his eyes. No, it's just as well that Amanda, with her human grace and wisdom, was the one to carefully guide Spock on behalf of human kind. She tried her best to give Spock a positive picture of his own half-human, half-emotional nature. She reminded him, no doubt, of his heritage as best she could.

But Spock had to live in a Vulcan world, not a human one, so, like all of us, he developed as best he could in order to be accepted, in order to be a part of the society around him.

Perhaps the knowledge of that can lead us to understand more about the Spock/McCoy relationship and how it works to bind two such "contrary" characters into an unlikely friendship. It's a funny thing about Spock and McCoy. Though their relationship is not very often the focal point of an episode, its undercurrent is so strong, so subtly pervasive, that it stands out in the memory of even the "fringe" Star Trek watchers. There is a reason for this, and we will get to that in a moment. (And wouldn't it have been nice, just once, to have seen an episode in which these two are thrown together alone for a good length of time in a hazardous or troublesome situation, where they could have discovered the "selves" in one another more openly. I suspect it would have happened if the series had been allowed to continue, or if it hadn't been necessary to give Mr. Shatner so much film time. We "almost" had it in "The Tholian Web," but someone somewhere along the line evidently felt that the audience only wanted to see the two of them bicker and make up.)

Leonard Nimoy and DeForest Kelley work well together. It is clear that they have great understanding and respect, not only for the characters each portrays, but for the character of the other. Perhaps that is part of that heretofore "unsung" Kelley/Nimoy magic: They each appreciate and perhaps even envy the character of the other. As actors, each clearly enjoys what the other does with his character—and they like to see that character do well. This makes for good underplaying of a delicate friendship. (Kelley's class and ability to underplay are his crowning glory in *The*

Search for Spock. Though many scenes in that movie were his, they were also Spock's. Kelley never forgot that, and he played it that way. It is his finest work.)

Because Nimoy and Kelley have taken the time and effort to understand what the contrast of their respective Spock/McCoy characters is all about, they have gradually established that offbeat friendship as one of the major, if less swashbuckling, themes of Star Trek. In fact, we can pretty safely say that Kelley and Nimoy, more than any of the writers, producers, or directors of Star Trek, are primarily responsible for the development of that friendship. Some of the finest moments in film have come across this way—more through the patience and understanding of the creative mind of the performers than through anything blatantly intentional. And in a recent interview, Kelley reveals how closely he and Nimoy worked on the Spock/McCoy friendship, and that they would have liked to have done more were it not for Shatner's demands.

But the fact remains, regardless of all the nit-picky attitudes that may get in the way, that Nimoy and Kelley have worked consciously and unconsciously to create one of the most worthwhile, complex, and enjoyable subthemes in Star Trek. They have portrayed for us the existence of the differences within us all: the man in the mirror. With insight and warmth, they have taken part in the creative process, becoming true authors of the mood of friendship in Star Trek. They have taken the raw clay of Spock/McCoy and molded it into something very fine.

More important, they have provided, in Star Trek, the kind of theme which can either be enjoyed on the surface (the Spock/McCoy, Doc/ Festus clashing of temper and wits) or appreciated on deeper thematic levels. The Spock/McCoy personality is itself a theme in Star Trek. An old theme, placed on science-fictional terms to make it all the more effective. As the "literature of ideas," science fiction and fantasy are extremely fertile grounds for the study of human personality. And it may be a lucky coincidence that Kelley and Nimoy seem to have a keen interest in the kind of acting which delves into the inner workings of the character. They both had a gut instinct for their characters . . . and what they mean to one another. There is no doubt that their portrayals of their respective characters are greatly responsible for the gradual script development and enhancement of the Spock/McCoy theme. After all, when Star Trek began, it was generally thought to be William Shatner's show . . . a fact which, whether Shatner accepts it or not, changed markedly, very soon.

Even as early as the first season, writers were taking advantage of the Spock/McCoy "feud" by allowing it to develop into something deeper. While in most first-season episodes the two seem to spend more time bickering than anything else, we do see a gradual development. We see them learning about themselves (and so, each other) in episodes like "Miri," "City on the Edge of Forever," and "Operation Annihilate." Not to say there is anything all that profound in the Spock/McCoy friendship in the first season. There isn't. But in the episodes mentioned, we do see the development of the McCoy character. We see his inner workings a bit more (the troubled McCoy of "City," the self-sacrificial McCoy of "Miri" who tries the antidote on himself).

In "Operation Annihilate," McCoy and Spock come closer than ever before in the sense of the mirror personality. Spock's courage in the face of pain is one of the main themes of the episode, as is McCoy's desperate struggle to save the Vulcan. And when the doctor experiences failure and (with a little encouragement from Kirk) guilt for having blinded Spock, we see his very, very human capacity for a kind of self-indulgent pain. When the doctor thinks he's responsible for blinding the Vulcan by acting too quickly to remedy his ailment, he becomes morose. It would seem outwardly ironic that Spock is the one who tries to reassure him. Ever so logically, he reminds McCoy that it is better to be blind than dead.

Could it be that Spock here is acting the part of the rational human mind? And that McCoy is portraying the emotional part? Why not? If you look at Star Trek as something more than just another action/adventure TV show, then it's hard to ignore what's going on here. We have the two most basic parts of the human personality juxtaposed. The ability to reason, the need to feel. And, by giving us clear, sometimes painful portrayals of the Spock/McCoy personalities, could Star Trek also be presenting us with a study of our own selves?

As a reader and writer of Star Trek articles and fan fiction, I've had occasion to talk to fans about this. It has been a favorite, secret topic of mine, one that seemed worthy of study. And over the years I've heard two recurring tales from Spock and/or McCoy fans. From avid McCoy fans I hear stories like this: "I was an isolated individual, shy, not used to admitting my feelings openly. But as I got into Star Trek, and watched McCoy work on Spock, I began to listen to him and apply what he was saying to myself. It's as though, in speaking to Spock, he was also talking to me. After a while, I began to look at myself more objectively. Maybe some of the things McCoy was saying to Spock applied to me as well. I began to examine my own outlook on life and open up a little bit. This may sound silly, but somehow McCoy made me like myself a little more. He also made me appreciate people more."

From the Spock fans, it goes something like this: "I guess I'm a Spock fan because I've never been a person who has a good deal of control over my emotions. I'm like McCoy gets sometimes, hot-headed, too quick with a sharp word. But watching Spock, seeing how he handles McCoy, I began to try to use logic to deal with my problems. And even if I can't be as logical as Mr. Spock, I admire his ability to keep in control in pressure situations. I guess I envy him a little."

It all seems to boil down to this: "I admire McCoy's ability to be open, to show his feelings." "I admire Spock's ability to use logic to solve his problems."

Now, when you put those two qualities together, you certainly do have the two most important aspects of the human personality. Put in the very simplest of terms, you have emotion and logic. And it happens that in Star Trek, as in real life, you can't really survive happily unless you have a fair capacity for both.

And sometimes I'll hear from an individual who relates that the "dueling personalities" of Spock and McCoy remind him of himself. It's as though Star Trek had provided people with a split-frame view of the human personality and allowed them to examine it without inhibition.

If this all makes Star Trek sound very therapeutic, I think, at times, that it is. There's nothing very startling in that. All good entertainment is a kind of therapy. In fact, that is its reason for existence.

Talking about "dueling personalities" . . . That's really how the Spock/McCoy friendship got started, most noticeably in the first season in an episode called "The Galileo Seven." In this episode the two quarrel viciously (or at least McCoy does). McCoy comes down hard on Spock throughout, in a manner that nowadays seems out of character. But that's only because the characters were still developing at this early stage. In so many words, Spock is accused of being heartless, insensitive, ambitious . . . and maybe not so logical as he'd like to be. All because our poor, noble Vulcan is doing his damnedest to save the crew and the stranded shuttle, Galileo Seven! But the pattern is established throughout that Spock is the one who acts on logic, and unlike McCoy, will not let his feelings get in the way of his judgment.

McCoy is very much "the heavy" in "Galileo Seven" where his interaction with Spock is concerned. And you'd be surprised how that upsets people! Especially those fans who think of Spock as only a superhero type. As for McCoy—thematically, he can get away with being nasty once in a while. He's so damned human, it's in his nature. If he gets cranky or blows his stack we tend to forgive it in him as we would forgive ourselves. It's natural for humans to "lose it," and we accept it, but when Spock of Vulcan does something "illogical"—look out! Some fans find it absolutely unacceptable, even insisting that it must have been an error on the writer's part.

Spock does something "illogical" in "Galileo Seven." He takes a chance when all else has failed. The shuttle is in a helpless position, unable to contact the mothership, the *Enterprise*, and so as a last-ditch effort, Spock ignites the last of the shuttle's fuel, causing a blast of power which is meant to tell the *Enterprise*, "We're here! Help!" The odds of the *Enterprise*'s receiving Spock's dramatic message were . . . well, we don't even want Mr. Spock to figure those for us. Let's just be glad it all worked out.

Nevertheless, Spock's behavior brings a question to mind. Was his action one of emotion or logic? We all know what McCoy would say: Deep within that logical Vulcan exterior lies a human's instinct to take a chance. There's no doubt that McCoy (never one to keep cool in a crisis) was more than a little pleased by Spock's very human behavior at the end of the episode. And while Spock insists that his last-ditch effort was really an act of logic, we find a kind of irony in knowing that it was in fact a very "McCoy-like" thing to do. Humm . . . is the cranky doc actually getting to him a little bit? And so early in the series?

Maybe, maybe not. But in episodes like "The Galileo Seven" and "Operation Annihilate" we can see that Spock is certainly getting to McCoy. The Terran physician seems to have been in the fleet for a few years, but somehow Spock has more of an effect on him than the average alien. There may be a reason for this. To McCoy, the physician, the psychologist, Spock is no more classified an "alien" than Uhura or Sulu are classified as part of the "third world." Spock is an intellient being, a patient, and gradually, a friend. Spock's Vulcanness doesn't bother McCoy—his humanness does!

Like Spock's mother, Amanda, McCoy wants the Vulcan to appreciate his own human heritage. It's very likely that McCoy even believes that of all the crew of the *Enterprise*, only one is a true bigot: Mr. Spock. For in rejecting his own human half, he is rejecting his Terran heritage. He is virtually saying to Kirk, McCoy, and the others, "You are my inferiors."

McCoy just doesn't seem to be the type to sit still for being called an "untouchable."

And yet, when you really think about it, he allows Mr. Spock to get away with a great deal. It's as though the doctor senses that the Vulcan needs someone to "berate." At least that would serve to make him a bit more human. So McCoy serves as a kind of therapeutic punching bag; someone with whom Spock can express all his rational and irrational fears about the state of being human. Like so many of us, Spock is terrified of being human, and more than anyone else aboard the *Enterprise*, McCoy seems to understand that. He understands it so much that he insists on calling Spock out on it—as would any good psychologist. Spock's struggle with his human nature has become such an important theme that it has now been the backdrop for two of the Star Trek films: *Star Trek: The Motion Picture* and *The Search for Spock*, although it might be more appropriate to say that *The Search for Spock* is specifically about Spock's struggle (and powerful friendship) with Dr. McCoy.

But in the first season episodes we see more of McCoy's view of Spock than Spock's view of McCoy. McCoy just doesn't seem to be a topic of discussion for those first season writers. They were too busy giving Kirk the lines and scenes Shatner wanted, and Spock the lines and scenes the fans wanted. No time for the eccentric ex-cowboy from the South. McCoy's main purpose (with a few exceptions, like "City on the Edge of Forever") seems to be that of providing tension—which he does well from the season's first aired episode, "The Man Trap," to its last, "Operation Annihilate." In some of these episodes, in fact, you're not all that sure which side the doc is on. He blusters, threatens, pouts, and explodes with a stubbornness and impetuousness which is almost a caricature of the McCoy of later episodes.

No doubt about it, McCoy had some growing up to do—and it is to DeForest Kelley's credit that McCoy did grow tremendously. He certainly got little help from script writers and producers. But McCoy had one thing going for him all along which none of the other characters did, not even Kirk.

McCoy had Spock. He had the Vulcan's continuous inner struggle with his human half. If Star Trek writers were going to explore the Spock personality, they needed some poor sap there to be the mirror of the mind, "emotional brat," the "friendly antagonist." Kirk couldn't do it. Nobody would believe it. Kirk was his friend! They needed a mirror-man to help Spock (and so the viewers) explore the humanness within himself. And for that, they needed a character who could be at once sympathetic and abrasive. They didn't need a hero, they needed an actor.

It's been said before, but it bears repeating here: Leonard McCoy is the most keenly developed, most well-rounded and complicated character of Star Trek. He has the advantage over Kirk and Spock in that he is not a hero as the Saturday matinee goers define heroism. His knees shake and his stomach quivers . . . and sometimes he wishes he were back home. And that makes him real enough, human enough, to represent that "other" side of the man-in-the-mirror friendship of Spock/McCoy.

As Spock, in many ways, is the man we would like to be, McCoy is the man we are.

Now, of course, some fans don't like that. They don't even like to "think" that they should relate to a character who is ill-tempered, sharp-tongued, distrustful, who can be openly afraid, who admits to feelings of inferiority, who . . . well, the list goes on. The being that Bones McCoy is doesn't appeal to those who turn to a hero for self-image. Nor has the good doctor won friends and influenced people by his open honesty with the good Captain Kirk. They see him (as have certain Star Trek writers, directors and producers) as being "too hard on Kirk." Many excellent scenes have been axed at the outset by persons who so identify with the captain that they cannot stand the thought of McCoy facing him with that powerful, often too-forceful honesty. McCoy sees too clearly, it seems, for the Saturday matinee audiences. And as we view the pulp-oriented Star Trek of the eighties, we can't help but wonder if the doctor belongs there at all.

The second season of Star Trek opened with "Amok Time." McCoy certainly did belong there. It was the doctor who first observed that something was troubling the Vulcan when Spock began to suffer the symptoms of *pon farr*. Unlike Kirk, who thinks of his friend Spock as being almost invincible, McCoy knows that he is, in essence, no different from anyone else. McCoy knows that the Vulcan has a breaking point, has weaknesses. It is only natural. And what concerns him throughout Star Trek is Spock's seeming denial of his own fallibility. McCoy is again the mirror-man, who sees the danger of that "other" part of the self: the logical, achieving part. The part which says, "I must succeed, I cannot be found out a failure." The part in each of us which, with all its logic, illogically maintains that fallibility is a sign of weakness. As if there were some great sin in being less than perfect.

As in *The Search for Spock*, the tension between Spock and McCoy is purposely underplayed in "Amok Time." The two are at odds, but quietly, and for one simple reason: each knows the other very well. Perhaps it's because they are men-in-the-mirror that they can see through one another's facade so easily. Kirk, for example, is too convinced of Spock's overall superiority to notice that there is a problem, while McCoy has been concerned about it for some time. Indeed, he's tried to get the Vulcan in for a checkup—only to be threatened ("You will cease prying into my personal affairs, Doctor, or I shall certainly break your neck!").

But don't feel sorry for Bones on that count. Nothing could please him more than seeing the Vulcan blow his cool! Just once, even!

That fact seems to bother many Star Trek fans. And again we'll hear complaints about this or that episode where "McCoy was too hard on Spock." Poppycock! "Amok Time" is a perfect example of how McCoy's supposed "roughness" on the noble Vulcan is actually just the opposite. It is the truest sign of friendship.

Look at it from McCoy's point of view. He is a doctor, a friend (as Spock goes out of his way to acknowledge in "Amok Time"), and in a figurative way at least, he is the emotional side of that man-in-the-mirror who is Spock/McCoy. He has a deep, perhaps instinctive need to speak to the logical Vulcan from his own emotional perspective. At this stage in Spock's life, the only way he can experience emotion is through the man-in-the-mirror. McCoy, quite frankly, is his tutor.

He is shaking Spock to wakefulness at times, as one would shake a friend out of a dangerous stupor. It all makes even more sense if we look at it figuratively, digging a tiny bit below the surface of any given episode. Just as we'd dig beneath the surface of our own waking mind to find the secrets that lie within. So let's put aside our human prejudices for a time and think of Spock and McCoy not as two characters, but as a single mind, not totally human, not totally alien—one half ruled by the unswerving, comforting laws of logic and order, the other half its opposite, ruled by feelings that run deep and sometimes chaotically with impulse and emotion.

The cool, green-blooded Vulcan. The fiery, red-blooded McCoy. One may well represent our future, the other, most certainly our present. Together, on a figurative level, they could, indeed, represent those aspects of the mind which deal with logic and emotion. Like any single mind, they have their ups and down, but mostly they work together well.

It's the popular thing these days to speak of the aloof Mr. Spock—his nobility, his isolation, his grand heroism in the face of a strange, often threatening universe. But the circumstances of Star Trek give one cause to wonder if that is so completely true. After all, our Vulcan is the embodiment of logic in a world where logic, order, and science have come to reign. From the "mental" perspective, he would be more at home on the *Enterprise* and in the twenty-third century than his mirror image, Dr. McCoy. Most of the time he is. His logical, scientific mind virtually lives and breathes the work to be done on the *Enterprise*. He thrives in the science of research. Yet, there are times (such as in "Amok Time") when we know all is not in perfect balance. We detect a loneliness, perhaps even a fear which, put in everyday terms, is childlike and vulnerable.

Could it be that the Spock we see at such times is the Spock of the figurative Star Trek? The "logical" half of the mirror-man? Look at him in "Amok Time": frightened, nearly out of control because of his lack of understanding of the ways of passion. And look who discovers his problem first: McCoy, the other half of the mirror-man. Here, perhaps, representing that part of the mind which recognizes, accepts and appreciates the passions of love and sex. In that case the "emotional mind" of "Amok Time" is quite literally taking charge, doing its best to handle that for which the "logical mind" is inexperienced and unprepared. The "emotional mind" does indeed take over in this episode of Star Trek, because it is in "its" territory. McCoy is able to save both Kirk and Spock at the end of the episode by injecting Kirk with a neuroparalyzer (to stimulate death, thus ending the "fight to the death"). He acts here as a passionate man, a friend, who is so "comfortable" with his feelings of love and fear that he can act for the good despite their influence. His mind is not "clouded" with emotion, but directed by it.

We see it happen again in many other episodes. Emotion takes over where logic fails, logic takes over where emotion fails. In "The Deadly

Years," when Kirk, Spock, Scotty, and McCoy are exposed to radiation which causes rapid aging, Spock's logic carries the burden as long as it is physically able, but as the confusion of old age hits him, he is deeply troubled and distrustful of his own mind. In short, he's not used to being forgetful, or intellectually fatigued. But McCoy, always the emotional and erratic one, seems the least susceptible to senility. Well . . . maybe we should put it this way: If he's becoming senile, it doesn't bother him much. In his own, emotion-guided way, he takes his aging in stride. Of all who are affected, he alone retains the capacity to laugh at himself.

And if ever there was a clue to the most valuable aspect of human emotions, McCoy has just hit on it. McCoy, unlike Spock, has the ability to laugh at himself. And a man who knows enough not to take himself too seriously has a mighty edge indeed . . . regardless of what time he is living in!

But even that is not enough, in this century, or in the twenty-third. McCoy knows that, and despite his stubborn outward desire to "put logic in its place," he recognizes that Spock's devotion to logic and order is to be respected, even envied by the supposedly more "sensitive" humans. McCoy, the emotional side of the mirror-man, has learned some hard lessons. He has grown to understand.

But McCoy hasn't learned the easy way. The emotional half, after all, is the part which has learned the fine-tuned and very intricate rules of the "game" of caring. So when it comes up against a strange, undiscovered "new" way of being—the way of logic—it faces a kind of psychic shock. Why is McCoy at first so leery of the Vulcan, Spock? Because while Spock is half human, he does not play by McCoy's "rules" at all. He doesn't even think much of them. And in his own, icy, standoffish way, Spock ridicules (without benefit of true experience) the very essence of McCoy's emotional being. It becomes a clash of souls.

It seems that as far as Mr. Spock is concerned, McCoy can do nothing right. Roles are strangely reversed. McCoy, the man of old Earth, is out of his territory, blasting into the unknown on a Starfleet ship built by the science of mathematics and logic, dedicated to the kind of discoveries most appreciated by the physical sciences. One wonders, at times, as Spock must have wondered in the early days: Why is the doctor even there?

But we discover, along with Spock, why McCoy is there. We see him wrestle with the mighty force of pure logic, we see it change him, mature him, guide him to believe at last that there is, indeed, something "more than the universe." Gradually, as the series develops, McCoy's distrust of Spock's logic becomes a grumbling admiration. Not only does the doctor see through Spock's outer facade of isolationism, he begins to understand that they are not so different after all. And McCoy will doubtless not forget that often it was as much Spock's logic as Kirk's courage which saved the day. In fact, in every episode from "The Man Trap" to *Star Trek: The Motion Picture*, Spock employs logic to help find the answers. But through his adventures Spock learns to work his logic carefully where McCoy is concerned. McCoy, it seems, must be dealt with on rather unusual terms. His friendship is a puzzle . . . even to the Vulcan.

In "Bread and Circuses," McCoy confronts Spock in one of his most angry, dramatic moments. He challenges Spock to "feel"—dares him to admit that he feels the human bonds of friendship for Kirk and himself. And when he chides Spock, saying that he "wouldn't know what to do with a genuine human feeling," the Vulcan takes it with a calmness and steady-mindedness that serves the mirror-man two ways. It shows McCoy, once and for all, that he is wrong. That if Spock at one time did not feel for his friends, he does now, despite the pain (and perhaps even shame) it causes him. Secondly, Spock's tremendous self-control provides a buffer for the powerfully emotional Dr. McCoy. Seen from outside, as a single mind working to keep balance, we can see that logic saves the entire spirit from a kind of hopeless self-destruction. Its purpose now, with the Spock/McCoy man-in-the-mirror, is to save the whole, when the part might cause serious damage.

Think back to some of the angriest moments of your life, whether it be anger with a loved one or heated frustration with traffic. Haven't you just once wished you could do or say something regrettable in a moment of anger? Something violent, irrevocable. Kind of makes you appreciate that logical side a little more, doesn't it?

Spock-the-prophet of *Star Trek II: The Wrath of Khan* gives McCoy a warning when the doctor gives way to one of his outbursts of emotion. They are discussing the horrible potential of the Genesis Device, and McCoy blasts angrily at Spock, saying, "Logic? He's talking about logic! We're talking about universal Armageddon!" Spock listens as a friend, clearly now enjoying McCoy's outburst, almost as one might relish the freshness of an unexpected thunderstorm. Then, with almost offhanded calmness, he issues a friendly warning:

"Really, Dr. McCoy. You must learn to control your emotions. They will be your undoing."

No kidding, Spock. No kidding.

Because Kirk's emotions are more tempered with logic (he is not part of the mirror-man), he was able to deal with Spock's death. He faced the pain and found reason to go on with his life. As Spock would have wanted. McCoy, on the other hand, was nearly dealt a death blow. Figuratively, without the "other side" of the mirror-mind, he was lost. As representative of the man of our own century, in Spock's death McCoy lost something which was too important. He lost

Future; the part of the mirror-mind that represents the ability to control destiny.

At first, he was buried in grief, and in the turbolift scene which was cut from the third film, he showed that grief to Kirk. Maybe, if we're lucky, we'll get to see it someday. We only get a hint of it in *The Search for Spock* in an early scene where Kirk mentions his concern with the crew's "obsession" with Spock's death.

But that's just McCoy's luck, isn't it? It turns out he isn't so much "obsessed" as "possessed." Why is it that so often those horrible things that befall the emotional side of our natures turn out to be for the best? And why is it we can only see that after the emotional pain is over?

I suppose old Spock, if he'd been in a more corporeal condition at the time, would have calmly brought McCoy's own words back to him. "Remember, doctor, a little suffering is good for the soul."

McCoy's soul, coexisting with Spock's, is suffering as never before. And Kelley, under Nimoy's insightful direction, play it with taste. (Though there must have been a few good laughs about the doc's situation between takes!) And through McCoy's journey of the mind, we discover the profound connection which has really always existed between Spock and McCoy. In *Star Trek II: The Wrath of Khan* we saw, in a few good scenes, Spock's gentle affection for the crusty, outspoken Earther. We see that Spock genuinely enjoys McCoy for the man he is and that he seems to represent something of unspoken value to the Vulcan. After the V'Ger experience, Spock has learned to respect the intense existence that is the emotional McCoy. He knows now that McCoy has presented him with the best of humanity and that, despite the doctor's human failings, man has not been found wanting. He appreciates McCoy—as we all learn to value that part of us that dares to feel . . . that part of us which makes us civilized. Perhaps, on some deeper level, the Vulcan has come to understand that McCoy had contributed so much to his own "emotional upbringing" as to be considered a pychic part of him. Perhaps in this one way, McCoy has become closer to Spock even than to Kirk. Certainly no two beings understand one another better than Spock and McCoy.

In *The Search for Spock*, McCoy becomes all. He is the mirror-man complete, struggling for survival in a world which doesn't even believe in his existence. (As Kirk's superior told him, "I never understood Vulcan mysticism, Jim.") It is a death struggle supreme, a battle to achieve peace, at the least, and the survival of the soul, at most. It may seem strange to some fans that McCoy was "chosen" to carry the soul or *katra* of Spock, but not when seen from the literary or interpretive sense. No good writer would have it any other way. There's just too much fertile ground, too much to explore, too many questions which can be touched upon, then left for the individual mind to discover more deeply. That's what science fiction, the "literature of ideas" is all about.

This all provides groundwork for another article, I suppose, on the Friendship of the three—how it works, and why Kirk can truly say that to have left Spock on Genesis would have meant to destroy his own soul. He knows about the mirror-man, all right. And he knows that the mirror-man, while not dependent on him, is still essential to his existence. He is tied to Spock and McCoy just as all the cosmic laws of the universe are tied to one another. His perspective is different; based on a greater balance now than either Spock or McCoy. He is the one in control, the one who dares to save this "new being" created by the meld of Spock and McCoy. He knows his friends well enough to accept that together, they just might be capable of pulling off a miracle. Always the Prometheus and the man of adventure, he senses the greatest discovery of all, and risks everything to achieve it: the discovery of Immortal Soul. Kirk, the true adventurer, represents in *The Search for Spock* that part of the human mind which has so far saved us from self-destruction. He believes in the friendship of the three of them, even when there is only reason to doubt McCoy's sanity, only proof of Spock's death. He is the "pure knight" of *Star Trek III: The Search for Spock*, the one capable of finding the chalice. Lucky for us that Kirk has always been the one to dare to reach outward, beyond Doubt . . . that ancient enemy of man's divinity.

The real beauty of McCoy's "sacrifice" in *The Search for Spock* is its human, down-to-earth perspective in a space-age setting. For on close inspection, McCoy's sacrifice is no sacrifice at all. As part of the mirror-mind of Spock/McCoy, his effort to save Spock is almost instinct. An act of survival. He is bound to Spock now through the meld in such a way that to separate their minds—other than through the Vulcan ritual of refusion, *fal tor pan*, would mean insanity and ultimate death. Like any man, he dwells, within the mind, in his own universe of life experiences. He cannot dwell eternally with that other universe that is Spock. There is too much subjective experience, translated—for the lack of a better word—as "difference," between any two minds, even the most tolerant, for long-term coexistence. That's why the Vulcans are so reluctant to perform the mind meld: to do so is to intervene in another's complete universe and to impose your universe on him! A painful, dangerous experience.

For McCoy, separation from Spock is the only answer. And it must be done carefully, for Spock is now virtually a part of him. His inner balance has been disturbed, then changed, so that to suddenly rip away the Vulcan's *katra* would be as destructive as allowing it to remain. This also serves to reinforce the concept of the mirror-man. On a figurative level, logic and emotion are separate functions, critically interdependent. To rip one carelessly from the other, just as to allow one to dominant the other, means insanity, psychological death.

So McCoy's stewardship of Spock's *katra*—his ultimate "sacrifice" on the altar of logic to Spock's rebirth—was simply the practical, natural thing to do. He didn't do it for Spock, although Spock must have known (at the time of the meld) that he was willing to, or he wouldn't have placed his *katra* with McCoy. McCoy did it for himself. To survive. And so mankind has taken another step. It has discovered that the "need" to give is a selfish thing. A matter of survival. It is a kind of evolution. A discovery, at least, of the necessity to care for one another . . . because it is logical.

In Star Trek, trust and friendship are practical concerns. Spock trusted McCoy with his soul, and his reward was the greatest gift of all: McCoy's open confession of friendship. And for all his blustering about "Vulcan logic," when McCoy found Spock had entrusted his essence in the most human hands for safekeeping, he held tight to that powerful and frightening "logical mind" . . . and carried it gently home.

It was the logical thing to do.

STAR TREK IN THE CLASSROOM

by Jeffrey H. Mills

Did you ever wish that you could major in Star Trek in college? Or at the very least, take a class wherein Star Trek was discussed seriously, enthusiastically, and on an adult level? Well, some time back students at Oberlin College in Ohio got just such an opportunity, thanks to the efforts of Jeffrey Mills. He tells us something of his experiences guiding a class of eager students through discussions about Star Trek and its "cultural relevance." We think you're really going to enjoy this article, and we suspect that it just might stir enough interest so that similar classes may appear in colleges and universities throughout the nation.

Imagine meeting twice a week for three months with twenty other people who are as delighted by or intrigued with Star Trek as you are: you watch episodes and talk about the development of the characters, you debate the significance of Federation principles and institutions, you discuss the importance of Vulcan philosophies and seek to understand the relationships between the world of the twenty-third century projected on the screen and the world we live in today. Sound like ecstasy?

Well, it *was* ecstasy, of a sort, for me to be able to bring all of the above to a group of students at Oberlin College in Ohio. Like many schools in the Midwest and elsewhere, Oberlin has an academic organization that allows students and townfolk to offer classes of varying subjects to other students and townfolk (and occasionally professors)—sometimes for credit, always for fun and the delight of learning. Thus, it was in spring of '84 that I taught a course through Oberlin's Experimental College (EXCO) called "The Cultural Relevance of Star Trek."

Why would I want to do such a thing? And what *is* the cultural relevance of Star Trek? (These two questions were asked me eternally throughout the course of the semester when people discovered that it was I who was teaching *that course*.)

When the EXCO catalogs first came out, the appearance of something called "The Cultural Relevance of Star Trek" was greeted by a fair amount of laughs. "This is to be a serious study of the popular television show, Star Trek," my course description began. (Giggles.) "By looking at the characters, cultures, institutions, and events of the Star Trek universe, we will examine the various social, historical, moral, political (etc.) implications—or the *meaning* behind Star Trek." (Belly laughs, some rolling on the floor.)

In short, my course offering was responded to by many with cries of "Come on—let's get serious" (my intention exactly) or "Oh, God, those Trekkies are at it again."

I have always been fascinated by the fact that for every person who can't get enough of Star Trek there is another person who cannot get too little of Star Trek. There are quite a few people out there who despise everything about the show and who feel deeply offended if they are forced to watch even the tinest fragment of an episode. I have never really understood these people (and they aren't always the same folks who hate science fiction in general) nor the great love-hate relationship between Star Trek and the viewing public that they help to create. As Spock would say, it is like nothing I have encountered before.

It wasn't these people I hoped to attract to my course—they would never sign up. There is another class of viewers that I hoped to attract. These are people who watch Star Trek and poke fun at it—filling in key moments with their own dialogue, pointing at alien makeup and costumes (pajamas, of course), laughing at tender moments and suggesting alternative motives to explain the actions of the heroes and villains on the screen. If you've ever watched Star Trek with a crowd on a public television, especially on a college campus, you know the type.

Along with the true fans of Star Trek, it was these people I had hoped to attract to the course. In fact, I got the idea for the course and the incentive to teach it while sitting through one of those public viewings. All around me there were people competing with one another to insert the best line the next time Kirk opened his mouth to speak. These viewers, I feel, do not understand Star Trek. They see a series of plot events tied together by a pretty neat ship, funny costumes, an arrogant captain, an eccentric doctor, and "that mellow pointed-eared dude." They do not see, and thus cannot appreciate, the things that Star Trek is saying—sometimes blatantly, more often with subtlety—about being human and living in society. Without understanding there can be no appreciation or learning. I had hoped to change that through "The Cultural Relevance of Star Trek."

As you readers and true fans of the show know, Star Trek is sophisticated. Despite the restrictions of prime-time television, Gene Roddenberry and his creative core (the writers, directors, production people, and actors who worked together to shape all that is Star Trek) managed to say some very interesting and provocative things about relationships between individuals, cultures, and nations; about the link between people and their machines; about alienness and the importance of preserving uniqueness about social and political problems like racism and sexism. The institutions and philosophies presented throughout the show speak of mankind's problems and potentials. And though it projects the world of the twenty-third century, Star Trek teaches us important lessons about life in the twentieth century—lessons as relevant to the mid 1980s as they were to the late 1960s. Star Trek is not only sophisticated—it is intelligent.

As such, Star Trek is as at home in the classroom as it is in the convention hall. The voyages of the starship *Enterprise* provide us not only with excellent stories, but with valuable lessons as well. There is much to be gained from the formal approach.

Just as Star Trek is well suited to the classroom, the classroom is an arena well suited for Star Trek. Not only do students gain from regularly reading critical literature (of the sort found in *The Best of Trek* and elsewhere) and sharing the insights of a zealous course instructor, but they gain—tremendously—by throwing around ideas with one another. If you've ever talked with a friend about the themes and issues raised by Star Trek you know how enlightening it can be to share another person's ideas. Now imagine that multiplied by a factor of twenty or more. . . .

The act of teaching Star Trek in the classroom is a perfect, living example of the Vulcan philosophy of IDIC. The twenty students in my class came together to create great diversity: each of us brought different histories, different biases, different *uniqueness* to the classroom. There, our ideas built upon one another like bricks in a wall. Even when we disagreed (perhaps *especially* when we disagreed), or arrived at no conclusions, we understood Star Trek—and the world around us—all the better. True to the Vulcan IDIC, the meeting of minds (so to speak) fostered by the academic arena allows great possibilities for knowledge and meaning, and the beauty of understanding.

"The Cultural Relevance" was designed to study Star Trek concepts both for their intrinsic value—that is, how they relate to one another within the world of the twenty-third century—and for the insights they give us concerning life in the twentieth century. After all, you need to know what a "power principle" and a "prime directive" are before you can use them to understand situations in our own time. Thus, EXCO 282 was designed to study both the world of Star Trek and the world at large.

As a class, we met twice a week—once to watch (slightly edited) episodes aired from a local station and once to discuss the themes and issues raised by that episode and others like it. If I had my druthers (attention, all you potential course instructors) the best way to teach Star Trek would be to videotape the important segments from several episodes and group together those scenes which illustrate a particular point. It is a much more effective teaching method to have important scenes played out in front of students' eager eyes (e.g., "Here are some reasons you might call the Federation an imperialistic organization.") than it is to verbally remind everyone of these segments. Unfortunately, I did not have the resources for videotaping episodes (nor am I sure if it's even legal), but I was thankful for the weekly airing of Star Trek. It would be next to impossible to teach a weekly course on Star Trek without some sort of active viewing.

In a way, the opportunity to teach "The Cultural Relevance" was a dream come true for me. Ever since my high school days when I watched Star Trek episodes sandwiched between "Sesame Street" and "Space 1999" every afternoon (what a lineup!) I have studied the show and gained many insights into its significance. Star Trek is as dear to my heart as anything. Thus it was a great pleasure to be able to share my insights with others.

Yet the real pleasure (and the real challenge) was in allowing others to understand Star Trek for themselves. Rather than launching each class with a lengthy lecture, I most often eased into our subject by referring to a few episodes and dropping a few provocative thoughts. Then, if the discussion weakened, I inserted a fresh idea or a different angle to stimulate the conversation toward a new direction (as any good helmsman will do). This strategy I used for two reasons: First, by not overwhelming students with my interpretations I encouraged the shier people to take risks and suggest their ideas to the class; secondly, I felt it was important to stress the fact that different interpretations could be equally valid.

Some people came into "The Cultural Relevance" expecting to be *told* what *the* meaning behind Star Trek is. That is, what (specific things) were Gene Roddenberry and his creative core saying?

This was a misconception. There are, in essence, as many meanings to Star Trek as there are people. It is the same way with life. Many people run around trying to sell us their versions of life's meaning. But no—we must make our own meaning in life. We are all unique.

Star Trek is like a piece of art. Its shapes and faces are recognizable—as they are, say, in an impressionistic painting—yet the relationship between them defies objective meaning. The significance of a Picasso or a Monet depends on the viewer. And who could say, objectively, what the meaning behind Kubrick's *2001: A Space Odyssey* or Melville's *Moby Dick* is? We each do—in our unique ways.

One does not need to know the intentions of the writers and creators in order to gather meaning from Star Trek (or any other piece of art). If it is meaningful for you to understand the combined personalities of Kirk, Spock, and McCoy as a working model of human psychology, then it doesn't make a bit of difference what Roddenberry or anybody else had in mind. If you feel that the *Enterprise* represents elements of Motherhood, then it doesn't much matter that its designers might not have thought about it.

And isn't that the beauty of it? Star Trek means different things to different people. As well, it can mean different things to us at different times in our lives. (I find, for instance, that the older I get, the more value I place on the relationship between Kirk, Spock, and McCoy—and the principles of friendship and loyalty they espouse.) Star Trek suggests different ideas, draws different connections, raises different feelings, depending on who you are and what you're all about. Star Trek can be a very personal experience.

There *are* parts of the show, of course, which suggest only one interpretation—the racial hatred in "Let This Be Your Last Battlefield," for instance—yet it is in how we apply these events and images to other parts of Star Trek and to our own lives that subjective meaning has its place. (The events of a single episode are, of course, less open to creative interpretation than the themes which run through several episodes.) For instance: Are there forms of prejudice within the Federation which this episode is inadvertently underlining? How is racial hatred an issue in the world today? And how do *I* deal with it? These are the questions which people will answer according to their own beliefs.

In order to prevent some students from becoming discouraged during the course of the semester by interpretations too abstract or radical, I made it known during the very first class that something as broad and complex as Star Trek can be interpreted on many levels, and that the act of doing so can be a very personal and subjective process. (This also meant that all interpretations were fair game, which allowed for more vigorous debate.)

To underline the point, I read to them a quote from the inside page of Karin Blair's *Meaning in Star Trek* where Gene Roddenberry says he learned much about Star Trek and himself from her book. Here we have the *creator* of Star Trek saying he learned a lot about *his creation* from a book written several years after the show had been cancelled!

Had Roddenberry missed something along the way that Blair's book enlightened him about? No, he was simply being introduced to another interpretation, another *meaning*, of Star Trek. Nor did he necessarily have to agree with her views in order to have learned something about his creation. (In fact, many of my students did *not* agree with Blair's views.)

This is because the classroom is in many respects similar to a shopping market. When we go into the market we see thousands of different items displayed on their racks and shelves, yet we purchase and bring home only those particular pieces which fit our personal needs and desires. But by knowing what other people eat and wear—we are all the more enlightened. The classroom effectively exposes the student to a wide spectrum of postulations and theories about Star Trek (or any subject). It is the task of the dedicated student to not only take home those interpretations which fit her personal needs but also to seek to understand those interpretations which don't jive with her own.

Why is this important? Why should we bother to understand alien ideas (alien here meaning simply "not one's own") which bore us or which seem ridiculously wrong? There are two main reasons. The first is knowledge for the sake of knowledge. Many people believe (and Spock is certainly to be included among them) that knowledge is in some respects a measure of self-development. In other words: *To know* is *to be*. The more we know, the more complete we are, the greater our possibilities are. (This is very much related to the Vulcan IDIC.) The act of learning—even learning about things alien—is an act of *becoming*.

Western culture has long taken great stock in knowledge. Learning was the greatest passion of the ancient Greeks. Ever since the scientific revolutions of the Renaissance, we in the West have been very busy performing our experiments in an attempt to understand the natural world around us. (Examination of the inner world of the human soul has, unfortunately, lagged behind.) The spirit of confronting the unknown (and overcoming the unpleasant) which sends the backpacker out into the forbidding wild (and sends starships out into the Big Black Beyond) is as much a cultural phenomenon as it is, say, a psychological phenomenon.

Roddenberry recognized the value of knowledge, and our thirst for it. "To explore strange new worlds, to seek out new life and new civilizations. . . ." If you consider the *Enterprise*, for a moment, as a *person*, her mission describes our own lives from Day One. We are born into a "strange new world" and begin a process of exploration which doesn't cease until we do. Roddenberry recognized that confrontation with the unknown is not only a very useful dramatic tool, but an essential human need, as well.

Of course, Kirk and his crew didn't always like what they found when they went exploring, just as students don't always like what they hear in the classroom. But (violations of the Prime Directive aside) the information brought back was still useful to the Federation. Ah, to know, to understand . . .

But knowledge for the sake of knowledge is not enough. (Yes, that was V'Ger's ultimate realization.) We must also know how to act. And thus, the second reason we must embrace alien viewpoints in the classroom (and in the world around us) is a matter of pragmatism. When we understand the full range of issues surrounding a Star Trek theme we can communicate more intelligently in circles where Star Trek is discussed. (And because many of Star Trek's themes are relevant to our own world, we can communicate more intelligently in circles where Star Trek is *not* discussed.) More important, we can better understand those people with whom we disagree and thus become better equipped to relate to them.

The importance of understanding other peoples' viewpoints as a guide to action cannot be exaggerated here. It is anthropology's greatest teaching and one of Star Trek's most useful lessons.

Picture the cultural anthropologist in the field, studying individuals of a primitive culture. The natives dance. They howl. They perform violent rituals and exhibit social patterns far different from our own. On the surface it all seems very strange, even perverse.

Yet when the anthropologist learns to see the world through their eyes, suddenly the dancing and howling and violence all seem to make sense. The anthropologist joins in their rituals and learns to relate to them without causing insult. And when he is immersed in the native culture, he sees that from *their* point of view it is *our* social patterns and violent rituals which seem so very strange, even perverse.

Now picture James Kirk in the mine shafts of Janus VI. He is faced by the rock-dwelling Horta which has killed several of the planet's inhabitants as well as members of his own crew. His first impulse (and official order) is to destroy the alien on sight. But he doesn't.

At some point during the search, Kirk becomes curious. He knows the Horta is not killing without reason. And he hears the troubled words of his first officer bemoaning the loss of uniqueness which the Horta's death would cause. So what does he do? He avoids the impulsive action.

By ordering Spock to mind-meld with the Horta, Kirk is seeking to see the world from the alien's point of view. And suddenly—the killing makes sense. From the Horta's viewpoint, it was the miners who had been killing. Though "The Devil in the Dark" is, on the surface, about the efforts of a starship captain to protect a group of miners (and later the life and offspring of an alien), this episode is more broadly about the wisdom of taking other people's viewpoints into consideration when finding solutions to interpersonal or international problems.

When the captain's life or ship are not in danger, he can compete with the best of anthropologists. Kirk's compassion (call it humanitarianism if you like), seen in his desire to save the Horta, or to save Charlie X from the Thasians, or in his decision not to kill the Gorn, comes partly from his ability to see the world as others see it. If not, what would be the difference between the Gorns' blowing up Cestus Three and the Klingons' blowing it away? The difference is that the Klingons would destroy the base just to undermine the Federation (or just for fun), whereas the Gorn truly believed they were protecting themselves. This suggests that Kirk believes in an ethical system based upon intentions rather than results. Poor Charlie X, for instance, didn't know any better.

To see the world as others see it. This is the key. The anthropologist in the field and James Kirk in the mineshafts of Janus VI both represent a model for the way we should lead our lives. The person who watches "Devil in the Dark" (or any other episode which explores the topic of "otherness") can apply its lessons immediately to becoming a better social creature—a more understanding father, mother, or child; a more insightful employer or employee; a better friend.

This same lesson has enormous possibilities when applied to a larger scale. Democrats and Republicans are more prepared to make productive compromises when they understand not only *what* the other wants, but *why*. If the global powers would seek to understand their adversaries (and not only around election time) rather than (un)comfortably standing behind their own dogma, the world would be a safer, more prosperous place. Conservative/liberal, capitalist/communist, Arab/Jew, black/white— all would benefit from taking the time and effort to see the world as their traditional rivals see it. Prejudice feeds on ignorance and fear. Kirk's treatment of the Horta presents an alternative.

This is not to say that understanding another's viewpoint will eliminate opposition. But it will help. With understanding comes a reduction in conflict. With a reduction in conflict comes an increase in the total harmony of the universe. With an increase in the total harmony of the universe . . . well, who knows the limitations of that one? It certainly sounds logical, though.

This is what I mean by the "cultural relevance" of Star Trek. Not only does Star Trek make intelligent statements about important issues of our day—issues like war, power, and prejudice—but it also offers us insights into the little problems we face in our daily lives. "Little" problems such as love, alienation, aging, loyalty to friends, and values. Both politically and personally, Star Trek offers us options for our own lives.

When we view the world as our alien neighbors do, we come to understand that there is more than one way to see an issue or an event. We come to understand that there are many spectrums which describe human thought and action, that differences are legitimate and special. Episode after episode, we are presented with intelligent and inquisitive aliens, cultures with different ways of thinking and acting, as if to say, "Look at all the variety of life out there!" By exposing us to such a great variety of possibilities, Star Trek helps us to appreciate the uniqueness of others, and the alien aspects of ourselves.

It's *okay* to be different, says Star Trek. It's okay to practice different beliefs or different rituals, to have different aspirations, to *physically be* different in a society dominated by norms. In fact, it's not only okay, it's great.

In Star Trek, such differences are not the cause of destruction but are instead a source of *con*struction. Earth of the twenty-third century is a *United Earth.* People of different ethnic backgrounds, of different politics, have embraced one another in peaceful and prosperous coexistence. They have reached out to unite with their alien neighbors in space. The many cultural backgrounds represented aboard the *Enterprise* (and presumably in other Federation vehicles/offices) is symbolic of the usefulness of differences. As Roddenberry says, if mankind survives to the twenty-third century he will learn to take delight in differences.

We have, of course, a long way to go in the next three-hundred years. Differences in our society are more *tolerated* than they are a source of delight. Our American Constitution has the roots for such delight, for instance, in its preservation of freedom of speech and religion, yet we have a long history of persecuting our minorities and singling out those who are different.

There is often great pressure to conform in our society. It is something Alexis de Tocqueville called "the tyranny of the majority." It is the phenomenon which causes millions of people to wear the same brand of clothes, get the same haircut, believe the same beliefs.

Star Trek tells us not to be afraid of the unique. It's okay to be a Vulcan on a vessel packed with humans. (This message is especially attractive to young people, most of whom are in constant search for identity.) To commit yourself to a fad or mass belief (simply for the sake of belonging—whether you realize it or not) is essentially to become "of the body," an automaton without individuality, dominated by something other than your own initiative. (I would bet that a statistical analysis of Star Trek's greatest fans would find them to be, more often than not, the type of person who does not fit into the common social cliques or easily participate in fads. Star Trek speaks to these people.)

Be yourself, says Star Trek. Allow differences to be not a source of alienation but a springboard for growth.

By watching Star Trek, studying it, and applying its lessons, we can make the world a better place. In this light, Star Trek almost becomes a sort of Scripture, doesn't it? Like the Bible, Star Trek has excellent stories with heroes and villains; it contains important messages and occasional thou-shalt-nots. What the Bible does in sixty-six books, Star Trek does in seventy-nine episodes. Of course, the focus is often different, but the method is the same: What remains up to the individual is interpretation and application.

Granted, the lessons in Star Trek are not perfect. Joyce Tullock has written in these pages about the tendency for Kirk and the Federation to "humanize" the aliens they encounter. This analysis is quite legitimate and is one example of how many of Star Trek's lessons are sometimes realized imperfectly. In other words, the Federation doesn't always practice what it preaches.

The same fault that occurs between theory and practice in American constitutional values occurs also in the realization of Federation values concerning the alien. "Where I come from," Kirk tells Alexander in "Plato's Stepchildren," "size, shape, or color make no difference." Yet equality is *not* fully realized within the Federation. Not until the movies, for instance, do women seem to have the same opportunities as men. (Neglected minorities are as alien in practice as outworlders.)

One of our best discussions in class concerned the image of women in Star Trek. The female has long been presented through the media (i.e., in advertisements and on prime-time television) as a seductress or a servant to the male will. Star Trek's treatment of women doesn't go much further than this.

Where do you place the blame? Place it partly on the audience that rejected the pants-wearing Number One (from the first pilot); partly on the businessmen who control what we see on television; partly on a long-standing imbalance in our culture.

Another Federation tenet not fully realized is the Prime Directive. On a few occasions Kirk interferes with the affairs of alien planets which he feels are not experiencing "normal development" (though Kirk and some viewers, in all fairness, may consider these actions to be "creative interpretation" of the Prime Directive rather than interference). Quite often the issue for Kirk is one of freedom. For instance, even though the people of the Vaal enjoyed a society without disease, social violence, or war, they also had no choice in the matter. Kirk felt his job was to give them back their freedom, even though he would introduce all the historical evils into their society in the process.

By policing the freedom of other peoples, Kirk's actions take on American overtones. American foreign policy in the last twenty years or so has basically been to go into an alien country and slap some American freedom on it. The critics of this policy speak of the right of self-determination and argue against our version of "freedom" as a standard for other societies. The Prime Directive was designed during the Vietnam era with these criticisms in mind. Thus it is interesting that the show's producers allowed Kirk to violate the rule *at all.* (It is also interesting to note that most violations of the Prime Directive occur in the second- and third-season episodes, when Roddenberry had less creative control over the show.)

The occasional gaps between what the Federation preaches and what it practices are both disturbing and refreshing. They are disturbing because we don't like to consider our heroes as hypocrites; we don't want to believe that the noble values they subscribe to are unattainable. These faults are refreshing at the same time because we know our heroes are operating in the "real world." If everything the Federation or its representatives did was perfect, Star Trek would be reduced to a utopia; it would lose credibility and thus its ability to give us hope. As it is, we understand that mankind is still evolving in the era of Star Trek, still pushing toward the (elusive) ideal. We take comfort in, and are challenged by, such progress.

Since the filming days of the late 1960s bits and pieces of progress *have* been made toward realizing the Star Trek dream. Technologically, certainly, we are miles ahead of where we were. With the advent of the space shuttle, we have broadened our grasp on space, thus providing the next link in the (oh so achingly slow) evolution toward starships. The omnipresent computer seen in Star Trek has made great advances in the last sixteen years, changing the way adults fight wars and conduct business, the way youngsters play and learn. The computer has so very rapidly come to be accepted in our society that if Star Trek episodes were made today I imagine we would see errant computers more often *reprogrammed* than illogicked to death.

Social and political progress, unfortunately, does not occur as rapidly as technological progress. Human society is still plagued by war, greed, violence, and a whole scorecard of "isms." Faces have changed in sixteen years. Themes haven't.

It is a credit to the timeless quality of Star Trek's lessons that episodes filmed in the late 1960s can be used to illuminate problems in the mid-1980s. One student of mine, for instance, wrote an excellent paper in which he used the episode "Errand of Mercy" to examine the recent turmoil in Central America. In his analysis he used "Errand of Mercy" as a study of occupation and colonialization.

In this episode the Federation and the Klingons were competing for influence over Organia, just as the United States and the Soviet Union are competing for influence over El Salvador, Nicaragua, and much of Central America. This student concluded that from the point of view of the occupied party there isn't much difference between being occupied, or influenced, by one side or the other. (The Organians certainly didn't feel a difference.) The basic reality—stripped of all subsequent consequences—is that self-determination is lost. In practice, Central Americans have much in common with Organians. Not that they are twinkling

energy forms of pure th...
the process of having their
nologically superior) superpo...they are tech...
Was the Federation on Organi..."enhanced
native people (promising defense, ...ctuall...
interest involved? This question must ...ne,

Another student wrote a similar ...asked...
Cloudminders" to examine apartheid in S...using the
circumstances which drive the exploited Tr.frica. By ex...
terrorism one might also employ "The Cloudmi...s to commit...
examples of terrorism in Ireland or in Lebanon." to explain mode...

Part of the beauty of Star Trek is this capacity to ...tinue to examine
cultural situations which occur years after the episodes ...er...filmed. This
timeless quality is one reason why Star Trek still flourishes ...n the air-
waves after so many years.

The "Star Trek phenomenon," it is called. It is the phenomenon which
sees a mere three-year television series burst into record-breaking popularity upon syndication and draw an ever-increasing base of fans (not just
viewers, but *fans*) year after year. It is the phenomenon which brings
characters back to the screen ten years after they believed they had left it
for good. It is the phenomenon out of which arise hundreds of fan clubs
and fanzines, conventions and collectors. It is the phenomenon which
causes Star Trek to be the subject of major theses and, yes, academic
coursework.

The classroom is one of the many places where fans can learn to
appreciate and understand this wonderful thing we call Star Trek. The
classroom is an excellent arena for the serious study of Star Trek. It
allows students from diverse backgrounds to come together to watch episodes and share ideas. It encourages the review and production of critical
literature. It engenders many of the values upheld throughout the series
and opens up options for use in our own lives.

I am not the first one to offer a course in Star Trek—and I won't be the
last. Wherever and whenever they come together, students of Star Trek
all have one thing in common: Not only do they study the Star Trek
phenomenon, but they themselves are very much a part of it.

SPECULATION: ON POWER, POLITICS, AND PERSONAL INTEGRITY

by Sharron Crowson

Star Trek fans just don't consider the "why" of something, they take that one, but very long, step further and consider the "what"—that is: What was the cause of this event or action, and what will the ramifications of this event or action ultimately be? This is the kind of thinking which went into the whole Star Trek concept and many of the best scripts. In this article, Sherry Crowson gives some of the elements of Wrath of Khan *and* The Search for Spock *just such an in-depth examination.*

Speculations are conjectural considerations of a subject, and as such are often personal and subjective. As I watched the last two Star Trek movies, *The Wrath of Khan* and *The Search for Spock*, I was first caught up in the action and the adventures, in the wonder, humor, terror, and even grief that were part of the experience. After several viewings of both movies, I discovered I had time to look beyond the story and I found myself considering certain events and attitudes, speculating on causes and effects.

Consider Genesis. What are its causes and what effects will it have? Carol Marcus proposed the original project, the Federation funded it, and Starfleet provided men and material for it. Why?

Th.
thoug...
would mea...

At worst, Ge...ic effects of...
dreadful weapon," ... custom-
matter restructured into a... initial...

Planets, resources, and peo... more natu...
The Genesis Wave created the p...us said, "be p...
But whose order?

Evidently Federation officials felt the...
reponibility and directing such power, that...
risks. However, they kept the research under...
Starfleet both as workhorse and watchdog for the...
presence made the younger members of the Genesis te...
Why should they have such an attitude? Carol Marcus was will...
Starfleet the benefit of the doubt even when it seemed about to overstep
its authority and take control of Genesis. The other members of the team
were furious that their work would be taken from them, but didn't see...
at all surprised at such a turn of events.

If you set aside the natural animosity which occurs in any situation
where a person has to give up some control of his work, for security or
funding or any other perfectly acceptable reason, the hostile reaction of
the Genesis workers is still all out of proportion to the cause. Is it
possible that the younger team members have some just cause to mistrust
Starfleet? If so, what could it be?

To answer that question, it is necessary to take a good, hard, objective
look at what we are shown of the Federation and Starfleet.

When the Federation suspects there might be something wrong on
Regula One, Starfleet sends Kirk and his "boatload of children" to look
into the situations. They are sent not because they are best suited for the
task, but because Starfleet *has* to know what is happening to Genesis.
Even Kirk, who is not known for patience, seems to question the wisdom
of sending a training ship on a possibly dangerous mission. When he asks
Spock for reassurance about the cadets, he gets command of the ship
instead. It must have seemed like a mixed blessing at the time. Genesis
must have made Starfleet "nervous," and with good cause.

Khan steals Genesis despite tough security for the whole project. An
oblique example of that security is the fact that Spock, "beyond the
Biblical reference," knew nothing of the Genesis project until it became
necessary for him to know. Spock was not only a top-ranking Starfleet

...nds. We are
...peculate that he
...eed to know" when
...ized. A madman, out to
...*Reliant* and nearly destroyed
...cadets. When Khan realized he
...apon, the *Enterprise* and its crew

ut also one of the Fe...
ng to figure out how...
n touch with Carol M...
roject was first intro...
Now the Federation's
evenge himself on Ad...pock.
the *Enterprise*, killing
could use the Gene...
was saved only by...s potential, creating a world and a small
The Genesis D...the Mutara Nebula. The premature detona-
sun from the...rimental protocols and was monitored only by
tion discarded...ged sensors. Even given the evidence, as in *The*
the *Enterpri*...at Genesis might be flawed, the idea, the basic prem-
Search for...gh to guarantee that someone, somewhere, might find a
ise might...t work. There is a state of the art to scientific endeavors
way to...ous to ignore.
that is

So...tarfleet and the Federation found themselves in the unenviable position of trying to jam the lid back on Pandora's box. And how did they go about it? They panicked. They closed off the Mutara sector, tightened security, ordered the *Enterprise* personnel not to discuss Genesis, and scheduled a whole raft of hearings and debriefings. Sulu was replaced as captain of the *Excelsior*; Starfleet announced that the *Enterprise* would be decommissioned. Starfleet and the Federation were desperately trying to regain control of the situation, while Kirk and his crew paid the price.

If the Genesis Device hadn't been stolen and used as a weapon, the Federation might have had time to deal with the consequences of its success. There might have been time to answer questions such as: Who accepts responsibility for using Genesis? Who pays for it? Who decides when and how it will be used?

Saavik thought it might be possible to recreate the Glaezivers' home world, so that they might not die as a race. Even so noble a motive would take some examination. Those who control Genesis control power of a sort that's almost beyond comprehension.

And suppose, for a moment, that Genesis should fall into enemy hands—a distinct possibility. Valkris obtained a briefing tape that showed her the bare bones of the Genesis project (though not the technical data).

What would the Klingons do with Genesis? They would use it as a weapon. The Federation was forced to consider that possibility almost before they had time to realize that Genesis worked. The permutations of the process are endless and terrifying. Genesis could be used to destroy living worlds, create slave races to carry on the battle, manufacture gems, crystals, and precious metals enough to disrupt entire economies.

Stories 349

348 THE B

how row   or to my
allows   omulan
aholet   et.
          elp:
          d

So the Federation had to deal with the res
monitor what Genesis created and try to kee
ship and crew were assigned to take Saavi
research the Genesis World.

Whom and what did the Federation send to dea
sive crisis of the century? They sent a single ship, the F
ship *Grissom*, commanded by J. T. Esteban. They were cer
Esteban would not act on his own initiative—he didn't have a
couldn't breathe without calling Headquarters to see if it was allow
Esteban was sent *because* he could be relied on to carry out policies and
orders without hesitation, because he didn't have the imagination or courage
to do anything else. Starfleet was taking no chance that it would not
remain in complete control of the situation. Starfleet did, however, fail to
realize that it takes courage and imagination to deal with the unexpected.

Commander Kruge's cloaked Bird of Prey was certainly unexpected.
Though the *Grissom* probably had little in the way of defensive capability
and even less offensive capacity, it would have been interesting to see
how Kirk might have handled that situation. Kirk did manage to destroy
a good portion of Kruge's crew with next to nothing functioning aboard
the *Enterprise*. His actions took courage, initiative, and imagination—
qualities singularly lacking in Captain Esteben.

Captain Styles, commander of the newest ship of the line, *Excelsior*,
was another officer Starfleet chose to deal with a crisis situation. According to the novelization, Sulu was supposed to command *Excelsior*, but
political fallout from Genesis made Starfleet back off and give command
of the ship to Styles.

Starfleet's choice seems rather odd. Styles does not impress an observer
as a man of action. He comes across as cool, and terribly smug, about the
ship and his responsibilities. His affected mannerisms, that electronic
swagger stick, for example, make him seem petty and a little ridiculous.
Styles could not imagine a situation calling for a yellow alert in space
dock. His lack of imagination made him slow to respond and slow to take
the alert seriously. When finally convinced of the crisis, the theft of the
Enterprise by Kirk, he checked out his equipment and admired it, yet you
never heard him ask after any member of his crew. The yellow alert
occurred during the night shift, and surely some personnel must have
been off-duty or away from their stations.

Captain Styles relied on equipment (his "beautiful machine") and the
new drive, rather than people and tested methods. He might have been
able to catch the *Enterprise* on warp drive, or come pretty darn close,
but, to satisfy his ego or curiosity, he used the transwarp drive, even if it
meant overshooting *Enterprise* and doubling back. Kirk and Scott both
seemed to understand Style's mentality and took cruel advantage of it by

establish authority on the basis of one's biological sex is a rather illogical custom.

If one discards this limiting notion, a rather more intricate view of Vulcan life and society can be suggested.

Star Trek offers a firsthand view of Vulcan in "Amok Time," and it provides our first view of Vulcan authority in T'Pau. Here, Hoffman eloquently describes T'Pau's claim to power, and eventually attributes that rise to her individual abilities, abilities allowed to express themselves because of Vulcan's belief in equality of the sexes. To my mind, this belief in equality is in itself a denial of a patriarchal *or* matriarchal structure in Vulcan society. T'Pau is powerful because her talent and force of personality are undeniable. Her sex is immaterial.

Sarek, Spock's father, is possessed of a similar strength of character. Early in the series his son alludes to a resemblance between Sarek and the alien commander Balok ("The Corbomite Maneuver"). The resemblance is obviously not a physical one, but one of personality.

Sarek's demeanor in "Journey to Babel" fully corroborates Spock's view of his father as a forceful individual. Seen as just that, an individual rather than a male, Sarek's character has no relation to either a patriarchy or a matriarchy.

But there are many sources for authority, and personality is just one of them. Sarek is accorded military honors upon boarding the *Enterprise* (an action much regretted by the ship's surgeon, clad in dress uniform). These signs of respect had little to do with Sarek's personality (as yet unknown to the crew) or to his sex (women such as the Elaan were accorded respect as well). Sarek merited this reception because of his position as an ambassador from a powerful Federation planet.

In addition, Spock accorded his father respect (when they were talking) because Sarek is his parent. Again, this action can be seen as gender-neutral. Spock evidenced equal respect, if less formality, to Amanda as his mother. Any difference in their interaction is quite justified given that Amanda is a human and much less austere than her husband.

This Vulcan respect for family may also serve to explain the perceived power differential between Amanda and Sarek. In her own human way, Amanda is no less forceful than her Vulcan husband, but she does accord him with a noticeable public deference. She comes at his bidding ("My wife, attend") and bows to his wishes. The basis for this *public* acquiescence (in private she seems much more outspoken) may be due to his role as ambassador. However, it could also be due to an inequality of rank because of class or clan.

Sarek comes from a powerful Vulcan family, and a kinship with T'Pau might bestow a high rank on all members of her family (more on the nature of that status later). However, Amanda, as an outsider, has no such Vulcan connections. Therefore she could bring no status of her own into the marriage. On Vulcan, this difference in rank would probably be common knowledge and her deference properly interpreted. The human crew of the *Enterprise* (and the human viewers of Star Trek), true to their patriarchal origins, misinterpret this inequality of rank as a sign of sexual inequality.

Much has been made of the physical distance that separates a Vulcan husband and wife while walking. Again, taken at purely face value as shown in the televised episode, their action is easily attributed to Sarek's position as an ambassador.

However, if one considers the production scripts to be a part of the Star Trek canon (I don't), then we must believe that a Vulcan woman "habitually walks behind and to the side of any man, but especially her husband." Like a glass that is half empty and half full, a verbal description of this proximity in human language brings an emotional connotation to these words. Just as easily, it can be said that the Vulcan male walks ahead of his wife. *Why* he does this is never explained. To automatically interpret this distance as a sign of patriarchal prerogative is pure cultural bias. (For instance, early animal studies of primate troops, conducted by male anthropologists, often stated that males led the group and were thus dominant. Later observations by female scientists indicated that the males may have been in the front in the group's movement but that the females actually dictated the direction.)

Hoffman herself points out that the Vulcan custom may have its origins in pre-Reform times when a man would walk ahead to protect a woman from danger. Based on the few Vulcan individuals we have seen, there is some evidence for a slight sexual dimorphism in the Vulcan species. Sarek, Stonn, and the attendants at Spock's marriage ceremony are all tall and well muscled. Spock is more slender, perhaps because of human inheritance, but all Vulcan males are undeniably strong. T'Pau and T'Pring are hardly frail by human standards, but they are certainly less muscular than their men. And while modern times may offer fewer dangers to a physically weaker woman (wild sehlats having become increasingly rare), the custom may yet persist. "Be prepared" is not an unlikely Vulcan adage.

In "Journey to Babel," Kirk observes that Sarek's "request" for Amanda to continue her tour sounded much more like a command. Amanda replies to the implied question "Why does it sound like a command?" with the words "He is a Vulcan. I am his wife." Her precise answer is in keeping with her long residence on her husband's planet. She correctly interpreted her husband's words as a request, but Sarek's statement *sounded* like a command because Vulcans do not say "My dear, don't mind me and my long estrangement from our son. Please continue with your tour while I pull myself together." Though Amanda is not a Vulcan by birth, she has married a Vulcan and accepts his culture. She does not expect human courtesy.

After Amanda reveals Spock's childhood fondness for a pet sehlat, Sarek reprimands her for embarrassing their son: "Not even a mother may do that." Hoffman sees this as "an unlikely restriction in a matriarchy." She misses the point. Sarek certainly doesn't mean that he, as a member of a patriarchal society, does have the right to embarrass his son. Rather, he means that *nobody* has that right, not *even* a mother. This implies that a mother has the greatest rights of all but that they do not extend this far. Actually, one could use this incident as evidence that Vulcan is, after all, a matriarchy.

But another explanation is available. Because of the telepathic powers of their race and their physical proximity during embryonic development, Vulcan mothers may develop especially strong ties with their children. This biologically based intimacy may result in a very strong maternal involvement, and a high status within the family circle, but does not necessarily have any bearing on the allocation of power in the society at large.

In "The Savage Curtain," the last episode of the series to depict Vulcans, the image of Surak serves to illuminate portions of Vulcan moral and ethical development. Violence and the emotions which endanger violence were rejected. Given his role in instigating the Reform movement, Surak is rightly viewed as "the father of all we became." After all, it would be silly to call him "the mother of all we became." "Father" is used as a precise description of "male parent." There is no direct mention of how this pacifist philosophy affected the power structure within the society.

In typical sex-obsessed human fashion, Star Trek viewers accord the Vulcan *pan farr* with far-reaching significance. However, the occurrence of this mating fever has no necessary impact on the allocation of individual or institutional power and authority. On the contrary, the manner in which Vulcans deal with *pon farr* points to a respect for both sexes.

The bond which joins a Vulcan male and female serves the avowed purpose of bringing the couple into great communication. A bonded, yet unmarried, couple will "both be drawn to *koon-ut-kal-if-fee*." However, upon marriage this light bond will undoubtedly deepen, perhaps reaching the intensity to be found in a mind meld. Certainly one purpose of this bonding is to transform what might otherwise be rape into a telepathic sharing of uncontrollable passion. A patriarchy could take this sexual union as a right, but Vulcans have developed an intricate ritual which assures the male of a sexual partner yet protects the female from unwelcome intercourse by promoting a mutual arousal.

If a Vulcan woman chooses not to enter into this prearranged union, the male's sexual passion must be directed away from her. Unfortunately, the most likely way to channel a male away from his sexual lust is to arouse him into a bloodlust. The two states are physiologically similar, involving increased respiration, heartbeat, physical activity, and emotional upheaval. (Presumably, running a marathon just won't do.) Since Vulcans have a deep respect for pacificsm, it is not surprising that a challenge is very rare.

Despite the *pon farr*, a regular and embarrassing lapse from Vulcan reserve, men have not been denied a place in the Vulcan hierarchy. After all, it could be logically argued that Vulcan men are too emotionally unstable to govern. However, with typical Vulcan pragmatism, there is an apparent acknowledgment of the infrequent occurrence of the *pon farr*. Presumably, as long as a male keeps track of his seven-year cycle, he can be trusted with positions of responsibility, such as ambassador.

How then to explain T'Pau's question to T'Pring? "Thee are prepared to become the property of the victor? Not merely his wife, but his chattel, with no other rights or status?" The origins of this phrasing might be found in pre-Reform ritual which has been changed. Or, since the words were spoken in Vulcan, the ship's translators may simply have been unable to find human equivalents. More likely, however, is a return to the ideas of Vulcan status and rank.

The concept of status as seen through human eyes is concerned with wealth and privilege and as such is probably of no interest to Vulcans. Rank based simply on inheritance would also be seen as illogical. Under this system, undeserving individuals would inevitably be accorded respect above that of someone more ethical or responsible than they.

Vulcans are much more likely to see rank as an indication of the level of responsibility expected of an individual or family. High status brings a great burden of duty, not personal gratification. Thus, signs of respect are a constant reminder of this responsibility, not of privilege. T'Pau, by her very success, has committed her family members to a high standard of conduct. Sarek has upheld the family honor and expects Spock to do the same. Amanda had no family honor to uphold, but presumably has gained status over the years through her actions on Vulcan and her marriage to Sarek. Still, her rank will probably never approach that of T'Pau or Sarek, both of whom are many years older and have a good head start on her.

So what does this tell us about T'Pring? "Thee are prepared to become the property of the victor? Not merely his wife, but his chattel, with no other rights or status?" T'Pau does not pose this question until *after* T'Pring's challenge.

T'Pring, by reneging on her marital contract, has *lost* her status. A challenge, as discussed above, is not to be undertaken lightly and is a negation of the promise she made in the initial bonding ceremony. Presumably, if she had bothered to break the engagement earlier, a Vulcan equivalent of an annulment could have been arranged. But by waiting until Spock is well in *pon farr*, she has placed his life and the life of her champion in jeopardy. Surely that constitutes a sufficient reason for loss of respect. Like Amanda, she will enter her chosen marriage with no family-based honor and will defer to the greater honor of her husband. Unfortunately, ancient Vulcan rituals have no provision for Kirk's equal lack of status, unless his close relationship with Spock (the captain is "best man" at the marriage ceremony) bestows a modicum of rank.

Thus it can be shown that using the same incidents discussed by Rebecca Hoffman, one can nevertheless support a theory that Vulcan is not a patriarchy, or even a matriarchy. Rather an entirely different, and more subtle, view of Vulcan character and culture is possible.

Vulcans deal with authority in a decidedly logical manner. Power is invested in an individual or clan that has proved its abilities by its actions. The signs of respect given to the members of this family are symbolic of the burden of responsibility which they have assumed. Thus rank and status are earned, rather than inherited on the basis of sex or "noble" bloodlines. They can just as easily be lost by dishonorable action.

Biological sex is irrelevant authority except when directly pertinent to a situation, such as in the close ties between mother and children. The physical distance between husband and wife when walking in public serves a protective function and carries no connotation of societal authority.

The mating cycles of Vulcans are primarily a matter of reproduction and continuance of the species. They do not determine delegation of authority. Very likely, when the cycle occurs, the Vulcan husband and wife are *both* permitted a temporary leave of absence from their ordinary duties so that they can deal with their shared passion in privacy.

All things considered, we humans could learn a thing or two from Vulcan culture.

THE STAR TREK FILMS: VARIATIONS AND VEXATIONS

by Mark Alfred

Did you ever turn to the person watching a movie on TV next to you and say, "I don't remember that part!" Well, sometimes a faulty memory can fool you, but if such a mystery scene popped up during a Star Trek movie, then maybe it wasn't really there when you saw the film in the theater. In the following article, Mark Alfred explains how and why missing scenes suddenly appear in network and videotape prints of some Star Trek films; and, for those of you who missed them, he outlines exactly where and what those scenes were.

Thanks to an unsung hero at the ABC television network, Trekkers have been able to see more of their favorite universe: the universe of the twenty-third century, the universe of Star Trek. New footage was added to both *Star Trek: The Motion Picture* and *Star Trek II: The Wrath of Khan* when they aired on ABC TV. This article's purpose is to describe those additions (and minor exclusions), and along the way point out some flaws in continuity and some technical errors that made it onscreen.

Before we begin our discussion of the films, however, we must realize that *STTMP* and *Wrath of Khan* were not the first Star Trek to exist in different versions.

DIFFERING VERSIONS OF EPISODES

After a ten-year wait, the original version of Star Trek's first pilot, "The Cage," was finally shown at a New York City Star Trek convention in January 1985, as reported in *USA Today*. There are a number of differences between this original version and the version existing as part of "The Menagerie." The major differences are a striking special effect in which the *Enterprise* became semitransparent during warp drive, and the original ending which showed Chris Pike watching Vina return underground with his illusory double.

As described by Allan Asherman in his excellent book *The Star Trek Compedium* (Wallaby/Pocket Books, 1981), the second pilot, "Where No Man Has Gone Before," exists in two versions.

The untelevised version included William Shatner's familiar "Space, the final frontier" voiceover, included more footage in the show's first minutes, and was divided into four acts like such Quinn Martin series as *The Invaders* and *The Fugitive*.

Observant viewers will note that Kirk's tombstone reads, "James R. Kirk, C 1277.1 to 1313.7." The mistake concerning Kirk's middle initial was made by someone at Paramount who had not paid attention to format (or, to be charitable, is perhaps an indication that Gary Mitchell's memory, at least, is not godlike). The dates are stardates, as shown by Kirk's final Captain's Log entry, dated Stardate 1313.8.

STAR TREK: THE MOTION PICTURE

Star Trek: The Motion Picture was released on December 7, 1979, and was shown on commercial television by ABC on February 20, 1983. The film as broadcast ran two hours and twenty-three minutes, or thirteen minutes longer than in theaters and on cable TV. The response of fans, as described later in this section, demonstrated that the longer version was vastly preferred to the original. Paramount, to its everlasting credit, re-released *STTMP* in its longer version on video.

Interestingly enough, the versions shown by ABC and re-released on video, while containing the same added footage, are not identical. ABC's copy was very dark and dingy, to the extent that Kirk's and the crew's light blue uniforms appeared light gray.

ABC's broadcast version of *STTMP* also differed in the panning-and-scanning techniques used to prepare it for telecast. [Because the television image is much smaller than the film image, the camera must be focused on whatever part of the movie image is deemed most important. This technique is called scanning.—Ed.] Some of the most obvious examples follow:

On Epsilon 9, ABC showed the English readout of the Klingon transmission, whereas the video version shows the Klingon's face.

ABC cut to the far right side of the frame to include the black crewman saying, "I have an exterior visual."

In Kirk's beaming to spacedock, ABC showed the transporter operator; the video version shows Scotty, who stands beside her, instead.

After the wormhole debacle, ABC cut to the right and eliminated McCoy's face as he tells Kirk that his wits were casualties.

In a few places, ABC chose to show close-ups of characters as opposed to original wide-angle shots, as when Sulu says, "Thrusters at station-keeping," in drydock, and when Chekov and Spock meet at the primary hull's docking port.

However, ABC's pan-and-scan techniques are not our main topic. Here are the additions and changes made in *Star Trek: The Motion Picture* to create "the complete version," as well as some of the "bloopers" that made it onscreen:

The first item is a possible continuity error. When Scott and Kirk arrive on the *Enterprise* via travel pod, they debark from an airlock numbered 5. Then a computer voice announces that a travel pod is available at "cargo six." This appears to refer to airlock five, the one Kirk and Scotty entered through.

The first instance of new material occurs while the *Enterprise* is still in drydock. After Kirk has ordered Chekov to assemble the crew on the rec deck and disappeared into the turbolift, Sulu states, "He wanted her back; he got her." Actor Billy Van Zandt, played a high-pated Rhaandarite, asks about Decker's status. Uhura retorts, "Ensign, our chances of returning from this mission may have just doubled!"

In the rec room sequence, more shots of the assembled crew have been added, so that some of the 125 Star Trek fans used as extras can be identified. Among those visible in the ranks are Bjo Trimble, David Gerrold, Millicent Wise (the director's wife), Susan Sackett (Roddenberry's secretary), and Marcy Lafferty (Shatner's wife, playing Chief DiFalco, who later takes over Ilia's post).

The next addition occurs on the bridge after Kirk leaves to meet McCoy in the transporter room. Decker instructs Sulu to "take Lieutenant Ilia in hand," and our suave swashbuckler is transformed into a klutz by Deltan pheromones. Ilia makes a verbal jab at Decker concerning "sexually immature species."

Meanwhile, new footage in the transporter room shows how McCoy won't beam up until, according to an ensign, he sees "how it scrambles our molecules."

When the *Enterprise* leaves drydock, the navigational deflector at the fore of the secondary hull is shown as red. Throughout the film (and in

Wrath of Khan as well), it alternates between red and blue, for no apparent reason. Since it is self-lit, the color variations are not due to reflections of exterior light sources.

A continuity error may be seen in the moments after the *Enterprise* escape from the wormhole. In a wide-angled shot we see the bridge leveling off. Across from the camera, Decker and Chekov are at the weapons console. The next shot, a closeup of the two, shows Decker's hand still firmly resting on the console.

After Kirk, Decker, and McCoy depart for Kirk's quarters, on the bridge Sulu gives an order to Ilia which she does not at first notice; it is obvious she is concerned for Decker. This is new.

Also added is more discussion in Kirk's cabin between him and McCoy after Decker departs. McCoy gets Kirk's attention by telling him that he is "now discussin' command fitness."

More insight into McCoy's concern for Kirk is shown in the officers' lounge after Spock has left them. Kirk has said he can't believe Spock would put personal interests above the ship. McCoy retorts, "How can we be sure about any of us?"—meaning Kirk's selfish obsession with "his" ship.

When V'Ger's first energy blast is on its way toward the *Enterprise,* its transit time is extended while new dialogue is added concerning such things as evasive action, notifying Starfleet, and yaw and pitch.

After Chekov is zapped by the effects of the first plasma bolt, Dr. Chapel and a medtech are shown entering; Uhura directs them to Chekov, Ilia rises from her chair and informs them, "I can stop his pain." She does so: Chekov thanks her fervently.

A few sentences concerning the attributes of V'Ger's transmissions are added.

Then comes a major continuity error, to the effect that Ilia is two places at once. While Spock is speaking of sending *Enterprise*'s friendship message at the proper rate of speed, a camera angle from his point of view to Kirk shows Ilia's bald head at the navigator's console, while she is still fifteen feet away at the weapons console with Chekov. Indeed, the very next shot shows her getting up to return to her chair.

After Spock's message has been received, Spock speculates on the intruder: "It has a highly advanced mentality, yet it has no idea of who we are." Its plasma bolts were not a warning, for that would presuppose an emotion, which Spock senses no indication of.

More reactions of the crew to the V'Ger flyover are added. Uhura speculates, "It would hold a crew of tens of thousands," McCoy, returning to the bridge with Chekov, replies, "Or a crew of a thousand, ten miles tall." Spock observes that V'Ger's forcefield is "greater than that of Earth's sun."

A major mistake included in the film is the final version of the energy probe sent by V'Ger onto *Enterprise*'s bridge. This is one of the few special effects designed by Robert Abel and Associates that remained in the finished film.

The probe, according to Walter Koenig, consisted of an eight-foot-high tube of neon gas with handles on one side. An effects person would carry it vertically as it glowed, thus simulating the probe's movements about the bridge. Originally, the effects man wore white, so as to be "washed out" by the tube's brilliance. This didn't work, so it was tried with him wearing black clothing. He was still visible. The final course taken is painfully obvious, especially in one wide-angle, left-to-right pan. With the effects man standing to the right of the probe, a take was filmed as the probe crossed in the foreground. Then the scene was reshot with the effects man standing on the probe's left. Then the film was sliced in half vertically, and the halves without the technician were married to produce, theoretically, a perfect illusion. Unfortunately, the takes do not match: Kirk in his command chair is suddenly about six inches narrower and eight inches taller after the probe passed "in front" of him. A much cheaper and more effective means of achieving the effect would have been simple animation, as was used for the probe's "tendrils." This sequence is almost painful to watch because of their definitely substandard special effect.

An interesting slight error can be seen as the probe reads out the *Enterprise*'s memory banks. Instead of blueprints of the uprated *Enterprise*, the viewscreen shows the six-year-old blueprints of the television *Enterprise*! (By the way, look at these blueprints closely. They are the only place we'll ever see a bathroom in Star Trek.)

More additional footage shows McCoy coming onto the bridge after DiFalco arrives; Decker instructs Uhura concerning sending a message beacon to Starfleet.

A major sequence was added after Spock is discovered to have taken a thruster suit. Kirk suits up, follows him, and actually has him in sight before Spock ignites his thrusters. It is also interesting to note that Kirk moves forward by using thrusters at the front of his suit, thereby violating the laws of motion and action and reaction.

Some playful special-effects workers were no doubt responsible for the two fantastic characters encountered by Spock in his journey to V'Ger's heart. If you will watch carefully while Spock is saying the lined "I am witnessing a dimensional image," a reflection at the left of the screen on Spock's visiplate looks remarkably like the helmeted visage of Darth Vader! Further, immediately upon Spock's line "But who or what we are dealing with?" the attentive viewer will note the face of the Muppet Miss Piggy rapidly appearing, rolling down and out of the bottom center of the screen.

The scene in Ilia's cabin concerning the Deltan headband is expanded. The Ilia-probe states that V'Ger knows the Creator is on the third planet. It then asks why carbon units have entered V'Ger and what their purpose is. McCoy retorts, "Their purpose is to survive!" The probe responds that V'Ger will survive by joining with the Creator.

It will be noted that this scene, located at this same point, also in Roddenberry's novelization, was inserted in *STTMP*'s original release between Spock's neck pinch at airlock four and Spock's first speech on his suit recorder. The new dialogue indicates that the correct place for this scene in Ilia's cabin is here, not in its earlier position.

A rather noticeable error in continuity is apparent in sickbay after Spock's return. We see Spock's right profile as he lies in a diagnostic bed with Kirk on his right side. Spock's sideburns are distinctly squared at the bottom, yet, minutes later, when Kirk orders the bridge cleared. Spock's sideburns are back to their regulation pointed shape. (Perhaps a quick shave?)

At the same time, the Ilia-probe is stating that only V'Ger and similar life forms are "true." Then, McCoy deduces, V'Ger's god might be a machine.

After Kirk instructs the bridge crew to resume duty stations, he tells Scott to prepare to execute Starfleet Order 2005, the self-destruct order. An engineering crewman asks if they will thus destroy V'Ger too: Scott replies, "When that much matter and antimatter get together—oh, yes, we will indeed."

More activity by the bridge crew is shown concerning crew status, remaining time to V'Ger's orbital devices' equidistant orbits, and the fact that the ship is seventeen kilometers (ten and a half miles) inside the alien vessel.

Kirk asks Spock for an evaluation, and the most affecting addition to the original film is seen: Spock swivels in his chair to expose tear-stained cheeks. He is weeping not for their plight, but for the waste of V'Ger's vast potentialities. "As I was, V'Ger is now," he says. "Logic and knowledge are not enough." McCoy asks, "Are you saying you've found what you needed?" Spock nods and continues talking about each person's search for the meaning of life. This brief scene and Spock's conversation with Kirk in sickbay are the keys to Spock's final integration of his personality as evidenced in *Star Trek II: The Wrath of Khan*.

However, we journey from the sublime to the ridiculous when Kirk and company ride an elevator to the personnel hatch atop the *Enterprise*'s primary hull. Imagine the top surface of the primary hull's saucer shape to be composed of three levels: The top level is that of the bridge; the middle level contains the officers' lounge; the third level is the vast sloping shape of the saucer itself. Yet, when the Ilia-probe and followers emerge into the oxygen-gravity envelope surrounding the ship, the special-effects modelers omitted the second level, and the large lower level of the hull is forced inward at a sharp ascending angle to meet the bridge level. Many viewers noted that the saucer looked "funny" here; this is why. The primary hull is not the same model seen through the travel pod's windshield during Kirk's trip to the *Enterprise* at the beginning of the film.

Another mistake is put into the mouth of Commander Decker, when he states that Voyager VI was launched "more than three hundred years ago." Moments later, Kirk states that Voyager VI was "a late-twentieth-century space probe." This places *STTMP* in the late twenty-third century. This conflicts with the carefully researched and Paramount-approved *Starflight Chronology* of Stan and Fred Goldstein (Wallaby/Pocket Books, 1980). This meticulously worked-out timeline places the action of *STTMP* at A.D. 2215, toward the beginning of the late twenty-third century. We must assume that in the excitement Commander Decker became a bit tongue-tied, and that he meant two hundred, not three hundred, years.

A final change in the expanded version of *Star Trek: The Motion Picture* is a minor one: The background music heard as Kirk, McCoy, and Spock return to the bridge at story's end continues throughout their ensuing discussion; it originally faded out until Kirk's final lines.

Almost immediately, the fans responded positively to the new incarnation of *Star Trek: The Motion Picture*. A letter to *TV Guide* stated, "A terrible disservice was done to the movie when it was originally edited. . . . This was the first time that it all really made sense. And Mr. Spock with a tear on his cheek! Paramount left *that* on the cutting-room floor!"

Writers to *Starlog* also expressed general approval. One wrote, "It seemed as though all the scenes deleted from the movie's initial release contained just those little touches of humor, character development, and plot explication that the film was originally criticized for lacking." Another correspondent said, "Thank you, ABC, for treating all the Trekkers in the nation to extra footage. Thanks also to Paramount Pictures for releasing the extra footage. . . ."

Happily, Paramount re-released *Star Trek: The Motion Picture* on video with all the added footage. This is the version "now available at stores everywhere," for as low as $24.95—definitely a bargain.

STAR TREK II: THE WRATH OF KHAN

Star Trek II: The Wrath of Khan was broadcast on the ABC network on the evening of Sunday, February 24, 1985. Some Trekkers, having read all ABC's advertising and finding no mention of added material, were caught off-guard at the sight of the words "Edited for Television" that appeared onscreen. Usually, this phrase means that something has been cut out. It transpired that only two brief sections were excised, amounting to perhaps five seconds of screen time (the two bits actually showing the Ceti eels entering and exiting Chekov's ear); but some anonymous Santa Clauses at ABC and Paramount had also added three or four minutes of new footage.

Sadly, however, ABC followed its own *Star Trek: The Motion Picture* precedent and broadcast an extremely dark and muddy print. Further, from the point where Kirk's shuttle heads for the *Enterprise* until the point where Khan states the Klingon proverb concerning revenge, the broadcast sound was shaky and draggy, as if a tape reel was dragging.

The first incident of note in *Wrath of Khan* is not an addition, but an obvious boo-boo. In the *Enterprise* bridge simulator, as on the real *Enterprise*, there are two turbolifts. As Saavik orders the simulator into the Neutral Zone, over her shoulder we see that the starboard door's turbolift insignia is covered by a large, rectangular section of what looks like duct tape. This patch is about eight by ten inches and quite visible in the background. Yet, seconds later, when Kirk has entered and walks beyond Saavik, the same insignia is now completely visible, and the gray mask is gone. This sort of maintenance does not take place in battle.

When Kirk reads the label of the Romulan ale, he reads the date, 2283, aloud, and McCoy comments that "it takes the stuff a while to ferment." Since our characters are living toward the beginning, not the end, of the twenty-third century, we can only assume that 2283 is a date of Romulan reckoning. This only makes sense, since it is illogical to assume that Romulans would label their product with the Federation's *lingua franca*, Standard English.

Immediately following is the first addition of new material. McCoy tells Kirk that the glasses are "more than four hundred years old. It's hard to find any with the lenses still intact." He has to tell Kirk, "They're for your eyes." McCoy's statement concerning the glasses' age would place their manufacture at around 1800.

Due to some odd value judgment concerning the relative offensiveness of profanity, ABC allowed McCoy's various "damns" to remain in this scene, but looped out a preceding "God" when McCoy is describing Kirk's relations with a computer console.

The next technical slipup is one familiar to the hearts of all fans of the TV series. On Ceti Alpha V, which is shown possessing only one sun, Chekov and Terrell cast multiple shadows. This is caused, of course, by Nick Meyer's policy of filming these scenes on a Paramount soundstage, not at some desert location. The multiple shadows are most noticeable when Chekov and Terrell ascend the final ridge before seeing Khan's cargo-hold containers.

An incident upon Chekov's and Terrell's capture by Khan has caused much speculation. How did Khan recognize Chekov? In William Rotsler's highly recommended *Star Trek II Biographies* (Wanderer/Pocket Books, 1982). Chekov, in a Starfleet debriefing, says, "He recognized me! I have no explanation for that, as I came aboard the *Enterprise* after the contact with the *Botany Bay*. I recognized him from ship's records and from historical photographs. But he is a kind of superman and . . . he might have memorized the face of the entire Starfleet." Vonda McIntyre, in her uneven novelization of *Star II: The Wrath of Khan* (Pocket Books, 1982), states only that Chekov "remembered the incident itself with terrible clarity," thus contradicting Rotsler.

Exactly how Khan recognized Chekov must remain a mystery, since two different and contradictory Paramount-authorized accounts exist.

Khan states, "On Earth, two hundred years ago, I was a prince with power over millions." Since Khan is referring to the 1990s, before his exile in 1996, this conflicts with Commander Decker's statement in *Star Trek: The Motion Picture* that Voyager VI, a late-twentieth-century space probe, was launched "more than three hundred years ago." Again the Goldsteins' *Spaceflight Chronology*'s dates—that the events of *STTMP* and its sequels takes place in the first third of the twenty-third century—are more acceptable.

After Ricardo Montalban has, with the aid of an unseen hoist, lifted Walter Koenig off the floor, it is obvious that he has to pull Koenig down. This does not go along with the law of gravity. Better for the off-camera technician to have simply let Koenig down on cue, and Montalban to have followed that lead.

Scotty's nephew, Peter Preston, is finally identified onscreen, and the added scene where Kirk baits him with the statement that the *Enterprise* is a "flying deathtrap" is a wonderfully warm moment. We can imagine a young Midshipman Kirk reacting in just such gung-ho fashion on his first voyage—you will recall that Kirk described himself in "Shore Leave" as an "absolutely grim" student.

A few seconds are added to the possessed Chekov's first communication with Dr. Carol Marcus. Chekov attributes *Reliant*'s new orders to "Starfleet General Staff"; then, pinned down by Dr. David Marcus, he admits, "The order came from Admiral James T. Kirk."

The next change in *Wrath of Khan* is not the inclusion of additional material, but the inclusion instead of a variation on an original scene. You will recall that the "joke" scene in the turbolift between Kirk and Saavik was all of one take: Saavik stood at the left of the screen and Kirk was on the right. This single-take procedure was to show off the different corridor seen when the doors reopened, enhancing the illusion that the turbolift had actually moved vertically. The video release of the film cut right and left to show Kirk and Saavik. The ABC version, on the other hand, used a different take featuring full-face camera angles. Saavik's apparent come-hither looks at Kirk are nowhere more prominent than here.

The "pawns of the military" scene on Regula I now ends with Carol Marcus telling her workmates to pack what they can. "Where are we going?" someone asks. "That's for us to know and *Reliant* to find out," she replies.

More welcome dialogue appears in Kirk's cabin after the three friends have watched the Genesis proposal. Spock agrees that Genesis, in the wrong hands—"Whose are the right hands?" McCoy breaks in. A few more moments of argument are added before the scene returns to familiar material.

Upon Khan's sneak attack, added material in engineering makes it more obvious that Preston has gone out of his way to save a crewmate's life. Scott's voice is heard crying, "Get back to your posts!"

In sickbay, after Peter Preston's death, McCoy asks how Khan knew about Genesis. Still, he tells Kirk, the *Enterprise* gave as good as she got. No, Kirk replies in frustration, they are only alive "because I knew something about these ships he didn't." Scott states that the main engines will have to be taken down for repairs.

A noticeable continuity error has its inception in Preston's death scene. The bloody handprint the young man leaves on Kirk's uniform blouse is roughly halfway up the exposed portion. Immediately thereafter, when Kirk steps onto the Bridge, the handprint has moved six inches higher, is smaller, and is much lighter in color!

Another slight error is only evident when the film is shown on a wide screen. When Kirk and Co. are in the anteroom to the Genesis Cave and David Marcus says, "We can't just sit here," Kirk is shown putting on his glasses to look at his wrist chronometer. Then, seconds later, we cut to a wide-angle shot. Kirk's glasses have disappeared from his face, and he is still sitting in the same position with no movements to indicate he has replaced them in a pocket.

The next insertion of new material is a brief scene back on the *Enterprise* after Spock has informed Kirk that the turbolifts are inoperative below C deck. They ascend through the same vertical access tube later used by Spock in his descent to engineering. Kirk says, "That young man—he's my son!" Spock replies, to our delight, "Fascinating."

When the ship goes to Red Alert status, various crewmen are shown at their Red Alert tasks. One is carrying the same vacuum-cleaner backpack seen used at the film's beginning in the background while Kirk and

Spock discuss the *Kobayashi Maru* scenario. I find it hard to believe that a vacuum cleaner is a Starfleet-authorized piece of emergency battle equipment.

The final bit of extra material is added as the *Enterprise* is trying to lure the *Reliant* into the Mutara Nebula. Saavik asks, "What if the *Reliant* does not follow?" Spock replies, "Remind me to discuss with you the human ego."

As you can see, some of these changes and additions are more noticeable and important than others. Still, all are nice touches, whose exclusion from the original release print I, for one, cannot explain. The total time taken up by the additions amounts to but three minutes; surely no one could argue that such a small amount of footage, spread over a 113-minute film, could slow the action.

Further, since the total running time of *Star Trek II: The Wrath of Khan* was only extended by a small amount, it is virtually certain that Paramount will not run the large expense of re-releasing the film on video in an expanded version. However, it will likely be repeated as a rerun, and, now forwarned, more Trekkers can see for themselves Scotty's nephew call Admiral Kirk blind as a Tiberian bat.

STAR TREK III: THE SEARCH FOR SPOCK

Star Trek III: The Search for Spock has only recently been released on video. Paramount has, according to the April 1984 issue of *Video* magazine, an exclusive contract with the Showtime and The Movie Channel cable networks for the film's first TV showing, scheduled for July 1985. As with the previous films, at that time it will probably appear in its originally released form. However, when it appears on network television in a couple of years, we can only hope that more "outtakes" will be reinstated.

It would be fruitless to speculate at this time what material might be added to *The Search for Spock* at some point years away, but this viewer for one noted a few mistakes and continuity errors that are interesting to point out.

The alert viewer will note that the layout shown on Chekov's security scan, indicating a life form in Spock's quarters, is from the TV blueprints, not the updated blueprints issued after *Star Trek: The Motion Picture*.

After Kirk's unsuccessful discussion with Starfleet Commander Morrow, he enters a turboshaft with Chekov and Sulu. Chekov is told to inform Dr. McCoy of their plans. Yet, when they arrive to rescue McCoy, he acts completely surprised, not forwarned.

Once more, the "exterior" shots on Genesis provide cast members with multiple shadows, evidence of soundstage "on location" shooting.

Another Genesis question: All views of Genesis show only the plant itself and its sun. It has no moon, and the flaming gas sheets of the ex-Mutara Nebula were condensed to form the matter of the planet and its sun. So where, then, does the nocturnal illumination, bright as that of Earth's full moon, come from?

When Saavik is awakened by the eruptive falling of a tree just before she notes that Spock's *pon farr* has come, a sloppy film editor inserted a momentary glimpse, from the rear, of a Klingon warrior being buried under a treefall. This brief clip belongs much later in the action.

In "Amok Time," the first incidence of *pon farr* in Spock, we can safely assert that he is at least thirty to thiry-five years Terran years old. Yet, a young actor playing Spock at the age of seventeen (according to *The Search for Spock*'s credits) undergoes the throes of *pon farr*. How can we resolve the one with the other?

When Kirk and company depart the *Enterprise* for the last time, the quick-eyed viewer will note that the transporter room walls have been changed, again. In the first film, the walls were a dull gray color. Nicholas Meyer's passion for little blinking lights caused the transporter room walls as shown in the second film to be covered with tiny panels, each flickering madly. Now, in *The Search for Spock*, the transporter room is back to its original appearance as seen in *Star Trek: The Motion Picture*.

As you will also recall from *Star Trek: The Motion Picture*, the self-destruct contingency of the *Enterprise* involves the uncontrolled conjunction of matter and antimatter. The very detailed and useful "cutaway" painting of the *Enterprise* by David Kimble, released as a poster after the release of the first film, clearly indicates that the antimatter pods and the matter/antimatter mix chamber are located on the lowest levels at the very front of the secondary hull. Since this would be the source of an explosive reaction, that is of course the first place where damage would become apparent to an outside observer. Yet in *The Search for Spock*, it is the primary hull which explodes in separate detonations; as the *Enterprise* plunges toward Genesis's atmosphere and begins to heat up, the secondary hull, the location of the matter/antimatter pods and the very heart of the self-destruct system, is shown to be completely intact. Once again, *The Search for Spock* has violated established (and Paramount-approved) continuity.

My final observation is but a minor quibble. A scene present in both DC's comics adaptation and McIntyre's novelization is the brief appearance of a Vulcan child who says, "Live long and prosper," to Spock's empty body while it is being carried up to Mount Seleya. It is not present in the film. Even so, the girl, Katherine Blum, is given credit in the cast list.

Many of the continuity difficulties of *Star Trek III: The Search for Spock*—the use of TV blueprints; the age of Spock at *pon farr*; the source of the *Enterprise*'s self-destruct explosions—could have been resolved had someone simply intended to check everything with what had gone before. Other errors, in all three films—moving handprints to multiple shadows to nonexistent moonlight—must have their origin in sloppy filmmaking.

There is so very much to love and thrill to in the (so far) three Star Trek films: characters old and new, costumes, spaceships, triumphs and tragedy. It's a shame that errors, large and small, detract from the fantasy that what's up on that screen is possible and real. My hope is that Paramount, the producers, writers, and directors will find it necessary to budget the time and expense to get it right. Further, it is a shame that Paramount, with so much money and materials invested in the Star Trek property, does not consider it worth its while to police the various products it licenses to make sure they are consistent with each other.

Nobody can get it right the first time. Now that Paramount has had twenty years of practice, this Star Trek fan is hoping that some of the obvious blunders and conflicts such as those listed above will be very rare (dare I hope nonexistent?) in *Star Trek IV* and beyond.

About the Editors

Walter Irwin has been writing professionally for almost twenty years, and has authored over 100 articles, features, and short stories. He became active in Star Trek and comic book fandom in 1970, culminating in the publication of *Trek* in 1975. He is currently script editor and head writer for Mediaplex Film Corporation. In addition to editing *Trek* and coediting the *Best of Trek* volumes, Walter continues to publish short fiction and novels. He married longtime Star Trek fan Lauren Johnson on Halloween in 1987, and they currently live on a ranch in Valley Lodge, Texas, with hordes of horses, dogs, and cats.

G. B. Love was one of the Founding Fathers of comics fandom and was also a Star Trek fan early on. He began publishing the seminal fanzine *The Rocket's Blast* in 1960, and eventually became one of fandom's first enterpreneurs, organizing some of the first comic and Star Trek conventions, and publishing over 100 books and magazines. G. B. began editing *Trek* in 1975, and continues to coedit the *Best of Trek* volumes to this day. G. B. is happily single and lives with his faithful dog Rip in a house full of comics, books, and toys in Pasadena, Texas.

Although largely unknown to readers not involved in Star Trek fandom before the publication of the *Best of Star Trek #1*, WALTER IRWIN and G. B. LOVE have been actively editing and publishing magazines for many years. Before they teamed up to create TREK® in 1975, Irwin worked in newspapers, advertising, and free-lance writing, while Love published *The Rocker's Blast—Comiccollector* from 1960 to 1974, as well as hundreds of other magazines, books, and collectables. Both together and separately, they are currently planning several new books and magazines.